Electra

Books by Kerry Greenwood

The Delphic Women Novels
Medea
Cassandra
Electra

The Phryne Fisher Series
Cocaine Blues
Flying Too High
Murder on the Ballarat Train
Death at Victoria Dock
The Green Mill Murder
Blood and Circuses
Ruddy Gore
Urn Burial
Raisins and Almonds
Death Before Wicket
Away With the Fairies
Murder in Montparnasse
The Castlemaine Murders
Queen of the Flowers
Death by Water
Murder in the Dark
Murder on a Midsummer Night
Dead Man's Chest
Unnatural Habits
Murder and Mendelssohn

The Corinna Chapman Series
Earthly Delights
Heavenly Pleasures
Devil's Food
Trick or Treat
Forbidden Fruit
Cooking the Books

Short Story Anthology
A Question of Death:
An Illustrated Phryne Fisher Anthology

Other Novels
Out of the Black Land

Electra

A Delphic Woman Novel

Kerry Greenwood

Poisoned Pen Press

First U.S. Edition 2013

10 9 8 7 6 5 4 3 2 1

Library of Congress Catalog Card Number: 2013941226

ISBN: 9781464202117   Hardcover
       9781464202131   Trade Paperback

Poisoned Pen Press
6962 E. First Ave., Ste. 103
Scottsdale, AZ 85251
www.poisonedpenpress.com
info@poisonedpenpress.com

Printed in the United States of America

Cast List

GODS

Adonis   the slain God, identical to Osiris; the Summer King, slain and resurrected every year

Aphrodite   the stranger, Lady of Cyprus, goddess of love

Apollo   sun-god, the archer

Artemis   the hunter, sister of **Apollo**, a virgin goddess

Athene   mistress of battles, daughter of **Zeus**, also a maiden

Demeter   goddess of the Earth, also known as **Gaia**, the mother

Dionysos   god of wine and madness

Hades   Pluton, the rich one, lord of the underworld, husband of **Persephone**

Hera   wife of **Zeus**

Hermes   messenger of the gods

Pan   god of forests; he and **Demeter** are the oldest gods

Persephone   Kore, the maiden, daughter of **Demeter**, married to **Hades**

Poseidon   Earth-shaker, god of the sea

Thanatos	angel of death, brother of **Morpheus** (sleep)
Zeus	the father, son of **Chronos**, lord of the gods

DEMIGODS

Asclepius	son of **Apollo**, father of medicine
Calypso	nymph, rescued **Odysseus** from the sea
Circe	sorceress, turned **Odysseus**' crew into pigs
Erinyes	the furies, revengers of blood
Eumenides	the kindly ones, ex-furies and harvest goddesses
Heracles	hero, famous for his labors
Hygeia	daughter of **Asclepius**, patroness of medicine
Macaon	son of **Asclepius**, father of surgery; died at Troy
Polidarius	son **Asclepius**, father of herbal medicine
Tiresias	philosopher, half-man half-woman, consulted by **Odysseus** in **Hades**' realm

THE HOUSE OF ATREUS

Aegisthus	son of **Thyestes** by incest, revenge-child, **Clytemnestra's** lover
Atreus	twin to **Thyestes**, cooked his children and was cursed
Agamemnon	brother of **Menelaus**, King of Mycenae
Chrysothemis	daughter of **Agamemnon** and **Clytemnestra**
Clytemnestra	daughter of **Leda**, sister of **Elene** of Sparta, wife of **Agamemnon**
Electra	see **Laodice**
Hermione	daughter of **Menelaus** and **Elene**, betrothed to **Orestes**
Iphigenia	daughter of **Agamemnon**, sacrificed for a wind to Troy
Laodice	called **Electra**, daughter of **Clytemnestra** and **Agamemnon**
Orestes	last son of **Agamemnon**
Thyestes	brother of **Atreus**, father of **Aegisthus**

TRAVELLERS

Cassandra	daughter of **Priam**, healer of Troy, captive of **Agamemnon**
Diomenes	called **Chryse**, 'golden' healer, priest of Asclepius, from Epidavros
Eumides	Trojan sailor, once a slave in Mycenae

OTHERS

Abantos	slave and cook to **Electra**
Achilles	'Swift Runner,' the hero
Achis	of Thrace, a trader in herbs
Agenor	sailor on **Laodamos**' ship
Alceste	slave to **Electra**
Andromache	widow of **Hector**
Arion	the bard, dolphin-rider
Aulos	slave to **Pylades**
Autesion	son of **Gythia** and **Taphis** of Corinth
Azeus	son of **Clonius**, freeman working for **Pylades**
Cilissa	nurse of **Orestes**
Chryseis	'golden' (fem), wife of **Diomenes**
Clonius	freeman working for **Pylades**
Cyclops	giant with one eye, which **Odysseus** put out in a cave on Crete
Dion	priest of Poseidon, lover of **Cassandra** in Troy
Eleni	priest of Apollo in Dodona, twin to **Cassandra**
Glaucus	master of Epidavros and **Diomenes**' teacher
Graios	slave to **Pylades**
Gythia	wife of **Taphis**, herb-merchant of Corinth
Hecabe	queen of defeated Troy and mother of **Cassandra**
Hector	prince of Troy, brother of **Cassandra**
Laodamos	sailor friend of **Eumides**
Laphanes	slave in Mycenae, in love with **Electra**

Lysane	slave to **Electra**
Menon	apprentice to **Arion** the bard
Metrodorus	pirate of Troizen
Molossos	counsellor of Epirus
Neleus	head man of Artemisi
Neoptelemus	son of **Achilles**, King of Epirus
Neptha	**Electra's** nurse in Mycenae
Nestor	old man of Mycenae
Odyesseus	prince of Ithaca, of the Nimble Word
Pariki	'Purse,' son of **Priam**, brother of **Cassandra**
Peirithe	wife of **Scamandros**, Queen of Troas
Penelope	wife of **Odysseus**
Priam	'Priamos,' the ransomed, king of Troy
Pylades	of Phocis, cousin to **Electra** and **Orestes**
Scamandros	king of Troas
Staphylos	inventor of wine, Minoan king of Blue-Green Island, now title for all succeeding kings
Taphis	the Corinthian, an herb-merchant
Telemachus	son of **Odysseus**
Tydeus	of the lyre, Orphean bard

ANIMALS

Racer	a half-wolf bitch
Banthos	'Dapple,' **Electra's** gelding
Nefos	'Black Cloud,' **Cassandra's** horse

BOATS

Waverider	**Emides'** galley
Dolphin	**Arion's** ship
Farseer	**Eumides'** first boat
Hand	a pirate galley belonging to **Metrodorus** of Troizen
Phoebus	**Laodamos'** galley

Chapter One

The Gods were quarrelling, as the Gods often do. Olympus, the abode of Immortals, was crowned with the marble cirque where the Wells of Seeing lay, deep waters wherein the Makers could view the earth. Aphrodite the Stranger, Goddess of Erotic Love, and Apollo Sun-Bright, God of Learning, son of Zeus, had not resolved their wager.

Cassandra, daughter of Priam, and Diomenes the Argive, the Healer-Priest of Asclepius, had been their puppets, acting out the play of the Gods through war and the fall of Troy. The city lay in ruin, and enslaved Cassandra was being brought to Mycenae by Agamemnon, the victorious king. Diomenes followed in the wake of the army. Aphrodite had wagered the golden apple on her own power, that of love. Apollo had set against this fate and death, and the outcome was still in the balance.

The golden apple spun in the air, the gage of Aphrodite's wager with Apollo Sun-God. As he reached out a hand to catch it, a great bell sounded, shivering the drowsy eternal afternoon.

'Children,' announced Zeus the Father with solemn majesty. 'Leave your squabbling over the daughter of Priam, much-tried Cassandra. Troy is dust. My son Apollo, your favorite, Diomenes Chryse the Asclepius-Priest, shall love or not love as he wishes. Your favorite, Lady Demeter, Cassandra, captive of Agamemnon, shall live or die as fate wills. Cut the strings of these minor puppets, children; make peace with each other. There is a greater matter to be considered. Your intervention has woven their threads into a tapestry in which all the Gods are interested.'

'Lord?' asked Athena of the glittering helmet. 'What matters?'
'The House of Atreus,' the great voice intoned.
The golden apple fell to the marble floor unheeded.

Electra

I knew she was going to kill him when she laid out the sacred tapestries.

I stood at the head of the marble stairs and watched them unroll across the floor, blurred by the feet of the children of Atreus. Intricately embroidered, many-figured with holy beasts— bulls and lambs and horses dancing to the altar to die in the worship of the Gods. Black like the splashed blood of the sacrifice.

Before dawn the watchers had cried that the signal fires were burning to announce the return of Agamemnon, son of Atreus, from the sack of Troy. I went out, wrapped only in a thin chiton, and sighted the points of greedy light on the surrounding hills. He had been long away, my father, the King of Mycenae, and many things had happened in his absence.

She had taken a lover. Queen Clytemnestra, my mother, had welcomed into her bed the revenge child Aegisthus, my uncle. He was the son of incest between his father Thyestes, brother to my father, and his own daughter, a priestess of the river. He existed to enact his father's vengeance on the House of Atreus, for Atreus' murder of Thyestes' children. Before he came, I had not known how well I could hate.

I hate very well.

Part of me did not really believe that she could kill him. My tall father, dazzling in his bronze armour, tall as a giant, strong as a bull. When he had gone with the army to harry Troy, ten years before, I had been twelve and a child, believing that the world was a safe place for Laodice, called Electra, Princess of Golden Mycenae. I had given him my bunch of windflowers and he had fastened them on the shoulder of his harness. He had picked me up and hugged me, smelling of leather and wine, and I had snuggled closer to him, begging to be allowed to come, at least as far as Navplion and the beaches where the black ships lay, keel to keel, waiting for the wind.

Later I was glad that he had denied me that sight. We sent my sister Iphigenia, my gentle, beautiful sister, out of the gate of the lions, with rejoicing and the music of bells, for her marriage with the hero Achilles. Instead she had been espoused by Thanatos who is Death, the Dark Angel. She was sacrificed on the altar of Boreas, the north wind, so that my father's ships could sail to Troy; so that the revenge of the sons of Atreus for the kidnapping of the faithless Elene should fall on that stone city.

The nightmare began the night we heard of her death.

My mother Clytemnestra did not scream or cry. No tears fell from eyes that became more and more stony as the days went by. She did not speak or eat for three days, then she arose and stalked the walls. She stared out, towards the sea, towards Tiryns where Dikaios the Just ruled. I did not know what she was looking for.

Now, ten years later, I know. The beacons were blazing for the return of the king. My mother's order, my mother's fire, whipped on by her will. From Lemnos to Athos, Makistos to Messapion across Euripos, Kithairon to the Gorgon's Eye, burning Ida to the Black Widow's mountain, Spider Peak above Mycenae, which always threatens to topple but never falls.

The cloth was laid for the sacrifice; the double axe was in my mother's hands. I shivered in the chill light of dawn, looking out over the silvery olive groves, my hands on the balustrade thawing the ice-rimmed stone, and listened to the morning noises.

A cock crowed *kou kou ra kou*! I could hear Orestes, my dearest brother, singing the morning song to Eos, who is the dawn. Somewhere a man was whistling on the cold hills; a goatherd was piping calling-tunes to his herd. Running feet, well shod, sounded in the chill courts of Mycenae and I smelled hearth smoke and the scent of baking bread. But there was a misplaced sound among the morning noises, a suave, gritty, sliding sound just behind me.

With mountain-stone and virgin oil, Clytemnestra was whetting the axe.

Cassandra

The bearers stopped for breath at the foot of a steep gravel path in the middle of what seemed to be a market. I looked out of the litter, in which I was tethered by a chain about my neck. A captive of Lord Agamemnon must not be allowed to escape. She might be valuable, especially if she is—was—a princess of Troy.

The traders cried firewood and skewers of meat and sandals and tripods. I could smell dust and roasted flesh and charcoal fires, unwashed humans, pine trees, wine, and amber oil. Now that the religious hush which greeted the return of the Great King had passed, the noise of the crowd hurt my ears.

I looked up to a narrow gate, surmounted with two lionesses carved out of grey granite. For a moment I flinched. The massive walls seemed about to fall and crush me. The road wound past the feet of the Cyclopean walls and curved up the hill. The bronze doors were open.

Above us the city rang with harping and singing, and some enthusiast was hooting through a bronze trumpet. Long strips of delicate weaving, blue and black and crimson, fluttered from the walls and flapped in the chill breeze. Mycenae was evidently pleased that Agamemnon was home in triumph from Troy.

I was part of his triumph. A most unwilling part. I had seen the city—my city—sacked and burned. Agamemnon's army had slaughtered my brothers and taken my sisters as slaves. He had taken me also, disgraced Priestess of Bright Apollo, torn me from my twin Eleni, who was closer than any lover. Agamemnon was bringing Cassandra, daughter of Priam, home to his queen and his city, to draw water for his horses for the rest of my days. I listened to the sea-sound of wind in the olives, remembering Ocean, and the buzzing of flesh-flies in the pines.

I had almost escaped. The priest of Asclepius, Diomenes called Chryse, and the Trojan ex-slave, Eumides, had fished me out of the water. Agamemnon, however, had not drunk any of the drugged wine with which I had put my ship to sleep. We heard a bull's roar over the water, 'Find Cassandra!' I had slipped back into the ocean, to avoid compromising my friends. Even then I swam quite a way to shore before they caught me.

Chryse and Eumides had sworn, in hurried whispers, that they would follow and rescue me, but I had seen nothing of them on the long road. I did not expect help from them. I trusted their good hearts, but anything might have happened to them—storms at sea had scattered the fleet, several ships had been lost, and we had been repeatedly attacked by bandits on the long road from Navplion.

I recalled the chain of little hot lights, fire speeding across the mountains to announce the return of the Sons of Atreus. Kind Agamemnon had sighted them too, far out on the wrinkled sea, flat as a plate, the seamen grunting at the oars.

'There goes the message of my victory,' he said, and grinned.

I hated him. Big as a bull, strong, coarse, brutal, cunning king. He had tried to rape me the night of my recapture, but I had called on the black aspect of Gaia the Mother, the Goddess Hecate, Drinker of Dog's Blood, and the proud phallus had shrunk and fallen under her black regard, the snake-haired one.

For disgraced or not, captive or not, exile or at home, I am still Cassandra, daughter of Priam of the Royal House of Troy, Priestess of Apollo, and I can call on the gods. They owe this to me, who have wounded me almost beyond bearing.

Agamemnon had attempted violation again the next night, when I was seasick; perhaps he thought that I would have less power if I was retching helplessly. The other women had urged me to co-operate, saying that he would beat me, but I would not. He disgusted me, his matted chest, filthy skin still smeared with Trojan blood, and his grasping, sweaty hands.

And when he shoved me down and knelt again between my thighs to no effect, he did not beat me. He got up clumsily, made the sign against evil—and evil was certainly there in that loot-filled cabin—and pushed me out to sleep with the captives.

Thereafter he did not speak to me. If I looked at him, he avoided my gaze.

Slaves have but small triumphs.

The journey from the port was slow, because Agamemnon's treasure had to be transported, loaded on every horse and mule in the Argolid. The loot from Apollo's temple alone burdened ten ox-carts. Oh, Ilium, all that remains of you is golden vessels and the frail flesh of your children, and how long will we last? Gold melts and flesh dies. In a generation all memory of Troy will be gone. No one will speak of it except to say, 'This was Troy, once a great city, which the Sons of Atreus destroyed because of faithless Argive Elene.' It was not Elene. We never had her. It was greed that destroyed Troy, all its wisdom and wealth spilled on that blood-soaked plain, because the Argives did not like to pay our tolls for passing the Hellespont. Eight years of piracy and two years of siege, and now the treasuries of Agamemnon brim with our gold.

And Troy is gone, gone utterly.

Oh my twin, my lost Eleni, taken by the son of Achilles. My arms ached for him, my mind sought constantly for the spark of his mind. It was there—a flicker, just a flicker. A desperately miserable and humiliated Eleni lit a small corner of my mind. I hoped that he could not feel my rage, my burning fury. I would not add to his burdens. He was a slave and I was a slave. But we were in good company.

The women of Troy are valuable throughout the world. They call us the well-skilled women. In the baggage train there were almost a hundred of us—spinners, weavers, two jewellery-makers, a dozen house-builders and the best potters in the city. Our skills would not die, provided we were allowed to them to another. For we worked and moved and even breathed now at the behest of our masters, and we had not been slaves before. We talked when we could, to comfort each other. Perhaps half were resigned enough to settle down in their new lives, but three had already been murdered by their Achaean masters for being insufficiently meek.

I did not hold out great hopes for the rest.

The happiest of Ilium are the dead, and there are so many dead. Hector, my brother, tall as a tree, sun-golden, with his great beard. My mother and father, my brothers, all dead, all gone. I could feel Eleni, my twin, by our god-given consciousness. He was just existing, but he was still alive, the last son of Priam.

Eleni was still alive and I was about to die.

By the God's vision I knew. I was certain. If I went up that hill I was going to share Agamemnon's death. The woman was waiting for him. She would strike once across the belly and then as the guts spilled and he bowed before her, with a skilled woodsman's stroke she was going to cut off his head.

And mine. I heard my own dying cry and smelt blood so strongly that I choked. The water of the bath lapped like a red tide. I clutched at my throat, cleared my voice and cried, 'Stop!'

My bearers, both Achaeans, looked around inquiringly. Achaeans are infallibly curious. It is their only charming characteristic.

'Why did you say "Stop!" Lady?' one asked.

'If you take me up into the city I will die,' I said. They were sorry for me, and the left one patted my hand soothingly.

'Slavery is not good; no one desires it. But in life there is hope,' he said.

'I mean, soldier, if I go up into the palace I will be killed,' I elaborated.

The patted me again and said, 'Lady, we are ordered to take you up into the city.'

'Listen, idiots, don't you understand me? I thought I spoke clear grammatical Achaean!' They stared at me stupidly. 'There's a lake of blood up there. I can smell it so strongly that I can hardly bear the stink. I am a Priestess of Apollo and he gave me clear sight and I tell you, the king must die—will die—I can see the manner of his death now as clearly as I see you. If you take me there she will kill me too, so put the litter down.'

'The Lady is distraught,' said one.

'Women, even priestesses, are excitable,' said the other, lifting his end of the litter so that I was flung backwards by the length of my chain.

'The Priestess is overcome by the horror of her situation,' said the first, hoisting his end to a muscular shoulder.

We jolted up the steep path to the Lion Gate and I occupied myself in prayer. Not to the new cruel Gods, Apollo or Artemis or Hera, but to the familiar Lords of my destroyed city; Gaia the Earth, Mistress of Animals, and Dionysos the Dancer. I shut off the vision of blood and recalled, instead, sitting on Hector's shoulders with my twin Eleni, hands clasped across his golden head, while he argued with a ship's crew about a missing amphora of honey from Kriti. I closed my eyes.

Electra

He was coming home, my magnificent father, victorious and bringing captives and treasure, and I wanted to rush out to meet him. He would render justice to me, roast Aegisthus over a slow fire, kill the unrighteous queen.

I dressed in my finest chiton, of delicate rose with a blue mantle, colored my lips and cheeks with cherry juice and outlined my eyes with Egyptian kohl. I brushed my dark hair until it shone. I laced on my best sandals, a present from my father and too small for me, but decorated with little bronze rosettes. My nurse, Neptha, showed me my face in the bronze mirror and told me I was beautiful. I heard the trumpets and the drums. The Great King was returning.

Then my nerve failed. As others had turned from friends to monsters in a moment, might not my father change as well? My trust wavered. I could not just leap into his arms as I had once. I was not his little daughter any more. I was flustered, confused and afraid. My golden eyes were not innocent. I knew things, I held secrets, who had once been as clear as water.

So I crept, not to the main wall, but to the women's quarters, under the mountain called Spider. I saw the baggage train gleaming with gold, heard horses neighing and men shouting and wooden wheels groaning on the uneven road. I smelt dust and roasted meat and a waft of wine and swallowed tears, tasting salt. The Triumph was filling the flat space before the city and overflowing up the hills on either side, a confusion of animals and people. There was a hush as a bronze-clad man walked proudly and alone up the path. His helmet was plumed with bright feathers, he clanked as he moved, but I could not see his face.

Then my father passed out of sight and the noise came back.

Surely she did not really mean to kill him. She was just sharpening the axe for the sacrifice of the bull to welcome the king. Surely she could not manage to kill him, so tall and magnificent, so strong?

I could see all the way across the valley to the mountains beyond. Grey-green with white stones knuckling through thin earth, that is Mycenae. The wind always blows here.

Two young men looked up as I looked down. They were a contrast. One was a sailor, by the look of him. Curly dark hair, dark eyes, gold rings in his ears which glinted as he moved; compact and strong, like an oarsman. The other was taller, slimmer and chryselephantine. Ivory and gold. His skin was pale and smooth and his hair was as bright as the sun, like a statue of a god. He did not smile but looked at me gravely, and I did not retreat. He did not feel threatening.

The dark one was equipped with a long plaited line with a grappling hook on one end, dangling from his hand. They were actually attempting to climb into the women's quarters.

'The penalty for what you are intending is death,' I informed the golden man.

'The penalty for living is death,' he replied evenly. 'It is a common fate.'

'But not so surely or so soon,' I told him.

I should have called the guard, but they were all at the Triumph, welcoming my father back into the city.

'We have to get into Mycenae,' said the golden man.

'Why?' I asked, surprising myself. Ordinarily I never speak to men.

'It's a long story and this is an exposed place for tales. Let us in, maiden, and we'll tell you all about it,' said the golden man calmly.

I did not know what to do. A memory was trying to surface in my mind. I had seen that golden hair, that cool profile, somewhere before. A long time ago. When?

I had been waiting at the gate of the city with my mother and my sisters when Iphigenia was alive, when I first saw Argive Elene, the most beautiful woman in the world, or so she seemed to me, a little girl. We were handing out coins and bread to those who had survived the plague. There had been a very riotous bard called Arion, and a bearded Master of Epidavros called Glaucus. Prince Odysseus had just left, who had brought me a sea-shell the color of sunset from a shore on the other side of the Pillars of Heracles. Yes. The memory was becoming clear. I do not like memory and try to avoid it if I can. But here it was. A sunny day, and the procession of cured ones are coming, led by a boy no taller than me, a boy with straight golden hair and tired eyes. Diomenes. They called him Chryse, 'golden', and he was made a healer priest because of that battle with the plague of Apollo on the hills outside Mycenae.

I winced and said, 'Chryse?'

'Princess,' said the golden man. 'Electra, daughter of Agamemnon, you know me. I am Diomenes, called Chryse the Healer, Priest of Asclepius. This is my friend Eumides, who was once a slave in this very city. We must enter. Help us, or at least do not call the soldiers.'

I stood in thought, rasping my palm over the clean edge of the tiled wall. They stared up at me, the dark man and the golden. I was powerful. I could scream—it was my duty to scream—and even amid the rejoicing the armed men would run to my aid, bronze weapons clattering on marble, and cut the intruders down on my order…

I exclaimed in pain. A sharp edge of tile had cut my hand. A little blood dropped onto the stone. It was an omen.

I did not speak but stepped away from the wall. The grappling hook flicked up, grounded, scraped and held under the weight of two climbing men.

They were over the wall in an instant, the agile Eumides hauling Diomenes up by the arm. They were taller than they had seemed on the ground. They loomed over me and I backed until I came flat against a wall. The usual draperies were gone to furnish the Triumph, and the stone was very cold. The sun had not reached the megaron yet.

'Princess,' said Chryse, 'allow me.' He took my hand and turned it to examine the palm. There was a thin cut, already closing. His touch did not disgust as much as that of men usually did. His hands were deft, and he bound my wound with a strip of linen from his bag.

'Maiden,' begun Eumides hurriedly, 'we must find the Trojan prisoner Cassandra, daughter of Priam.'

'The captives will be brought to the Great King's hall, the audience chamber. Who is this Princess? Has my father taken a concubine?'

'Not if Princess Cassandra had anything to do with it,' grinned Eumides. I flinched away from his knowing smile.

Chryse Diomenes noticed this and said gently, 'She is a Priestess and has prophesied the death of Agamemnon your father. She has spoken truly for all of her life and she said in the gateway that a woman would kill both her and the King.'

'How do you know?'

'We heard her. We've followed the army from Troy, travelling among the traders. Watching all the way, looking for a chance at rescue,' said Eumides impatiently. 'We won't fail now, eh, brother?' Chryse took the offered hand and held it and I perceived that they were close—very close. Speech came to me in a rush. For some reason I wanted to help them.

'The King goes to bathe. I will show you the place. There's a server's door in a narrow passage, I know how it can be done. They'll bring the Trojan slave there to be purified if she's lain with the Kind. There will be no one else there, just my mother, she said she would tend him herself and she's sent all the slaves away. You can take her, this Trojan Princess. We don't need Trojan women here; Troy has fallen and is dust.'

They said nothing. The knowledge I had suppressed smashed through the barriers that guard me against feeling. This prophetess was telling the truth—they said she always did. My mother was going to murder my father. I froze, trying to find words, then gabbled, 'Save my father, Healer, you must save him.' I pleaded with him, even touching his shoulder in the suppliant's gesture.

A line of pain divided his smooth brow. 'We can try, Princess, but Cassandra prophesies truly, and we may not succeed.'

'We have to try, come, hurry!' I said. I turned and ran through the maze of the women's quarters and they followed me, far too slowly.

The palace of Mycenae may not have a labyrinth, like the fabled Palace of Minos, but it has been added to by successive kings since Perseus, and it is said that no one can find their way through unless they were born here.

The passages are unlit, except by occasional light wells. They dip below ground at unpredictable intervals, have distracting flights of stairs which seem to lead nowhere and odd corridors which conduct the poor lost ones out of their way and them strand them in the wine cellar. Without my help the men panting behind me would have been utterly confounded, but I had been playing in the mazes of the city since I was a child, and knew them like my own hand.

I slid to a halt before the water-carrier's door. I heard voices, one calm and one cold.

'Come, Princess,' said the cold voice, 'Will you not walk on the cloths? My Lord does so. Is it for his slave to disobey?'

'I will not walk on the sacred tapestries,' said the other voice. I heard in it exhaustion and determination. This was a woman who knew she was going to die, had accepted it, and would not be further compromised. If she said she would not do something, then she would not do it. Eumides and Diomenes leaned forward, listening. On both faces was an identical eagerness and joy, so that for the first time they looked alike. They loved her, this Trojan slave who was my Royal Father's concubine. I shivered and tasted metal in my mouth. The corridor was musty and damp and stank of mould.

'My Lord, will you not order your slave to tread in your footsteps?' insinuated Clytemnestra the Queen, my mother. I could imagine the flush of malice on her cheek, my beautiful mother with the long ringlets of ebony hair, the pale, skilled, pink-tipped fingers. There was a time when I thought her more beautiful than Elene, wife of Menelaus of Sparta.

I found the catch and allowed the door to open a little way. Eumides and Diomenes pressed against me, and I had no room to recoil from their warmth.

Three figures were standing on the steps leading up to the great bath. There was my mother and there was my father, armour removed, clad in a stained tunic.

He was not a giant as I remembered. He was an ordinary man, man-sized, an old man sagging at the belly. His black beard and hair were streaked with grey. I could not see his face.

'Enough, woman, let the slave do as she likes,' he grunted. Then I knew it was indeed my father. Just so had he grumbled if his wine was too hot, or his favorite horse had been badly groomed. I think I almost smiled at the memory.

He was standing on the sacred tapestries, brought out only on festivals, which only the priests were allowed to handle. She had tempted him into blasphemy. The gods would never forgive her. Neither would I.

If I could have reached her, I would have killed her then.

The slave stepped back, allowing the King and then the Queen to pass up the stair to the bath. She was a tall woman of no particular beauty. Her hair hung loose like a maiden's and her face was as still and white as a marble statue before the painter has applied the tincts of nature. She looked like a Kore, Persephone the Maiden, in a green chiton, loaded with gold jewellery, chiming with bangles.

I heard Eumides and Chryse draw in a breath when they saw her.

Then she raised her head and cried out in an unknown tongue.

Eumides shoved the door open and plunged onto the stair. I followed and Diomenes came behind.

At that moment Clytemnestra turned her head and saw us.

The King was plodding up, oblivious. Her black eyes raked us, cataloguing each person; golden man, dark man, Trojan prisoner, her own daughter, with equal calculation. I could almost hear what she was thinking. She had not expected witnesses to her dreadful act. However, if she stepped down to kill us, she would lose her main prey, my father. Like a hawk who lets four mice escape in favor of a hare for which it has whetted its beak, she held us all for a long moment and then released us, turning back to the King.

Eumides, one arm across his face to fend off those Gorgon's eyes, seized Cassandra by the shoulder and she came to him. She seemed to be tranced, for she said no word as they pulled her through the doorway, pushing me before them.

'Father!' I screamed, struggling past them and gaining the stair. 'Help! Help!'

There was a thud and a great cry, then another thud.

Diomenes lifted me, flung me through the water-carrier's door, shoved it shut and leaned on it.

'Let me go!' I struggled frantically, ripping at his face with my fingernails. He trapped my arms by my sides in a wrestler's grip and clapped a hand over my mouth.

Cassandra the slave came close, so close I could smell perfume and wine on her, and said, 'He is dead, Electra.'

Her eyes were unfocused, as if she was dreaming, or saw things other than with sight. She stilled me. I was not resigned or calm, I was boiling with fury and loss, but I could think again. All my thoughts were of revenge for blood.

'We must leave,' said Diomenes shakily. 'Now, before the murder is known and the gates are shut.'

'Good counsel,' agreed the sailor, one arm around Cassandra and one around his friend. He seemed to be dizzy.

Cassandra began retracing my journey, which was fortunate for I had lost my way. I did not recognize any landmarks. I groped along in an ocean of darkness. I heard the unsteady steps of Eumides and the steady pace of Diomenes, burdened with his friend. After a while he recovered and walked on his own. I watched while he recovered and walked on his own. I watched the sure feet of the Trojan slave, moving like a dancer.

We skirted guards, avoided pitfalls, doubled back and went on after the fluttering green chiton and the faultless pace. She did not pause until we were back in the megaron. Then she stopped suddenly and fell. Diomenes caught her as she crumpled in a jingle of gold.

'Cassandra,' he said, and shook her almost roughly, so that the jewellery rang like bells. 'This is not time for a prophetic swoon! Wake, Lady, we are in deadly danger.'

'Princess,' said Eumides gently, 'Wake and smile, Lady, on your suppliants.'

'Oh, my dears,' she said, sliding an arm around each neck and drawing their faces down to hers. 'Oh, my golden ones. My most faithful. I had given up hope. Did you follow the army all the way from Troy?'

'Every weary step, though we did some trading on the road. Come, can you stand?' Eumides encouraged.

'I don't know.' They lifted her and she shook her draperies into place with one brisk, cat-like movement.

'Princess Electra,' she said. 'Come with us.'

'Why?' I hung back from her warmth, stubborn and shocked.

'Because your mother may find your presence inconvenient,' said Eumides grimly. 'She kills people who inconvenience her. The boy, too—the son of Agamemnon—what is his name?'

'Orestes,' I said numbly.

'Do you think he will survive the death of his father?'

'The death of his father?' I repeated stupidly.

'Come or stay, Princess. We are leaving,' said Eumides, unwinding the plaited line from his waist and balancing the grappling hook.

'Where are you going?' I asked, forcing the words past stony lips.

'Delphi. If you are coming, fetch the boy and bring some provisions for a journey, and change your sandals, they aren't fitted for the road. And hurry!' he shouted after me as I ran from the room.

I found Orestes, gathered his clothes into a bundle and thrust him before me into my room, all without a word. I clawed three chitons from my chest, rolled them in a blanket, and stuffed a handful of gold inside. At the last moment, I took my doll Pallas and laid her in the bundle as well as the sandals my father had given me.

I left all my remaining possessions on my bed for Neptha. Small things, but precious to me, hard to leave. Neptha would understand. I dressed for a journey and took Orestes' hand.

We climbed down the wall, unnoticed, and picked our way across the rocky slopes. It was getting dark. A child wind struck and numbed all exposed skin. With held breath we drifted through the market traders and the ox-carts and continued through the undergrowth. I saw that Cassandra was unveiled, wrapped in Eumides' cloak and openly holding his hand like a whore. I heard the noise of running water, the stream beside the road.

I was leaving Mycenae and my father was dead.

Chapter Two

Odysseus

The wine from the attack on Ismarus was good, but the Cicones had contested possession of it and their wives and livestock. I would not have attacked them, but my coarse and brutal crew had to be pleased with the spoil. We had buried our dead in the bosom of Poseidon, who hates me. I, Odysseus, Sacker of Cities, The Sly One, Odysseus of the Nimble Tongue, Wise and Much-Enduring, Odysseus of Cunning Counsel. I won the battle, broke the siege, and destroyed Troy, his city. A terrible gale struck the Ionian ships, driven along before the wind under the flapping rags of the sails.

A god's hatred is a heavy burden, but heavier to leave the land of the lotus eaters, who sup on honeyed fruit on those pleasant shores. The men wept as I compelled them back to their ships, calling them weaklings and scoundrels. I chained them to the oars as we rowed out.

Penelope, my wife, and Telemachus, my baby son, are waiting at home for me now as my ships approach Kriti. And I am Prince of Ithaca. I will return, though Poseidon blows me all over the world.

Electra

There is no cover on Spider Mountain. Though the scrub is dense and hardy, it is only half of my height, barely thigh-high to tall Cassandra and Diomenes. I was cold. Orestes had not spoken, not even asked a question. He dragged at my hand, stones turned under my feet, and even on the path we stumbled and lagged.

My sandals were made to glide over the marble floor of the Palace of Mycenae, not to walk the road like a common market-trader. I had never been so far from the women's quarters on foot in my life, and of course, as a Princess, I was unused to walking. Only female slaves and whores walk.

Slaves, whores, escaping prisoners and exiles walk.

I grasped my chiton and mantle in one hand and pulled Orestes along. It seemed as dark as the inside of a fish and I listened for other feet on the beaten earth.

As my eyes got used to the night I began to pick out images. Ahead of me was a strange, starfish-shaped monster, and I stopped in horror.

It halted also, broke up, and pieces of it came back toward me. I caught Orestes close and stifled a scream. Then I realized that the creature had been three people walking with their arms shamelessly around each other. I heard them laughing.

'Maiden, you are slow,' said Eumides impatiently. 'We must get in out of the night and it is still a way to the hut. Can I carry the child?'

'No!' I gasped.

'Come, boy, will you walk or ride?' he asked, smiling, and Orestes let go my hand. 'Ride, please.'

Eumides hoisted my brother without effort onto his shoulders, creating another weird shape. I picked my way behind him, hurt that the child had abandoned me so easily, trying to find a smooth path among the stones. Thorns caught my garments. At first I stopped to undo them, but I was tired and shocked and miserable and after a while I just let them tear.

Orestes was almost out of sight when someone ran lightly back and took the bundle off my shoulder. It was Diomenes and he offered me his arm.

Leaning on him, I managed to complete the journey.

'There's our stopping place just ahead, Princess, we can light a fire and you can sit down. But we must get you some strong sandals. Those will never carry you far.'

'I am not used to walking,' I gasped. 'I am a Princess of a royal house.'

'Indeed,' he replied, and did not speak again.

Around the shoulder of the hill we came upon a small house, built perhaps by goatherds. It was set back into the cliff, under the protection of a huge ledge of rock. A little light glimmered inside it and Diomenes led me to the door. I sank down onto an earth floor, exhausted. The hut stank of goats and smoke.

Orestes was sitting on the other side of a charcoal brazier, watching the roasting skewers of meat as though he had been a kitchen boy all his life. His pale, delicate face was sharp with attention. Orestes always concentrated completely on whatever he was doing. He was thin, with a ruffle of dark hair and beautiful eyes. I used to think that my golden eyes, which gave me my name—Electra, 'amber'—were unique in the House of Atreus, until I saw Orestes'. He gave me a brief smile and returned to the cooking.

I took off the ruined sandals and massaged my poor feet, bruised by stones and stuck with thorns, to distract myself from the indecent threefold embrace in the center of the small room.

They were sitting in a group, arms around each other, mouths almost touching. Each hand caressed a throat or a back. They were continually in motion, dark hair mingling with golden, kisses laid gently on pale, scented whore's cheek or rough unshaven fisherman's. Bracelets jingled on narrow wrists as Cassandra cupped both faces, stroking them with aching tenderness, as though she had never expected to touch them again.

'Netted like a fish,' said Diomenes softly, and kissed her bare shoulder. 'A very valuable fish.'

'Such a catch I never made in all my life, dark seas and pale, high waves and flat calm,' said Eumides, and kissed her other shoulder.

'Oh, my golden ones,' she said, kissing each mouth carefully.

Then they all clasped thigh-to-thigh in so close and convulsive an embrace that I turned away. After a moment, they separated reluctantly.

'Now, let's dig up the wine,' said Diomenes. 'Take off all that gold, Lady; we shall have enough trouble with bandits on the way.'

'To Delphi?' she asked, unfastening her earrings.

'To Delphi. We should be able to manage that journey and there we must take the lady Electra and Orestes, son of Agamemnon. I fear that the Queen of Mycenae may pursue us.'

'Why?' I asked.

Diomenes said, 'We must tend you, Lady,' and came to me with the healer's bag. I drew away from his touch, because he had come to attend me straight from the embrace of the slave. He did not appear to notice my reaction, but sat down composedly and began to extract thorns with a pair of golden tweezers.

'Why? Because we know she murdered her husband,' said Eumides, who was digging for the cellar of the little house. He knelt up, triumphantly producing an amphora of wine, on which he broke the seal.

'She will not hide it,' I said, flinching as a thorn slid out of my ankle. 'She will proclaim it.'

'She'll proclaim it?' asked Cassandra.

'Yes.' I tried not to move under the little stabbing pains, but he was hurting me. I felt my face assume its mask, and the pain ceased to matter. Cassandra was looking at me. Her eyes were brown and very deep.

'Chryse, you're too rough,' she told him. 'Gently.'

'Get me some more light, then,' he grumbled. 'And the stonecrop ointment.'

'Do you use stonecrop for bruises? Surely not on broken skin,' she took up the small oil lamp and crouched to shed light on my foot.

'What would you use?' he asked, drawing her wrist and the light closer.

'Wound-herb, pounded with sea salt, then stonecrop once the punctures are closed.'

'Trojan practice, probably good, but I have no wound-herb. Take my pestle and make some fine salt and we can clean the injuries, at least. Then the ointment shouldn't sting too much.'

I objected to them working on me without so much as a word in my direction and said, 'I can bear pain.'

'Of course, but healers are devoted to the philosophy that no one bears pain needlessly. There. A good pair of sandals—boots would be better—and you'll not be so wayworn tomorrow, Lady.'

He smiled at me but I could not smile back. What company had I fallen into? Women walking openly with men, male and female healers consulting each other as though they were equals? It was unthinkable, impossible—against all order.

Cassandra filled a bowl with hot water and washed my scratched with salt. It hurt, but I did not really feel it. I never do, in that state. I can make myself numb.

She anointed me deftly. Then she gave me a wet cloth to wipe my face and I found a comb and gave it to her.

'It's a pretty comb,' she said, looking at it and then at me.

'My hair…' I turned to give her space to work and then turned back as Eumides laughed.

'Lady, have you never combed your own hair?' he chuckled. 'Fishermen's girls can plait theirs when they are six. I think the Trojans were right about the Achaeans. Their women are so pampered, they said, that they don't even wipe their own…'

'Eumides,' said Diomenes hurriedly, 'is there anything to eat? I'm starving and we have to leave at dawn.'

'Yes, of course, our young cook here has done good work. There's bead and there's meat and there's wine. What more could we ask?'

I could have asked for a lot more. My hair was not properly arranged and I was tired and sore and had no one to attend me. The meat was half-burned and half-raw, the bread several days old, and the wine cheap and sour. But Orestes and Electra, exiled children of the House of Atreus, choked down a sufficiency and fell asleep, side by side, on the floor of the goatherd's hut. I felt the warm breath of my little brother on my shoulder as he slept, not for the first time, on my breast.

I dreamed.

I was sitting in the courtyard with my nurse Neptha, learning how to weave. We set the looms outside in the spring, when the wind ceases for a while in windy Mycenae. Neptha was a plump and comfortable woman, a slave from the far north, where the stars are cold and close, she said. Her hair was grey and she bore a scar across one breast, the legacy of the pirate who had raided her village and taken her prisoner. She had proved barren, and my mother had bought her cheap as a nurse for the youngest royal children.

Chrysothemis, my sister, had completed her lesson and was sitting on the warm marble step, shelling nuts. Her hair glowed in the cool light. She was humming her favorite song, a long ballad made by the bard, Arion, about the nymph, Salmancis, who petitioned the gods to be united forever with her lover and who had been transformed into a hermaphrodite.

'Together in truth were Hermia and her lover,' sang my sister, cracking nuts and spitting out the shells. 'Beware, lovers what you pray for, for you may get what you want.'

'You sing better than you weave,' commented Neptha, peering at the web on the practice loom and picking at the knots with gnarled fingers. 'Electra, pull out the last ten rows and we shall begin again. Now, you lift the weft with one hand, push the shuttle through, then release the weft and return the shuttle. Try not to pull it too tight—yes, like that. It helps if you sing. Your hands must flow, gently, gently, like the tide.'

'What's the tide?' I asked, biting my lip and trying to loosen my grip on the shuttle. I was trying too hard and the warp was puckering.

'Ah, children, that is the sea, the great water of the river Ocean which encircles the world. Every day the water rises on the shore, cleaning the beach of lost things and dead things, and every day is falls again, exposing the smooth sand. I miss the sound of it still. It used to lull me to sleep. There, Electra, I declare that you have learned the beginning of weaving faster than any child of mine. Look, Chrysothemis! Ten years old and a straight, smooth, even cloth. Aren't you ashamed of all those knots?'

'It's very nice,' agreed Chrysothemis grudgingly. I glowed with pride and smiled in my sleep.

Cassandra

I was exalted at my rescue. I had seen the death of Agamemnon so often that I was not even mildly surprised at it. I had expected to die. I had heard my own death cry and was prepared for it. I had not died. I had been freed. Hecate had come and disconnected me, possessed me, at the moment when I would have resisted rescue because of the danger that my followers were in. I might have pulled away and bidden them run before they shared my fate, but the gods had wrapped me in trance and I had allowed them to take me from the altar. I was a slave of the Palace of Mycenae no longer. I was out on the road with a destination and some chance of peace and delight. Now, beside me, wine cups in hand, replete with goat-meat and bread, were my dear ones, my unutterably faithful Chryse and Eumides, smiling, touching me, real, not visions.

And the haughty Princess Electra and her silent brother had finally fallen asleep.

I had put the gold aside; now my movements were silent. Eumides unfastened one brooch and Diomenes the other. The chiton fell to my waist, and I lay back on my thick sheepskin mantle and held out my arms.

One face dark, on pale; golden silk and curly fleece, smooth, smooth skin, as they shed tunics and lay down beside me. I stroked them. Palm down, my hands moved along slender thigh and muscular thigh, along flat muscles which grew rigid under my touch.

It had been so long since someone had loved me that I took a moment to identify the thrill running along my nerves as a mouth closed around a nipple.

I clutched a handful of curly hair and tried not to cry out.

Then it was all firelight pictures, scenes from a Dionysiad, the Three Days when Troy was mad and lived for nothing but mating. I tasted grease and honey on someone's mouth; hands touched, slid, skin grew hot then wet as we rolled, curled, curved, pressed close. I held one phallus, hard as metal, and the other pierced me, there were thighs between mine, a strong body, a gasping breath, an urgent mouth. A heart beat wildly under my cheek, and another pulsed inside my flesh.

Then the charcoal glow blurred, and I would have screamed, but a mouth sealed mine. Oh, honey and fire, I melted into the light. Diomenes lay beside me, cradling my body against his, and Eumides on the other side shuddered and was still.

I lay in the goat-scented hut in this dual embrace and wept with pleasure and release, and they kissed my tears away.

'Lady,' said Eumides, 'we are yours now.'

'My loves,' I said, touching one flank and the other. 'I am yours.'

We could not bear to be apart, and fell asleep where we lay, in the warm darkness, wrapped in the mantle which was once the gift of King Agamemnon to his captive.

◇◇◇

I woke in cool grey light. Diomenes had rolled over in his sleep and lay with his head on my thigh. My cheek rested on Eumides' chest. I was warm and sated and unable to account for what had woken me.

Eyes, for there were eyes on us, inimical, horrified. Golden eyes of the small woman clutching the boy on the other side of the room. I felt for the source of her disgust, trying to find what had shocked her, and recoiled from a burning rage, deep as a pit. I had not felt such a thing before.

I was suddenly very awake. I sat up, dislodging my lovers, and said, 'Lady, we must take the road again.' She did not reply.

The boy wriggled out of her too-tight embrace and said calmly, 'Electra, you are hurting me.'

Chryse woke, kissed the thigh he was lying on, then hauled himself and Eumides to the crouch which was all the hut allowed a tall man.

'Morning,' he stated.

'Again?' groaned Eumides, ran a hand through his hair, and smiled at me so that my heart glowed.

'Perhaps the Princess can make a fire, we'd better cook the rest of the meat, while I go out and find a leather-worker. If you will give me your sandal, Lady, I'll get you some boots.'

'I can't walk further,' she said angrily.

'Perhaps…horses? Mycenae won't need them now that the treasure's in the city,' suggested Diomenes.

'I'll try. Give me four gold bracelets. And the sandals. Stay quiet, Cassandra,' Eumides said to me. 'We won't be long. The traders know us.'

It was the first time he had used my name.

Electra

The whore and the two strangers had mated in my plain sight— I had heard their breathing, their gasps, their laughter—I was revolted. Into such company my mother's actions had thrown me, and I had to rely on them, for I was so still that I could hardly move and I did not know the way to Delphi.

Therefore I said no word to the slave Cassandra as she blew into the brazier and made the coals glow. The hut, which stank of humans and goats and mating fluids, began to smell of roasting. Orestes took a skewer of meat from the fire and sat down to eat it. He was dirty and dishevelled but he seemed composed, licking his fingers as the grease dripped down.

I was not used to sitting on the ground and my legs cramped as I tried to move. I crawled to a crouch and snagged my feet on a trailing edge of my chiton. She reached out a hand and hauled me to my feet—she is very strong—saying, 'We will have to shorten these garments, Princess. Court robes are not suitable for the road. Have you a needle amongst your things?'

'I think so.' I had to talk to this degraded woman. I found two needles and gave her one, and she sat down to bundle up the hem of her delicate robe with uneven stitches. I did not like to see beautiful weaving so mishandled, so I said, 'Let me do it.'

She smiled at me. 'I have never managed to learn sewing. I'm a healer, that's my skill,' she observed, shedding the outer robe so that I could work on it. Her body was almost bare under the northern chiton, which is slit up to the thighs on both sides, a garment that only a heterai, a courtesan, would wear.

I made a neat seam along the chiton and the undergarment, then started on my own. She watched me and commented, 'You sew beautifully.'

'It's easy,' I said, for it sounded like an honest compliment. I had not had much to do with other people. My mother's house was not happy, but it confined me in propriety to her company and those of the slaves. This woman was neither sister nor slave and I did not know how to talk to her. I had never met a courtesan before. I said, 'See? Just don't drag the needle through and it won't snag.' She began to copy my action, though she was clumsy.

'This must be your skill,' she commented, sucking a pricked finger.

'You said that before. Not my skill alone, but the skill of all women. We are required to spin, card, weave, and sew to supply the household. It is the mark of a good woman.'

'Good as in virtuous?' she asked.

I nodded. 'Good women do not stray abroad, gossiping; we do not visit other women and drink wine, even at festivals. We stay in the women's quarters, make clothes, supervise the slaves, and make all comfortable for our Lord when he returns.'

'I see. So you have no learning?'

'We do not need learning,' I said, a little stiffly.

She nodded and asked, 'Who tends you in childbirths? Physicians?'

'Indeed no, what an idea!' I exclaimed, shocked. 'Good women must never look into the eyes of a man, not even a relative, not even her husband. Midwives and wise women come to a birth. Of course, the baby is not named until the father has accepted it.'

'What if he doesn't accept it?'

I realized that she was a complete stranger to all civilization and went on, talking more than I usually do. 'Then it is exposed, of course. That's why women say that one must not get fond of a child before it is a week old, because it may be rejected.'

'Princess, are you telling me that unless an Argive father accepts a child, it is killed?' she asked, abandoning all attempt at hemming.

'Not killed, exposed, laid out on the hillside. If there's anything wrong with it, too, if it's deformed or a girl. Fathers require sons. My family is unusual because there are three girls before… No, there are two girls now.'

Cassandra did not speak, but held my hand gently as I remembered that one of the daughters of the Royal House of Atreus had been sacrificed by her own father. Iphigenia, my favorite sister, so gentle and beautiful, who had taught me the fast looping hemstitch which I was using. I had a rare flash of memory. The dark hair falling glossy from the silver fillet, her almond eyes bent on me, her red mouth smiling. A smell of spring in the air, and the tinkle of little bells as my sister moved. 'Now, little Electra, don't pull the thread so tight, and the material will lie perfectly flat. If you finish the whole seam, I will give you a bit of honeycomb which father sent from Troizen.' My mind shied off the thought of our father's death. That was something which I must not think of yet. I dragged myself back to the present and said, 'You will need to learn it all, Cassandra, if your Lord marries you to an Argive.'

'I have no Lord, and I will never marry an Argive,' she said firmly. I realized that she was mad, and I was sorry for her.

When the men returned they found us sitting like friends at the hearth, sewing cat-scratch stitches on Orestes' spare tunic.

'Good news and good bargaining, we have horses and I think we'd better go,' announced Eumides. Cassandra rolled her possessions into a compact bundle and swung her heavy cloak over her shoulder.

'Just how good a bargain?' she asked suspiciously, and the sailor grinned, showing missing teeth.

'A very good bargain,' he emphasized.

'Come along, Princess.' She rolled my burden for me. 'Eumides' very good bargains can cause trouble.'

She extinguished the fire and we left the hut, blinking in the sunlight. It was a cool spring day and the hills were covered in flowering nettles.

Four horses stood outside. On one of them Diomenes was riding, with Orestes sitting before him. Cassandra, laying her bundle on a tall black horse, leapt unaided onto its back. She gathered up the reins like a man and said, 'Hssh, beast.' The horse, which had reared, came down onto all its hooves again, looking embarrassed. Eumides secured my burden to the saddle with straps and then lifted me up. 'I can't ride!' I gasped as I came down astride and blushed for shame.

'You'll have to learn,' said the sailor impatiently. 'It's too far to walk. And we'd better get away before…'

'Before those horse-merchants find out that the gold was actually bronze?' suggested Cassandra.

'Copper,' he corrected her, and she laughed aloud.

I was travelling with a mad whore and an escaped slave and a thief. However, it was pleasant to be out of the hut, though I was so high up that I clutched the saddle in fear. Orestes looked happy. He was sitting almost on the horses' neck, with Diomenes' arm around his waist so that he couldn't fall, and he was looking eagerly along the road. I heard him say, 'Look, Lord! Smoke!'

'Now I wonder what that can be,' mused Diomenes. 'The road's taking us there, so we'll find out. Listen, son of Agamemnon. I know you're a prince and a child of the House of Atreus, but you will have to obey certain rules if we are to arrive in

Delphi alive. The first rule is that if we say run, then run, run and hide. Don't stop for anything. Is that clear?'

'Yes, Lord,' said my brother.

'The other is that we do not announce who we are, our names or lineage, to any chance-met companion. Enemies may be looking for us to do us harm.'

'But, Lord Diomenes,' Orestes said, a little shocked, 'names and titles must be proclaimed at first meeting. It is a matter of honor. It is the duty of all men to be honorable.'

'We are aiming to be both honorable and alive at the end of this journey, Orestes, and that may require some ingenuity. Did you ever meet Odysseus, Prince of Ithaca?'

'Yes, certainly. He was a friend of our father; he used to bring us presents from the other side of the world.'

'The Lord Odysseus of Ithaca employs guile, and his honor is intact—so far.' Said Diomenes drily. 'So shall ours be. Off you go, horse.'

Cassandra, observing me in difficulties, gathered up the reins of my horse and said to it, 'Come along, *Banthos, Dapple*. Don't be difficult,' and the animal, which had been dancing on its hooves and trying to scrape me off against a tree, became biddable and followed along after Cassandra.

'I think I'll call this horse *Nefos*,' she said, managing her own beast and mine with ease. 'Black cloud, it's a good name and fits his temperament. You've never ridden before, have you? It's not difficult. Sit down on the horse and dig your knees into its sides. If you think you are going to fall off, sit up straight. If you start to fall off, sit up straighter, grip tighter, and don't grab for the mane. There, see? Easy. And more pleasant than walking on those sore feet.'

It was, as she said, much better than walking. Once I found the trick of balancing, the easy pace did not jolt me, and I had time to look around. The valley was wide and beautiful, shimmering silver with olives and green with vines. The sun warmed my back and the horse was behaving. I had never been so far in the open before. The world was unexpectedly big and interesting to someone who had looked at walls all of her life.

The road was smooth and empty. Although I closed my eyes when *Banthos* strayed too close to the edge, where fallen rocks lay among trampled weeds to show how steep the slope was, I was not very frightened. One of my chambers had been painted with a fresco of flowers. Tall purple loose-strife, small purple orchids, yellow daisies, rock roses and red poppies, the blood of the Slain God, Adonis. The colors had always seemed overbright, but now they burned on the mountainside, real, sharp, almost blinding to sheltered eyes.

I drew my veil aside for a moment and blinked in the sun. I think it was happiness that sent a shaft through me. I haven't much experience of it so I don't know.

We had travelled around the bulk of the mountains on thin, winding goat trails when we smelt smoke again. A strong stench of mingled flesh and wood. Cassandra jerked at the rein, bringing *Banthos* and me close to *Nefos*. The horses whinnied, and Cassandra called, "Chryse, I know that smell.'

Ahead of her, Diomenes replied, 'So do I. That's the stench of war, or I never smelled it. How well does the maiden Electra ride?'

'She's staying on,' said Cassandra. 'Shall we dare it and ride through?'

'The road takes us there, and there's no other path—I doubt we could get the horses over the mountains.' Said Eumides. 'Surprise is best—they will probably be feasting in the ruins, Argive dogs! There was a village here, just goatherds and fell-mongers. They sold us good leather to make bags when we came through. I remember the road. If it's blocked, we'll make a fight of it—they're just bandits.'

Cassandra gave me the reins and, of all things, accepted a bow which she bent and strung in a most professional manner. She was not just a slave and a whore, but an Amazon. She tied back her hair at the nape of her neck. Her eyes were hard. I was wary of her.

'Maiden, listen,' said Eumides to me, speaking slowly. 'Soon we'll come into a village. The road runs out on the other side of the square. All you have to do is dig your heels into your mount and go straight for the road. Don't wait for us. We'll be right behind you.'

'That is true. I have not been rescued from slavery to be stopped by any Achaean bandit,' Cassandra said through her teeth. 'Come on.'

We increased speed as the road flattened out and widened, and came suddenly into what had been a small settlement, made mostly of mud houses with wooden roofs. These were aflame. I heard wailing in the ruins, the scream of a woman, and saw a partly armoured man lift his helmet from a pile of broken potsherds and cry a warning. Shouts rose from the wreckage. Three men with spears came running.

I sat down on *Banthos*, kicked him hard, and he galloped. I could see the opening between two burning houses, and in a gush of flame which singed my veil, we were through the gap and into the road.

I would have turned back, but *Banthos* had been goaded into running and kept running, despite my tugging at the reins. I was jolted and bounced out of breath and so bruised that I could hardly find a spot that didn't hurt by the time I brought him to a halt. He walked a little onto the verge and began grazing. I did not want to get off, because I doubted if I could get back on again, so I sat uncomfortably in the saddle and listened for a sound on the road behind as the heartless beast cropped mouthfuls of rich grass.

I was just telling *Banthos* that I was a princess and that he ought to do as I so civilly requested, when the others caught up. Orestes was wrapped around Diomenes, his head against the Asclepid's chest and his arms around his neck. I hauled *Banthos* out of the hedge and turned him. Diomenes saw my face and said quickly, 'No, maiden, he's not hurt, I bade him hide his face. There, boy, you can look now. We are all safe and we'd better keep going.'

'The village? Who did it?' I asked. 'Surely not the victorious army?'

'Bandits. Agamemnon was gone so long that the old order has almost broken down. There was a drought two years ago, and the crops failed. Since then it has been banditry on the land and piracy on the sea. The state of the Argolid is very evil. Luckily Cassandra is Amazon-trained and a dead shot. I would have been more careful, Lady, when I spoke to you over the walls at Troy, had I known you were so good an archer.'

'Even an unskilful archer cannot miss a target barely an arm's length away from her,' she said. 'I fought with Hector in the battles, of course, but only as a rear-guard. I was never more than a passable shot.'

'You fought in the battles, Cassandra?' I asked, nearly dropping a rein.

'Yes, that is our custom. Trojan women fight in their own defense, Electra.'

'Are there really such people as Amazons?' asked Orestes. 'Surely there are no women who can fight.'

'If I had not hidden your face, boy, you would have seen the Lady Cassandra fighting. Of course the Amazons are real. I myself saw them at Troy.'

'Tell me about them,' insisted Orestes.

'As we ride,' said Diomenes. 'We've got a long way to go before dark.'

Chapter Three

'I have won my bet. Cassandra and Diomenes are lovers now.' Aphrodite said.

'Very well, Lady of Cyprus,' said Apollo, baring perfect teeth. 'You may keep the apple, but I will not forget. Your Princess is not safe yet. There are many perils between Mycenae and Delphi.'

'Make your peace,' grumbled Demeter, Earth-Mother. 'Leave the poor mortals alone. Their life is short enough, their danger immediate, their chance of lasting satisfaction sketchy at best. They have suffered enough. Merciless and cruel, that is the nature of the children of Zeus. Besides, you are bidden to attend to the fate of the House of Atreus, more wicked, more dreadful even than gods. Did not Atreus cook his wife's adulterous fruit in a banquet for his brother Thyestes? Did not Thyestes then rape his own virgin daughter, Poseidon's Priestess, to father the revenge-child Aegisthus? And isn't that Aegisthus now lying with the Queen Clytemnestra in her husband's heart's blood? Do these outrages, and your Divine Father's order, mean nothing to you, children of Chaos and Death?'

'The child Orestes and the maiden Electra are alive,' said Athena. 'There will be revenge.'

'There has been too much revenge,' said Demeter.

Apollo's laugh was as child-like and as sweet as the sound of little bells.

Cassandra

I don't like war. I shot that bandit when he was so close that I could see every missing scale on his stolen mail-shirt. They weren't soldiers; they were just hungry men, driven to desperation by Agamemnon's neglect of his kingdom. But I killed the man, anyway, before he could throw the spear which was aimed directly at Eumides' back. The others ran away, which was sensible of them.

We came without harm through the ruin of the small village and I wondered how many more would lie between us and the Isthmus of Corinth. Eumides took my hand as we rode along narrow paths.

'I owe you my life,' he said. I patted his unshaven, olive-tinted cheek.

'And I owe you mine. That Queen of Mycenae was going to kill me.'

'Oh, those eyes—those hawk's eyes—yes, she would have killed us all,' he shuddered. I changed the subject. I was curious about our travelling companion.

'Eumides, what do they say about Argive women?'

'That they are so lustful and uncontrollable that their husbands lock them in their houses and chain a big dog across the stairs to discourage adulterers. Seduction is punished by death. Achaean women are never allowed out, not even to go to the market, not even to fetch water if there is a slave to do it for them.'

'That sounds more like the husband's fears than the wife's unfaithfulness,' I commented.

'Yes, I never believed it, and that maiden Electra is proof—cold as ice. She squeals at the slightest approach. You're a living affront to her, lady.'

'Me? Why?'

'You are Trojan, Lady, and Trojans are free women,' he said patiently. 'Achaean women don't even see each other, except at festivals. They never see another man, only their fathers and brothers and husbands. There was an Argive once whose friends told him that his breath was foul and bade him clean his mouth. He went home angrily to his wife and demanded to know why she hadn't told him. She said, "I thought all men smelt like that".'

We had come up to the others, and they heard this anecdote.

'She was a good wife,' commented the Princess Electra approvingly, silencing my incredulous laughter.

'Because she had never been near another man?' I asked.

'Yes. I was never in the presence of a young man except my brother until I travelled with you,' she said. 'All my life I have lived with women, my family and the slaves. But I used to look out of the window into the city sometimes, though it was forbidden.'

'Oh, Electra,' I said, filled with pity. No wonder she was narrow, prudish, and uneducated. 'The Trojans believe that there is no virtue in ignorance.'

'Chryseis was the same,' said Diomenes, then fell silent.

'Who is Chryseis?' I asked, after we had clopped along mutely for some time.

'My wife. Palamedes gave her to me. She is dead,' he said, and we did not talk any more until Orestes demanded first a drink and then to get down, so we stopped at a convenient stream which leapt down the cliff.

It was snow water, chilled and delicious. Chryse and I spoke, almost together.

'Don't drink it too fast or...' We stopped and looked at each other. 'You'll get cramps,' we concluded.

'Don't get sick on this journey, Orestes,' said Eumides. 'We have two healers, and they'll probably quarrel about the treatment.'

'Tell me about Trojan medicine,' said Chryse. He seemed unsettled since the mention of his wife. I wondered if he had loved her, this human reward whom someone had given him, who cannot have seen him before she lay with him, and to whom 'consent' was only a word. I began to ransack my knowledge of herbs, identifying them from horseback. I saw a cluster of familiar dark leaves.

'*Solanos*,' I said, and he said, 'nightshade.'

'Poisonous and to be used in the last resort,' I continued. 'Used for malignant fevers and the ague. Brings down a terminal fever.'

'Causes a terminal fever,' he argued. 'Treatment if ingested; induce vomiting with mustard and water.'

'Or *lychnis*. Aloe is good, too.'

'Yes,' he agreed, 'If you can get the patient to swallow it. What's *lychnis*?'

'There's some, growing next to the *mentha* near that stream.'

'Soap-leaf, growing next to mint,' he corrected me. 'Do you use Heracles' herb?'

'What's that?' I asked. He pointed to a tall plant with pea-shaped pink and white flowers. 'Oh, you mean wound-leaf.'

'This is going to last for the whole journey,' muttered Eumides. 'You're going to arrive at Delphi an expert on herbs, boy.'

'It's interesting,' responded Orestes. I looked at him properly for the first time. He was a thin child, with alert eyes, solemn and slightly frail, as though he might have been ill as a baby. I smiled at him and he smiled back, an enchanting, innocent smile which lit up his whole face and made his uncanny golden eyes shine.

'We used eye-in-the-grass for bleeding noses,' offered Electra.

'Yes, that's periwinkle. It's used in love potions, too,' said Chryse, smiling. It was an unwise thing to say, for the princess went straight back into her shell.

'I call it *vinea*,' I said coldly, annoyed with him. He shot me a wary look.

'What about these?' He leaned from the horse and plucked a flower, which he handed to me with a flourish. 'We call it *orchis*.'

'We also. We use it for scabies and cradle-cap in babies—and for love-potions, as well. But I've never seen *orchis* this color before. We used to go out and gather them in spring on the slopes of….' A lump rose in my throat, cutting off speech. I would never see that mountain again. Troy was destroyed. The Lord Agamemnon had seen to that. The very stones of the city were scattered.

'The *orchis* will bloom there again, Lady,' said Eumides. 'They grow fast on the bones of the Argive dead.'

'Yes, I saw them, a carpet of little wine-red points on the burial mounds,' said Chryse. 'Troy is avenged.'

'Avenged or unavenged, Troy is gone,' I said. 'Soon all who remember the city will be dead, and no one will speak her tongue again. We have been absorbed, swallowed.'

'You should not have stolen Elene,' said Orestes.

There was a silence. They were leaving it to me to explain, even Eumides, who was as Trojan as I was.

'We never had her, Orestes. My brother Pariki ran away with her from Sparta. It was a most dishonorable act, though I believe that she wanted to escape from Menelaus. She never entered the city of Troy and you have my oath on it. If we had had her, don't you think my father, King Priam, would have given her up to save the city?'

'Then...my father and my uncle must not have believed that you didn't have her,' he reasoned.

'They neither believed nor cared. They wanted the wealth of Troy, and they have it. They wanted to obliterate Troy, and it has been wiped off the face of Earth as though it had never been.' I was not going to tell this little son of Atreus that Troas, daughter of Troy was, I hoped, flourishing with those who had escaped long before the city was sacked. Little sons of Atreus grow up into monsters. Perhaps even this docile child would fall under the curse which had eaten the male issue of that most bloody of families.

'So it was just.' His brow was wrinkled. 'What my father and his brother did was just.'

'I think the Lady Cassandra has answered enough questions,' said Chryse.

'No, it was not *just*, Orestes. There are no just wars. Just death and loss,' I said, and my vision blurred, though not with tears. The gods were with me again. Not Hecate or the Maiden, that the Argives call Persephone, but Gaia the Earth, patient and generous.

'Daughter,' was all she said, but I was suddenly as cool as if I had bathed in spring water. I was soothed as though some ointment had been applied to my pine-cone nerves. I smelt woodbine.

When I was aware again, the others were discussing a place to rest.

'There is a village not too far from here—we have a reason for returning,' said Eumides. 'It is called Artemision. There we should also ask about…other travellers.'

'We have heard nothing behind us,' objected Electra, looking nervously back.

'There are faster ways than the road. A runner on foot could be before us. Perhaps I should just ride into Artemision and see if there's any trouble,' he said airily, and then galloped off before we could stop him.

'Curse this Trojan courage,' fumed Chryse.

'We'd better wait here,' I decided, and drew Electra's horse off the road. It instantly dipped its head and began grazing, and I only dismounted in time to snatch a nightshade plant from its insatiable jaws.

'Foolish beast, that is poisonous,' I scolded, and Electra said, '*Banthos*! I'm surprised at you.'

She was getting the idea about horse-management, because *Banthos* knew her voice. He raised his head and looked at her, before returning to his ingestion of anything edible in the immediate area. He was the greediest horse I had ever met.

'You must have been bred from King Diomedes' stable,' she said, referring to the famous flesh-eating mares which Heracles had tamed.

'Oh, yes, this is Heracles' country, isn't it? I learnt about his labors from my nurse.'

'Was she an Argive?' asked Electra.

'Yes. She told my twin and me many tales about Heracles. He must have walked this road,' I said, tugging at the spiritual cord which found Eleni and me together. It was thinned to spider web now, but he felt me and thought of me, as I thought of him.

'Heracles is bound up with Troy, too. My nurse Neptha told me about how he killed the sea-monster, and then, when the Trojans would not pay, he killed the King's family, all except one boy...' Electra replied.

'Whom Hesione, the princess, ransomed with her maiden-head. Priamos, the ransomed one, they called him. He was my father, King Priam the Old.'

'I miss Neptha,' she added, and Orestes said, 'Don't be sad, Electra.'

'I'm not sad.' She gulped and made herself smile. 'See? I'm smiling. Do you want another story, Orestes? I'll tell you about Heracles' first labor, the slaying of the Nemean Lion.'

I was very pleased when Eumides returned, because we had run out of the labors of even that indefatigable hero by then.

'Old Neleus has dug up some wine for us, in exchange for some metal-work on the village's weapons,' he said. 'They're expecting trouble, it seems. He won't lodge our women with his women, he says, as they might get foreign ideas, but he's lent us his brother's house, which is new and empty. Don't look at me like that, Lady Cassandra, I am merely repeating the ignorant words of a stubborn Argive peasant, which do not reflect my own opinions.' He managed a creditable bow and kissed my hand. We rode into Artemision.

There are eleven villages called Artemision in the Argolid. It's very confusing, though devout, and I am sure that Artemis appreciates it.

One description will do for all. Artemision has a central square, with slightly wobbly brick houses all around. The occasional house is of stone, but stone is usually reserved for temples to Artemis, of which there is always one, and sometimes a subsidiary one to Zeus, Poseidon, or Athena. There is a well in the square, with a bucket and windlass, and a trough for wash-ing (unless there is a river). There are benches made of wood outside a wine seller's shop, and there is some sort of storehouse for grain, olives, and whatever the village sells collectively to Mycenae, Argos, or Tiryns. Add to this a few dogs, the odd lost goat or ass and a few females who vanish under their veils as soon as a stranger arrives, and you have all of the villages called Artemision. The predominant smell is of cooking beans, sour milk, dung, or burned dust, depending on the weather and the prosperity of the particular Artemision.

This one was nervous but not hungry. My stomach growled as we rode in. In response to the Lady Electra's imploring looks, I had pulled a corner of my mantle over my face and head, so I saw little as I was ushered inside the new house. I could smell bread baking and I was suddenly very hungry.

'The horses stay with us,' I said.

Chryse asked, 'Travel sense or intuition?'

'Intuition,' I told him. Chryse nodded and lifted Electra down from the saddle. She was so muffled in wrappings that it would have taken a seer to identify her.

'No one's looking,' said the Asclepid patiently. Electra shed a few ells of peplos and shook her head. 'Oh, I'm so stiff!' she complained.

'Horses always come first,' I said. Diomenes and Eumides went out and shut the door behind them, leaving only two small openings to shed light on the interior, which was entirely empty and newly whitewashed. The floor was of beaten earth and I knew that horse-dung and water was mixed with it to make a hard surface which can be swept. Our mounts added considerable flooring material as I taught Electra and Orestes how to unsaddle and rub down the beasts.

'You must always clean out the hoof,' I demonstrated, picking up *Nefos'* back foot. He did not like this but he had been tended before and was resigned to it—as long as I didn't extend the process unduly. 'Just pick out any mud or stones, and watch the creature's reaction. See, look at *Nefos*. His skin is twitching and his ears are laid flat. If I don't give him his hoof back, he's going to kick.'

He did, but I dodged, and the hoof hit the door, which boomed.

'Instructive,' said Electra. 'Now, *Banthos*, you're not going to kick me, are you?' She put her arms round the horse's neck and he lowered his muzzle and snuffled her hair. Being *Banthos*, he might have thought it was edible. But Electra was touched and proceeded to groom him to a gloss which the Amazon cavalry might have appreciated.

Orestes was willing, but not strong. Once we finished with the horses, our next need was water.

An amphora stood inside the door. I hefted it. It was almost empty.

'Will you go for water, or shall I?' I asked. Electra blushed fiery red, as though I had offered her a terrible insult.

'I will not,' she managed to say. Orestes was also staring at me. Deciding that all Argives were quite mad, I lifted the water jug to my hip.

'Take my veil,' she offered, draping it over my head. My arms were full of terracotta so I let it stay, walked into the square, and filled the jug from the well. There were ten men in the square, shepherds and farmers. They followed my every move, some levering themselves off their bench to try and stare through my veil. They talked about me as though I were not there, though luckily their dialect was so thick that I could not understand all the words. They seemed to be discussing my childbearing potential. They stared at me, those peasants, as though I were carrion and they were crows. Comforting myself with the reflection that I could kill any one of them with a single arrow, I paced back to the house and Electra let me in.

It was not at all amusing to be an Achaean woman. I resolved to stop doing this as soon as I could.

Electra

I had never ridden on a horse before. It was exhilarating, though I was still unsteady and I hadn't even dared to inspect my bruises. Orestes was interested in the conversation and looked well, though I kept listening for his cough. He had coughed all the time as a baby, until Neptha had declared that my mother would never raise him.

Banthos let me groom him. I found something very soothing in brushing the horse's coat with a wisp of plaited straw until it began to shine. It was as satisfying as raising gloss on worked leather, and the technique is the same, except that this was a living beast who enjoyed the attention. He turned around and nudged the hand to keep going even if the wrist was tired, which mine was.

I had become almost reconciled to poor mad Cassandra, who had been quite entertaining company during the day and very brave in the village, but then she suggested that I fetch water.

I just stared at her. She must have realized her error, because she went out herself. It probably isn't her fault—she is a barbarian, a stranger, and a captive—but I didn't know what to say. Neither did Orestes. Slaves fetch water. Only slaves.

When she came back she seemed short of breath, but she didn't say anything, and we watered the horses. I found that *Banthos* could drink out of a dish, such a clever creature. That used up all the water, so Cassandra hoisted the amphora and went out again, unveiled. I heard silence fall in the square outside. This time she came slowly back, not hurrying at all.

'Didn't they stare at you?' I asked. She laughed.

'Oh, yes,' she said indifferently. 'I don't mind being stared at, as long as I can stare back, and not one of them would meet my eyes. Hecate is with me. They might have sensed that.'

'Hecate? You are a priestess of the Black Mother?' I pushed Orestes behind me. Hecate's worship includes human sacrifice.

'No. I was a priestess of Apollo—but I have belonged to the gods since I was a child. The gods of Troy are Gaia the Mother, and Dionysos the Dancer. But the others are there if I need them,' she said, grimly pleased, and tipped some water into the dish to wash her face.

Diomenes and Eumides returned laden with bread and wine and a squashy basket which proved to be full of soft sheep's-milk cheese. We sat down on the floor and shared it out, and it was delicious. The wine was better than the night before and the bread was crisp and hot from the oven. I ate my share and gave

Banthos a crust, which he took off my palm with great care. His lips were soft and he snuffled.

'Now, we're off to make spearheads,' Diomenes said. 'You can sleep, Maiden. Cassandra will watch.'

'So she will,' said Cassandra flatly. 'Be alert, friends, I don't like this place.'

'I'm coming too,' Orestes insisted.

'No, you'll stay here with me,' I said. He set his jaw and said, 'I am a man. I should be with the men.'

Diomenes knelt down until he was eye-to-eye with the boy. 'Possibly, little brother, but not this time. If you are lucky enough to travel with a prophetess, then it is wise to listen to her. She says this place is unsafe. Therefore, you will stay here with the women, on guard. You have your knife?' Orestes nodded, one small hand to his hip. He had a dagger such as is used at feasts to cut one's meat. It was a present from the King, bronze work of Mycenae, set with running bulls. A pretty toy for a lady. A weapon for a boy.

Cassandra, noticing me vainly trying to order my hair, took the comb from me and in a few rapid strokes had it tamed and coiled. She divided it into three strands and began to plait it, quickly and without pulling. I wondered that someone who could not sew could be so deft.

'I used to plait my little sister's hair,' she said, looping the ends back through the tail.

'What was her name?'

'Polyxena. My doomed little sister.'

'What happened to her?'

'Agamemnon sacrificed her on the grave of Achilles.'

'Then we are bound together,' I reasoned.

'How?' She did not sound either friendly or unfriendly.

'The same man sacrificed my sister Iphigenia for a wind to Troy, and they told us that she was going to be married to Achilles. She died, like your sister.'

We did not say anything, but our hands crept out and clasped, warmly, in the darkness. We sat like that for a long time, then I lay down to sleep and she sat upright, watching, in the night.

The attack came without warning. I was jolted and rolled face down on the floor, breathing mud. I heard Cassandra shout a sentry's warning like a soldier. 'Ware enemies!' and there was a solid thud as her attacker hit the wall. I heard the grunt as he fell.

My assailant, strong and drunken, hauled me up and grappled me close to his sweating, stinking body. Wine fumes almost overcame me. I sagged, fainting, and he chuckled, 'Mine, stranger-woman.' I was powerless, sunk in horror, which stole what feeble strength I had.

He shoved me into the coign of two walls. His breath was on my face and I gagged. His hands tore the front of my chiton. I had no escape.

And I lost myself. I felt a shriek rip my throat. Thereafter I heard nothing and saw nothing until I was sitting in the sunlight in the square, with Cassandra bathing my face and hands.

The water in the dish was red with blood, but I seemed uninjured. Sound came back to me. Chryse Diomenes, tall as an offended god, shining in the new light, was reproving the elders of the village called Artemision. His face looked like an ivory carving, set in stern lines.

'You broke in to violate a guest, fracturing all the customs and rules of Achaea, where strangers are sacred,' he was saying. The elders looked sullenly at their feet. They were old men, as crooked as their shepherd's staffs. In a house on the opposite side I heard female voices raised in a lament for the dead. Their keening underlay Diomenes' words.

'You have been suitably rewarded. We would have given you gold for your hospitality and friendship, but you decided to take our women and our treasure by force. Truly it is said that in the land of the Argives there is neither honor nor trust.'

'One of us is dead,' muttered the oldest man.

'You are fortunate that the rest of you are alive. Don't you recognize the Goddess when you see her, blind men of Artemision?' All eyes swung, not to me, but to Cassandra kneeling at my feet. Her hair was bright gold in the rising sun. She did not look at them, but turned her face away.

'Could a woman have so torn that man? Could a wild beast? He was almost rent in half, disembowelled, by a slight maiden with no weapons. Only the gods have such power. I am a priest of Asclepius the son of Apollo, from the Temple at Epidavros. My brothers were Macaon and Polidarius, my sister Hygeia. I was dedicated as a child and I have been to the slaughter at Troy, and yet I have never seen such injuries. You named this village after the Virgin Hunter, Artemis. You defile her worship by attempting rape. You are punished.'

'We will tend our sister, possessed by Artemis. When we are sure that she is well enough to travel, we will leave. You will occupy yourself in prayer. A sacrifice must be made to the Divine Hunter, her temple must be cleaned and repaired, and you must fast for three days. No woman will work in that time, for you have offended Her. You will carry water, men of Artemision, wear the veils of maidens, and you will repent to the depths of your hearts, or the game will desert your slopes and this time next year men will say, "Here was Artemision, but it is empty now, except for the Iean corpses which the famine left." Signify your agreement.'

They all nodded and shuffled away. Cassandra emptied the bowl and refilled it. There was crusted blood all over me, from thumb to shoulder and all down my breast, but I felt no injury.

'Return to your hearth, husband!' shrieked a woman in the shuttered house. 'Go not to Styx, the cold river of the under-world. Aie!' she keened, and other voices joined her. 'Aie! Aie!' they wailed.

There was an odd edge of glee to this female chorus, which made me uncomfortable. 'What happened?' I asked. Cassandra touched my wrist, felt my forehead and examined my eyes, then gave me a brisk pat on the cheek.

'Electra, you've come back. You don't remember anything?' I shook my head. She continued, 'The villagers of Artemision tried to attack us in the night, first plying our escort with much wine. Three broke in. I flattened one and Orestes stabbed another in the thigh, which was as high as he could reach—he's a good boy,' she said, casting an approving glance at my brother, who was sitting on the edge of the well, being washed by Eumides. He was unhurt as far as I could see, though white and shaking. 'Then one attacked you and, before I could come to your rescue, you were possessed and you tore out his guts with your hands,' said Cassandra matter-of-factly. 'Of course, it wasn't necessary to kill him,' she added, sluicing clean water over the rest of the stains. 'Go and sit down on the bench and the wine-seller will give us warm wine and honey, then you must eat something. A maenad rage is very exhausting. Have you had them before?'

'Never.' I did as I was told and sipped at a cup handed to me by a man ludicrously draped in a woman's veil. My hand slipped a little on the kylix and cringed away from my touch. I considered the implications of all that blood on me and the dead man being mourned, and delved for some feeling about it. I couldn't find anything.

'This tale will follow us to Corinth, with any luck. I think we may avoid attack in future,' commented Eumides, scrubbing my brother clean with someone's precious linen towel and throwing it down. 'There, boy, you did well, have some wine.' Orestes sat down at my feet, cradling his goblet. 'Lady sister, how fare you?' he asked formally.

'I fare well, my Lord brother,' I replied. 'Orestes, were you hurt?'

'No, Electra, but I was scared in the dark.'

'So was I,' I said, to comfort him. But I hadn't been. Something had taken control of me.

I drank more wine and was hungry enough to eat bread and cheese. Then I changed into a clean chiton and gave the bloody one to a hovering elder to wash.

Cassandra sat on the elders' bench, combing her golden hair and considering the veiled men coming to the well, like a well-fed fox watching grazing rabbits.

Chapter Four

Odysseus

Captive in the cave of the Cyclops, I told him my name was Nobody, and thrust a fiery stake into his single eye. I led my shipwrecked and terrified men out as the giant howled in pain, and when the others asked what was wrong, the simpleton cried that Nobody had wounded him. Nobody had hurt him!

I obliged my crew to remember that I am Odysseus of the Nimble Word, when they asked how we had been saved.

'Wine, a talent for impersonating sheep and superior linguistic ability,' I told them.

Poseidon, Lord of the Sea, Earth-Shaker, take your hand from above me. Though you sink my ships and swallow my treasure, I will not beg for your mercy. You have none.

Cassandra

Making a mental note that I should never, never back the Princess Electra, daughter of Agamemnon, into a corner, I watched the shoemaker of Artemision as he fitted soft boots onto her dainty feet. She was small, like the figurines that they make in Tanagra, with delicate wrists, a tiny waist, and little feet, still bruised and cut by thorns. How could such a diminutive woman, who did not look strong enough to harm a flea, have disembowelled a grown man fuelled by lust and wine?

It was impressive. I had heard her shrieking, then silence had fallen, except for certain revolting noises which I now understood and which rendered me unlikely to really relish red meat for the foreseeable future.

Eumides had brought the lamp into the melee when it was all over, and the floor had been swimming with blood. Wrist-deep in the victim's abdomen, Electra had frozen, seeming to be tranced, and had not resisted when I led her gently out of the house. The man who had attempted to rape her was more comprehensively dead than any fallen soldier, and I did not know what to make of it. I had to unfold her fingers to make her release the unidentifiable piece of squashed tissue, which might have been his heart.

Chryse was sitting behind me and I leaned back against his warmth. I felt his heart beating.

'Are all Argive women subject to such rages?' I asked.

'No. I believe that it was a trance such as maids sometimes have, women who dance for the God Dionysos. It usually takes them three days of fasting and wine to work themselves up to this fury, and they have hunted men and killed them in mistake for deer, but always in a pack. Each one encourages the other. I have never seen it happen to one alone.'

'Perhaps it was the god,' I said in all seriousness, and he laughed.

'Lady, surely you do not believe in the gods?'

'Lord, surely you don't disbelieve in them? They are all around.'

'I have only seen one god, and his name is Thanatos, Death. All other gods are constructed by men, who wish desperately to explain the random workings of chance.'

'Chryse, look at me.' I shifted my position so I could look into his eyes. He seemed sincere. 'I have seen the gods since I was a child. They are a fact. I do not need to believe in them, I can see them as clearly as I can see you.'

He laid his palm on my forehead. I held his hand between my own, compelling his attention.

'I have no fever and I am not mad. The gods are there. They move men. I saw the Bright Lady distract my brother Hector in single combat, so that Achilles killed him. One is not mistaken about things like that.'

'Is one not?' he asked quietly. 'I cannot see them.'

'That is your way of seeing. Mine is different. But both are equally valid.'

'I cannot believe in the gods, Lady, however much I love you.'

'You don't need to, as long as you have no objection to me doing so. Do you have color-blindness among the Argives? In Troy it was always an affliction of men. A man who cannot see the difference between red and green is likely to deny that they exist, but that does not affect the existence of either red or green.'

He stroked my cheek very gently.

'You are wise and merciful, Lady. We shall agree to differ. Did you see any god with the Lady Electra in her rage?'

'None at all, but I was occupied.'

He smiled and shook back his hair, seemingly relieved.

'Well, Healer of Troy, if she was your patient, how would you treat her? With mistletoe?'

'Ordinarily, or maybe basil—what do you call that?'

'The same, king of herbs, revealed like valerian to Asclepius by Apollo himself. It may be significant that it grows by the basketful in the fields around Epidavros.'

'Possibly. You will get no praise from me for Apollo. But she doesn't seem unwell, Chryse. Look at her. Her color is good, her breath comes easily, she is steady and she ate a good breakfast.'

'Perhaps it is a matter of pressure. Pain or fear builds up inside her, becomes unbearable, and when it is discharged, she feels relieved.'

'Like the release of urine in dropsy. Yes, possibly. But what pain or fear could be so dreadful as to make a slight maiden strong enough to tear a village bully to bits?'

'The Asclepids would put her to sleep in the tholos, to learn from her dreams,' he said earnestly.

I replaced myself in his arms. His hand lay upturned in my lap. A healing hand, strong and well made. I saw that the first boot had been laced to the princess' imperious approbation and mused, 'That might be a good idea. She is nervous, certainly, starts at most sounds and is very protective of her brother. She is not ready to consider the death of her father yet; we must let that lie until can speak. She is uncertain in the world, but that could be expected in an imprisoned woman who has suddenly been set free.'

Chryse shifted a little against the warm wall. 'We call them secluded, not imprisoned. She reminds me of my wife, Chryseis. She had never learned anything or seen anything until her father gave her to me. But she picked up languages with astonishing speed, and she was arguing points of philosophy with the old men before the year was out.'

'But she died?'

'In childbirth.' I felt him tense, ready to withdraw again into his memories.

'There are always some we cannot heal,' I said, not looking at him. 'They are always the ones we remember. One by one, Healer, I watched my people die and no effort of mine could save them. We must comfort one another, Chryse,' I said, very deliberately, 'for no one else can understand what we suffer.'

For a moment his voice caught in his throat, then I felt him lean down until his face was in the hollow of my shoulder. His mouth moved and I heard him say, 'That is true, Healer. I will try to comfort you, and you will try to comfort me, for our loss is almost beyond bearing.'

We sat until noon in the sun, in the central square of Artemision, embracing, and did not speak further. Eumides was engaged in forging himself a short sword on the pattern of Orestes' knife, and the boy was helping, fetching and carrying. After the boots were finished to her complete satisfaction, Electra joined them in the smithy.

Chryse and Cassandra, who had watched an army and a city die, who knew that there were gods and that there were no gods, drowsed together in the light of the sun or Bright Apollo and, for the first time since the destruction of Troy, I felt loved. I had been aroused and satisfied by my lovers in the goatherd's hut, but now I felt simply loved, without having to move or speak, without needing to caress or be caressed. The touch of sun-glow and pine-shade, the breathing heat of Chryse behind me, the scent of quenched metal, the inventive Trojan blasphemy from the smithy and the veiled men balancing jugs—all of this formed a bizarre but fascinating pattern which effortlessly included Cassandra, the stranger, and made her feel whole.

It was growing cooler as we set out for the next Artemision with an escort of boys, who followed in a silent, dogged group, perhaps to make sure that we cast no more spells on their cursed village. We had been generously supplied with figs, olives, wine, and bread. A small price to be rid of such disturbing travellers.

I had gone into the house of mourning. Though I doubted that the man would be much missed, I had a suspicion that widows might fare very badly in Achaea. The woman was doubtless mourning for herself as much as for her husband. I was reinforced in this opinion when I dropped a handful of coins in her lap and the disconsolate face brightened instantly. Thereafter, the keening for the dead had a certain theatrical vigor which had been lacking before.

I still had all my golden ornaments to use as currency. Gold would have been of no value in Artemision. One of my Mycenaean earrings, figured with golden bees, would have bought the whole place, with change over for a flock of goats and my own weight in barley.

We rode gently along, spitting olive stones over the edge of the path, and within a few hours came to another village almost identical to the previous one.

This time we rode in together. Eumides went first, sword in hand. I followed with arrow on string. Electra and Orestes were next, and Diomenes brought up the rear. He had no weapon and would not carry one, saying that it was against his oath.

I may be cynical in suspecting that word had got to this Artemision before us, but the villagers welcomed us with open arms. Not a glance was cast at Cassandra's unveiled head, and a house was cleared of occupants for us.

Electra

This Artemision was poor. The children were swollen-bellied with hunger and I noticed that some of the roofs showed signs of recent burning. I could count every rib on the elder who staggered up from his bench as we came in.

'Greetings and peace to all here,' said Diomenes, sweeping to the front. 'We are travellers to Corinth and wish to stay the night. I am a healer of Epidavros. Is there disease here?'

'No disease that a harvest wouldn't cure,' replied the old man. 'Welcome. Have you any news, travellers?' This was evidently a ritual question. I allowed Eumides to lift Orestes down. He stared at the hungry children, their hollow eyes and wrists like sticks. Orestes had never seen such a thing before, and neither had I. Cassandra dismounted and led my horse into the little house, where I could get down decently. The door was open and I could smell cooking, an unpleasant whiff of something bitter.

I asked Cassandra what it was. 'Nettle soup,' she told me. Then she sniffed and added 'No, it isn't. It's solanos, what did Chryse call it? Nightshade? They are preparing poison. Is it true that the Argives, in times of famine, kill the women and the girls?'

I remembered my father talking about cities under siege. 'Yes. Each man keeps one woman to fetch his water and bake his bread, and the rest go to the temple and drink the draught.'

'By the Goddess, Electra, I don't like Achaea. Even Hecate, Dark Mother, couldn't really approve of Achaea.' She rubbed both hands over her face. I could not understand her reaction. No man really needs more than one woman, and most of them would keep a mother or a sister, not a wife. New wives could be stolen or bought if the village survived. However we felt about it, women were possessions, to be disposed of as the master saw fit. We expected no voice in our fate. Cassandra went back to Diomenes and the elders, striding like a man over the beaten earth. I followed her.

'Troy has fallen,' said Diomenes. 'Agamemnon has returned.'

'That,' he said, looking significantly at the burned roofs, 'we know. We have also heard that Agamemnon is dead. The bandits came and took what little we had left, last night. We are preparing to sacrifice to Hades, to Pluton the Rich One. Then we will wait for our last hope.'

Cassandra mixed wine and water for us as we sat down in the square. I wondered that I had lost so much of my mother's training in such a short time. Princess the Lady Electra, daughter of Agamemnon, raised in the strictest propriety, sitting down in public view and drinking wine with unrelated men! I would not have been able to entertain the thought a few days before.

There is nothing to be said for the strictest propriety. There is no safety behind those thick walls and heavy doors. I drank, remembered my mother, and choked down a burning wave of rage and horror.

The old men had accepted a little of our wine. I noticed that they were sipping sparingly and wondered why they did not take more, for we had plenty. We produced bread and shared it, and again they mouthed only a token crumb.

And they were hungry. Their faces were carved with deep lines of privation.

'When do the markets begin?' asked Eumides. 'There should be grain soon.'

'Perhaps there will be food to buy in Argos, Guest, but we have nothing to exchange. There are enough provisions in the South Village to feed us all, but we have no treasure. The barley failed, and then the rye failed. We have been scavenging for purslane and roots, acorns and pine-seeds, and if the next crop does not grow we will be finished. The beasts are starved as we are. Now that the rain has come, we can sow one last crop.

But it takes ten men to drag our ploughs, we are so weak.' He said this not in a boasting or a self-pitying tone, but perfectly calmly. I remembered Father saying, 'The common people are hysterical, volatile, prone to despair.' If this was despair, it was very controlled.

Orestes walked over to the nearest child and crouched down on his heels. He broke his lump of bread in half and gave it to the boy. The child stared for a while, his eyes glassy with starvation. The he ran into the house. I heard a woman begin to cry.

'But we would not fail in hospitality, our sacred duty,' the old man was continuing. 'A goat shall be slaughtered.'

'It shall not,' said Eumides gently. 'We may not eat meat tonight, for we are under blood-guilt until dawn. Put off your sacrifice to the Underworld, men of Artemision. That would not be pleasing to the Goddess. Instead you will send some men to the South Village, and buy grain and oil for us, also figs, wine, and perhaps honey.'

A wretched mule was brought. It was, however, healthier than its owners, due to its ability to eat grass. Diomenes gave the three men some coins, and they set out, wearily, the mule plodding behind them.

'They are mountain-born,' commented the old man. 'They will not fail and they will return by morning. Lord,' he touched Diomenes' sleeve, 'will you ask the Lady for us how we will fare?'

'The Lady?'

'Our Lady, the Hunter Artemis. She is travelling with you, like a mortal, for a time, for her own good purposes. She is just as the priests said; tall and proud with golden hair, and a glance to strike fear into men. The Divine Hunter, bent bow in hand. We knew her immediately. We are her faithful people.' Diomenes hesitated and Eumides said, 'If she wishes to speak, old man, she will speak. But I think that she is pleased with her reception into Artemision.'

Cassandra inclined her head gravely. This was blasphemy and I wondered if I should tell them that she was an escaped slave of my father's. Eumides caught my eye and shot me a warning scowl.

I went to find Orestes.

He was in the first house. A woman so thin that her bones thrust against her tight-drawn skin was heating a little milk over a smoking dung fire. As I watched, she poured it into a clay dish, over the crumbled bread which my brother had given to the first child. The woman knelt down to distribute it, spoonful by precious, slow spoonful, to three children. They sat around her, mouths opening like little birds, and she wept as she fed them that she had no more to give.

I collected my little brother and crept away. What was a little Goddess-impersonation compared to this suffering?

◇◇◇

The three men returned as promised. I woke abruptly, and the three lying together on the one mantle stirred.

'Morning,' stated Diomenes, and Eumides buried his head in the Asclepid's shoulder and said, 'Again?' as he always did.

'The men have returned, bringing—how much did you ask them to buy?' I said from the doorway. The mule was sagging at the knees under many sacks and what looked like an amphora of oil. The men were dragging a travois with more sacks. Diomenes joined me and gave a pleased grunt.

'Yes, that should supply them until the first barley ripens. Come on, sailor, get up. Lady, perhaps you could pour some nice cold water on him.'

'I'm up, I'm up, barbarian! Well, this Artemision didn't try to rape us but it has the fiercest fleas in the Argolid.' He stripped off his tunic and captured the insect, cracked it between his nails, and yawned. There was straw in his coal-black curls. He was a disgusting sight.

'A picture of Trojan elegance,' commented Diomenes indulgently. 'Put on your tunic, you'll shock the maiden. Let's go and examine the load. They've made a bargain almost as good as one of yours, Eumides.'

'Those were authentic silver coins, not convincing tin,' he protested. 'You can't make a very good bargain with real money.'

'You're a scoundrel,' said Cassandra fondly. 'I must speak to the village. Come with me.'

She had let down her waist-length hair and she shone like gold as she walked into the square. She had dressed in a tunic and peplos, as Artemis is always drawn. Her strong arms were bare. Her eyes were grey. She looked like a goddess.

The voices, exclaiming at all that food, died away as she came. She walked to the very center of the village and said, 'I am pleased with you, Artemision. You have made me welcome with all you had. Therefore I say: all will be well. The barley will grow. You will eat of my bounty until then. I require this of you; feed your women, for only thus will you breed strong sons.'

She went into the little temple and came out bearing the cauldron full of nightshade broth, and poured it out on the ground. Eumides and Diomedes unloaded the produce and allotted one sack of grain and a little oil to each house. There was also a handful of figs and one dish of honey, and a measure of strong winter-wine. We would have enough bread to take us to Corinth once they had ground and baked our single sack of barley.

Cassandra did not come back into the little house, but perched on the well-coping until the women, veils awry or missing in their excitement, carried their grain down to the grinding stones.

Then she sat down as though she was used to such labor, and rolled the stone for each woman in turn, so that all the flour had been sanctified by the Goddess.

'Artemision will never forget this,' I said when she returned. Orestes was eager to watch his friend eat his first full meal and followed the women back to their houses.

'True. They will feel strengthened in future misfortune by my fraudulent presence. They will treat all strangers well, in case I sent them. Their barley will surely grow and they will boast of this visitation for generations,' she said. 'Also, their women are saved and they will recover faster because they believe. Or does that not accord with your philosophy, my Lord?' she said to Diomenes.

I could not get used to the way she spoke to men—mockingly, like another man.

'They will certainly heal faster because they believe,' said Diomenes. 'Every Asclepid knows that. Will you come with me, Lady? I want to search for plants. They'll need some tonics and some purifying herbs. I've already told them that they can only eat gruel today, and a little bread and oil tonight. Luckily some of the goats are still in milk.'

She laughed. 'Yes, I shall spread some divine radiance on the hillsides, and Eumides shall have a lesson in herbalism. Will you come, Maiden?' she asked me.

No one had ever asked me before to make a choice if I came or stayed. I had been doing exactly as I was told for my whole life, and I did not know what to say. I was comfortable in the square and I liked watching the people, so I ventured, 'I think that I would like to stay here.'

It was easy. Cassandra said, 'We will return soon,' and they went away.

Cassandra

Tearing off his dirty tunic, Eumides flung himself down into the rich spring green and complained, 'I tire of land.'

'How can you tire of it when it's so beautiful?' asked Chryse, doing the same and lying down beside him. 'Sniff, Trojan! That's a mountain bouquet out of Achaea that a princess might gather.'

'A princess has gathered it,' he grinned as I dropped flowers onto his naked chest.

'Orchis for male potency, primroses for sweetness, daisies for the sun, fieldfares for wealth, cyclamen for hidden loves,' I chanted, scattering them. Eumides took a deep breath. The rings in his ears glinted, and the purple orchis was netted in his hair.

'It's beautiful,' he conceded, 'but I belong to Ocean, the salt river that encircles the world.'

'We shall have sea enough soon,' said Chryse. 'We must reach the Isthmus of Corinth and then take a boat for Khirra, thence inland to Delphi. The gods only know what the roads are like.'

'And the Corinthian Gulf will be swarming with pirates,' commented Eumides. He did not seem unduly disturbed by this prospect.

'Do you think it was improper of me to impersonate a goddess, Chryse?' I asked. Eumides pulled me down to lie between them and I smelt mint and flowers, crushed by our weight. 'You are the goddess,' he said, kissing me. He exuded a sleepy heat. Eumides would never engage in deep philosophical debates, he would never worry about an ethical problem, and questions of honesty would never keep him awake at night. It was part of his disreputable charm.

'The women of Artemision would have died tonight,' said Chryse judiciously, his tone oddly unsuited to someone lying half-naked in spring pasture. 'And you didn't present yourselves to them as a goddess; they made that assumption themselves. So I believe that you did right. Their women live, the village will survive, and they will consider themselves blessed. Unless they are so boastful about their divine visitors that their neighbours rise up and massacre them out of sheer envy, they will be fat and insufferable in a year's time. I think you did well.'

His opinion mattered to me. 'Lord, I thank you. Now, if my status as a Divine Virgin is not to be blasphemously imperilled, we must get up and pick herbs. What are you looking for, Chryse?'

Their arms released me reluctantly. I was equally reluctant, but I did not want to risk the wrath of vengeful Artemis if she noticed that her avatar was playing spring games on a flowery hillside.

'Aha, borage,' he pounced on a plant with small dark-blue flowers and greying furry leaves. 'What do you call this, Lady?'

'Rabbit's ears. Blood purifier. Now if we can find some all-heal...'

'Valerian?' he hazarded. We strayed down the mountain and I found a large stand of it. I dug carefully with my knife and broke off a piece of root no longer than my hand.

'That will be enough for the whole village. You want to calm them, don't you? Perhaps we should give some to our friend?'

Eumides, perhaps a little elevated by the scented meadows, was dancing along the goat-path, singing a very rude Thracian song.

'I'd make a decoction and add this to their barley gruel,' I said.

Chryse beamed. His rare smile was to be treasured. He seemed to radiate joy.

'Healer, I thought that was my own discovery. Though I would add basic for healing and moisture—their stomachs must be shrunken and dry—and, let's see, it's too early for birch sap; we'll have to use young nettles for strength.'

'Basil is an excellent idea, but I haven't seen any nettles.'

From the goat-path we heard a thud and a torrent of exceptionally complicated oaths in a variety of languages.

'I think Eumides has found some,' said Chryse calmly.

The avatar of the Goddess Artemis laughed so much that she had to sit down.

Chapter Five

Sunlight poured down like honey on Olympus, home of the Gods, but a dark cloud threatened from the east. Zeus, Father of Laws, was concerned.

'The House of Atreus is cursed,' he rumbled.

'Then cleanse the earth of them,' urged Apollo. 'Strike with your lightnings, remove the dreadful Queen and her lover, demonstrate the justice of the gods.'

'And what is to become of this poor Princess Electra and her brother?' asked Aphrodite, rolling the golden apple along the floor.

'This matter has lasted through many generations,' commented Athena. 'Tantalus, intending to offend the gods, offered baked child to them and now spends eternity in Hades' kingdom, thirsting, hungering. Then Pelops, his son, restored by your direct orders, Father, killed his father-in-law and married Hippodameia. His sons were Atreus and Thyestes of bitter memory. We helped Atreus' children to reach Troy and the city is obliterated, and many of my heroes are dead. The army that went with him is decimated. Because of the sacrifice of Iphigenia and her own wickedness, Clytemnestra the Queen has murdered her husband. Now a new revenge-child, strangely conceived, is journeying to another death. Finish the House of Atreus, Zeus Father. I weary of their crime.'

'They are my children,' said a scornful voice. They turned and recoiled. Hecate, Drinker of Dog's Blood, stroked a hissing snake back behind her head-dress. 'The House of Atreus is mine. I have helped your Cassandra to escape, Aphrodite, because it pleased me

and she called on me. She belongs to me, as the sailor is Poseidon's and the Asclepid is Apollo's. She is a priestess of the Mother, and I am the Dark Mother aspect of Gaia. I will protect her. The House of Atreus must fall, finally and forever. Mycenae shall lie empty to the crows and the snakes. My Erinyes will punish crimes of blood. To a dark ending, to irreparable guilt and grief, are these pitiful Atreidae travelling.' She bared pointed teeth, flicking her serpent's tongue. 'Oppose me if you dare.'

Electra

The next Artemision was a whole day's journey away, the goat-path endlessly winding along the slopes of a mountain and then wearily down to a little stone village in the valley. We were all tired as we rode into the main square and dismounted stiffly.

We were met by the elders of the demos—old men, prosperous and fat, their skins shining with oil. The village, they said, had been blessed with a bumper olive harvest and was thriving. So much so that they had bought five new slave-women, and proposed to house us with them.

I was eager to get inside, away from the gaze of all those eyes. The village brought water and ceremonially washed our hands and offered us bread and salt, making us xenoi, guests, under sacred law and not to be molested. The air was full of the comfortable smell of everyone's food cooking. Children played with a dog in the dust outside our door and I sat down to watch them, after I had groomed my faithful *Banthos*. It appeared that they were playing Heracles and the dog was cast as the Nemean lion. It kept forgetting to be fierce and licking them. They were charming. Their laughter, high and innocent, followed me inside as it began to get dark.

I rolled myself in my cloak and lay down on the Artemision's sheepskins, favoring my bruises. I noticed that after only a few days I was becoming stronger, more able to ride for a long time, less sensitive to the strong light and the wind and the rigours of travel. It was a really interesting world. I had never watched it from the outside before.

I woke in the dead of night because someone was crying. Not loudly. Crying like a child or a slave cried, muffled for shame, trying not to attract attention. I touched Orestes but he was asleep beside me.

I had to do something. Tears started in my own eyes in response. I had cried many nights like that, my face buried in my pillow or my doll, hoping that no one would hear and ask me why. I had to help her.

I crawled to the brazier, which had a glow right at the center, obtained a coal and lit the oil lamp. A tiny bead of flame illuminated the house. White-washed walls. Cassandra, Chryse Diomenes and Eumides clasped together under their cloak. Four slave women asleep in a row, snoring.

One maiden curled up in a ball, weeping as though her heart would break.

I knelt beside her and whispered, 'What is wrong?'

She opened her wet eyes and said miserably, 'It is nothing, Lady.'

'No, it is something,' I said as gently as I could. I noticed that she was hiding her right hand, and touched it. 'Are you hurt?'

'My mistress ordered me to weave an ell of cloth today,' she muttered, allowing me to unfold the injured hand and look at the red mark across the knuckles. She was badly bruised and must have been in considerable pain.

'And you could not do it, and she struck you?' I asked.

'She struck me so that I could not do it. Tomorrow she will flog me for not completing my task. She is an old wife and there is an old master and he favors me,' she said very quietly. 'She will maim me if this goes on, and then the old man will sell me, and what use shall I be? I might as well be dead. I can't please the mistress by refusing the master or he will beat me.'

'We can at least prevent tomorrow's beating,' I said. Poor maiden, she scraped back her dark hair and stared. 'How?'

'Where is your loom?'

'There against the wall, Lady, but you can't…' she stammered. I smiled.

'Can't I? And we will wake a healer to look at your hand. In the morning I will speak to your mistress. What's your name?'

'Clea, Lady.' As I stood up, she embraced my knees in gratitude, though it was a small enough favor.

I woke Cassandra from between her lovers and she sat down to compound an ointment for the injury, while I stood to the loom. I examined the rows which had already been woven. It was a simple pattern, a herringbone weave very common amongst the poorer families in Mycenae. It is very satisfying to weave, and I could manage it half-asleep in the dark.

I unpicked a couple of miswoven rows, wound the shuttle to the correct tension, and began to weave. I found myself singing Neptha's work song as the heddle lifted and fell with the correct flat clack against the wall, indicating that the line of wool was absolutely straight.

> Until the light fails,
> Pallas is weaving.
> While the sun lasts,
> Pallas is working,
> Weaving a fine cloth
> For her brother,
> A fine red cloth
> For a healer's gown.
>
> While the light lasts,
> Pallas is weaving.
> While the rain falls,
> Pallas is working,
> Weaving a fine cloth
> For her little sister,
> A thick warm cloth
> For a baby's gown.
>
> While the sun shines,
> Pallas is weaving.
> While the wind blows,

Pallas is working.
Weaving a fine cloth
For her grandfather,
A double woven cloak
To warm his bones.

While the sun shines,
Pallas is weaving.
Until the dark comes,
Pallas is working,
Weaving a fine cloth
For her lady mother,
A purple brocade
For mistress' gown.

I heard Cassandra's quick voice cease. She was listening, although it was just a work song, such as women and slaves sing to wile away the weary days and regulate the work of their hands. It is the work of women's hands which clothes and feeds the world. Clea's injury, if it proved permanent, would lower her value to that of a water-carrier, indifferently fed, unsaleable, despised.

The cloth grew under my hands. I stopped to rewind my shuttle—if the wool was of Clea's spinning, then she was an excellent spinner—and resumed my song.

Until the light fails,
Pallas is weaving.
When the snow comes,
Pallas is working,
Weaving a fine cloth
For her bridal,
A red gauze veil
For Pallas the bride.

I wove and sang my way through all of Pallas' relatives, refilling the shuttle as the cloth grew. I sang of her brother, the soldier, and her uncle, the potter, and her friend, the maiden, and then the verse describing the making of the ceremonial cloth which we weave every spring for Persephone, Kore, the Maiden, for the festival which celebrates her return from the underworld.

> Until the light fails,
> Pallas is weaving.
> While the wind howls,
> Pallas is working.
> Weaving a spring cloth,
> A cobweb tracery,
> A sacred offering
> For Demeter's child.

I rolled up the completed cloth, re-hung the loom, and tied off my ends. Clea was gazing at me as though I had done something miraculous. Her cruel mistress would get a surprise in the morning.

And it was morning. Birds were singing outside and a cool light was bleaching my little oil-lamp's flame. I had stood and woven all night. As I stretched, taking the stiffness out of my back, I saw that all the people in the room, even sleepy Eumides, were smiling at me, and I blushed.

Then I said to the Healer, 'How can we save Clea?' and Cassandra smiled and said, 'I think we shall have another miracle.'

Cassandra

I had been woken by an imperious voice saying, 'Get up, Healer!' and I had extracted myself grumpily from between the two warm, breathing bodies. Eumides, who sleeps as though he and the Achaean God Morpheus have a close personal understanding, did not stir, but Chryse woke and asked, 'Cassandra? What is happening?'

'Sleep again,' I said. 'The princess requires my attendance.'

He muttered something abrupt about making her comb her own hair this time and subsided again into the sailor's embrace.

But it wasn't a trivial matter. A sobbing girl held out a wounded hand for me to treat. The bones were not broken but it was a very bad bruise, and I found the stonecrop and the pestle and mortar and the remains of Eumides' third-best tunic, which was frankly only fit for bandages, although he insisted that it had a few seasons' wear in it yet. The little light wavered in the cold air—it was very late. The girl seemed faintly astonished at being tended so carefully, and I thought better of Electra for having noticed that the maiden was injured. I hadn't. Slave women seek anonymity and after a few villages, I had ceased to really look at them. I sat on the floor pounding rendered lard and the herbs together, deeply ashamed.

Then Electra, standing at the loom, began to sing. She had a high, clear voice, very precise and true, and she sang a weaving song. She was not thinking about her performance or she would not have dared, but the song went with the work. Her hands sped almost without her volition, automatically, and she moved with the grace of a dancer, shifting her balance as the shuttle moved across the warp and the cloth grew as inexorably and effortlessly, it seemed, as a wave. Cream-colored wool moved up the web like magic.

I bandaged the girl's hand, told her that she would not be permanently crippled, and then fell silent under the influence of Electra's song. In the dark and the cold, in the warmth and the sun, Pallas wove, endless cloth for endless purposes. A vision came to me as I sat on the earth floor with the sobbing girl's maimed hand in my own. The vast tapestry of the world, tree and star, flower and human and stone, all woven by women such as these. Clotho who spins, Lachesis who measures, and Atropos who cuts the thread of life; the moon-spinners, the Fates.

By dawn, Electra had woven a cloth as long as her out-stretched arms; one ell.

In the morning we spoke to the master of the house and his wife, and expected that Clea would have no further trouble. Few weavers have ever had the favor of Arachne, who came in the night to miraculously relieve the distress of an injured slave.

Electra

We passed through seven small villages before we came to the outskirts of Corinth polis, and never a whisper of pursuit from Mycenae. I could not believe that my mother would let us escape so easily. When I was a child fleeing punishment for some misdeed, I had never managed to hide from her. She had found me even in the mazes of the under-city, dragged me forth whimpering and spanked me. I almost expected her to do that now. I was still amazed that she had let us escape at all. We were easy to find; the passage of the Goddess Artemis through her people was whispered from one goatherd to the next all the way, I expect, to Argos.

I was confused. All the rules I had learned didn't seem to apply to the world outside the Palace of Mycenae. I had been told that a woman could never be happy outside her own house—that that was her place. But Cassandra rode laughing in the sunlight, between her two lovers. I saw women working in the fields, riding donkeys, sitting under the trees in the spring sun. We stopped on the road to ask directions of one group of maidens. They wore scarcely enough between them to make one respectable tunic, were burned brown by the sun, and they were happy. They offered us berries. Their mouths were stained purple with juice and they exchanged teasing words with two goatherds higher up the hill. They were easy with travellers, friendly and easy and fluent. Offering to show us the turning, one maiden climbed on Eumides' horse and rode the little way to the crossroads.

I began to understand about Europa. She had been a girl like these. When the great bull from the sea had come, she had clambered, laughing, onto its back and been borne away. I had been taught that all women who speak to unrelated men are whores, but these were not whores. Neither was Cassandra.

Perhaps they had lied to me about whores as well. I had never met one. They had lied to me about a lot of things in my mother's house.

My confusion grew, but so did my pleasure in being outside. At first I had been intensely uncomfortable in the open, but now I began to feel constrained in a house. I did not know if I was being set free or going mad. I talked to Cassandra in one drowsy noon rest about where we would be happy. She was leaning against an olive trunk, combing her hair, and I was sitting down with Orestes asleep in my lap. The air smelt of honey and the bees of the Mother buzzed in the early flowers.

'I need a place where we can all live,' she said, 'where we can all be accepted. I don't mind where it is. What would you like, Electra?'

'I would like…a white house, like those, but bigger,' I said, considering, for it was not something I had ever thought about before. 'With an olive grove and three good fields for corn and a vegetable garden. I would like a stable for *Banthos*, and a clean wall for my loom. And a bench to sit in the sun and embroider. I would like a window with shutters and a stout door between me and the night.'

'And who would live in the white house?' she asked.

'There would be the master,' I answered. 'A kind man, a good trader. And perhaps he would be away a lot. But it won't happen,' I said.

She asked me, 'Why not?' and I could not answer. I could not tell this foreign woman why no one would ever marry me. Then *Banthos* snatched at someone's linen, which had been laid on a hedge to bleach, and we had to stop to retrieve it and apologize to the outraged owner. We didn't speak about it again, though I remembered my white farmhouse every time I came into a village.

Banthos and I were now close friends. I had never met a horse before—horses in Mycenae are the province of men. I had assumed them to be fierce and dangerous, needing to be overborne by a mastering will. But I found that they were tractable beasts, not very clever, perhaps, but willing and helpful, within their limits. He knew me, turned when he heard my voice, and loved my touch.

In the next village I saw an elder chastising his daughter. This would usually be done behind closed doors, but the girl had run into the square and he had followed her, beating her with a stick.

The girl screamed and cried. Cassandra took a step forward and both Eumides and Chryse laid hold of her.

'Princess,' said the sailor, 'this is not our argument.'

The girl fell to her knees, her chiton torn away from her shoulders. She cried to the old man, 'Yes, yes! I will do as you order!' and he threw the stick away and gathered the girl into an embrace, pressing his white-whiskered lips to a weal on her breast.

That night the dreams began. A feeling of dread had been on me all evening. I don't remember dreaming, but I woke horrified, sore, to the exhausted faces of my companions. I forgot my joy in being free, because I was no longer at liberty. My dreams bound me like a chain, and even Orestes could not comfort me.

Banthos was nervous as we came into Corinth, shying at every line of washing and chewing his bit. I was dreadfully tired and only pride stopped me from asking Cassandra to take the rein, as she had on that day when we had escaped from my mother's crime. Homicide. Regicide.

I dreamt every night. It seemed that the things I could not bear to think about were surfacing in my sleep. I had dreadful visions, which I could not remember. They said that I screamed in my sleep, struggled and cried for mercy, for vengeance. Eumides still bore vivid scratches where, apparently, I had clawed for his eyes. He was in favor of binding me, but Cassandra and Diomenes would not allow this. They sat up with me, one after another, as I wept and writhed. Or so they said. I only know that I awoke every morning exhausted and bruised, and that my escort was getting more short-tempered as the days wore on and village succeeded village.

They didn't seem to like me anymore, but that did not surprise me. Only Eumides was sleeping at all, and he remained obstinately cheerful, which was irritating the others. *Banthos* tossed his head, almost hauling the rein out of my grasp, and Cassandra flicked him with a luggage strap and growled 'Behave!' in such a dangerous voice that he lowered his neck meekly and behaved. And he is my horse. I was about to remonstrate with the Trojan woman about her handling of *Banthos* when we heard a shout from ahead on the mountain road.

'Thalassa, thalassa,' Eumides cried, reining the horse. 'The sea!' Orestes, who had greatly taken to the sailor, pointed and I looked.

Blue as the sky, blue as borage flowers or eye-bright, shadowed with islands, it was the salt river Ocean. I had never seen it before. It was vast. I heard the cries of strange white birds, raucous and sad. I strained my eyes to see the other side, and couldn't.

'Up there is the Corinthian acropolis,' Eumides told us. 'And down there, at last, is the port and that is where we are going.'

'You go and find us a ship, and we'll look for a lodging,' offered Cassandra, red-eyed and haggard. I had reduced her to this state, but I could not feel that it was my fault. I hoped I could die in one of those nightmares, and relieve them of my company. They had been kind to me beyond my worth, and kind to Orestes. They would look after my little brother. I sagged in the saddle, rubbing my eyes.

'Don't pay more than four obols and look for me in the temple of Poseidon,' he advised, and kneed his horse into a gallop, taking my brother with him. I watched the dust cloud on the white road. My heart sank. I was so tired of the wideness of the world, the unsafety outside walls, that I was almost longing to be back in my mother's house.

'Come along,' said Cassandra briskly. 'We need a place to stay and a stable for these tired beasts. Tonight we will all get some rest, if there is a herbalist in Corinth who sells the herb I am looking for.'

'Which?' asked Diomenes dully. 'I might know the Argive name.'

'It's a black sticky substance made of the sap of the Asian poppy. We call it earth of poppies.'

'Here we call it lethos, and it's dangerous.'

'I know that,' she snapped. 'But with milk and wine, honey and vervain, it's the strongest sleeping drug I know. Electra must sleep in peace, and so must we.'

'Vervain should abolish the visions,' he said, without anima-
tion. 'Milk and wine will be nourishing to the spirit, and honey
will render it palatable. We'll try it. Taphis the Corinthian should
have some, and we can lie in his house. He supplies many rare
herbs to Epidavros. I came here with Master Glaucus before I
went to Troy—he should remember me.'

I had never been in a city before. Corinth sprawled down
from the white pillars of the acropolis to the edge of the sea, a
maze of little houses and taller temples, built to no plan. The
street was paved as we went on.

The walls of Corinth are high and well-made, but the town
has grown outside it. If attackers ever come from the shore to
sea-bordered Corinth, then there will be a massacre.

This did not appear to concern the citizens. The streets were
full of people, all selling something or carrying something
home. Women shoved past us bearing amphorae of wine and
oil, heavy water jugs and armloads of bread. Slaves dragged new
pithoi, taller than me even sitting on *Banthos*, newly fired from
a smoking kiln. The air rang with hammering from a carpenter's
workshop, asses complaining that their loads were far too heavy,
and talking, talking, endless voices, in a cacophony of known
and unknown tongues.

A man with a wheeled cart shoved against Nefos and shouted
at Cassandra in some language, and she astonished him by
shouting back in the same speech. He then blocked the street
by bowing in a strange foreign fashion, allowing us to pass.

'What did you call him?' asked Diomenes. 'I mean, I know
the words, but…'

'The son of a pine-tree. It's a very nasty insult in Phrygian. It
means illegitimate. It's the standard reply to what he called me,
which was daughter of the cavern, where the Phrygians throw
their deformed children.'

'And the comment that caused him to bow?'

'I reminded him that Phrygians were known for their execrable
manners.'

'And for their perversity?'

'Just so,' she said.

'You are a woman of many talents,' said Diomenes, admiringly.

We had to dismount a little further along and lead the horses through a market. I had never seen so many people together in one place, and I was shaken and frightened. Cassandra reached back without looking and took my hand, Diomenes took hers, and we moved slowly through the agora of Corinth like a chain of sacred dancers in the circle-mazes of Mycenae.

Faces, so many faces! Women sold woven cloth, leather boots and sandals, bronze ornaments, and potions. An old man and three huge, grinning sons sold every possible type of pot, from lekythoi to hold tears or perfumes, to amphorae and jugs and rhytons, flat kylix wine-cups, goblets, cauldrons, earth-ovens, pots with ears and pots with feet, and pithoi big enough to take a whole cargo of wine. A man with a tray sold honeycomb in squares—'Only one obol, Kyria!'—and another was tied all over with ribbons, precious and paltry, of all shades from pale to startling red, fluttering in the breeze. I saw a baker dwarfed by a tower made of the flat barley loaves that Corinth consumes by the wagonload, and a winemaker with a whole vat of reeking raw new wine. There were oceans of honey, mountains of grain, harvests of olives and fruits, including strange preserves from distant Libya that smelt sour and exotic—long, yellow, flat, dry things and round, red, flat, dry things. There were golden apples from Libya, sharp and juicy, and enough well-woven and dyed cloth to wrap the city of Corinth in.

People let us pass, linked hand to hand, and the horses followed us. We did not slow until we were across the main square, through the stoa's colonnade of shops under cover, and onto a side-street. There Diomenes knocked at a large wooden door with a stone lintel and an intriguing image outside it. It was the carved head of a man—rather handsome, with a hawk nose and deep eyes, but halfway down the otherwise undecorated pillar there was an erect phallus. It seemed an odd place and the wrong season to find a prop from the Dionysiac mysteries, and I said so.

'It's a herm—it signifies that a citizen lives here,' said Diomenes shortly.

'If that is all it takes to become a citizen…' began Cassandra
coarsely, when the door opened and we were ushered inside.
The yard door was shut and the rage of the market was subdued.

The courtyard was cool. It was paved with creamy polished stone. There was a marble bench under a vine, and
the slave motioned that we should sit there while his master
was called.

The slave was very dignified but his master was less so. He
hastened into the courtyard, a tall man with bronzed skin and
strong, corded forearms. He was wearing a spotless tunic, but
had not even waited to put on his sandals as he rose from his
noon rest. 'Chryse, my dear,' he exclaimed. 'Can you stay with
me? It's been years, boy, you've grown.' Diomenes nodded at
the invitation and Taphis ordered the horses to be tended and
wine to be brought immediately. He also, to my astonishment,
called for his wife Gythia.

'You must be Chryseis,' he said to Cassandra. 'He told me
how beautiful you were, Lady. He spoke the truth.'

'No, Lord, Chryseis is dead,' said Cassandra quietly, as
Diomenes did not speak. 'I am a priestess of Demeter, as is my
companion. We are travelling to Delphi with the Lord Diomenes
and Eumides the sailor, who has gone to find a ship.'

Taphis, recovering gallantly from his error, poured unmixed
wine for us and we sat down. 'Delphi, Chryse? Why are you going
to Delphi? Is it Troy that had burdened you with blood-guilt?'

'Too much blood, Taphis,' he replied soberly. 'Far too much
blood.'

'How is your master, Glaucus?'

'He lives and is well, I believe. I have not been back to Epidavros yet. Perhaps later. Also, I need to buy some herbs.'

'My storehouse is yours,' he said formally. 'What are you
looking for?'

'Lethos.'

'I have some. Chryse, is it for you?' Taphis looked worried and took Diomenes' hand in his own. 'You look tired enough to sleep, Asclepid, without such strong measures.'

'No, old friend, for one who shrieks all night in unbearable dreams. The Lady here is my patient. We will mix lethos with honey, wine, milk, and valerian root.'

'An interesting compound. Ah, here is my wife Gythia. She will care for your companions.' He very carefully did not use any of the terms which would imply any close or marital relationship between us and Diomenes. Taphis the Corinthian was a tactful man.

Gythia, unveiled, was a brisk woman of perhaps forty, with long braids and bright brown eyes. She led us up the stairs to the women's quarters, talking all the way.

'Such a hot day and you have made a long journey, Taphis says.' She did not even use the honorific 'my Master' or 'my Lord' about her husband. 'I shall have them draw a bath for you at once, honored ladies, and some food shall be brought. Would you care to unveil, Lady?' she asked me. 'There are no male eyes here, except that of my son.'

As her son was presumably the fat, dark-eyed child presently taking her basket of wools apart quite methodically, I decided that he was no threat to my propriety and put back the veil. 'You are ill,' she said. 'I am sure that Taphis and Chryse Diomenes will be able to help.'

I wondered what she had seen in my face.

Cassandra

The Princess Electra shrieked and struggled in her sleep every night. She could not be left because she would tear off her garments and run out into the night, ripping at her skin with her nails and crying, 'No! Don't!' Something about Eumides attracted her especial hatred. After she had attacked him, trying to claw out his eyes, Chryse and I shared the watch and sat between her and our comrade. Orestes, questioned, said that he had never seen her behave like his before. Eumides took over the care of the boy, and they grew closer together. So did Chryse and I, watching and wearying over the tormented princess.

'What can have happened to her?' I asked for the seven-hundredth time, as we wrestled her to the ground in another shepherd's hut in another Artemision. I lost patience and sat on her, pinning her to the earth floor. Sometimes this calmed her back into sleep.

'She must have been tortured. I feel now that your disapproval of seclusion is wise, Cassandra. Lock creatures up in close cages and they will attack each other.'

'Her mother? You think her mother did this to her? Certainly the Queen is a woman of strong passions, but why should she bother to torture this meek daughter, when she had a whole city full of slaves? Besides, she has no scars. She has not been beaten or whipped, Chryse. It is something else. She is full of self-loathing.'

'Is she re-living the death of her father, do you think?'

'No, I have not heard her say one word about her father. It is her mother she hates most bitterly.'

'You knew,' said the Princess Electra, clearly, as though she had been listening. 'Mother, you knew. You knew! And you didn't save me!'

'Didn't save you from what, Electra?' I asked softly, hoping to talk to the undermind.

'Him!' she screamed, stabbing a finger in the air. 'Him, him!'

'Him?' I asked, but she was lost again in a dream.

'Him?' repeated Chryse. 'Does this mean that she isn't a maiden?'

'Surely no one could have…not in her mother's palace…' I hesitated.

'She says that her mother knew,' Chryse reminded me. 'Perhaps there was a lover. Even in a palace such things are known, sometimes.'

'Possibly, Chryse, but she would not be so wounded if she had voluntarily taken a lover, even a secret one. This sounds like rape.'

'She's over twenty, isn't she? When did you first lie with a man?'

'When I was fourteen, I made the sacrifice and joined the Mother. What about you?'

He leaned into my arms in silence. I could not see his face. I wondered if he was about to disclose the secret which he was clearly keeping about this, but all he said was, 'I was thirteen.'

'But I was in Troy where women are free, and you are a man. This stiff little princess would never have dared to take a lover, I can't believe it. She shrinks from any contact with a man. She believes in all the rules of propriety. Also, she has been watched by that hawk-eyed queen since childhood, so she hasn't a particle of initiative. She must have been given away, or waylaid in some dark place in Mycenae. It has enough dark places.'

'In the women's quarters, with all those guards outside?' objected Chryse, running a hand over his tired face. Exhausted and red-eyed, he was just as beautiful to me, the golden Asclepius-Priest, as he was when he had been alight with joy over my rescue. I remembered coupling with him in the goatherd's hut and suppressed a desire to bind Electra and down in his arms. His linen tunic, much stained with travel, had fallen away, revealing his throat and the pure lines of his chest. I dragged my mind away from Dionysos and concentrated on Asclepius. We had a patient and she had to be cared for, which meant we had to get to the bottom of this problem.

'Agamemnon has been away for a long time, since this princess was about eleven, I suppose. Would there be any way for her mother to find her a husband, or is that just the province of Argive fathers?' I asked.

'Her oldest male relative would arrange the marriage, and the princess would have a great dowry. There would be feasts and everyone would know. As far as the world knows, the Princess Electra is a virgin.'

'Ah, yes, the Achaean obsession with virginity. Instruct me, Chryse, I am ignorant. What would happen if the Princess had been raped? For she is behaving as violated women do.'

Chryse was too tired to notice the irony in my voice. 'Happen? She would be dishonored and the rapist would be fined. Rape is not such a terrible crime in Achaea. A seducer makes the woman fall in love with him and is therefore punished with death. A rapist makes her hate him and therefore her affection remains with her husband, so he is fined.'

'But the victim would be dishonored?'

'Yes. "Virginity gone, honor gone," that's what the Argives say. It would require a hefty dowry to bribe any man to marry her.'

'Have I told you how much I don't like Argive ways?' I asked, disgusted. Chryse smiled tiredly.

'Yes. Fortunately, you like at least one Argive.'

This was true. I stroked his hair. 'Why don't you sleep? I can watch her.'

'Provided that you call me if you need help.'

'I promise.'

When I was sure that he was asleep, his head on Eumides' shoulder, I lay down with the Lady Electra, breast to breast, measuring my body against hers. Then I called on the goddess that the Argives call Menmoysyne; we have a sacred name for her. Sometimes I had been able to make a link between my own mind and the mind of a patient. I was reluctant to do it without the support of another priestess, but this could not be allowed to go on. If someone wanted to capture us, we would be easy prey. We were so exhausted that only Eumides would have been able to put up a fight. And our Trojan sailor was growing fretful, urging us to leave this inconvenient, maddened princess in some village, saying we should otherwise bind her with ropes and gag her so that we could sleep. I saw his point but I could not do that. She would not survive alone, and her silent little brother would not leave her. If we abandoned her she would die.

The most difficult task was to sink into the sacred state and not fall asleep. I quickly gained the cloudy space where the souls of humans walk when they are not awake, and there she was.

Poor princess. Secured by wrist and ankle to a bed, spread-eagled, naked.

'He's coming,' the phantom whispered.

'Who?' I asked, trying to untie the bindings. They snaked away from my touch, sliding, unravelling. I have some power over this realm. I touched each bedpost and ropes hissed at me and retreated. The princess lay as rigid as a two-day corpse. Her eyes were wide open, the pupils dilated black with horror. And her pain flooded me—corrosive, bitter. I cried aloud under the burning. I wondered how she had managed to live in this state, in agony.

'You can move,' I told her. 'Sit up, Princess. Fight. Run.'

'The door!' she screamed, and I heard the click of a bolt being drawn.

A misty form blocked the doorway. Electra's fear was so strong that I was compelled out of communion and snapped back into my own body with force enough to bruise. I lay shaking beside the Argive princess, her mystery still unsolved.

The next day, Eumides addressed Electra as 'Maiden' and she shrieked at him. 'Don't call me that!'

Thereafter he awarded her the usual word for women of all conditions: Lady. The dreams went on. And so did the journey.

'Perhaps at Delphi they will be able to cure her,' Eumides said. He was sitting on the harbor wall outside the Temple of Poseidon of Corinth, eating olives and spitting the pits into the water. It was an impressive temple. The marble pillars were painted in Poseidon's colors, green and blue, in patterns like waves. From the temple came the scent of roasting fish; the noon sacrifice. Despite the Mycenaean restrictions on women, no one had challenged me as I walked alone through the crowded streets. There was a babble of tongues from traders of all nations in sea-bordered Corinth. Unless a woman was wearing the purple chiton of a whore, consensus said that it was unsafe to meddle with her. The general view was that an unaccompanied woman might easily turn out to be either heavily armed and Amazon-trained, or the personal property of some particularly ill-tempered foreign god. I, as it happened, was both, and no one bothered me.

Eumides looked unhappy. He had endured our long, tedious journey with the half-mad girl with as much patience as he could muster. The only reason he had not run away to his beloved Ocean was the love he bore for Chryse and me, and I was grateful.

'Have you found a ship?' I took an olive and bit it appreciatively. Kalamata. The best olives. I spat the stone into the sea.

'An old friend is going to Khirra, the port we need, in three days' time. Have you found a lodging? Not in one of the waterfront hovels, I hope. I've already been bitten by every flea, tick and louse in the Argolid. This is not a country I wish to see again.'

'No, we'll lodge in the house of an old friend of Chryse's, Taphis the Corinthian. And tonight, sailor, we will all three sleep together, and the Princess Electra will be tended and quiet.'

He brightened and grinned.

'I missed you,' he said, using the collective 'you'. 'But the boy is a good boy. Solemn, sorrowful little Orestes. Apollo talks to him, he says, urging him to revenge. I told him to think about it when he's a cubit taller. I have made him laugh once or twice, though. I hope that he comes into his kingdom in time.'

'I just want to get to Delphi and leave them there. The fate of the House of Atreus is not our concern.' I was very tired, and leaned my head on his shoulder. He shifted a little to embrace me. We sat there for a while, listening to the market and the soft voice of the sea.

I looked into the temple, over his strong shoulder. I could see into the sanctuary. There was Poseidon, a resplendent new marble statue, painted in gold and blue. Round his altar were many offerings, cloth patterned with fish, jugs painted with octopi, seashells from the children, a blue vase of the stone the Egyptians call 'glass' and a model boat made out of driftwood.

For some reason the boat caught my attention. It was well made, the keel following the natural shape of something which had probably been a tree-root. The sails were of painted cloth, red-and-white striped, such as Corinthian vessels often display.

Someone had spent a lot of painstaking work to get it right, this thoroughly acceptable gift for a god of the sea.

Why did it hurt me to look at it? Why were my eyes stinging?

Then I remembered. Just such an offering had been taken by the maidens, I amongst them, to Poseidon's temple when I had brought his worship back into Troy. Apollo had cursed me for it. I remembered exactly what the temple looked like, remembered my lover Dion, who was Poseidon-Priest, Dion of the kelp-brown hair and eyes, who had fled to Egypt before the city fell. I remembered my twin, golden Eleni, his closeness and his smooth skin and the scent of his hair. I searched for him and found only a desperately unhappy shade, a ghost of my bright twin. Then it struck me like a knife in the heart.

Troy was gone.

Eumides held me tighter, sensing that something was wrong. 'What is it, Cassandra?' he asked. I could not speak for a moment, then I said in my cradle-tongue, into his neck, 'Troy is no more.'

'Troy is no more,' he agreed in the same language. 'I will never sail my boat *Farseer* into the harbor again and see the walls rising sheer from the Scaean Gate, nor hear Prince Hector, Priam's son, calling for news from Libya, a golden child on either side of him and Stathi the cat perched on his shoulder. I used to dream about you, Princess, when I was enslaved in Mycenae. I dreamed of coming into the harbor again and finding Troy as I had left it, tall and proud and impregnable. I would swagger in, I thought, and drink mead in the tavern below the acropolis and boast of the wide world, having come home. But freed against all hope by an apprentice healer, I returned to a siege and saw the death of everyone I knew and the loss of everything I loved—except you, Princess, except Chryse and you.' He kissed me, and I tasted salt; his tears, not mine. My grief was too great for weeping. Eumides clutched me by the shoulders and stared into my eyes. His agate gaze held me fixed in his regard. His face was wet. 'The city is destroyed by Agamemnon and his army, the people are scattered or enslaved and all the sons of Priam are dead. But so is Agamemnon, slaughtered like a beast by his wife at the height of his arrogance. His damaged, half-mad children are now our companions, dependent on us to get them to Delphi alive. And Troy has not perished, Princess, Priestess, Cassandra of my heart, while we are still alive.'

I had never heard such a flow of words from Eumides. I dug my fingers into his arms, dragging him closer into an embrace which was almost an assault. His answering grasp bruised my skin.

'We belong together,' I said, realizing that this was true. 'While you live, Troy remains.'

'Agape mou,' he said. 'My love.'

'I love you,' I replied. I had no better words. There should have been one in some language to describe how much I needed him, liked him, wanted him, valued him. Eumides the sailor, my companion in the Dionysiad, sharer of my Trojan speech, my rescuer, scoundrel, trader, old friend, thief, with eyes like black honey and hair that curled like bracken. We strained closer. I breathed in the scent of his skin, salt and pine-resin.

I do not know how long we sat there on the harbor wall, embracing in full view of the scandalized citizens. A passing sail cast a cold shadow over us and we blinked and shivered.

'Come along, Lady,' he said, lifting me to my feet. 'Taphis the Corinthian has a good name and my friend Laodamos supplies him with the best of Kriti wine. We can have a rest, then dinner, and then some more rest.'

Taphis had given his male visitors a large room on the ground floor. It was paved with marble—the herb business was obviously prospering—and scattered with sheepskins and woven rugs in bright colors. We made a bed out of these and lay down together.

'Where is Electra?' asked Chryse sleepily.

'I left her with Gythia, Taphis' wife. I have told Gythia that the lady is prone to nightmares and should be watched constantly, and she has promised to care for her. She is a strong and intelligent woman with a large number of female slaves, including a very tough old woman who nursed the Lady Gythia and looks equal to anything, and she can manage.'

'Even if she can't, it will wait until morning,' he said, removing his outer tunic and yawning.

'Chryse?' I asked as he lay down beside me. I was flanked with warm muscled bodies and I found it hard to concentrate.

'Lady?' His golden hair tickled my face.

'Why did you follow the army and rescue me? You could have just gone home to Epidavros.'

'Because I love you,' he said, as though he was prescribing for a headache. 'I spoke to you over the walls and admired your wisdom and your courage, beautiful Princess, Healer of Ilium. You saved my life when the Amazons would have shot me like a roosting bird and you spoke to me most courteously when you gave me back the ashes of my master's son, Macaon. I nursed your twin brother, Eleni, when the arrows of Apollo struck the army. I looked into his face, which is also your face, and I knew that I loved you. I had not thought to love a woman again, after Chryseis left me,' he said sadly. 'But she will understand. Why, Lady, don't you love us?'

'Yes,' I agreed. There was an interval while we shifted under the woven blankets, finding places better for knees and elbows.

'Why did you say you were a priestess of Demeter?' asked Eumides, snuggling down beside me. My eyes were closing. I was blessedly comfortable, bathed and clean and scented with sweet oil instead of travel-dust.

'Simple, Trojan,' I laid my head on his smooth chest. 'Argive Priestesses of Apollo have to be virgins. My companion does not qualify, and neither do I. I would have had to lie apart even from the children, alone with the Princess Electra in virginal seclusion, instead of with you.'

'I have always been devoted to Demeter,' lied Chryse sleepily.

Chapter Six

Odysseus

Of course my greedy crew, thinking that I was cheating them—
How could they think that of me?—opened Aeolus' bag of winds
and we flew to another island.

Strange, rosy smoke encircled the valleys as we climbed to
Circe's house. Birds sang there, unafraid. Flowers blossomed
under her feet as she came out to greet us, a slender maiden with
a waterfall of rich black hair. She invited my dirty, squabbling
crew into her marble house, fed them soup, and watched them
become pigs—not a long journey for most. They dropped to all
fours, snorting and grunting, and she penned them firmly with
the swine. Indeed I was tempted to leave them there.

But I smiled at her and she softened. She was lonely with only
gods for company. She washed me clean of sea-rime and filth,
and sang to me. Her black hair flowed across my face as she lay
down with me, scented with dittany, herb of immortality. She
was smooth and warm and responded to my caresses, which I
had learnt from many women in the islanded sea. When she
was pleased and sated, I kissed her and asked her for my crew
again, and for directions home.

She loved me and tended me, but she sent me sailing into
Hell.

Electra

I heard the latch click. I woke in terror and the dream went on. I saw his black curly hair, felt his hand slide along my hip, and lashed out with both feet. This had never happened before. The only resistance I had managed in my mother's house was to cry, to beg, to whimper, to try and push him away, and it had never worked.

The figure recoiled with a cry, but there was no thud as he fell. I was still dreaming. But he did not return. The horror faded a little, and I wandered off into a green landscape, empty of people. I remember dipping my hands into a stream, feeling the coldness of the clean water. Then I knew no more until morning.

I woke feeling unusually well. An old woman, toothless and wrinkled, was sitting by my bed. She laid a work-worn hand on my forehead.

'Good,' she said, in the Corinthian dialect, which is thick and hard to understand. 'You have no fever. You slept well, Lady?'

'I slept well. Have you been here all night?'

'Indeed, Lady. The Lady Gythia instructed me to watch you carefully. You struggled and screamed a little, early in the evening, but you have lain sweetly all of the night, and now, see? It is morning.'

Bright light was shooting through the shutters, stripping the floor with gold. The old woman was nursing two people. The bright-eyed child was lying in a basket at her feet. As though he had felt my gaze falling on him, he awoke and awarded the world a demi-god's smile. The old woman allowed him to scramble out of the cradle and he padded away toward the Lady's apartment, planting each sturdy little foot as though he had a good solid grip on the earth. I blinked back unexpected tears.

'The Lady Gythia's son?'

'The son of the household. His mother was a slave. She died in childbirth and the Lady took the child. He is called Autesios; a fine strong boy! Taphis has no other son. He hopes he will show promise with herbs. He is curious and bold, and we love him very much. Taphis loved his mother, too. Children conceived in love have a sunny nature.'

I changed the subject. The gods alone knew in what emotion I had been conceived. 'The Lady Gythia. Has she been married long?'

'Twenty years. The Lord depends on her. He knows herbs, but she knows people! She knows who can pay, who is reliable, which shipmasters are pirates, which will deliver their cargo on time. All the women of Corinth come to see her, and she has her finger on the pulse. She listens. She was a fine child, too. I nursed her at my own breast. Ah, well, I'll nurse no babes from these withered teats. Come along, Lady, there is a bath for you, and my Lady will be anxious to know how you passed the night. That is a strong infusion. Only an Asclepid would dare to administer it. They are under the protection of Apollo, and the Bright One would not let them make mistakes. A little dizzy? That is to be expected.'

I let her lead me to a fine bronze bathtub and two slave girls poured hot water scented with roses over me. I was revising my opinion of Cassandra again. If the Lady Gythia was valuable to her husband because of her knowledge and her ingenuity, then there might be something in the Trojan woman's talk of skills. And the Lady Gythia and her husband were familiar together, like old friends. I had never seen this before. My father never asked my mother's opinion about anything, and she was, of course, never seen at counsels where there were men. My hostess was visited by all the women of Corinth and had retained her reputation. Perhaps the rules were not as strict as I had thought.

I was hungry enough to eat a good breakfast of yoghurt and honey. The yoghurt was chalky and not very fresh but the honey was excellent, herb-scented. I realized that it was the famed Kriti honey, gathered by the Goddess' bees from the sacred thyme. Weight by weight it is worth more than gold. This was a wealthy household.

Orestes said that he had slept well and he certainly ate enough. He was looking healthier. One night's sleep can erase a week's privation in a child. His hair had regained its wave and his face was filling out from that white, pinched look that had wrung my heart. He, it seemed, was also worried about me.

'Did you sleep without dreams, Sister?' he asked.

'I slept well, Brother,' I replied. He leant into my lap and looked up into my face. His eyes, as always, were deep and solemn.

'Electra, why are we going to Delphi?'

'Because we will be safe there,' I said, and he drew away from me a little, putting both hands on my knee.

'And from there?' he asked. My shadowed little brother, the darling of my heart. Orestes was the reason, I believe, that I had not taken my maiden's girdle and…my mind shied away from the memory.

'There we will stay,' I said. 'When you are settled, I will leave you there and come back to the Palace of Agamemnon.'

'Why?' he asked.

I wiped a smear of honey from the corner of his mouth and said, 'To kill our mother and her lover.' He thought about this.

'The Queen, our mother, killed our father, didn't she? That's why we ran away.'

'Yes.'

'Do you know that she killed him?'

'I saw her kill him.'

'I think,' he said gravely, 'that I should be the one to go back and kill them.'

'You?' I almost laughed. He was so delicate, so thin and small. He had never practiced at sword play with the other boys. His wrists were as slender as mine.

'Because the Lord Apollo says that it is for me to do. I hear him, when I am sleeping. And, Sister, because to do this deed will attract a dreadful curse from the Gods. I can bear it if you will look after me, but I cannot tend you, Lady Sister Electra.'

'It is my task, Lord Brother Orestes,' I said.

He did not reply, but walked away, down the stairs from the women's quarters.

The old woman came back. She had veiled her head, though there were no men around, and the glimpse of her face that I saw was very pale. Her hands shook as she took away my plate and brought me warm and much diluted wine. I wondered what was wrong with her.

I dressed in a clean chiton—it was pleasant to be back in civilization again—and went to find my travelling companions. This meant that I had to go downstairs to the main room of the house, where the master Taphis and his clerks were engaged in classifying and packaging a shipment of herbs from Thrace. I covered my head in the presence of the male household.

The courtyard stank of medicinal scents. Diomenes, Cassandra, still unveiled, and Eumides the sailor were sitting together on a marble bench, drinking wine-and-water from terracotta wine cups and quarrelling amiably about herbs. They looked pleased with themselves, close and warm. I surveyed them bitterly. The most unlikely conjunction possible—a sailor, an escaped royal slave, and an Asclepid from Epidavros—were pleased in each other's company, valued each other, were delighted in each other. It was utterly immoral. Disgusting. One man for each woman, that's what I had been taught. Now this Trojan whore had two men, and they both sought her company; they both liked her. There are no rewards for virtue. I comforted myself with the thought that they would desire wives and legitimate children, and would abandon her at Delphi. The she would be alone indeed. The priestesses of Apollo must be virgins, and over fifty, and Cassandra was neither.

'It's Asme,' said Cassandra, sniffing at a spray of flat green leaves on a reddish stem.

'It's Percicarion,' insisted Diomenes.

'Well, what use is it?' asked Eumides.

'If it had been dried in the sun, it would be useful for toothache, and when made into a decoction, it kills intestinal worms,' said Diomenes.

'And if you rub it on a saddle gall it will keep away the blow-flies,' said Cassandra. 'But this has been desiccated in an oven and is quite useless.'

'We agree on that,' said Taphis. 'Who sent it?'

The bald, worried clerk consulted a clay tablet and said, 'Archis of Thrace.'

'He usually deals better than this with me. Perhaps he just hoped I wouldn't notice. How much did we pay?'

'For the whole cargo, Master, seven Corinth ship coins.'

'Well, well, that isn't too much, provided that there is something we can use,' said Taphis, rumpling his thinning hair. 'That Hermes' leaf looks better. What do my guests think?'

'Dried in the shade, as the mentha should be,' said Cassandra, breaking off a leaf, crumbling it, and licking up a little from the palm of her hand.

'Still green,' commented Diomenes with approval. 'For bruises and dropsy.'

'Only if steeped in wine,' said Cassandra. 'Made into a decoction with spring-water, it's good for the ague and marsh fevers.'

'Being cold in the third degree,' agreed Diomenes, bowing. 'As the most learned healer says.'

Cassandra returned the salute, as though she were a man. Then they caught sight of me and stopped smiling.

'Ah, the Lady Electra,' said Diomenes, getting up. 'How did you sleep?'

'Well, thank you.'

'Will you join us?' asked Cassandra, shifting on the bench to make room for me. I was not going to make a spectacle of myself, sitting down with her and her clients.

'Have you seen Orestes?' I asked.

'He is in the kitchen, I think.' Eumides did not like me, and I did not like him. He was too solid, too strong, for my comfort. His hair curled too freely, his body sweated and smelt like… like…I could not complete the thought.

I walked through the main courtyard, hearing the conversation go on without a break, as though I had never been there.

'Crane's bill,' said Diomenes, 'for fluxes and internal bleeding.'

'Dove's claw,' insisted Cassandra, 'for inward wounds and hemorrhages.'

'Barrakion,' he said, slicing open a wrapped bale of stinking yellow flowers.

'Frog's foot,' she answered. Since barrakion means a frog's foot in Achaean, they had agreed on a name at last, and I went out on a wave of their laughter.

Orestes was not in the kitchen. Three slaves said that he had been there but had gone out into the city, alone, and not one of them had thought to stop him. I ran back into the courtyard, interrupting a discussion about something called colt's hoof (or, as Diomenes insisted, lung-leaf).

'Orestes—he's gone out into Corinth on his own!' I cried. They seemed unimpressed.

'He's ten, Lady,' said Eumides. 'He'll be all right. He's probably gone down to the harbor, all the boys of the city play there. Can he swim?'

'No, why should he be able to swim?' I was suddenly frantic with fear. Cassandra was watching me narrowly.

'It's all right,' she said. 'Eumides is going to visit his old friends on the waterfront. He'll find Orestes and bring him home.'

'It's time I was going,' said the sailor, responding to Cassandra's nudge. 'I can't add any profound knowledge to this feast of herbal wisdom, anyway.'

He kissed first Cassandra and then Diomenes Chryse on the mouth, as though farewelling a spouse. Then he threw his new, flame-red cloak around his shoulders and said, 'I'll find him, Lady. Don't fret.'

I climbed the stairs to the women's quarters, sat on the bench which commanded a view of the street, and worried.

Cassandra

After a day spent agreeably, arguing about the properties of Taphis' shipment of herbs, Chryse and I took our supper with the herbalist and his spouse. I gathered from the Lady Electra, still sulking upstairs, that it was unusual for husband and wife to eat together in Achaea. No wonder they had such difficulties in being friends, these men and women. Eating at the one table has always been a pact of peace—at least for the duration of the meal—and a primary method for getting to know another person. This separation of the sexes meant that there were no shared activities. No man relied on a woman, or woman on a man, to help or guide in any task.

As I took another helping of fish I remembered the best weapon-smith in Troy, working together with her husband at the forge making helmets. 'Bronze needs love,' she had declared to me through the steam of quenched metal, hefting her hammer. 'Silver needs care and gold needs attention, but to make good bronze you must have love.' Her big grimy husband had grinned and agreed. I recalled the Egyptian weavers, husband and wife, working at the same loom, passing the shuttle from left to right across the wide weft, as they made 'woven air,' the best gauze, both sets of hands working with unthinking speed and grace.

And with Chryse as my fellow healer, I could battle a plague, tend the wounded of an army. There was a saying in Troy which applied to all trades. 'Bare is the back that is comradeless.'

In Achaea all backs were bare and I did not like the thought. Without that fellowship, there could be no friendship between men and women, only the stud relationship of dam and sire. The only free Argive women seemed to be priestesses and whores.

However, Gythia was highly respectable and she and her husband appeared to be friends, in a way. He condescended to her and she always deferred to him, but she clearly had a strong will and a lot of business sense and she always got her way.

'Achis sent two bales of herbs which cannot be used,' he said loudly. 'We will not trade with him again.'

'It shall be as you say, Lord, but he did send fifteen bales which were in excellent condition, and the shipment only cost seven trading coins,' she said quietly.

'A package of Ares' root which was half furze, and a bundle of Percicarion fit only for kindling,' he puffed. She ordered his wineglass filled with an unobtrusive flick of her finger, and said sweetly, 'And the best barrakion we have seen for three seasons and some very clean iris corms. Come, husband, I think you can forgive the Thracian. He has served you well in the past and it is not fitting for so important a merchant as yourself to take offense over a trifle.'

Taphis immediately began to thaw.

'And you can send a stern reproof to him by the shipmaster,' continued Gythia, offering him a plate of olives. 'What do you think of these? I had them from a trader just up from the Argolid, and I am wondering if they are good. You know how I value your opinion, my Lord.'

Taphis' complacency increased as he absorbed this shameless, skillful mixture of praise and advice, poured upon his head like the best virgin oil from a great height. I shut my mouth and refrained from comment. If this was the way to rule a household in the Argolid, I could not see myself ever managing it. Between complete subjection and this honeyed persuasion, I might almost have chosen subjection. But Gythia was important and had position amongst the women of Corinth, and she had made the best of her life.

I did not despise her, but I resolved that her fate would not be mine.

We were just reaching the end of an excellent meal when Eumides returned. We heard him returning.

Two voices, one alto and one bass, were raised in an extremely indelicate Trojan sailor's song, the chorus of which went 'drink, drink, drink,' which made it easier to remember if the singer was inebriated, which these singers definitely were. I hoped that we could get to them before they embarked on the verses, which related to the amorous properties of various races of women all around the sea of Aegeus, and were not fit for any respectable household. We bade our host goodnight with some celerity.

Then Chryse and I hurried into the courtyard and found out who the other voice was.

A small boy was partially supporting our friend, who was elevated and flushed. Orestes was also pinker in the face than I had ever seen him and giggling freely.

'Oh, Gods of all nations, what is the Princess Electra going to say?' muttered Chryse. 'You take Eumides, Lady, and I'll see what I can do about the boy.'

'She's got him back safe, and he isn't hurt,' I objected, accepting the wine-full sailor into my arms. He was very heavy, being almost completely relaxed. I tried to stand him up and he folded at the knees.

'That's not how she is going to see it,' said Diomenes. 'Come along, Orestes, let's get you a clean tunic and wash your face. Someone has spilled wine all over you.'

'Nice boy,' said Eumides owlishly, as Chryse led Orestes away.

'Where did you find him?' I asked, gathering him closer as he tried to slither bonelessly to the floor.

'Sitting on the temple wall looking at the ships. Didn't want to go home. Sad about something. Took him along to a tavern or two and then to Laodamos' house. One of his houses. Can't be sad there. Had Carian wine. Strong. Got to sit down,' said Eumides, and I hauled him into our room and sat him on a bench. He grinned at me, a fine, wide, intoxicated grin.

'Drink some water,' I said, holding the cup for him. He drank obediently, closed his eyes, and fell asleep abruptly, like a baby. I woke him for long enough to get him to the mattress and he slid down, unconscious before he touched the sheepskins.

Chryse came back after half an hour.

'I washed the boy and gave him back to his sister, and she was so glad to see him that she didn't scold him. But Eumides is likely to have his ear chewed off tomorrow.'

'By then he'll feel so awful that it won't matter,' I said. We looked at our friend. He was sleeping on his back, perfectly relaxed, breathing wine fumes into the warm air, with a smile on his lips.

Chryse and I stripped and lay down together. We had been too tired the previous night to even notice how much we desired each other.

Argive and Trojan, we had much to teach, and much to learn.

He was naked, lying on his back, and I began by kissing him, as I and the maidens had done when we lay together in the palace of the king and wondered about the love of men. I tasted his skin, herbs and honey, as I mouthed down his chest to the thighs and felt the tendons tighten. His hands stroked my hair as I found the phallus, left it and buried my face in his belly, then slid up his body again and found his mouth.

He tasted sweet and dangerous, aroused and breathing hard. I took his hand and laid his fingers to the object which the Trojans call the goddess' pearl.

'What is there?' he asked into my neck.

'The pearl,' I said, catching my breath. 'Stroke it gently and feel my pleasure.'

He lay with his cheek on my stomach and I felt a circular, fiery touch which made me shiver. His fingers were sensitive and he learned very quickly, gauging my reaction, listening for the gasp. I shuddered into a climax and held out my arms, and he moved inside me as the muscles flexed and pulsed.

'Cassandra,' he whispered, as I locked my thighs around him, my hands on his buttocks, thrusting him deeper into my body, which bloomed around the phallus like a flower. We fitted together as though we had been forged in the same fire.

He lowered his head, almost sobbing with desire. His face in the pale light was bronze and gold, his hair falling to my breasts, each movement bringing my wave closer to breaking. His grey eyes closed, every muscle tensed, and I sucked in seed, the gift of the sky to the field, the earth to the sea.

Morning was announced by a green-faced blur transiting to the bathroom like a comet. Eumides emerged some painful moments later and sank down into our bed again, squinting as though he was unable to focus.

'You've been loving while I've been sleeping,' he said accusingly, sighting the red mark of a bit on Chryse's throat and a matching one on mine.

'You've been sleeping so deep we couldn't wake you to join our loving,' Chryse pointed out soothingly.

'Leave me alone,' said Eumides, lying down with wincing care. 'I want only to die.'

I got up, found my tunic, and called for the slave.

'I need some things from your master's stock,' I said. 'Chryse, what do they call Lord's leaf here?'

'I never knew the Trojan name. I'd use jaundice-herb and mint, and a little honey and mead in a lot of hot water.'

'Sounds suitable,' I said, irritated that I could not prescribe for Eumides until I learned the Argive names. The slave brought a bunch of familiar leaves, as well as a jug of mead, and honey in a little pot.

'That's Lord's leaf,' I said. 'Cooling and cleansing. Shall I make the infusion?'

'If you please, Healer,' he replied politely, lifting Eumides to a half-sitting position against his shoulder. I recalled the delicacy of his touch and smelt his scent on my hands while I heated the water and made the decoction. As the steam rose, refreshing and medicinal, I felt good. Troy was gone, I still knew that. But there was nothing fate could do to the past and it was still there, preserved like wheat in tree-resin, in the mineral they called amber, like Electra's eyes. Now was all I had, and all I wanted. Eumides' grumbling, the smell of the morning, the babble of the market outside, the calm voice of Chryse and the sight of his unbound hair brushing his bare shoulder—all things combined to make me happy, who had not thought to be happy again.

Despite his feeble struggles, we got fully three-quarters of the brew down Eumides' protesting throat and left him to recover a little.

'Drink some more water,' ordered Chryse, from the door.

'Leave me—that's right, leave me alone to my demise,' he said bitterly.

'All of us die alone,' said Chryse unexpectedly. Eumides cast him a startled look from a bloodshot eye and forbore from further complaint.

'Cassandra,' said the Asclepius-Priest as we came into the courtyard, 'I am afraid.' I stopped with my hands on his shoulders, looking into his face. He was pale.

'What are you afraid of?' I said, surprised.

'I am afraid to lose you, lose him. I am suddenly and dreadfully afraid to get close to anyone. I have lost them all; the first woman who loved me, then Chryseis. I can't bear to lose you and Eumides as well.'

I altered my sight, casting about for the gleam of silver in the air which meant that the gods were interfering in my life again. Not a glimmer.

'The first woman and Chryseis were taken away,' I agreed. 'I lost my city, my family and my lovers. If I let it, my grief could consume my life. I am afraid too, Chryse, but we cannot be afraid, we must not be afraid. *Agape mou*,' I kissed his mouth, soft as silk. 'My love, my heart. If the gods make us too terrified to trust, too frightened to risk loving something which must die, then they will have destroyed us.'

'That is true,' he said, and tentatively returned the kiss.

Eumides emerged at noon, much recovered and demanding food. Orestes, it appeared, was being kept close to his sister's side, and neither of them came to eat with us. Our host and his wife were busy with negotiations on behalf of Epidavros with several Kriti merchants with thyme to sell, so we dined alone.

'He's a strange child, Orestes,' said the sailor, engulfing large quantities of bread and sheep's-milk cheese. 'I found him sitting on the temple wall, looking forlorn and overburdened. I asked him what was troubling him, and he said "Murder." Then he wouldn't tell me any more. So I took him with me, as he didn't want to go home. Did we make an exhibition of ourselves?'

'You certainly did. We could have sold tickets. Crowds would have flocked to hear your sparkling rendition of "Aegean

Women," said Chryse. 'Don't gobble all the cheese, Sailor. There are others at the table who like feta as well.'

'Heartfelt, too,' Eumides said complacently. 'I made up several new verses on the subject of Trojan women, who inspire me.'

'I'm deeply honored,' I said, removing the cheese and sharing the remains with Chryse.

'But that boy—I've never met a boy like him. So withdrawn and strange. Yet he brightened up and sang along. I didn't give him much wine, only one cup.'

'That's enough for someone a third your weight,' said Chryse. 'Why strange?'

'I really think he was considering murder,' said Eumides slowly. 'He's very truthful. Whether self-murder or other-murder I'm not sure. Anyway, despite what his sister says, I'm glad I found him and I don't think a small carouse will have done him any harm.'

'No, I don't think so. Unless you and your friends found him attractive,' said Chryse, with a cold edge to his voice. Eumides was as shocked as he could be with the remains of all that wine circulating in his system.

'Don't be disgusting. He's a child. Boys need to be at least fourteen and in bloom, and even then I would never force anyone. You should know that, Asclepius-Priest. Don't you remember the mountain outside Mycenae in the sunlight?'

Chryse's expression softened and he took Eumides' unoccupied hand.

'Yes, I remember,' he said gently.

'Did I hurt you or force you, when you were an apprentice healer who had bought me out of slavery?' Eumides was angry, and Chryse left his seat and knelt at his feet, bowing his head.

'I apologize, Eumides of my heart. Please forgive me. I didn't really think it was you or your friend, however drunk you were you would never hurt a child. But I washed Orestes last night, and someone has been…'

'Abusing him?' I was deeply shocked. 'A child?'

'I would stake my reputation on it.'

'Maybe that's why he was sitting on the temple steps, contemplating murder,' I said. Eumides dragged Chryse into a rough, forgiving embrace and hugged him hard.

'A dreadful thing,' he said solemnly. 'I must be careful of how I touch the child. He will be frightened of men.'

'No. He is frightened of whoever hurt him, but he likes you, Eumides. Treat him exactly as you have been.' I frowned and added, 'Now we have to decide whether to tell his sister.'

'Wouldn't she know? She clings close to the boy. Such a thing cannot be hidden from an anxious sister's eyes,' said Eumides.

'Not if she did not know what to look for. May all gods look down on us, what was happening in that accursed city? Were all the royal children treated like that?' asked Chryse, taking a goblet and staring into the wine as though he could see visions there and did not like what he saw.

'Mycenae is cursed, the sons of Atreus are doomed. I applied a lot of those curses myself while I was enslaved there, and it looks like they have worked,' said Eumides.

Chryse and I didn't laugh.

Chapter Seven

The gods looked into the Pool of Mortal Lives, where little ships scurried across the surface.

'It's easy,' urged Apollo. 'My Lord Poseidon. Bring a wave, drown them.'

'Why should I do that, Sun-God?' replied the Earth-Shaker. 'The sailor Eumides is a good sailor, and Laodamos of Corinth is devout in my worship.'

'We must complete the destruction of the House of Atreus, and you can erase the next generation with the flick of a finger, most powerful of gods.'

'Do not seek to flatter me,' growled Poseidon, shaking his kelp-crowned, shaggy head. 'I have no animus against them, poor little shivering children. If you seek to kill them in my domain, you will have me to deal with, as well as Hecate the Crone.'

'This story must conclude,' insisted Apollo.

Electra

I had only realized that I was resolved to go back to kill Queen Clytemnestra and her lover, the revenge-child, when I told Orestes. I should not have told him. Distraught, he had wandered out into the city, where anything could have happened to him, anything. He could have been captured and enslaved. We were fugitives, not citizens. No one would have defended us and I doubt that our associates would even have looked for us. They did not like our company. I would not have liked us, either. The kindness of strangers has its limits and they needed some sleep. Then Eumides had taken my brother to a succession of taverns in the lowest company and made him drunk. I was revolted and angry. Orestes could have been lost, hurt, taken away. He was instantly sick as soon as Diomenes had delivered him into my arms. I was distracted with worry over him and intended to tell him what a bad boy he had been when he was better.

But the next morning he was listless and his head ached, so I did not scold him much. I gave him the infusion of herbs which the old woman prepared, and he slept for much of the day. I did not move from the women's quarters, but took up some fine wool and spun. The thread made a perfect line down from the mass of white teased fleece to my spinning whorl, good stout thread, with never a knot or a break. I had spent my whole life spinning. I was good at it and it soothed me. I liked watching my fingers moving surely and cleverly, independent of my thought. My thoughts were of murder, of blood and revenge, for me and for my father.

'Lady, it is getting dark. Shall we bring lamps?' asked a slave. I realized that I had sat there all day and put down the spindle, breaking off my thread and winding it into a skein. I had spun fifteen ells of sound blanket thread.

'Lady, will you join the household at supper?' asked the slave, the old woman who had watched over me the night before.

'No,' I said abruptly. 'I will eat with my brother and then sleep. We are leaving in the morning. Is everything prepared?'

'Yes, Lady, all is prepared. Your sleeping infusion is here.'

'Where are my...travelling companions?' I asked. If they were out, I might venture down into the courtyard for a sniff of fresh air before it got too dark. There are only three occasions when a decent woman goes out into the night. When she is born and her father takes her outside to declare to the gods that she is his child, when she is given away and the maidens escort the marriage procession to her new house, and when she is carried to her funeral. I had never pined for the open air before, but travelling was changing me. I was uncomfortable now if I had been indoors all day, who had spent my whole life behind walls.

'Diomenes Asclepius-Priest is at the temple of Apollo, Lady, and the Priestess of Demeter and the sailor Eumides have gone to the temple of Poseidon. They will be back before long.'

She was looking at me, this old woman. I did not like her close regard and could not imagine what she wanted. She seemed to be waiting for me to speak. I had nothing else to say. I picked up my veil and went down the stairs.

It was pleasantly cool in the courtyard. I could smell roasting fish and someone was singing in the kitchen, a work song such as women sing.

> We rise at day and eat our Master's bread,
> We grind his flour and sweep his floor,
> We pour his wine and spin his thread.
> We carry his burdens and mind his door,
> We walk to the well with heavy tread.
> Weary, weary lives,
> Weary, weary lives
> Unfree, unfree…

The life of a slave is simple, I thought as I sat down, wrapped securely in my veil in case any men came in. They had merely to do as they were told, bear what had to be borne, and mostly they died blessedly young.

> Once I was a princess with a golden wreath,
> Once I was a prince with a golden spear,
> Once I was a maiden, once I was a youth,
> Once I was free, once I was free,
> Weary, weary lives,
> Weary, weary lives,
> Unfree, unfree…

So sang the slave in her kitchen, a lucky wretch who did not know what good fortune was. Rather be a slave than a princess with a golden wreath. Only a princess was truly unfree.

I heard the others coming back and I fled. I did not want to talk to them.

From the head of the steps I saw Eumides the sailor, carrying a large bundle, brush past the doorman and turn to speak to his companion, the abandoned Trojan healer, also heavy-laden. The torches had just been lit and I saw him clearly in the pool of golden light.

'I will not insult you by asking if your burden is too heavy, warrior-maiden,' he said, chuckling. 'But I might venture to suggest to the princess that she would like to put it down.'

'You may safely so venture,' she said, laughing, and dropped the parcel at the doorman's feet. He jumped back before his toes were crushed and laid his spear aside.

'Lady,' he said deferentially, 'allow me to carry this for you.'

'There are advantages in Argive manners,' commented Eumides, 'are there not?'

'No. None,' she snapped, lifting the bundle by main force and staggering with it into the room which they openly shared.

I wondered what they were carrying. Then I remembered how Eumides had looked beneath the torches and I sat down on the stairs, forced by that coincidental image to remember the first time I had seen the man who destroyed my life.

◇◇◇

He had been standing in the torchlight at the gate of Mycenae, under the stone lions. His breastplate gleamed bronze and his helmet plumes danced in the wind which always blows at Mycenae. I had been standing with my sister Chrysothemis on the balcony of the women's quarters. I remembered her saying, 'What a well-looking man,' as the tree-trunk gates swung open and revealed him. He had taken off the helmet. He had black, curly hair.

I would not name him. I would not soil my tongue with his name. His coming was my death.

The Princess the Lady Laodice, called Electra, daughter of Agamemnon, had been dead for a long time. She had died when she was eleven, when her father had gone in glittering armour to the harrying of the coasts, and finally to the siege of Troy. The creature who sat on the stairs and looked down into the courtyard of Taphis the Corinthian's house was a breathing corpse, who lived only for revenge.

◇◇◇

We were farewelled with great ceremony by Taphis, who saw our baggage loaded in Laodamos' ship.

Orestes and I found a place at the front, where we were out of the way. There was only room there for two, right in the eyes of the ship, which was called *Phoebus*. I hoped that Apollo would appreciate this. The others sat on the small deck at the back, close together as they always were. Our horses were tethered in the middle of the ship, seeming resigned to this odd method of travel. I saw *Banthos* raise his head and sniff, catching my scent, and hoped he would not try and come to me, or he would surely upset the boat. But he appeared pleased that I was there and returned to the trance-like state which horses drop into when they are forced to stand still for some time. The crew had boarded an were sitting at the oars, grumbling about wine-shops they had been dragged out of and girls left weeping for them. I did not believe it. They were coarse, unlovely, and unclean. The shipmaster was a short, cross-eyed man with a lot of missing teeth, and I did not like the way he looked at me.

Taphis' wife Gythia, delighted with my spinning, had given me a thick veil and several chitons. I was glad of her gift, for it was a cold morning and I felt very visible. I was wearing two tunics, the veil, and a peplos which covered my head. Not even Laodamos could see through all that. Not even Apollo could manage it.

There were twenty oars and two men to an oar. With Taphis calling to Diomenes, 'Come back soon, Asclepid. I'll send your letter to Master Glaucus. Good fortune, my friends!' the men backed oars at a command and began to row.

The sea was as smooth as a plate. Suddenly we were travelling much faster than walking pace, then faster than a running horse. Something was dragging us along.

'The current...' said Orestes. 'There is a flow of water from the outer sea and it is pulling us. When we reach the beacon at Eleon, we will turn and row until the opposite current carries us into the bay of Kirrha.'

'Who told you that?' I asked sharply, though I knew the answer.

'The Lord Eumides, sister. He knows all about this sea. He says that we will be able to sight the white tower on the cliff at Andromahi. There is a pharos, a lighthouse, there. Then we sail into the bay and land at the port of Delphi, Kirrha, which over-looks the plain of Chrysson. This is easier than riding, isn't it?'

It was pleasant. The sea lay wrinkled like molten metal, and *Phoebus* glided along like a water-spider, while the cliffs gave way to green banks, then cliffs, then meadows and little towns, and I fell asleep.

I woke with Cassandra bending over me, and jerked away from her touch.

'I have brought you some food,' she said simply, and was gone again, picking her way through the bare torsos and grasping hands of the lolling oarsmen. I heard a grunt and some swear-ing, and thereafter they did not offer her any insult. There was something admirable about the way she never allowed anyone to molest her, though I doubted that I could learn it. Orestes, who had stayed awake, said, 'There's bread and oil, Sister, and wine.'

'I wonder that you can bear to touch wine,' I reproved him, and he hung his head. I relented. He really was sorry and he was only a boy. We share the bread and he drank half the diluted wine. The landscape winged past. Strange birds wailed as they flew alongside *Phoebus*. They were white and had wicked, strong beaks.

'Seagulls,' said Orestes. He had clearly listened to all that Eumides had said, and I hoped that he had not learnt other, unsuitable things.

'That must be the beacon,' he told me with his mouth full, pointing. I saw a stone tower. The shipmaster saw it too, and yelled an order. The boat slowed, turned, and we began to row at right angles to the current, towards a shore which was only a distant shadow on the edge of sight.

It was hard work. The oarsmen had no time to speculate further on the identity of the woman under the veil. The oars slid forward, out of the water, the backs bent, the oars were hauled back with an explosive grunt, to be lifted and carried forward again. It was not an easy motion, a galley under oars. The sail had been bundled up. Orestes said it was useless, as the wind would not blow us in the right direction.

We were making good progress, or so shipmaster Laodamos was telling the crew, when Orestes said, 'Look! Another ship!'

'Where?' asked the man at the nearest oar.

'There, and they've got more oars than us.' I could see the ship too, speeding across the ocean like a beetle.

'Sail!' cried the oarsman to Laodamos. 'Sail to steer board, Master.'

'Eumides,' summoned the shipmaster. 'Look there.'

The mariner balanced easily, with one hand on the ropes which were strung from the mast, and called, 'You've got young eyes, Orestes, Can you see the picture on the sail?'

I grabbed the back of my brother's tunic as he leant out, shading his eyes. 'It's a hand,' he said definitely. I heard an intake of breath and someone began a prayer to Poseidon. Someone else was praying to Thanatos for an easy death.

'We're too far out to get back to Eleon,' said the shipmaster. 'We'd better try and go on, and hope the current catches us and takes us into Kirrha. All right, my strong men, my hearts. Bend your backs, bend your oars and we may get out of this with a whole skin. Pray if you like, but row. Row for your lives. You know who that is, that sail over there? That's Metrodorus of Troizen. He'll kill us all if he catches us.'

I had thought that they had been rowing hard before, but it was not so. Now I heard the groan of effort with every stroke, and the oars beat the water, throwing up spray so that Orestes and I were soaked. We huddled close together, wet and miserable, and the sail with the hand grew closer and closer.

Cassandra

The voyage had been delightful. I liked the notion of sitting still and skimming along the water instead of plodding the weary paths on feet. Chryse had prepared an infusion against sea-sickness for us and it seemed to have worked. My stomach was unruffled by the motion and my bread and oil remained where I had put them. The cliffs flowed past, melting into the green farmland, so rich that I saw olive trees leafy and fruiting with their roots almost in the sea.

We had settled down as comfortably as possible, considering the lumpiness of Eumides' baggage. He had collected it in great secrecy from the temple of Poseidon and would not tell us what it was, though Chryse and I had some shrewd guesses. I had prevailed on him to let me carry the smaller bundle, which was heavy for its size and chinked suggestively. All I allowed myself to say was, 'A very good bargain, Eumides?' and the sailor grinned in a way calculated to melt my knees and distract me from further questions. In that, the tactic had been entirely successful.

Electra had snubbed me, but I was not worried. Soon we would be at Delphi—one easy day's ride from the port of Kirrha, they said—and then I could leave the troubled children of the House of Atreus in safe hands.

I tried not to remember my captivity aboard the ships of the Achaean fleet. The day was clear, the sea calm, and the company excellent, though I had to plant a careless foot accidentally in the crotch of one oarsman who thought that unveiled females were fair game. He revised his views with satisfactory speed and I had no further trouble with the crew.

Then the sail came. We fled, but the ship was a trireme, and it gained on us steadily. Eumides came back through the rowers and told us, 'We've been unlucky. It's Metrodorus the pirate. He is notorious in these waters for his rapine and slaughter. Princess, do not be captured alive.'

'I do not intend to be captured at all,' I said tartly, stringing my bow and finding my arrows. 'But thank you for your advice.'

'Can you swim?' he asked us. Both Chryse and I nodded. I remembered with painful intensity my brother Hector holding my chin and my brother's as we floundered through the shallow waters of the Scamander delta. After we had gained some skill, Eleni and I used to race each other to the marker buoy on the first sandbank. No matter how hard we tried, we always landed, waterlogged and laughing, at exactly the same time.

'I've just remembered swimming in the river at Epidavros,' said Chryse in a low voice.

'And I, learning that same skill in the Scamander with my brothers. All lost, all lost. We are wounded, Chryse, but we are not dead. Yet. Will you fight?'

'I have no training,' he said, taking up a knife, 'but I will try. Since the Lord Apollo does not exist, he will not have to forgive me for breaking my healer's oath.'

'Since he does exist,' I asserted, watching the tattooed sail loom closer, 'he will forgive you anyway, for fighting for your life and the lives of others. That must be allowable. Then again, I have never found Apollo a merciful God.'

'Lord Poseidon,' said Eumides under his breath, hefting a boathook, 'have mercy on your faithful children. Look down, Master of Horses, on the fate of your devoted ones. Protect and assist us in our extremity as we rely on your mercy. Earth-Shaker, Blue-Haired Lord of the Sea, take us not down to death in the deeps, to be food for octopus and squid.'

'A cheerful prayer,' commented Chryse.

The trouble with sea battles is that they take so long to start. The rowers heaved and the ships moved, continually changing places and positions. After an hour, we were further across the Gulf of Corinth. We could see the white tower on Andromahi that marks the entrance to the Bay of Kirrha. But the sail with the hand was close behind us, and we saw no reason why it should not intercept us.

I would rather have dealt with any ambush or hand-to-hand fight than this slow chess-piece maneuvering. Close encounters either work, and one survives, or they don't work, and one is dead. In either case the action takes less than an eye-blink and there is no time for terror.

This board-game that both shipmasters were playing with our lives on the breast of Poseidon's country was blood-chilling. I slackened the strings of my bow and put it in my tunic to keep it dry as the ship heeled, turned, and wriggled to escape like a fish on a hook. Birds like scraps of white paper reeled over us. We could see the land quite plainly, but it was farther than it looked. I did not think I could swim that far.

I looked at Electra and Orestes in the eyes of the ship. They were huddled together like birds in a storm, these scions of the doomed House of Atreus. Unless the pirates were unlucky enough to back Electra into a corner, I did not think they would fight. Orestes was valiant, but small.

'What is the pirate trying to do?' I asked, noticing that the *Hand* was continually adjusting its position to remain at right angles to us.

'See that curved horn at the bow? That's a ram. They aim to hit us amidship and impale us, then board us and loot the ship while it is sinking. They will leave the men to drown, except perhaps little Orestes, and they will take the women. They will be sold when Metrodorus is finished with them.'

'I will not be a slave again,' I said. Eumides kissed me hard, his hand in my hair.

'Nor I.'

'This is a day as long as centuries,' sighed Chryse.

'If we can avoid him until night, we might slip into the harbor, but there is an equal chance that we will pile up on a reef in the dark. But he is gaining on us rapidly. I can't see what would delay him.'

The *Hand*, steered with skill and rowed with strength, became clearer and clearer. Now we could see individual faces, scowling with effort. The shipmaster caught sight of a black-bearded bald man and screamed, 'Metrodorus! Be forever cursed! May Poseidon break you with a wave! Are you a Libyan beast, to tear the flesh of innocent sailors?'

'Can we make a bargain?' asked Eumides. He did not shout, but his voice carried well. 'You know us, Metrodorus. Laodamos the shipmaster and Eumides of Troy. We drank together ten years ago in that tavern by the temple in Iolkos. What has turned you into a pirate, fisherman?'

'There are golden fish in the sea,' grinned the black-bearded man. 'Better fishing than ever since Agamemnon died. There is no law in the Gulf of Corinth now, Trojan. But give me all your gold and I might let you go.'

'Or you might just sink us anyway. Where's your home port, Metrodorus? Do they know that you're a murderer there? If you let us go, we can tell Corinth of your mercy. And the gods of the Sea can't be pleased with your actions.'

'I care nothing for Corinth, and I need no advocates. The Gods died with the King of Mycenae, and you are mine.'

The ships were sliding closer together. Metrodorus ordered his men to back oars, angling the *Hand* for the fatal ramming blow. I considered that Eumides had done his best for diplomacy and peaceful solutions, and strung the bow again.

An Amazon's bow, with a reverse curve. I wondered briefly where Chryse had found or bought it—living Amazons do not sell their weapons—then I bent it, laying an arrow on the string. Metrodorus made a lovely target, outlined against the dazzle of the water. He was too far away to reach, so I waited.

The air filled with sparkling silver light and silence fell. The Gods were with me again. I held my breath. Would they doom me or save me, Cassandra, Princess of Troy? Having destroyed my city, cursed my gift, murdered my family, stolen all my loves from me, had they still not finished with their plaything? I was filled with outrage. If this ship was to be taken because I was on it, then I would leap into the ocean. Too many people had died, far too many. Drowning was not an unpleasant death and at least then it would be finished, my story completed.

The sea was growing lumpy, like a decoction when a bubble is about to burst. I hear Chryse gasp, and Eumides cried aloud on Poseidon. Blue-grey and silver, shining like a fish, I saw a vast tail surface and slap the sea, halting the *Hand* with the backwash, though her oarsmen strained and groaned. Prompted or pushed, I loosed the arrow.

With God-sight, things move slowly. I saw the bolt curve up, level out, and fly steadily. The interval between *Phoebus* and *Hand* was crossed in jerky stages—far, further, yet further away from us, close and closer to the black-bearded man.

Then time clicked back into tune and the arrow buried itself up to the feathers in the pirate's chest.

'Ship, ho!' I heard, and the scream of disbelief from the *Hand* as Metrodorus the pirate fell, pierced through and certainly dead before he hit the decking. Another ship had come up from behind us and I found another arrow and turned towards it. It was a trading ship, deep-breasted and painted blue. Its sail was set and it must have followed us out of Corinth.

'*Phoebus* ahoy!' cried a great voice. I had never heard it before. It was a honey-voice, a rich, compelling, strong man's voice. It was impossible not to listen to it. Eumides and Chryse sprang to their feet, dropping their weapons, and shouted together, 'Arion Dolphin-Rider!'

'Well, well,' said the voice, amused. 'Chryse Asclepid-Priest and Eumides the ex-slave, my dears, my golden ones! Whither away?'

'Kirrha, then Delphi,' called Chryse.

'I, also. What shall we do with this pirate, Laodamos?' asked Arion. He was a big man, robed like a bard. Even Trojans had heard of the fame of Arion Badger-Haired, though his hair by now was almost white.

'Take him in tow,' said Laodamos. 'I'm glad to see you and we'll split the pirate's cargo. Just in the nick of time, Arion! I didn't know you were in these waters. I thought you had gone to Troy.'

'Oh, I had. Now Menon and I are going to Delphi. Where did you pick up your passengers? You were not used to carry royal cargo through these dangerous straits.'

Laodamos was puzzled. 'Royal? They are just my old friend Eumides and these religious people. One priest, two priestesses, and a boy.'

'All priests are the children of gods, how much more royal do you require?' asked Arion, preserving our disguise with admirable ingenuity. 'I'll bring in the pirate ship. Meet you on the quay, Asclepid!' he called, as his ship fell behind. I noticed that she had a wooden cut-out of a dolphin, beast of Dionysos, as her figurehead and thought it very fitting. Arion was known to be a devotee of that God. And Dionysos the Dancer had been a great friend to Trojans.

We caught the current into the Bay of Kirrha, to the noise of wailing from the bereft ship behind us.

Chapter Eight

Odysseus

Blood ran into the trench, steaming; ghosts gathered. Dead ones attracted to the scent of life, tasting and sighing, endowed with a little life for a little time. I was at the gates of Hades' realm, Pluton the Rich one and Persephone, his wife. I needed to find my home, and only the dead knew the way.

My mother's shade bent lovingly over me, her hands slipping through my shoulders with only a tingle. Tiresias told me to steer for Thrinacie and on no account to hurt Apollo's cattle grazing there. Then they came, the dead; Agamemnon slaughtered by his wife, Argive and Trojan from the siege and the fall, clustering, gathering, mournful and lost.

'Achilles!' I cried, sighting a shade clad in shadowy armour. I had his original golden war-gear. I hoped he did not know that I had stolen it. 'It must be wonderful to be Lord of the Dead amongst all these heroes!'

'I would trade it all,' said the ghost, 'to be the meanest slave, yet smell turned earth again, taste wine and bread, look at the ever-changing sky, feel loving fingers or cold water on my skin.'

We steered for Thrinacie, hoping not to join the illustrious dead.

Cassandra

We landed in the little port and tumbled ashore with relief. I did not go so far as to kiss the landing stage, as Diomenes did, but I was shaken and glad of land that stayed where it belonged and did not shift underfoot. We hauled the bundles of Eumides' bargain ashore and made Electra sit on them while we managed the other things that needed to be done. After an hour's frantic activity, most of which was occupied with convincing reluctant horses to put hoof to land, and arguing with tavern-keepers who saw in us a great opportunity to make an indecent profit, we found ourselves in a small, smoky inn, supplied with good wine.

Arion Dolphin-Rider was old. His beautiful voice was that of a man in his prime, but he moved as though his back hurt, and his hair was almost white. His nose was as beaked as a hawk's bill, and his bones were strong and rugged. The hands that lay on his knees were brown and weathered and knob-knuckled. He looked more like a soldier than a poet. His apprentice, a silent boy called Menon, cared for him jealously, finding him the warmest place to sit and hanging a blanket over the door to exclude drafts.

Electra and her brother had vanished into the women's quarters. Eumides came in after a refreshing argument with his old friend Laodamos about the division of the pirate's cargo, and put a golden wreath on my head.

'What's this?' I asked, lifting it down. It was fine Mycenean work, oak leaves and acorns in gold as thin as gauze, lighter than real leaves.

'Your share,' he said. 'You shot him, Amazon. A perfect shot.'

'The gods did it,' I objected. 'Didn't you see the triton's tail, halting my target in reach of the arrow?'

'That was a whale,' he said. 'But the timing might easily have been divine. And here is your share, brother.' He gave Diomenes a wreath of silver-gilt myrtle flowers. He placed another on his own head, a confection of bay leaves through which his live hair curled. He was beautiful. He sat down between us and we kissed him. 'Your share, Master Arion, is all bundled up in your ship.

They seem to have robbed a cargo vessel trading from Thrace with pretty things for Argos. I have not made any bargains with your share.'

'It is never wise to cheat a bard,' agreed Chryse, beaming his rare smile. 'Arion, Master-Singer, what brings you here? I left you in Troy.'

'That's where I thought I left you, and this Trojan scoundrel. And you, Lady Cassandra,' he took my hand and kissed it. 'I saw you over the walls, talking to this Asclepid, then later I saw your brother Eleni. I knew you at once—especially by your archery. How come you here? I thought you were Agamemnon's concubine. I expected you to be in Mycenae. I wrote a touching threnody for your untimely death.'

I winced.

'Agamemnon is dead,' said Chryse hurriedly.

'Dead indeed. And if I asked who your other companions were, Chryse Diomenes, the small veiled woman and the boy, would you tell me?'

'No,' said Chryse affectionately.

'I have kept worse secrets than the location of a runaway prince and princess.' The bright black eyes sparkled, and Chryse, unexpectedly, blushed. 'But I know that the Great King has been murdered by his wife. In fact, she is boasting of it.'

'We were told that she would proclaim it,' I said.

'Proclaimed and asserted, proved and done, and the badly hacked and undeniably deceased Agamemnon exhibited before the citizens. And not one voice raised in Mycenae of the Golden Walls in mourning for its king. I have a song—would you like to hear it? Menon, my lyre.'

'Of course we will be honored to hear the song, but first you must have some food and some rest, old friend,' said Chryse. Menon placed a platter of grilled fish in front of the old man and broke his bread into four pieces. Then he stood next to him, exuding determination. Clearly Arion was not going to get his lyre until all that fish was consumed. We were hungry, too, and ate in silence for a while.

The port was resounding with the news that the pirate was dead. I heard someone with a very loud voice declaring the news, and the hurrying of many feet. This was going to attract attention. I did not want any fame. I was supposed to be dead.

I sidled over to the shipmaster Laodamos and said quietly, 'That was a great shot of yours, Laodamos.'

'But Lady, it was you who...'

'No, on the contrary, it was you.'

He summed me up in a quick glance. Eumides' friends were usually intelligent. He cast a look around the room, where his crew were attempting to become absolutely sodden in the shortest possible time. 'It will have to be young Agenor,' he said. 'He has some skill with the bow. Very well, Lady, Agenor killed Metrodorus. With some careful publicity, Corinth might even give us a reward.'

'Will you be able to convince Agenor of his valiant deed?'

'He isn't very bright,' said Laodamos confidently. 'A few more jugs of wine and he'll believe that Thetis is his mother. The rest of the crew will believe what I want them to believe, especially with a half-share of the loot as a persuader.'

I gave him a silver coin of Corinth to assist in the process and went back to the fire, where Arion had prevailed on his apprentice to give him his lyre and was tuning it. The inn grew quiet, even as Agenor began to boast of his archery. The strings thrummed, a gentle, insistent note, then the voice began—quietly, but heard through all the room.

> 'I can smell blood, said the Princess,
> Disgraced Cassandra, captive of the Argives.
> 'Blood, a shambles, a slaughterhouse,
> The red tide laps at the bath's rim.
> Apollo. I go to the death prepared for me,
> Cruel Apollo, my death-cry your reproach.'

Tears came to my eyes. My lovers pressed close, holding my hands. It could have been like that. I had prophesied my own murder, heard my own scream. It would have been my death, if

they had not come for me. Now prophecy was gone and I was
alive, breathing, flanked by my rescuers.

> Myrrh, they said, splendor and wealth,
> A feast prepared for the great king.
> Then a cry, a sacrifice, a great cry,
> Then silence. The queen speaks,
> 'I cast the net and wound him close,
> My husband, murderer, monster!
> I struck once. Fountaining, his blood
> soaked my garment; again, and it spilled into
> my mouth.
> I drank it in as a fertile field
> Rejoices in the fall of spring rain.
> I flourish, I burgeon, I am filled,
> I glory in his wounds, the black blood drying,
> The water dyed red. Mine was the deed,
> Mine, mine. His concubine too,
> Dead. My heart is bronze. Judge me like
> No weak woman. Praise or blame,
> I care not. The King is slaughtered.
> I killed him. By Ruin, by Fury, the Gods he mocked
> When he sent my child to death on the mountain,
> I have justice.'

The hardened hands dragged a chord from the strings, desolate and plangent, and there was complete silence in the tavern.

I heard a shriek upstairs, and sent two house-slaves to attend
to the Princess Electra, who had evidently been listening.

Electra

One reaches the sanctuary of Apollo by following the sacred way.

Orestes and I had gone to bed early in the port of Delphi,
leaving the others to exclaim over their survival. Apparently the
travellers and the bard were old friends. I was sure that he had

recognized me, and my brother, too, though he had not seen me since I was a child and I had clung to my veil.

The talking and singing had gone on until late. I was annoyed that they would not be quiet when I asked them to and found myself in tears at some song the bard had sung. However, tomorrow I would lose the company of the Trojan woman, the sailor, and Diomenes, Asclepius-Priest. I would be glad to be rid of the first two, though I almost liked the third.

'Zeus the Father sent an eagle from each end of the Earth,' said the rich voice of the bard behind us. 'They met here in a wild flurry of feathers. Here is the center of the world, children. Here is *omphalos*, the navel of the universe.'

It was as though an earthquake had cloved the mountains in two. The plain of Chrysson was ordinary and flat, green with spring growth. We had skirted an equally ordinary mountain called Cirphis. On the opposite side, where the River Pleistos flows to Ocean, were two cliffs, very tall, silver and shimmering with old olive trees.

'*Phaedriades*,' said the bard. 'The Shining Ones. We stop here.'

He dismounted and the others got down. A stream of bright water leapt down the face of the cliff, splashing into a low basin. The horses dipped their heads and drank.

'This is the spring of Castalia,' said Arion. 'Here we wash our hands and feet, to prepare for the ceremony.' We did as we were told, awed by the mountains and the silence. Eumides lifted Orestes down and dipped him, clothes and all, in the spring. Orestes gasped but did not complain.

Delphi was visible as we left the horses with the Delphians who attended there and began to climb the hill. We passed a small temple of Athena, a colonnaded ring in which the priestesses dance. We climbed higher, along a road worn deep by thousands of feet.

There was only one gate in the temple wall. It was made of stone, placed carefully and with skill. The gap in it was broad. Over the lintel, as we passed in, I saw letters.

'What do they say?' I asked. Diomenes read aloud 'Know Thyself. Nothing in excess. And there is the letter E.'

'What do they mean?' I asked, and he answered, 'The seven sages alone know what they mean, Lady.'

It was very quiet as we walked along the Sacred Way. Delphi had this quality, that it can hold as many people as a small city and yet no noise disturbs the quiet of the god. The stones are well-cut, polished, and unfigured. The air is cool and clean, as though no creature ever breathed it before.

'It feels like a beginning, said Cassandra, and both Eumides and Diomenes reached out a hand to her.

'It is an ending,' said Arion happily, leaning on Menon's shoulder as he stumped up the path.

It did not feel like anything to me.

There were three temples to pass though before we came to the shrine where Pythia gave her prophecies. The first was made of laurel branches, freshly built every year, when Apollo left in autumn for Hyperboreas and Dionysos the Dancer ruled. It smelt dry, although it was early spring. We left our outer robes there, and all weapons had to be laid aside. All marks of distinction also had to be abandoned. No soldier comes to the god in armour, bearing a sword. No king can climb the rose-red hill with staff of rank or crown. Cassandra left her cloak, Eumides his knife, Diomenes his healer's bundle of herbs. I put down my veil and walked bare-headed, as the god requires, and Orestes abandoned his dagger.

The next temple was almost circular, made of beeswax plastered over wood and stuck with feathers—long white swan's feathers in patterns around the walls, which smelt of honey and were warm like flesh to the touch. Here we took off our sandals. I walked barefoot for the first time in my life, savoring the pink dust with my soles. There were people on the holy mountain. The priests of Apollo wear white tunics with no decoration, not even in the weave. They alone veil their faces, who have looked into the face of the god.

Orestes was interested, walking steadily, though I was tiring.

We came to the sanctum, a stone building with a hearth, sacred to the Goddess Hestia. Here we sprinkled incense into the flame, and it flared, burning blue. The attendant priest turned and surveyed us with interest.

He beckoned, and we followed him to the *oikos*, the outer chamber. Through the doorway we could see a little way into the *adyton*, the inner sanctum, where only the priestess could go. There was a gold statue of Bright Apollo. We heard water running, and strange exhalings from the earth. The air smelt of sulphur. Inside, I knew, was the navel-stone laid there by Zeus himself and the fissure from which the vapor came which Pythia would breathe, and be possessed of the spirit.

We sat down on stone benches. We had questions, and we needed to be careful about what we asked. They brought us a young goat. Eumides held it by the neck and it trembled. The priest sprinkled the beast with water, nodded, and the sailor cut its throat with one skilled stroke. The blood flowed into a stone dish set in the floor, and drained into the adyton.

'*Theopropoi*' came a man's voice. 'Oracle-seekers, ask.'

'Sibyl, speak—has Apollo forgiven me?' asked Cassandra evenly.

'Sibyl, speak—forgive an old man, and let me rest,' said the bard.

'Sibyl, speak—will I find a home?' asked Eumides, unexpectedly.

'Sibyl, speak—will I find revenge?' asked Orestes.

'Sibyl, speak—will blood wipe out my pain?' I asked, choking on the stench of the sacrifice.

There was a cry from the inner chamber, and a voice began to intone a verse.

'Dear to Asclepius, Diomenes is cleansed and blessed.'

Diomenes sighed and smiled.

'Apollo has released his faithless priestess, loved by Gaia.'

Cassandra gave a sob, then fell into Diomenes' embrace, weeping as though her heart was broken.

'Aphrodite's darling, return to Epidavros, bard grown old in her service. Arion will find peace, and after death an immortal home, singer to the Gods.'

Arion drew a deep breath. Tears trickled down his face, and hugged Menon to his chest. The boy looked stricken.

'Many seas you will sail, Eumides, by they will always be waiting. Those who love you, to welcome you home.'

Eumides knelt before Cassandra and the Asclepid and they accepted him into their arms. They were all weeping.

'Blood calls for blood, Orestes,' said the oracle. 'Blood will answer blood, tainted and cursed. Yet in the end there will be justice. In the end fate will relent. When Mycenae lies empty, shattered, and void, stone cast from stone as was the fate of Ilium, from the North the last son of Atreus, after long wanderings, will find his place.'

Orestes considered this. I was about to go to him when the oracle spoke again.

'Much-tried Electra, cruelly punished, until the ice melts from your eyes, cold-hearted maiden, blood will follow you, pain possess you. Footsore, weary, journeying long, no god can see your fate.'

There was nothing to say. I tried to hug Orestes, but he moved away from me. I don't know why I had expected better fortune.

We came down from the mountain, a hilarious group. The others were almost running along the pink-dusty path. We collected our sandals and our possessions, and walked down to the springs where we would remount and ride along to Delphi polis, to seek an inn. It was not seemly to laugh or dance in the temple, but I could see that this was what my companions were going to do as soon as they reached unsanctified ground.

'That was worth even an exceedingly expensive Delphic goat,' said Arion. 'Menon, we must go home. There is a little farm near Epidavros, and there I am bound, never to leave again.'

'Master, Arion, what of me?' wailed the boy. 'Can't I stay with you?'

'No. Old men speak to old men. I have much to say to Glaucus, Master of Epidavros. You shall conduct me home, Menon, and we will build you a lyre. Then I will stay and sleep in the sun and you will go on, boy, to wander these roads which I am abandoning, and become a great singer, bard of the Argives. You have my songs, son of my heart, and will make more of your own. Music-makers die, Menon. Only if someone still remembers their verses will they live. Do not weep,' he said gently.

'Apollo has released me,' Cassandra was crying and laughing at the same time. Diomenes and Eumides, one cleansed and the other comforted, hugged her from either side and they wept until they began to laugh and to dance, a Dionysiac dance of joy which reeled down the road.

None of them noticed me or cared for me. I mounted *Banthos* and took Orestes up before me as they recovered their senses and mounted as well, turning the horses' heads toward the town.

And there, in the road, I saw our cousin Pylades of Phocis, and I pulled *Banthos* up with a jerk which made the horse look around to see what had happened to me.

'Pylades!' cried Orestes, and leapt down. Pylades embraced him and said, 'What do you here, boy? And by all the gods, the maiden your sister as well.' He put Orestes away at arm's length and looked at him from sandals to face, smiling. 'You've grown, child. And the Lady Electra—Maiden, how fare you?' he asked.

'Better for seeing you,' I said, feeling a sense of great relief. Pylades the tall and strong, reliable, our cousin. It was wonderful to see him. He had known me since I was a child. He held out his hand to me, a worried line creasing his brows.

'Come, I have a house here—not worthy, small and rustic, but you cannot stay in a tavern, Princess. Say farewell to your companions, worthy people I am sure. He bowed to Arion, who as the oldest man in the group was responsible for me. 'I will take charge of the Lady and her brother.'

'Indeed, and who are you?' asked Arion sternly.

'He is the Lord Pylades, our cousin,' said Orestes. 'We can go with him. Lord Eumides,' he laid a hand on the sailor's boot. 'Do not forget me.'

'Orestes,' said Eumides, leaping down and kneeling in the dust so that he could see into the child's face. 'Do you truly wish to go with this man?'

'Truly,' said Orestes.

'Very well. I will never forget you,' said Eumides gravely, tugging at one finger. A ring came free, which he put into Orestes' hand. 'Wear this when you are grown. I do not know where I will be, son of Atreus, but if you need me, I will come. For the moment, you will find us in Delphi. Good fortune, little brother,' he said, and kissed him on the forehead.

They mounted and rode away, calling good fortune and farewell, and we followed our cousin up the mountain, toward a white house in a sea of olive trees.

Pylades' house was old, but sound and clean. He conducted me to the women's quarters' stairs, saying apologetically, 'I have no women here to care for you. I will find someone tomorrow, Lady.'

He was tall and slim. I had known him for years. His hair was the color of old chestnuts, a deep glossy brown, and his eyes were of the same color. He took my hand and kissed it very lightly, saying, 'I and all I have are at your service, Lady Electra.'

'My Lord Cousin, I need to sit down and be quiet for a while.'

'You have been to the oracle?'

'Yes, and she gave us riddling words, hard to unravel, cruel words.' I was sinking down onto the step. Electra, whose fate was unknown. I would almost have rather that the Pythia had told me of my death—at least that was a truth. And Orestes, the revenger...I began to weep.

Pylades did not attempt to embrace me, but gave me my veil and went away, returning with a cup of warm wine. I drank some. It was unmixed and strong and stopped my tears.

'Orestes, your sister is faint. Can you lead her to her bed? Then come down and talk to me.' For it would be monstrously improper for Pylades to enter my room.

I was too weak to stand, however, and he had to carry me, which he did with ease. As soon as he had laid me down and pulled a blanket over me, he left. Orestes stayed until I sent him away. I wanted to weep over our fate, most evilly treated of all the cursed House of Atreus, but weariness overcame me and I slept.

◇◇◇

I dreamed. In the dream I heard the screams again. It was the slave Laphanes of Paeus, lying with broken limbs outside the walls. They had thrown him down from the citadel, and no one was allowed to go near him.

The laws of Mycenae were strict. He who seduces a royal princess must die.

He took two days to die, and he screamed all the time. I could hear him as I lay in my bed. Laphanes with dark curly hair and black eyes, who had smiled at me from the courtyard, and sung love-songs in the city so they would come to my ears.

I could not even drag myself awake. I curled around the pain as I had done as a child, cradling the agony in my arms.

Laphanes screamed and, eventually, so did I.

◇◇◇

The next day, Pylades and Orestes came back from Delphi town with an amphora full of sleeping potion which he had obtained from the Asclepid Diomenes, who sent me good wishes. He also bought two women-slaves, one old and one young, to attend me. The old one was Lysane, a Corinthian, and the young one was called Alceste.

I heard them talking as they prepared my bath.

'It's a good house,' said Alceste. 'The walls are thick and the fields good. I think we will not starve, old woman.'

'And the master?' said Lysane slyly. Alceste laughed. 'I hope he will be kind,' she said. 'The last man I lay with liked to be beaten. I was glad when he sold me. He said I hit him too hard. I did, too.'

Lysane grunted and I heard water being poured into the bath.

'There, just the right temperature. What do you think of our mistress?' asked Alceste.

'They say she is possessed, haunted by demons,' said the old woman. 'She is very beautiful. I hope that she likes us. For we are isolated here, Alceste. If she is cruel then we might die.'

'She does not look cruel. They are memories, maybe, not demons. The Asclepius-Priest told us to be careful with the sleeping potion. Sleeping potions will not banish real ghosts. Her ghosts are in her mind, poor lady.'

'And the master—he is her cousin? And the child her little brother. They are singing songs in Delphi, Alceste, about the Princess of Mycenae and her brother the avenger.'

'But they will not find her here. She's been pleasant so far. And I have no mind to be stoned to death for slander. Let's wake her before the bath cools, Lysane. She needs our care, whoever she is.'

I started as if I had been asleep and they bathed and tended me, combing out my hair.

'The Lady is beautiful,' commented Alceste. 'Her hair is like silk, and so long and fine.'

'The Lady has been ill, or is in mourning,' said the old woman Lysane. 'She needs care. The Lord Pylades sent us to you, Lady. We are your women now. What are your orders?'

'We shall spin and weave and be at peace,' I said, leaning back as my hair was properly arrayed over my shoulders.

I looked around the women's quarters. It occupied the whole second story of the house. Below us were the common rooms, and above us storage for olives and herbs and grain. The walls were well built and thick, whitewashed this season, although there were no hangings. I resolved that it should be decorated finely. The floor was of well-cut smooth wood, as were the beds for me and my women, a large table, and several chairs. It smelled of spring and of the last of the stored grapes— sweet and clean. If I could trust the master of the house, I could be happy here. I had found my white farmhouse, the one I had spoken of to Cassandra the healer so long ago under an olive tree.

But humans are not allowed much happiness by the vengeful Gods, and I did not feel secure. I thought I knew Pylades, but I had thought I knew other people who had proved untrue.

'Where are Lord Pylades and my brother?' I asked my women.

'You may see them, Lady,' said Lysane. 'They are sitting in the sun.'

But they weren't. They had been. Two cloaks taken out as cushions were still lying on the stone bench. But Pylades had given my brother a wooden sword, and was teaching him to fight. On the green pasture, in the sun, the wooden foils cast shadows as long as spears.

Chapter Nine

'You released her?' asked Demeter, smiling at the Sun-God. 'That is a good deed and I will praise you for it, but why? You were not wont to be merciful, Apollo.'

'It is not mercy. Cassandra is of no importance to me now. She may find her own fate. The House of Atreus is my concern.'

'The tale and the curse has run on for five generations,' objected Athene. 'Why must it conclude?'

'Once more they will offend the gods by such a deed as will stagger men. They are vermin, irreparably wicked and cursed beyond repair. Their presence pollutes my shrine.'

'What, this poor little Princess and her eleven-year-old brother?' asked Demeter.

'Born in murder, conceived in murder, suckled on blood,' mumbled Ares hungrily.

'My Lord Ares, there has been war for ten years and the sea ran red with Trojan blood, with Argive blood. The heroes are dead and the world is poorer for it. No wars, not until they recover,' ordered Zeus Father.

'Cruel and young,' said Pan the Ageless. 'Young and cruel, these new Gods. I say this, Apollo. If these Atreidae flee into my forests, I will shelter them. If they thirst, I will give them water; if they hunger, I will feed them. No beast shall threaten them. They are possessed with nightmares, tender young creatures, not long to live.'

'And if they murder their mother,' said Hecate, 'there are those who will pursue.'

Behind her, black forms soiled the bright sunlight of Olympus. Serpent-haired crones armed with staves tipped with bronze; slavering, white-fanged dog's muzzles. They had small drums ringed with iron bells and they beat and jangled them, a tooth-gritting, toneless rhythm.

'Erinyes,' said Hecate. 'The Revengers of Blood.'

'Away with them,' Apollo waved a slender, marmoreal hand and they vanished. 'The children of Atreus are mine, hag. I have set them on to complete the story, and I shall save or punish them as I see fit. It is my voice the boy hears.'

'There is still law in Olympus,' said Hecate. 'By the law, if they do this deed, they are mine.'

Poseidon, sitting by the Pool of Mortal Lives, gestured over the water. For a moment the pool filled with a living picture. An elegant man in a fine chiton, his red hair bound behind his neck, his eyes brown and very seeing, stared up at the god.

'Odysseus,' grunted Poseidon, and the picture vanished. On the broad sea, as blue as Aphrodite's eyes, a ship the size of a pea pod was blown far off course by the god's breath.

Cassandra

There was no doubt, now, that we would stay together, live together. We knew that Eumides was a wanderer, but his question to the Pythia told us that he needed a place to return to, a safe home.

The discussion, which lasted far into the night, was not about whether we would make this unusual pairing, this tripling. It was about where we could all live.

Arion was going home to Epidavros, and I could see that Chryse longed to return there, though there was something he was not telling either Eumides or me. I could not go home. Troy was destroyed. But I could go to Troas, child of Troy, on the Hellespont, the new city founded before the destruction of Ilium. I could not seek my twin, for I did not know where he was, or even if he was still alive. The cobweb on which our communication depended had thinned to a wisp and then gone. I had woken the morning after Delphi to find myself, for the first time in my life, utterly alone. In losing prophecy and the anger of Apollo I had also lost Eleni. I was trying not to think about him. I nudged Eumides with my bare foot.

'What about you, sailor? Where do you want to go?'

'All land is alike to me,' he said. 'As long as I can find you again, I don't care where we live.'

'We could go home to Epidavros, to the temple of Asclepius,' said Chryse. 'I want to go there, to greet my master again and see that old rascal of a bard settled. He has been a good friend to me, and there are more songs to hear.'

'But the temple will not allow a woman to heal, will it?' I asked.

'No,' sighed Chryse.

'And if we go to Troas, you will not be accepted. Only women are healers in Troy.'

We stared into the fire and drank more wine in silence. Where would we be at peace? The Argives would consider me a sorceress, if not a whore. The Trojans would laugh at a man trying to be a healer.

'I have a solution,' announced Eumides unexpectedly.

'You have?' We stared at him. Solutions were not his main talent.

'We can go to Epidavros first, to take the bard home. Then, with all that treasure from my trading, we will build a boat in the shipyards at Corinthos Isthmia, at Kenchriae. Then we will go wandering. We will cross the Aegean to Troas, and visit there. On the way there are many places and islands which could please us. When we find a place we like, we will stay. Simple,' he said, pouring the last mouthful of wine into the fire as an offering to Morpheus for sleep.

Chryse and I looked at each other and laughed. Simple. Of course.

◇◇◇

The road to Epidavros was winding, leading through the mountains, but we had excellent company and we rode through the spring. We were not in a hurry. The old man was tired and ill, so we ambled a few miles every day, then sat for hours under the trees in some village and talked. When Menon judged him well enough, Arion would sing. His voice was compelling, dark-brown, a rich, unassailable voice. No one spoke while Arion sang, even if he whispered. Sometimes Menon rehearsed with him, learning songs line for line, word for word, hour after hour, until the pupil had the song exactly as the master sang it, intonation and note, and lyre accompaniment. To hear Menon was to hear Arion as a boy, his tenor voice clear and pure.

He was unwell, the old man. His lungs were not strong. He hawked and spat, and after any exertion he panted for breath. Chryse and I brewed various infusions, trying holly and lungleaf, sundew, and marsh-leaf.

'I'm afraid he won't last another winter,' I said, stirring a mixture of marsh-herb, colt's hoof, and honey as a linctus to soothe an over-strained throat.

'He's stronger than he looks. He survived pneumonia,' observed Chryse.

'How long ago?'

'Two years, no, three now. Chryseis and I nursed him in Master Glaucus' house. That's when…' he fell silent. A line furrowed his brow. I took his hand.

'Tell us,' I urged. 'We are your loving friends, Chryse. You will feel better if you tell us what is burdening you.'

'It is too bitter to tell,' he said simply.

To that there was no answer, and I returned to the linctus, which must not be allowed to boil.

Arion, sick and old, was nevertheless impressive. He was tall, heavy, and broad-shouldered. It was his eyes that held an audience, as well as his thrilling voice. They were black and bright, sparkling with intelligence and cynical humor. 'Aren't men strange?' they seemed to say. 'And aren't they comic?' He would smile a crooked grin—the Achaeans say that that lopsided smile is a mark of the favor of Aphrodite—which dragged all the world into his gleeful conspiracy.

He was watching us, Chryse and Eumides and me, as we lay together in the meadow, high on the bare hills. It was the tenth day of our journey, and we were rested, fed, and indolent. We shared the patch of green with seven goats and a wide-eyed small boy, who was licking delicately at a piece of the honeycomb we had bought in Corinth as though he had never tasted honey before. The old man's eyes widened as he saw Chryse lay his head on my breast, putting aside my hair, as though he was entitled to lie in my arms. Eumides was sitting up, plaiting flowers into a wreath, and my head was on his hard thigh.

Dionysos loves those
Who fear nothing,

sang Arion, grinning.

Dionysos loves those
Who lie down in joy.
Flowers are grown
Sweet for their bed.
The sky shelters
Their close-wreathed arms.
The sun warms
Their naked skin.
Rain will cleanse
Their locked-close mouths.
Their intertwined bodies
Embraced by the earth.

In his sight and the sight of the boys and the goats, to the music of the lyre, unaccountably, we began to make love. Dionysos was with us, honey-breathed one, golden among Gods. Arion had summoned him in his song, and Dionysos cannot be denied.

The thigh I was lying on flexed, turned, and Eumides stripped and then pulled away my tunic from under Chryse's head. He woke a little, his mouth seeking a nipple like a child's, and he sucked gently. We were slow, tranced, dream-like. The sun poured down on us. I smelled grass crushed by our weight. I stroked Chryse's hair and he blinked, opening wondering eyes. Eumides slid down, my face against his belly. I stroked languidly along his chest, down to the phallus nudging my cheek, and he lay with his feet toward me so that we were a triangle. I felt him kiss and caress, slowly and lightly, from the arch of my foot to the calf of my legs, from there to the knees and so upward, while I warmed in the sun to a fever heat and the lyre thrummed, constantly, until the sound entered our bones.

Chryse woke further, murmured, 'It is not…' I think he was about to say 'proper,' but hands were stroking him, lulling him into our embrace, and he forgot the end of the sentence and I forgot everything in the universe but the lyre and the insistent touch, the shine of sweat on perfect shoulder and thigh, the sweetness of mouths kissing and kissing, lazy and timeless, sweet as mercy, strong as wine.

We moved into actual mating without thought or check. Chryse was between Eumides and me and we locked close and hard, piercing and pierced, a tangle of limbs. We were inside each other, closer than humans ever were since the gods divided the sexes. Chryse's arms were around me so tightly that they later found his finger-marks printed on my back. I sucked Eumides' mouth and he bit me and someone snarled like a dog. I heard the maened shriek of triumph as I felt a climax as sharp as pain and my lovers shuddered under the goad of Dionysos the Dancer, Lord of Madness.

I was filled and wet, and yet the lyre pulsed and we moved again, so that Eumides lay with me and I buried my face in Chryse's loins, which smelt of my own scent and his lust, pungent and pure.

The lyre was fast, beating at our senses. It ruled our movements, quickening, hardening. As seed spilled into my mouth, Eumides and I were flattened by a climax that left us bruised and panting, and we lay like beached mariners, survivors of a shipwreck, battered and flung ashore by the waves.

I opened my eyes on a green hill in the sunshine. Two people and seven goats were staring at us. There was a naked man lying between my thighs, his head heavy on my belly. I was cradled against a smooth bare chest, sweat-dampened golden hair tickling my face, and we were all breathing as though we had run an Olympic race. A heart throbbed under my cheek.

I laughed aloud for the joy that filled my breast.

'Oh, my loves,' I said.

'Our maiden,' said Eumides, dragging himself into a kneeling position, then leaning down to kiss me carefully on my reddened mouth.

'Cassandra,' said Chryse, lifting his head. 'I love you,' he said, using the collective 'you.' Eumides stroked his shoulder and kissed the marks of teeth on his neck.

Chryse got to his feet, groaning, as I searched for my tunic and found it. A goat had started to eat it, and I fought a brief but fierce battle with the animal before I got it back, chewed but not damaged. Eumides dropped his chiton and laughed helplessly as I put the tunic on and patted the goat.

'You're a wicked old man,' said Chryse to Arion, kissing the bearded mouth.

'I was curious,' the bard defended himself.

'What were you curious about?' I asked, joining my fellow-healer and kissing the old man. He returned the kiss affectionately. He tasted of salt and wine.

'About you three,' he replied. Eumides conquered his mirth and knelt before Arion, and the old man kissed him as well.

'I was concerned for the Asclepid, whom I love like a son,' said Arion. Menon poured us some wine and we drank. I was still shaking from the embrace of the god and my lovers. My tunic was wet with seed as it had been with blood on the day when I joined the Mother. Eumides sat behind me, picking grass and burrs out of my hair, and I loved his touch, his ordinary everyday touch, more than I had ever loved a lover's ardent hands. I was joined to them, linked as by a chain. I had lost Eleni but I had found Chryse and Eumides. My hands reached for Chryse and he reclined into my arms without thinking, as though he belonged there.

'How, concerned?' asked the sailor.

'I have known him since he was a child. Women have always loved him. His first love was not his to keep—she was a gift to a boy almost too young to know what he had been given. His second was the golden maiden, Palamedes' daughter. He loved her and she loved him, they were as close as peas in a pod, completing each other's sentences, playing like children, learning how to live together for the rest of their lives.'

'But she died,' I said. Tears ran from Chryse's eyes and trickled down my breast, though he was not sobbing. The old man's face sharpened with sorrow.

'I thought he would die as well,' he said softly. 'He will mourn her all his life, Chryseis, the golden woman. She would have tended his hearth until he was old, growing grey together. That drove him to Troy.'

'Before that, he found me,' objected Eumides, untangling a long strand of my hair. 'In Mycenae, where he mended my broken jaw and bought me out of slavery. I lay with him and loved him on the hills above the city.'

'Ay, and I thought the love of men might save him, Trojan. You cherished him, loved him, but you knew that there was something missing, didn't you?'

'I knew; some deep sorrow. That must have been the first one of whom he has never spoken. She had his heart out of him even then. Otherwise I would not have left him, Arion Badger-Headed. You have clear sight, Bard.'

'That is my skill,' he agreed. 'No one love would be enough for him, I decided, as I watched him tend the wounded at Troy, men screaming and weeping and dying on those dreadful beaches amongst that stench—the Gods must have smelled it, rotten flesh stinking up to heaven. Then he rescued your brother, Princess.'

'Eleni?' I sat up. 'Yes, he tended Eleni.'

'He tended him in love, lay with him in love, and I hoped for him again. But not even that prince, not even that Trojan with the wicked eyes and clever hands, not even you, Lady, golden as Chryseis and wise as a goddess, would alone be enough to fill the void inside him. Too much loss, too young, too young, leaves a hollow deep as the sea. Then I sensed—I suspected, that you and the sailor had combined to love him, Chryse Asclepid-Priest, mourning his hollow heart. I wondered—gods, my restraint! I have been wondering about this triple since Delphi. And now I know. Dionysos is with me, sometimes, if I call him. If the light is warm, and the hills green enough. And I will never forget your beauty, the dance of your loves,' said the old man, giving his empty cup back to his apprentice. 'I will make a song for you, most favored of the gods, trios.'

He rose and bowed. But Chryse remained in our embrace and tears still fell from his eyes, soaking my stained tunic.

Epidavros is the most peaceful place in the world.

We came along the road from the village and port of Epidavros towards the temple as evening was falling. The road was white and we were dusty and tired, and the old man was coughing, so that Menon had taken his elbow and the reins of his horse. Chryse was worried, and so was I.

'The gates shut at sunset,' he said, riding alongside the old man. 'Come, famed bard of the Argives. My Master waits for us.' He chirruped to the horse and we picked up our pace until we were cantering. Thus we arrived at the gates of the temple and city of healers as the sun dipped below the horizon, and rode inside, the last of the suppliants of Apollo for that day. Behind us, the road was empty all the way to the turning. Owls began to hoot in the cypresses and the stars began to come out.

'Greetings and well met, Itarnes,' cried Chryse, leaping down and gathering the reins. There was a false note in his voice. It was over-hearty for the quiet-speaking healer.

'Chryse!' exclaimed a loud voice. 'Where have you been, boy, we have been praying for new of you? Master Glaucus asked Apollo only yesterday, and he said you were coming. I may have to start believing in gods if this goes on. Come, he will want to see you—and your worthy companions. Lord. Lady.' A young man bowed as Eumides and I got down, and then rushed to help Arion dismount.

'Noble company, I should have said,' Itarnes corrected himself. 'You are very welcome, Master Arion, Dolphin-Rider.'

'Arion thanks you for your welcome,' said the bard expansively. I was amazed. This man had sagged coughing over his horse's neck and seemed on the point of collapse for stadia. Now he sounded rested and confident and there was hardly a tremor in his voice. It was an impressive performance and I wondered how long he could sustain it. Menon was evidently wondering the same thing and said quickly, 'My master is tired and needs rest. Where shall we bestow the horses?'

'Leave them here,' said Itarnes, embracing Chryse and taking his hand. Two boys came out from the temple near the gate and led our mounts away. 'The boys will bring your saddlebags. Oh, my Chryse, my dear, it's so good to see you again! We heard the news of Troy, that you did great work there. Polidarius is always talking of your courage and your surgical skill. He says that by moving the army off the beaches and burning the dead you saved the remains of Agamemnon's army.'

'It was only what Apollo would have ordered,' murmured Chryse.

'If he had happened to think of it,' riposted Itarnes. It was evidently an old joke, for Chryse laughed, and I knew where he had learnt his disbelief in the gods.

But I have never felt them closer. It was a holy and a calm place, the temple of Epidavros. Not still like a cave under the ground, but cool and quiet. No strong winds blew here, I knew, as we passed along paved paths between the cypress trees in a cloud of medicinal scent. No snow fell, no heat burned in summer. Here all was ordered, quiet and gentle. Everything— even love and grief—in moderation.

I heard a gasp behind me and a flurry as Eumides and Menon caught the bard under the arms and bore him along, despite his cursing them in a croaking whisper by a remarkable number of

Gods and telling them that he could walk on his own, by the blue testicles of Hades, a religious concept new to me.

We came into a large courtyard lit with torches. It was set about with benches of white marble and planted with three ancient apple trees. On two sides were houses and in the middle was the pillared entrance to a temple, gleaming in the flickering light. Inside I could glimpse a golden and ivory statue. 'That must be Asclepius, a mortal beloved of Apollo,' I said to Eumides, who was bearing up under the bard's vituperations and his weight.

'Oh? What made him a god, then?' asked the sailor.

'Apollo murdered him,' gasped Arion. 'You know how Apollo treats his lovers, Lady.'

This was the first time he had spoken of my own past, and I wondered how much he knew about me. He was a wise man and very acute. He was also very ill and needed a bed and some more honey and lungleaf linctus.

At that moment, a tall man issued forth from the right side of the courtyard. He was thin, with long white hair and a flowing beard, and he moved so fast that his scarlet healer's gown billowed behind him.

'Bring him in,' he ordered briskly, 'Come in, please, most welcome travellers. Arion, you old scoundrel, you have been drinking again. Chryse, my son, my dear son, come in. The night strikes a chill; it is still early spring.'

He ushered us inside a fine house. The walls and the floor were of white marble, unpainted, though we had no time to inspect it as we were swept through the hall into the master's own apartments.

It was a large room, floored with plaited rush mats. There was a fire burning on the raised hearth in the middle, where a chimney pierced the wooden roof. Only a few lamps were alight. I smelled wine and old wood, a soothing combination. Eumides and Menon deposited the bard on a low couch and I rummaged in the saddlebags, brought by a boy, for the linctus.

I found it and sat down with my sailor on the padded floor, next to the old man. I gave him the bottle and bade him drink, and he must have been feeling very unwell, for he drank without complaint. Presently the coughing eased and he began to breathe more freely. Under my fingers his pulse fluttered, and when I listened at his chest I heard a scratching, like the noise of an insect trapped in glass.

Arion lifted one hand and stroked my hair, then the side of my face. His hands were hard but his touch was deft and affectionate.

'Tell me, Princess,' he murmured. 'Is it bad?'

'Not too bad,' I replied. He smiled his crooked grin and I felt my own mouth curve in response.

'I have come home,' he said, releasing me. I kissed his cheek before returning to the hearth. Eumides, uncomfortable, pointed toward Glaucus and our Chryse, standing in the middle of the floor.

'Sweet son,' said Glaucus, holding Chryse close. 'Son of my heart, my dear Chryse, I have been waiting for you, worrying for you, for a weary while. Agamemnon returned months ago— where have you been?'

'I returned with that king,' said Chryse, leaning his forehead on the old man's shoulder. 'I saw him die.'

'You saw him die? How, then, are you alive?'

'I was not worth killing.' Chryse closed his eyes and was embraced by strong arms. Glaucus looked down at him, intensely concerned, then patted his cheek.

'We will speak more of this,' said Master Glaucus. 'Now, introduce me to your companions. Arion I know too well, and Menon his faithful apprentice, but who is the lady?'

Chryse said unsmilingly, looking at us with empty eyes, 'This is the Princess the Lady Cassandra, daughter of Priam, Priestess of Apollo, and this is Eumides the sailor of Troy, my friends and rescuers. I would not be here, Master, if it were not for their care.' Chryse sounded unutterably tired. We stood and bowed to the master, and he scanned us, briefly but closely. I felt that he could look straight through me, bones and all. He seemed satisfied, however, after a very long moment, and clapped his hands, summoning slaves.

Within the first night-watch we had eaten figs, olives, excellent bread, green herbs of the meadows, and a soup of chicken, barley, and onions—most delicious. The fire flickered in the hearth and blurred before my eyes. I was suddenly very sleepy. I licked my lips. Had I tasted poppy in that broth?

'Do you think he will leave us?' asked Eumides, close to my ear.

'What?' I blurred up out of what I was convinced was a drugged sleep.

'Chryse. He has come home. What will he want with a couple of Trojan wanderers, bereft of city and lordship? He will stay here, and where will we go?'

'If he leaves us,' I leaned into his arms, resting my increasingly heavy head on his shoulder. 'If he leaves us, we will build your boat at Kenchraei, Sailor, and go home ourselves. To Troas, daughter of Troy. But I don't think he will,' I said with as much conviction as my stumbling tongue could manage.

It was not a great deal and Eumides was not comforted.

'You heard what the bard said,' I spoke directly into his ear. His curly hair was all that was anchoring my floating spirit. Indeed, I may not have spoken. I might have been dreaming. 'We fill the hollow inside him. Only we can complete him. By the Mother, Eumides, I am so drowsy that I must lie down soon or sleep where I sit, disgracing hospitality.'

The master had also noticed this, or perhaps planned for it. He spoke to me over Chryse's bent head.

'Princess, we have no fit place to lodge you.'

'I will lie with Chryse and Eumides,' I said, relaxing into the Trojan's embrace. I was not so somnolent that I did not catch the lightning glance which passed between Arion and the master. The bard nodded ponderously.

'We will talk in the morning,' said Glaucus soothingly. 'Now you should rest.' Eumides rose and dragged me to my feet. The master came behind with Chryse, who was walking purely by habit.

'This way,' said Glaucus. 'There are sheepskins to lie on, Chryse, and you are home.' He led us into a guest room. Our saddlebags were already there, and some prescient slave had made a bed for three out of fleeces and fine-woven blankets. I lay down on the left side and Eumides on the right and the master lowered Chryse to lie between us. I think he was asleep before his head hit the bolster, and Eumides was certainly embracing him in a dream.

'Has he told you, Princess?' The old man asked me. I forced my eyes open.

'No,' I stammered. 'Not all. There is something more, which he will not tell.'

'We will speak again,' said Master Glaucus. 'Sleep well.' In a sweep of scarlet robes he went away, taking the oil lamp with him.

The last thing I heard was the door closing.

I dreamed. Little pictures, not alarming in themselves. Not related to me, it seemed. Waves breaking over a smashed trading dock. A woman in the robes of Isis' priestess examining a handful of shells. A child climbing the hill to the shrine at Delphi. A white farmhouse, and the smell of charcoal fires and the sound of someone singing to the clack of a loom. Then I saw something which was close to my heart.

I saw a red-headed man on a white shore, escorting a bent woman veiled in black. It was my mother, Hecabe. I heard waves crash and birds crying, and the curses she flung at him, calling him pirate and murderer.

There was no expression on the mobile face. She might have been trying to provoke him to kill her, but he did not react. He seemed to be waiting.

Roughly clad fishermen came down to the beach, curious about the ship and the mariners. The red-headed one opened one man's hand and dropped coins into it, making some kind of bargain. The fisherman nodded and spat. Three shell-crowned women came walking through the dunes and took my mother by the hands, leading her away out of my sight, still scolding and weeping from a scoured throat.

'Remember,' said the red-headed captain. 'If anyone asks, she was transformed into Hecate's avatar Scylla, the black bitch with glowing red eyes, and she ran away howling into the hills.'

The fishermen nodded solemnly, his fist closed fast over the coins.

Then I was inside Eumides, my sailor, and he was dreaming of the past. In his little boat *Farseer*, he was sailing into the Bay of Troy. The city rose stone on stone, a great block, as the little boat wriggled through the break-water turbulence and came to the dock. There stood a tall man, golden hair and bushy golden beard. He was calling for news of Africa, and the grey cat Stathi sat composedly on his shoulder, grey eyes and green considering the world with interested good humour. 'Hector!' cried Eumides, leaping ashore. Then the city crumbled. Hector, my brother, fell to bones and then to ash with Stathi and the dockworkers and the women gathering seaweed, and there was a smell of bitter smoke over the fires still burning in the ruins of Troy.

I wept as Eumides wept for the loss and the pain. Our grief was greater than worlds.

We were in Chryse's dream, and he was dreaming of a golden woman, smiling up at him as he came into a little house and dropped a shell-shaped stone into her cupped hands. 'You smell of the mountain,' she sniffed delightedly. 'Of thyme and orchis. Come and lie with me,' she invited, lying back. Just as he knelt to lean into her arms the picture shattered and there was pain, a fire lit in back and belly, and the golden woman clutching his shoulders and weeping aloud. We heard Chryse telling stories, singing ballads, to the accompaniment of moaning. A woman's voice in agony, striving not to be heard. Our lips were bitten, our fists thrust into an abdomen whose burden strove to be free. We were Chryseis and Chryse, Eumides and Cassandra, writhing in pain.

Then something snapped, and we lay together in the dark under the ground, screaming with agony and loss, trying to die. The vision encompassed us all. We were walking along a dark path. The cold tunnel led to the Argive rivers, Acheron which leads down to Hades' realm, coming to Styx where an old man held out a calloused rower's palm for money. Eumides-Cassandra-Chryse-Chryseis paid him and sat down in the boat, looking down at our hands, which were transparent, feeling our humanity leech away into the misty water, hearing the barking of a three-headed dog just ahead and no other sound but the dipping splash of the oars.

We stepped ashore onto paved stones, walking without awareness of our body, until we came to another stream, Lethe, the water of forgetfulness, and knelt to dip up a handful. We were offered release from memory, from unbearable recollection, from living and from the pain that is living. We were offered final dissolution of all that was us.

But as we bent our head to drink, we heard a great cry from one male throat, vibrant and rich. '*Evoe! Evoe! Evoe!*' the triple invocation of Dionysos. Lethe water spilled from our hands and vines grew, cracking through the stony path; the ivy of the Lord of Madness and Wine, strong as a hawser, green as life.

Then we remembered the smell of crushed grapes, and drifted away into other unremembered dreams.

Chapter Ten

Odysseus

We sailed free, driven before a west wind, the rowers shipping their oars. We were being driven in exactly the wrong direction. A little boat was wrecked beside us, and we took a drenched and shivering survivor aboard.

'Odysseus of Ithaca!' he cried when he recognized me. 'You are long away.'

'I am, from no choice of mine,' I said. 'The anger of Poseidon is implacable. If we ever strike land again, you may go ashore.'

'Lord, you must go home,' said the man, as he clutched a cloak around his shuddering body. 'The dark-haired ones, Dorians from the north, ring your palace and besiege your wife, saying that you are dead, and that she must marry one of them.'

'Penelope will not believe it,' I said.

'No, Lord, she does not, but they need her to become lord of Ithaca, and thus to Zerkynthos and the mainland. She will not be persuaded, but she may be taken by force.'

Poseidon, Earth-Shaker, is it your will that strangers should conquer Achaea? They know no gods, Blue-Haired. It will be your own fault if you are forgotten.

Electra

I woke abruptly the next morning, starting out of sleep. I did not know where I was. I considered my surroundings. I was lying in a soft bed and the sun was coming in through a series of small windows in the eastern wall of a well-made house. The reflected glare from the uncovered whitewash had fallen on my face and woken me. An old woman clucked over a wooden floor, her bare feet making slapping sounds, saying 'It is all right, Mistress. We are here, Lysane is here. See, you are safe in the house of your own cousin Pylades of Phocis, and it is morning. The cook is making you some wheaten bread and shalt have honey.'

She sounded so like my own nurse, Neptha, that tears came to my eyes. She helped me sit up on her old arm and went on, 'And the Lord Pylades and your brother are already up and are out inspecting the vines. Here is a chiton, Lady. Alceste has washed your other clothes and they are out bleaching on the grass.'

'Whence came this one, then?' I asked, sitting up and allowing her to remove my sleeping tunic and dress me in a delicately made, rose-colored robe.

'My Lord Pylades ordered me to buy some chitons for you, Lady, and I have cloth for more. He was worried for you, child, not knowing how soon you might be fit to weave or spin. He is most concerned for your well-being, Mistress, and that is unusual in a man. Though it might be common among princes. I have never met a prince before. Come along now.' She led me toward a saddle-backed chair by the window. 'Cook is a Thracian, and you know how touchy they are. It's his own method of making bread, some Thracian secret. Now.' She laid a tray across my knees. On it was a cup of some infusion which smelt of mint, a terracotta plate with hot bread and honey, and a winter-stored lump of dried fruit. 'And here is your friend,' she said, putting my doll, Pallas, into the chair beside me. 'If you look out of the window, Lady, you will be able to see the men returning.'

I tasted the bread, which was excellent, and drank the infusion, surveying Pylades' land.

He had three fields. One was ranged with grapevines, budding along stone fences. They were coming into leaf, the pale new green of spring. Someone had taken a great trouble with the fields. They were drained by ditched and fenced from the depredations of the master's goats by stone walls and hedges. The furrows of the furthest field were greening mistily; strong spears of wheat breaking through the black earth. The closest enclosure was planted with all manner of vegetables and herbs for healing or cooking. A boy was weeding the red-flowering beans, whistling through his teeth. His back was bare and showed no scars of flogging. He was unobserved—he could not see me in the window—but he bent and pulled at weeds enthusiastically.

That was a good sign. When the king is cruel, the work is done reluctantly and in sullen anger—that is what my father had said. When the king is too kind and not interested, the work is not done at all and the city falls into ruin. But when the king is willing to work with the slaves, then the task is done whether he is watching or not, and he has no need to beat his workers.

I heard voices, and saw Pylades and my brother Orestes come into view. Orestes was leading *Banthos*—who was now, of course, Pylades' property—and our cousin was scrubbing mud from my little brother's side and shoulder. He had evidently fallen, though he did not seem to be injured. They were easy together, laughing, Orestes' face was turned up to Pylades, squinting against the early sun.

I felt a pang. Orestes had always been my own, and now he belonged to another. So did *Banthos*. That was perfectly right and in accordance with the laws, but I could not finish the bread and honey. When Lysane came to take the tray, she clucked again.

'Oh, Mistress, that Thracian will be angry!'

'It's the best bread I've ever tasted,' I said truthfully. 'Please, Lysane, you eat the rest and he will never know. Sit down, Lysane. Talk to me. Tell me about this estate.'

'It's in good heart,' she replied, sitting down on the floor at my feet and applying her remaining teeth to the bread and honey. 'There are seven people working here. Five are slaves, the Thracian, two laborers, and Alceste and me. The rest are free men who live under the protection of Pylades, as we are remote from Delphi polis and not under the government of their demos. The master has two pair of oxen, a good flock of both goats and sheep—fine wool there, Mistress—and his fields bear well. Clonius, the free man, tells me that we sell oil and honey—there are seven beehives in the vegetable garden—to Delphi, and we grind enough flour for a year. That's his son, there, weeding. He gets a loaf of bread for every row free of weeds and he's a greedy child who loves his belly—the best motive, according to Clonius. There won't be a shoot in the wrong place by noon.'

Lysane had clearly been investigating every aspect of Pylades' establishment, and had gained an amazing amount of information in a very short time.

'Is the Lady used to a farm?' she asked, licking up the last crumb from the red plate.

'No, the Lady is not,' I said a little stiffly. She was fishing for information about me, too. Then I considered the breakfast and the soothing words and the presence of Pallas my doll and said, 'The Lady is used to a palace, and you will need to educate her. She wishes to help her cousin in the running of his house, and she does not wish to make mistakes.'

Lysane considered me for a long moment. She had bright black eyes, white hair knotted behind her corded neck, and a nutcracker face. Her cheeks had fallen in with her missing teeth, and her hands were knobbed and bony. But her smile was sweet and she seemed to like me and want to care for me. She patted my knee with her old fingers and said, 'Then shalt be the mistress, Lady, and govern all as you like. And if you want my help, shalt have it.'

I came down at noon, when the farmworkers are fed their main meal. It would be my task to supervise their diet, make sure that they had enough to eat but to guard against waste and gluttony. I had girded the rose-colored chiton and put on my maiden's veil.

They all stopped eating and stared at me. I almost quailed under all those eyes. Then I gathered my courage and Lysane and I bowed to the master.

Pylades was deep in conversation with a man as gnarled as an old olive root and did not see us immediately. Alceste, who was laying platters of bread on the table, coughed, and Pylades looked up and sprang to his feet.

'I did not hope to see you today, Lady!' he exclaimed. 'Hear all men,' he said formally. 'This is my most noble cousin and the Lady of my house and you will obey her in all things.'

The workers scrambled to their feet and he introduced them by name. I could not imagine my father knowing the names of all his workers, but he had many, and I reminded myself that I was no longer in the palace of Mycenae.

'Clonius, the free man, and his son, Azeus. Aulos and Graios, they are slaves.' An old man and a boy bowed clumsily. Two young men avoided my eyes for some reason. 'This is Abantos, the Thracian. He is our cook.'

'You make very good bread,' I said to a huge man, big as a Cyclop. He was black with grime and he did not smile.

'Abantos, greet your mistress,' said Pylades with a hint of metal in his voice. The huge man muttered, 'Lady,' and bowed. Lysane glared at the cook.

'Will you eat with us, Lady?' asked Pylades. This was not entirely proper, but what had Electra to do with propriety anymore? The lentil soup smelled delicious and I was suddenly hungry. Orestes materialized at my side and took my hand, leading me to a seat at the master's left hand.

'I like this place,' he told me. 'My Lord Cousin is teaching me to ride.'

'Indeed?' I took up my wooden spoon so that the rest of the table could eat. Pylades had already gone back to a conversation about the best time to cut wood.

'It should have been done in autumn, Master,' said Clonius, the old man. 'Wood cut in spring is always sappy and will not dry.'

'But it was not cut in autumn,' replied Pylades patiently, 'and we must have wood. I need to repair the byre for the oxen and what if early snow catches the birthing ewes as it did last year? We lost three, and only managed to save one lamb.'

'We have women now,' the old man pointed out. 'Women care best for small creatures. Yes, very well, Master. I see what you are driving at. But if we leave the wood at least until high summer, there will be less sap and the planks will dry faster than if we cut it now. Unless you want a byre-roof which skews like rheumatic bones.'

'No, Clonius, I do not want that,' said Pylades calmly, sipping broth and reaching for another piece of bread.

'Or we could buy some building timber,' suggested the old man, gulping noisily. 'Stenor in the next valley has a pile of autumn-felled planks. He was going to build a new stable, but he killed his slave in a fit of rage, and he has no money to buy another man.'

'And none of his neighbors care to work for him,' put in Aulos. He was a slim young man with a brand on his chest and long straight black hair which was plaited into a braid over his forehead. Some kind of barbarian, evidently. Pylades replied, 'I know. He asked for the loan of you and Graios, and I refused.'

'Thank you, Lord,' breathed Graios. He was also slim, almost thin, though he had a deep chest and the strong sinews which Father had said made a good fighter. His hair was pale and cropped short, probably for some misdeed.

'I would not send you to him,' said Pylades. 'I will not have my men mistreated. Well, Clonius, that is an idea. How much would Stenor want for his planks, do you think?'

'As much as he can squeeze out of us, Master. He drives a bargain like a nail.'

'Misers die poor,' said the Thracian unexpectedly.

'And live miserably,' agreed Pylades. 'What are you doing this afternoon, Clonius?'

'Paring the sheep's hooves, Master. They overgrow while they are in stalls and tender feet in spring produce foot-rot by autumn, that's what my grandfather said.'

'He was a wise man. Very well. I'll pare hooves and you take the ass over to Stenor and ask about the wood. Get a price and inspect the planks carefully—no wormholes or cracked ones disguised with gum. If it seems expedient, ask the old miser to the noon meal tomorrow and we may get a better price if he is softened by Abantos' excellent broth.'

'He'd go anywhere for a free meal,' prophesied Clonius, grinning.

I had eaten my soup and two pieces of bread. Orestes was smiling at me. I was impressed by Pylades' handling of his men. He was authoritative but friendly. And I had no doubt that he would care competently for his sheep while his freeman rode over the hills on the ass.

Presently the meal was concluded and the men clattered outside. The sun was warm, but not hot. In high summer I knew that they would sleep through the hottest part of the day, as we had in the palace at Mycenae. The mastiff, Tauros, barked loudly, then put his head on his paws and went back to sleep. Clonius could be heard urging his son not to eat himself into oblivion while he was away, and I saw him bring out from the stable a fine, well-fed horse as to be saddled.

Alceste and Lysane cleared the table, scraping the uneaten food into the pigs' bucket and wiping the dishes clean. Abantos sprinkled ash over his kitchen fire, smoothing it into a glow which would be refreshed by new fuel for supper at nightfall. He muttered an excuse and left the kitchen, stalking into the courtyard.

'We'll have trouble with that one,' muttered Lysane, 'mark my words.'

'I mark them,' I said.

'Alceste, can't you do anything to humor him?' asked the old woman, bearing a pile of platters to a cupboard and piling them away. Alceste tossed back her dark-brown hair and put both hands on her ample hips.

'Me? Are you joking, old woman, or have you forgotten the lust of men? He'd crush me flatter than a grapeskin and split my belly—he's got a phallus like a flagpole.'

'Aha,' grinned Lysane. 'If you aren't interested in him, Maiden, how do you know that?'

'I must have a look at the stored wool,' I said, standing up. I did not like their conversation. 'Arcturus is rising, my women. We will have to work hard all summer if we are to clothe nine people for the winter.'

'They say it bites hard here,' said Lysane. 'The wool is stored in the roof, Mistress. Clonius, the freeman, says that no one has spun it for three years.'

'And before that?'

'Oh, the master had two women living here then—he bought them from Phocis, where they say he is a prince. They were called Perithea and Asia. He loved Perithea, the old man says, and she bore him a girl child, Tisimene, but they were all carried off in the coughing fever three winters ago. Their spinning and weaving tools are in the roof. Clonius says that the master ordered them put there, because he did not want to be reminded of them. This way, Mistress.'

<>‍<>‍<>

We began with the oldest bales. The spruce under the roof was stuffed with cleaned and tanned fleeces, goatskins, three ox hides for boots, and the household goods of the dead women. I found a basket of spindles and loom weights, three heddles for separating the warp, and all the instruments for carding and sewing. In the warm attic I considered a leather folder full of precious sewing needles. Someone, perhaps a child, had laboriously embroidered a flying bird on the front.

Impulsively, I kissed the bird, resolving that Pylades' daughter Tisimene should not be forgotten.

As chattering women do, as we spun endless lines of woollen thread we talked and sang and told stories.

And as women who must live together do, we exchanged our lives.

Lysane stretched and said, 'Ah, it is hard to be old and a slave.'

'How did you come to be a slave?'

'The fools of my village decided to get involved in a war between Athens and Tegea,' she said sadly. 'We lost. The Tegean women and children were made slaves. Ten years ago I had my own house, a son, and a grandson. Now they are dead or enslaved and I am here, Lady, and likely to die in slavery. But we take what the Gods send,' she said, winding wool around a shuttle. 'I am content.'

'And you, Alceste?'

'I was born a slave,' she said, shaking back her dark-brown hair. 'My mother was a bondswoman and I was her master's child. I lived with her until I was twelve, and then Master sold me to an old man. I did not like him. His breath smelled foul and he had…strange desires. Thus I was pleased when the Lord Pylades bought me. I will never be free, but no woman is free. I will do my best to serve you, Lady. And maybe I will catch the eye of a passing freeman who needs a strong wife. Here I will learn how to manage a farm.'

'And I…' I felt that I had to return confidence for confidence, 'I was a princess in a stone city. I was…misused as a child, in my mother's care.'

They were looking at me without blame, and I was encouraged to go on. 'That's why I have bad dreams. Then my mother…' I choked. Lysane embraced me and Alceste fetched me a cup of unmixed wine.

'We have heard the story, Princess,' said the old woman. 'There is no shame in being dishonored so young. The shame lies with your mother, for allowing such a thing to happen—ay, and on the man who did it, curse all of that sex for lechers and monsters. And revenge will fall on the house of Atreus, Lady. The Gods do not permit such misdeeds to go unpunished forever.'

We could see out of the window as the work of the spring went on. Pylades worked hard, tilling the vines, as the swallow cried mournfully.

'She is Pandion's daughter,' Alceste told me, as the sun crept across the floor. The spindle-weights spun smoothly as cream-colored thread wound around them.

'The swallow?' I asked. I had not heard the story.

'She was the daughter of Pandion the prince, so beautiful that the birds called to her across the meadows,' chanted Alceste. 'Her sister Procne married Tereus, the king, an unloving husband, and she sent for her sister Philomela to keep her company. She came, and Tereus fell in love with her, his wife's sister, forbidden to him by the wise gods.'

She stopped spinning to wind her wool into a skein, thumb to elbow in a smooth movement.

'What happened to her?' I asked.

'He waylaid her in a thicket and raped her, overmastered by lust as lawless men are,' replied Alceste. 'Then knowing what he had done would make him accursed, but not daring to kill her, not wanting to relinquish possession of her white body, he cut out her tongue so she could not tell and imprisoned her in a little house in the fields, a bride's house for his desperate bride. Blood filled her mouth and fear her mind, but stronger was her desire for revenge. When he came again she submitted to him, pleasing him with her hands, and asked him in mime for a loom and some wool, to occupy her until her sister's lord came again to invade her body.'

She impaled a bundle of fluffy white wool on the spindle-spike and drew out her first thread, rolling it between her fingers. I realized that I was holding my breath.

'Then she made a tapestry, an embroidered cloth, and sent it to her sister. The evil master had told Procne that her sister had returned home, so he had no reason to not convey the present to his wife. He mustn't have even looked at it, which is like a man. When Procne saw pictured on the cloth the rape and mutilation of her sister, she cried desperately on the gods for justice and they were turned into birds. Philomena cries for her lost love, men say, but I say for her lost honor, gone forever when Tereus seized her. The swallow's voice is answered by the nightingale, her sister Philomena, forever mourning, and the *hoopoe*, the evil king.'

'I do not like your stories, Alceste,' I commented.

That night the dream came again.

I was lying in my bed in the palace and I heard the door open. He came in, dark curls to his shoulders, placating smile on his face. I was pinned under his weight as Philomela under Tereus, and I screamed and screamed. Lysane came to me, and Alceste, and I slept uneasily under the influence of the drug, between their warm and breathing bodies.

The next morning I went to Pylades where he was sharpening a sickle and said, 'I must speak to you, Lord.'

'My Lady?' His smile faded as he saw my sad face. 'What is it, princess? Has someone offered you an affront? Are you not happy here?'

I am happy and no one has offered me an affront. You have all been very kind. But, Lord...' I groped for words. 'Lord, I wondered...if you might perhaps be thinking that I might make a wife for you.'

His eyes widened. 'Lady, I am honored by your presence in my house, I would not presume...'

'There is no presumption. What rank is Electra, now that her father is dead at the hands of her mother?' I snapped. 'But I have this to say, Lord. I like you, I am happy in your house, but I cannot marry you, Lord.'

'There is another?' he asked, his face stony.

'No, no other. I cannot marry anyone. Lord, I am tainted, contaminated, unfit to marry. I can never marry you, Lord Pylades, though if I could it would be you or no man.'

He was silent. Hollow and shaking. I laid a hand on his homespun sleeve.

'Shall I take my brother and leave, Lord?' I asked. That would be only fair. If I was unable to marry him, then I should leave my place to another mistress. But I was desperately reluctant to go. The farm had become dear to me and I felt safe, as safe as I could feel anywhere.

'Leave, Lady? By all the gods, not on my account.' He smiled at me. I liked the way the corners of his hazel eyes crinkled.

'Who else will mollify the cook? That Thracian will poison us all if I let you go.'

It was true that I had struck up what could almost be called a friendship with Abantos. For days he had ignored me. When I showed no signs of interfering in the management of the trade, however, he unbent enough to instruct me in some elementary skills. He was surprised that I had never cooked anything in my life and, I think, pleased that I confessed my ignorance. He found me, I believe, an apt pupil. After a few weeks, he began to smile at me, always disconcerting in that big dark man. He had such white teeth. We talked about the world. He had been captured in a border battle between the Thracians and the Epirotes, and had made his way from master to master all down the coast of Achaea to Delphi. He had been a famous cook amongst his people and was always, he said, sold for a higher price than before.

Pylades had bought him from his old master in the Delphi marketplace, outbidding several other farmers. Abantos told me proudly that he was worth five silver coins. I told him he was worth at least twenty for his bread alone, and he grinned at me for the first time.

He was worried by my thinness, which in Thrace is a portent of death. He made me eat bread and oil, and saved the fattest meat and the richest fruit for me. And he had gone to any end of trouble and experimentation to make for me the honeycakes of Mycenae, of which there are no better in all Achaea.

And I believe that the best honeycakes in the world are now to be found on the estate of Pylades, the Prince of Phocis, made by Abantos the Thracian, prince amongst cooks.

I smiled at Pylades as best I could.

'And Tauros likes you,' he added.

This was also true. Sharp-toothed Tauros, the guard dog, a mastiff almost as big as the bull after which he was named, had sniffed me suspiciously at first. But I was never afraid of animals. Men are much more dangerous. I had given him my travelling shift to sleep on and he had grown used to my scent. After a week he was taking tidbits from my hands, and licking my face. Yet he was wary or fierce with all other people, being the master's dog and proud of it.

'You are dreaming again, Lady,' Pylades observed. 'I can tell by the shadows under your eyes. I have a proposal. I think that you have been enclosed for too long. Reacquaint yourself with your old friend *Banthos*, Princess. Come riding with me and Orestes. He can ride now almost without falling.'

'He told me. But it would not be proper for me to be seen by the countryside riding astride on a horse, Lord.'

'Then we will go out early in the morning,' he said, 'before any but the hardiest are awake. I think you need to breathe free air, Lady.'

I agreed to try it.

◇◇◇

The days fell into a pattern. I find patterns soothing, being a weaver. Every morning I rose before dawn, dressed quickly, and met my brother and the Lord Pylades at the stable, where my friend *Banthos* and the others were waiting, ready-saddled by Graios, who slept in the stable to guard against thieves. By bringing a horse to Pylades' house we had doubled his wealth. That scoundrel Trojan Eumides had evidently made one of his very good bargains for him. Pylades said that *Banthos* was a warhorse from the king's stable, and had purchased a mare to be his mate, hoping for many fine colts if the gods were kind.

Graios boosted me into the saddle and then smiled at me as I settled myself and pinned my veil close around my head. He was always smiling at me, the young slave. His eyes followed me if I was in the room, though I was sure that he could not see through my firmly lowered veil. Alceste said—It does not matter what Alceste said.

Oh, it was fine to be out in the world again. I breathed the air, hampered by the veil. As soon as we were out of sight around the curve of the hill, I lifted it back and let the cold air rush past my face, scented with leaves and water. Orestes laughed.

'Here is my sister returned!' he exclaimed.

'She has never gone away,' I told him. 'She will always be with you.'

'Until the end, Electra?' he asked soberly, and I caught his hand, allowing *Banthos* to slow to a walk.

'Until the end,' I assured him. My little brother's eyes had never been the eyes of a child. They were golden and uncanny. They held divine secrets. I knew that the God Apollo must still be speaking to my brother. Pylades broke the silence, riding between us and urging his mount to canter.

'Come on, Electra,' said Orestes, and I kneed *Banthos* into a trot.

My Lord Pylades was right. The morning ride banished the black remnant of my dreams and I returned, veiled again, but awake and alert and ready for whatever work was toward. All through the spring, as Arcturus rose higher and the rhythm of the agricultural year quickened, I rode each morning with Pylades, Prince of Phocis, and I grew stronger.

The Thracian's feeding was showing results. At the time of the scything of the grain I pulled on the tunic in which I had arrived and found that it would no longer fit me. Lysane was pleased.

'There, Lady, my nestling, that's a good princess. See, you have breasts now, child, and hips like a proper woman.' Her hard hand ran approvingly down from my shoulder, cupped a handful of breast, and patted my buttocks. The touch sent a little warm tingle through my bones.

Alceste came up the stairs, announcing, 'The old man says that the snails have been climbing the stems, he says they are afraid of the Pleiades and it is time to harvest, and my Lord Pylades bid me to tell you that we will begin harvesting today.' She came close to me as I stood naked, waiting for Lysane to find me a better-fitting tunic, and said softly, 'My Lady is beautiful.' Her hand repeated the caress of the old woman's, gently stroking from shoulder to thigh, and I felt a stronger tremor, as though I was cold. Her hands were hard with work but their touch was pleasant. She allowed her hand to slide down to my belly, her fingers closing on the mount of Aphrodite, and she kissed me, a soft, delicate woman's kiss, not intrusive like the kisses of men—of the man.

Then Iysine came back with my tunic, and it was time to work.

The scythes were sharpened and the cook's temper was as black as his skin—or his heart, as Lysane mumbled. There would be twenty men to feed for at least two meals, and the fire had gone out. I could hear Abantos roaring as I came down the stairs, tying a coarse cloth apron around my waist. I ducked as a pot, flung at Aulos, hit the wall with a thud and bounced and clanged.

'Thracian, you will dent your master's pots,' I said peaceably. 'Come, leave flinging things. You sit down and drink a draught of the good wine—come, Abantos, sit here on this bench, fetch him some wine, Lysane—and Aulos will beg fire from the reapers.'

Somewhat to my surprise, he did as I told him. Graios, who ought to have been out in the field, was sitting on the back step, clutching his head.

Alceste examined him briefly, led him into the kitchen, and sat him down next to the huge Thracian, who snarled at him over the lip of the wine-cup.

'What happened to you, Graios?' I asked. Lysane took an old tunic and began to rip it into strips. 'I was in the way of the first pot,' said the young man, taking a blood-smeared palm away from the grazed temple and wincing.

'You shouldn't have let the fire go out,' grunted the cook.

'I didn't,' protested Graios. 'I was in the stable like always. You should have got Azeus with that pot. He was told to sleep here and mind the grate.'

Lysane brought water in a bowl and began to wash the bruise. Graios gasped at the cold, rough touch and I said, 'Gently, Lysane. I'll do it. You go and get the meal for the bread and measure it so that the dough can be ready when Aulos comes back with the fire. Alceste, can you find that boy, spank him, and make sure there is enough charcoal? There,' I soothed, stroking away the clotted blood. The young slave's skin was smooth and I was hurting him, though he was trying to conceal this. I put back his hair where blood matted it, and he opened his eyes. They were brown and soft.

I was quite close to him. He was no threat to me. He was in subjection, a branded slave, and in pain. His hands fell loosely between his knees and he would not dare to touch me. I leaning his head a little into my arm when the wound was clean, smearing on some of Lysane's stone-crop ointment. I wound the bandage around his head and secured it with a pin from my veil and he was docile under my handling, only wincing a little at the bite of the ointment.

'There,' I said. He looked into my eyes and whispered. 'Thank you, Lady.' Common words, but uncommonly meant. Abantos drained his cup and roared, 'More than a slave's head is worth, to be anointed by a princess. Get out to the fields, lazy one. And next time, when I am in a pot-throwing temper, Graios…'

'Yes, Thracian?' demanded Graios, getting to his feet, balanced, as if for a fight.

'Dodge,' the cook advised him. 'I'll make you one of the princess' honeycakes as an apology. Is that fair?'

'More than fair,' agreed Graios, and collided in the doorway with a fire-bearing Aulos, followed by the hod of charcoal with a howling boy underneath. Alceste had found Azeus, and spanked him.

I assessed the child as crying more as a matter of form than from any real injury, and joined my women at the long table and the meal-tub, where we were likely to be occupied all day. Abantos lit his fire again and began to concoct his famous bean soup, the secret of which, I hoped, he might one day share with me.

It was my household now, I realized. My people to be warmed and fed. My work to clothe them in my own spinning and protect them from winter and the heat of the sun. I was the mistress of the house, and I was suddenly very pleased.

Chapter Eleven

'Consider the race of men,' announced Zeus from his throne. The assembled Gods sat down in their places.

'A little thing, crawling between Paradise and Hades' realm,' said Apollo dismissively.

'With a divine spark,' objected Demeter, Earth Mother.

'So brave,' said Ares. 'I wonder with so little life that they spill their blood like water.'

'For greed,' said Hermes, bored. 'For acquisition, territory, and malice.'

'For an idea,' said the Lord of the Gods.

Cassandra

We found out the secret the next day. We were sitting in the master's own apartments when a boy brought in a casket. It was a large, well-made plain wooden box, closed with a clasp. He laid it beside Chryse and went away.

'What's in it?' I asked.

'It's mine. These things I left here when Chryseis died, when I left for Troy,' he said sadly, turning the box around in his hands. Healer's hands, large and strong, with straight fingers. I asked, 'Are you going to open it?'

'Yes,' he said on a held breath.

It was not even full. Eumides, who had been expecting treasure, sighed. There was a case, such as the Asclepids use to hold surgical instruments. Three folded tunics. A shell-shaped white stone, identical with the one I had seen in my dream. A very fine healer's chiton, embroidered with gold around the neck and in bands down the front. A chunk of rock with amethysts in it. Perhaps forty coins, some Phrygian trading silver and some gold of Mycenae. Chryse scrabbled under the tunics and came up with a pair of small sandals, worn through at the heels. He sat with them in his lap for a long time, and he did not speak.

I wondered for the first time about the string of amber beads which Chryse always wore around his neck. A charm-bundle was attached to them, something closely packed and precious sewn up in a bag of oiled kidskin. I had seen it a thousand times but never wondered what it was. Now I wanted to know. I wanted to know very badly.

Eumides caught my thought, but we could not break our friend's reverie.

Master Glaucus looked in and beckoned, and I rose and went to him.

'Princess,' he drew me outside into the dazzling hall. 'I ask as an old man, and one who considers Chryse his son. What is your will with him, Lady?'

I took no offense. He was plainly as worried about Chryse as we were.

'I mean to love him, my Lord, and I mean to stay with him and our sailor. I have lost Troy, Master Glaucus, and Priam and all his lordship have passed. I have no rank now. I am just Cassandra.'

'Arion says…' he paused, then went on, 'I have never known that old scoundrel wrong about matters of love or fate, Lady. That, perhaps, is what being a bard means. He knew that Chryseis the golden maiden would die—he knew it months before it happened.'

'He is a bard of great skill and his goddess is with him,' I agreed impatiently. 'What says the old man?'

'He says…that Chryse cannot stay here. Because you and the sailor cannot stay here.'

'Is Epidavros still afraid of the mere remnants of Troy, Master?' I was surprised and affronted. He laid an old hand on my shoulder.

'No, Princess, I do not explain myself well. You are a healer, a dedicated woman, a priestess of the Mother Demeter, are you not?'

I nodded.

'You could stay in the temple of the Mother in Epidavros village, tending to her worship as a true daughter of Hygeia, though you could not act as a healer in this temple. But you are a disgraced and dismissed priestess of Apollo also?'

'That is true.'

'This is a shrine of Apollo, Lady. He would not allow you to stay here.'

'In Delphi they said that he had cast me out,' I said. 'Pythia said that he had released me.'

'And yet, Lady.' His eyes were deep and wise, and I understood him. He was right. We had brought Chryse home, but I could not stay here. My eyes filled with tears against my will, and I turned my head so that the old man should not seem them.

Eumides, coming behind me, encircled my waist and demanded 'What have you been telling the princess, Master?'

'That she cannot stay here in Apollo's shrine. I am distressed to have hurt her, but my oath requires the truth. But there is nothing to hinder you going wherever you like, Trojan.'

'The world is wide,' he agreed, holding me close. 'But hollow without our Asclepid. He will pine without us, even in this peaceful place. Ask the bard, Master. I am only a simple fisherman and do not understand these great matters, but there are certain birds, Master, the soaring geese who mark the turning of the year for the Trojans. If one is shot, her mate will mourn until he dies, as she would for him. We have rescued the widower-bird, but it took two of us. He cannot live without us, Master of Epidavros. Nor we without him. We are trios.'

'So Arion says. But you may stay for at least a while, most welcome guests. You are xenos of the temple and you may not sail until the end of summer. I must accustom myself to losing my dearest son. And Chryse has something which he must face.'

'What is it, Master?' He gave us a long look, then bent and whispered. Eumides and I drew closer together.

We knew the secret, and it was a cruel one.

In a week we had learned the ways of the temple of Epidavros. The acolytes, some as young as nine or ten, were each allotted a tutor, and they accompanied him as he made his rounds, tending to the wounds of the world. Each suppliant was given that sleeping potion, and lay down in the tholos underground to wait for their cure to be revealed in a dream. Priests in masks confronted them on their journey into the Earth, so that they were in the proper frame of mind when the drug overtook them, and dreamed to a purpose.

It seemed pointless to me. Then I remembered my own teacher, Tithone, whose hair was considered lucky. She always tied it close and wore a veil, telling me with a wry smile that a charm, if it was to work, must be rare and hard to obtain. Thousands came to Epidavros with intractable illnesses and left cured. The method obviously worked. I hoped it would succeed with our friend.

We watched as Chryse was led by the hand by a child dressed like Hermes into the bowels of the Earth. Itarnes the Asclepid took us by a straight, paved path into the circular chamber and we sat down at Chryse's feet as he closed his eyes.

'We listen for his dreams,' said the priest, solemnly.

'How?' asked Eumides.

'He will speak,' said Itarnes. 'They all speak.'

For a long time we sat in the darkness and heard the sleepers moan. One cried out, shockingly loud in that confined space, crying for mercy, for help, and no one answered, no one soothed him with soft words or touch. Eumides held me in my place, stilling my urge to spring up and do something to stop that heart-racking scream.

Then Chryse began to talk. We leaned close to hear the words.

'Lost,' he mourned. 'Lost, lost, and they are alive?' Then he murmured so that we could not decipher any meaning, until he cried aloud, 'Oh, Chryseis, that you should die for them to live! Come Furies, come Strife and Chaos, kill them, they have no right to live, no right to live, no right...' he mumbled his way into incoherence again.

We sat looking at each other. It was worse than we had feared. It was not loss which hollowed our Chryse's heart. It was hatred. So deep that we had never felt it, burning out his insides.

We found the bard, Arion, sitting in the courtyard, tuning his lyre. He sounded better. His color was high and he breathed deeply, and I heard no wheezing when I laid my ear to his chest. He held my head close to him for a moment, then kissed my forehead.

'A song,' he announced. The three of us sat down on a bench in the sun and prepared to be amused, instructed, or enlightened as he wished.

> When the flesh is cold as stone,
> When the pulse of heart is gone,
> On cold pathways I will travel,
> Crystal waters I will drink.
> Then I will forget, forget,
> Then I will forget,
> Forget the flutter of maiden's tunics
> Forget the taste of wine.
>
> When the fire scalds out my eyes,
> When the blindness steals my sight,
> On hot winds I will be blown,
> Fierce furnaces will suck my breath.
> Then I will forget, forget,
> Then I will forget.
> Forget the wind, forget the clouds,
> Forget the scents of earth.

Therefore rejoice, living men,
Breathing ones with beating hearts.
Therefore rejoice in hearth and field,
Rejoice in byre and hall.
Remember flesh, remember love,
Remember the kiss of lips,
Remember grape and the taste of bread,
Rejoice in the hyacinth.

'I made that seeing the spring again, after Troy had fallen,' he said comfortably. 'Have some wine, Asclepid, you look pale. Have you heard the news? Odysseus is missing again. Someone sighted him off Circe's isle, heading west, but no one has heard of his landfall.'

'He will fall on his feet,' said Eumides admiringly. 'Or someone else's. That is a cunning man, the Prince of Ithaca.'

'And there is trouble at home. I hope he gets there soon. The dark-skinned ones, the Dorians, are threatening to take his wife, Penelope, and thus the kingship, saying he is dead. She refuses to believe it, but she may be overborne. And she is the only person that Odysseus Prince of Ithaca loves, his wife Penelope.'

'He spoke to me of her,' said Chryse, tempted into conversation. 'A woman of unparalleled beauty and virtue, he said. He will be furious when he hears. They brought him into the war by threatening his son, Telemachus. Penelope. Yes. He said she was the only human he trusted.'

'Not otherwise a trusting man, then?' I asked, hoping that he would continue to talk.

'No.'

'You met the monster Achilles, Chryse,' said Eumides. 'What was he like?'

'As beautiful as a girl, with long fleecy golden hair and strange grey eyes. And the gods had made a stone out of his heart,' replied the Asclepid, shortly.

Arion sent the boy back for some more wine and began to pluck the lyre again.

Elene of Sparta was fair as the morning,

he began, looking at Chryse.

Bright as the Goddess of Dawn.
Dangerous as an army with well-sharpened spears
Against whom no breastplate of bronze
would repel
The arrow that pierces the armored heart.

For some reason, Chryse slammed down his cup and ran out of the courtyard toward our room.

'What was that about?' I demanded, and the bard grinned his enchanting, lopsided, grin, settling his singing robes around him.

'It was an exceptionally well-made ballad about Elene of Sparta,' he answered, which was no answer at all.

Chryse dreamed, but we could not enter his dream. We could not soothe him and we could not seduce him, and we refused to make love with each other while he lay stone-faced and alone. He spent hours staring at the line of suppliants coming up the white road to the temple, and would not confide in us.

After a month of this, Eumides was getting restless. We were sitting together on the cool marble bench in the Master's courtyard when he said in Trojan, 'Perhaps I was wrong.'

'Wrong about what?'

'Wrong about Chryse. Perhaps we should leave him, Cassandra. Perhaps he will heal if we are gone.'

'No, we can't! What of Arion and trios? How can he live without us?'

'Is he happy with us?' he asked. I curled a strand of his black hair around my finger.

'No,' I agreed. 'But that is not us. The secret is eating him. He is here, in his master's house. He can no longer ignore it—ignore them. He must face it. And perhaps we are helping him, Eumides. Perhaps we are useful to him, just by being here.'

'And that is true,' said a quiet voice, in Trojan, behind us. Chryse stood there. He was as pale as the marble bench, his courage screwed together for some great test.

'Come with me now,' he said, and we came, going through Master Glaucus' hall and the main room and into a room behind. An old woman looked up in surprise brushing a squirming child's hair.

Chryse sat down on her bed, and two children leapt for him, fascinated by his golden hair and the amber necklace.

'They are my children,' he said flatly. 'They are called Chryse and Chryseis.' They were identical, golden-haired, with Chryse's wide grey eyes and strong, stocky bodies. '*Kala*,' they cooed, swarming up into his lap and stroking his face with soft little fingers. '*Kala*, pretty, pretty.'

'Their mother died bearing them,' he said in that same distant voice, as Eumides' hand met mine and clasped hard enough to hurt. 'I cursed them when they were born, and I have hated them all their lives. But it is not their fault that Chryseis is gone. They have a right to live, and a right to my love. I have let her go,' he said desolately. 'I have, at last, let my golden maiden go.' And he began to cry out his loathing into their golden curls, while they pouted at his tears and kissed them away like good children. Their nurse slid out from between Chryse and the wall and left the room without a word, returning with Master Glaucus.

And still Chryse wept as if his heart was broken, and the twins hugged as much of him as their arms could encompass. I was holding my breath that they would not decide to do something inappropriate which would break his relieving tears, but they were as close as Eleni and I had been. We must have appeared so, I and my lost Eleni. I realized that I had not thought of him in months, and began to cry as well, which brought Eumides in, and we all sat on the floor of the little room and wept for our lost loves, until Chryse and Chryseis, catching the mood, began to roar and hiccup, and Chryse, their father, stopped crying to comfort them.

The nurse brought honeycakes, which stilled our tears, and we talked to the twins.

They knew their names, their numbers, and Chryse broke into tears again when he heard his son declare, 'There are two herbs to be used in all cases, given to us by the Lord Apollo. They are vervain and basil, the king of herbs.'

After an hour, the Asclepid looked up at the Master and said, 'By the help of the god, Master, I am healed.'

This was evidently a ritual phrase, for Glaucus laid a hand on his head and replied, 'May health be yours for the rest of your life, and may you never need healing again. The blessing of the god go with you, my son.'

'Here is my replacement,' he said, patting his son on the belly so that the child giggled. 'And here is my Chryseis re-born. You will marry her well, to a kind man?'

'As if she were the daughter I never had,' said Master Glaucus.

'Then they are yours,' said our Chryse. 'And tomorrow, Master, we will leave.'

That night we slept wrapped together in relief and exhaustion, and never heard the cock crowing for our journey.

Eumides was occupied in Kenchraie, a typical seaside village. Stone houses, driftwood fires and the scent of drying fish. The boat-builder's yards were slowing down for high summer when we came and hired a space and bought the tools and woods we needed to build a well-found, hollow ship, the kind that the Achaeans call 'deep-bosomed.' Chryse and I were at a loose end. Chryse was not deft enough to please our shipwright, and although I could handle the tools, women were not allowed to build ships. So we sat in the market and solicited patients.

Healers were rare and we were well patronized.

I had been given an Asclepid's gown by Master Glaucus, a unique gift, after a long and learned discussion on the use of certain mushrooms as an antidote in poisoning cases. It was a fine garment, deep scarlet and flowing, but it produced such shock amongst the clients that I had one made for myself of my favorite dark green linen, easy to wash. Women who came to the market got used to me being there after a week, and before long the matrons of Kenchraie brought their troubles to a female healer, not midwife or witch but a healer like a man, and from Epidavros, too.

It was a fairly healthy place. There were accidents, of course, and the usual household burns and fractures. Because we had adopted the Asclepid's practice of only accepting what the patient could easily give, slaves came, and the poor.

As summer grew we acquired tenancy of a hut in the market from a seller of vegetables. We cleaned it and divided it down the middle, male on the right and female on the left. In any matter where we felt that we needed consultation, we would call each other in. I found that Chryse was better than I at wounds—this was perhaps not surprising—but that I had more patience with indeterminate complaints, where the patient feels not well but not exactly ill, head-achy and uncomfortable. For these I prescribed infusions of pleasant herbs and honey, though what I wanted to say to most women was they needed more rest and some care and consideration, which they were not going to get. One very hot day I called down the wrath of the gods on a stupid man who wanted his wife to submit to the rites of Aphrodite within two days of giving birth. The vessels of the body are open for six weeks, and that goddess can kill a woman with a newborn.

He gave me an argument, and I called Chryse, who listened, nodded gravely, and agreed with me. The man flung a coin at us and swore that she was his wife and he would use her as he wished. I lost my temper and followed him into the street, shouting, 'If you have any care for your health, freeman, you will let your wife sleep in peace. Her death may follow if you force her, and then your genitals will wither. Aphrodite the Stranger is a fierce opponent to those who would abuse her worship.'

The man collected his wife and scuttled away, followed by the laughter of the market women. I returned to my patients. Something was worrying me.

Since we had left Epidavros, Chryse had not lain with me. He was willing to make love; the touch of my fingers still brought heat to his skin, and he would caress me, please me; but he had not lain inside me. Eumides could receive his seed, but not I. I remembered that there was something that I had never told him. First there had not been time, and then I had not spoken, wondering how both of them would react. I prescribed absently for a baby with summer diarrhea, reminding his mother to feed him boiled water, and made an ointment out of lard which was melting as I pounded it. Sweat dripped down my face. It was as hot as a forge inside that hut and no one else was likely to come until the afternoon coolness.

I called through the curtain, 'Are you alone?' and a tired voice replied "Yes. Are you?'

'Come down to the shore,' I said. 'I need a wash and I have something to tell you.'

In a few minutes we were stripped of our robes and wading into the blood-heat water in a cove so clean that I saw his pale limbs through the sun-dazzle. He took my hand as we sank down into the blessed coolness.

No one was about. The citizens of Kenchraie had gone into their houses and shut their doors and were sleeping away the hottest part of the day. Dogs drowsed in the market, too sleepy to snap at swarming flies. I knew that Eumides would be comfortably drowsing under the half-built boat. It was delightful to be awake while all others slept, delightful to float free in the expanse of the sea and hear the little noontide waves laugh as they broke on the rocks. Chryse lay beside me, his hair floating like a triton's. A light breeze ruffled the water and made him sneeze.

'What did you want to tell me, Lady?' he asked.

I swam over to him and anchored myself with one foot on a reef. He embraced me and saw our hair mingle like seaweed.

'You need not be afraid to lie with me,' I told him.

'But...do I not please you, Lady, as it is?'

'Yes. But you are afraid, aren't you, that I will conceive and die as your golden maiden did?'

His face bobbed next to mine, but I could not read his expression.

'Yes,' he said, finally.

'Oh, Chryse, I will not die in childbirth. I did not know how to tell you, fearing that you would be terribly disappointed. But they told me in the temple of Gaia when I was cursed by the God. I'm barren.'

There was a splash, and I gulped water, to be hauled into a sandy wet embrace and kissed by a soft mouth bitter with salt.

'Is it true? Is it really true?' he gasped, as I coughed and shook my head.

'Unless you drown me, I'll live with you until we both die of old age. And you can bathe me in seed and I'll never conceive,' I said, spitting salt water down his back.

'Agape mou,' he whispered, finding my mouth and kissing me very gently. 'Oh, my love.'

I told Eumides that night, as we dressed the adze cut across his knuckles and listened to him explain how beautiful the new craft was growing under his hands and that of the sailmaster. He had curls of sweet-smelling wood in his curly hair.

'They'll bring the mast down from the mountain tomorrow,' he said. 'Barren, Princess? What did you expect me to say? That you are half a woman and we should cast you off? I've sown little Eumides all over the Aegean, Cassandra, from Phrygia to Epirus. Any common woman can bear me a child if I need one. But you are unique, healer, daughter of Priam, sweet princess, only priestess of my heart.'

And I lay with both of them that night, sweet sailor and grave Asclepid, still loved and valued, with my most shameful secret revealed and shared.

The summer was waning when we heard a voice raised on the other side of the market, and a lyre keeping time to one of Arion's most scandalous lyrics.

We ran out and saw Menon sitting on the sea-wall with a ring of delighted citizens around him.

'Cassandra!' he called. 'Arion Dolphin-Rider sent me, famed bard of the Argives.'

'Is he well?'

'Spends his time drinking wine in the shade of the vines. He has sent me away.' Menon's face crumpled for a moment, then resumed its performer's smile. 'We made my lyre and he told me to go forth and become a famous bard. "I've given you my songs," he told me. "Now make better ones of your own." I don't know if I'll ever be able to do that. But this is his last song, Princess. He sent me to sing it to you and the sailor and the Asclepid.' He tightened a peg, twanged a string, and began to sing. His voice was a tenor, clear and tuneful, but in it I could hear an echo of that honey-voiced old man, and see the glint in his bright dark eyes.

A thrice-woven cloth is warmest.
A thrice twisted thread is strongest.
Three, three, three is their charm.

The third day is fortunate
The third child is beautiful
Three, three, three is their spell.

The third wave is highest
The third horse is strongest
Three, three, three is their charm.

Two combined in man and maid;
Three combined the Gods ordained.
Three, three, three is their charm.

Two combined is husband and bride.
Three combined is unbroken joy.
Three, three, three is their charm.

Dionysos loves those three,
Three who lie together in love,
Courage and beauty shall they know.
Never to part; three is their charm.

When Thanatos come to take one,
The others will deny him,
Until the feathered Angel carries three.
Three, three, three is their spell.

Three, three, three is the charm,
Arion's blessings to the three,
Trios, God-protected, God-ordained.
Three, three, three is their spell.

We gave him a handful of trading gold and set sail for Troas
the next week.

Chapter Twelve

Odysseus

I spoke to a white bird, that which the sailors call the footless one, and it replied.

'Beware the siren voices,' said the lone flier. 'Bones strew their shore, bones of seamen who have listened and wrecked. Under their sweet seeming are the hearts of sharks. White teeth line their mouths and they savage as they kiss. Block your ears, Odysseus, Prince of Ithaca. The wind is carrying you to them.'

I rewarded him with a fish and began melting beeswax. If the Gods were sending me into every peril in the world, I would endure. And I could not pass the siren's isle without hearing their song.

But I was resolved not to die doing so.

Electra

The harvest was good. As the year grew warmer and drier, we threshed and winnowed, piling golden grain into sacks sewn shut to be stored. The grapes grew heavy on the vines and the olives plumped. I grew fatter and Orestes grew taller, until Pylades our cousin said one day, looking at us as we sat at supper over a laden table, 'Ah, you are the most beautiful of all your unhappy house.'

'The thistle is blooming,' the old man, Clonius, said, loosening his belt and leaning back against Aulos' shoulder. 'The cicada calls, the goats are fat, and women are full of lust.' He grinned at Lysane, who scowled at him. 'High summer, and nought to be done but sleep in the shade, boy—that's the time for a farmer. The hay's bleaching in the meadow, the wine's growing on the vine, and you can smell the sea. Gods help all poor mariners, who earn their living on the unchancy waves. Land's best,' said the old man, and staggered out into the men's quarters to lie down and sleep the heat away.

We women mounted our stairs and lay down on cool, well-woven linen—a gift from our master, Pylades—shaded our windows and sprinkled our naked bodies with well-water scented with roses. Lysane slept soon, and snored, keeping me awake.

'Is it true?' I asked a drowsy Alceste, who lay nearest me.

'Lady?'

'Is it true that in high summer women are filled with lust?'

In answer, she rolled over to me and kissed me on the mouth. It was a pleasant kiss, extended for a long time. I heard her catch her breath, but her lips left mine just as she found them.

'No, Lady,' she said, resuming her place and closing her eyes. 'It is not true.'

Yet when I came close to my own Lord, Pylades my cousin, there was something stirring in me, feeble and not often renewed, like a somnolent creature stirring in its sleep.

When the height of the heat had passed and Orion and the dog star Sirius were both in the sky, we cut our grapes, laying them on cloths for ten days in the sun and then five days in shade. Autumn was coming and beyond that, winter, when Boreas rules. But we were well stored. The crushed grapes yielded fine wine, our beehives gave us honey. The attic was stacked with sacks of grain, pickling olives, and tanned skins from the autumn slaughter. We could winter perhaps two-thirds of the flock. The rest must be sold or killed.

I did not go with Pylades and Orestes into the fair in Delphi. I had got out of the habit of wearing a veil around the house, and found it heavy. And there were tasks for me. Lysane, Alceste, and I were making cloaks and boots for the coming cold. Cutting and sewing hides is not as pleasant as weaving, and it is very hard on the hands. I was sucking at a punctured finger when a visitor was announced. I found a veil and flung it over my head and went down to the ground floor.

A welcome visitor indeed. It was Menon, apprentice of the famed bard Arion Dolphin-Rider. He was dusty, hungry, and tired, but we had food and wine in plenty.

Every evening, Lysane, Alceste, and I came down the stairs with our work and sat by the fire. Pylades would take off his boots and put his feet on the hearth and tell stories as we sewed. We would talk about the work of the farm, just us, for the slaves retired early to their own quarters, and Clonius and his son went home to their own house in the lower field. Sometimes we mentioned people we had known back in the city of Mycenae, which now seemed so far away. But we never talked of my mother or father. Pylades remembered things which I had forgotten; a stone-throwing game which the children had played on the pavement outside the temple of Apollo, for instance. One cast up pebbles and tried to catch them on the back of one's hand. I had forgotten it; but with Lysane and Alceste I recaptured my skill. He remembered Neptha, my nurse, too. I still missed Neptha. I hoped that she would approve of the conduct of my household. It was slow and comfortable speech. No one was in a hurry, and there were no surprises. I no longer started at sudden noises.

Now we had someone who would greatly enliven the evening. We were all tired with the length and the heat of the summer. And bards always had news. As it was a special occasion, the slaves stayed, sitting on their usual benches. Abantos brewed his spiced wine, which he alone knew how to compound. We waited while the bard removed his boots and Alceste washed his feet, gave him a clean tunic and fed him autumn honey and new bread. Menon was a tall young man, pinched with cold and hollow-cheeked. Tauros had bitten him on the ankle when he came in, unannounced, but the teeth had not broken the skin.

'I lost my way to Delphi,' he explained. 'I was astray in the dark until I saw your light. Praise be to all the gods for this food and wine!'

'When you are rested,' said Pylades, 'we would gladly know how your master Arion fares. He gave me a great gift once.' Pylades smiled at me and drew Orestes close. The boy snuggled into his arms like a puppy.

'He fares well, fat and sleepy,' said Menon. 'He lives on a small farm near to the temple of Epidavros, where he has friends. Diomenes called Chryse left there recently, with the female healer and his friend the Trojan sailor.'

'Where were they going?' I asked, remembering Cassandra. She had been kind to me when I was distracted and mannerless, and I hoped that she did not detest my name and memory. I recalled the smile of the Asclepid, too, and was even prepared to forgive his dark scoundrel of a friend.

'They were well and happy together. They were going to Kenchraie to build a ship. Odysseus is still missing. They sighted his vessel from afar, driven before great winds, in the height of the summer; but no word of him has come to Ithaca, where Penelope, his wife, walks a delicate line between suitors and civil war. The drought has been bad there, and most of the barley crop in the Peloponnese has failed. It will be a hard winter in the Argolid.'

He plucked at the lyre, flexing his fingers, and played a tinkling tune.

Joy comes rarely, flighty maiden,
Dances in on butterfly wings,
Can't rest for a moment and flies away.
But her sister, Woe, is a devoted damsel,
She comes to stay, and brings her spindle.

He added, 'And a whole bale of wool!' with such a doleful face that we all laughed. 'What shall I play, Lord?' he asked Pylades. 'Shall I sing of Troy and heroes for my most generous host?'

'No,' said Pylades instantly. 'Not wars and battles. Sing us a love song. If you please.'

Menon strummed for a while, adjusting a tuning peg, and sang of the maiden Psyche, beloved of the God Eros, son of Aphrodite. The god takes her to his beautiful palace, and only one promise is asked of her; not to hope to see him. Invisible hands caress her, an invisible mouth touches hers. She is altogether in love with him.

Warm in the darkness, flanks are aligned,
Warm in the darkness, mouth kisses mouth,
Sweet is the darkness to Psyche the nymph,
Weary the long day, waiting for night.

Then her jealous sisters nagged at the poor girl for not knowing what her husband looked like. Finally, greatly daring, she lit an oil lamp and looked at the man who shared her bed. He was as beautiful as a god should be; she fell in love him all over again as soon as she saw the long black, smooth thighs, the clever hands which caressed her, the smooth chin and soft mouth and curly hair.

But she spilt hot oil on him and he did not even wake as he vanished. She had broken her promise, and she was gone.

Then we followed Psyche on her long, long travail, trying to find Eros her husband, with his raging mother blocking every path, teasing and tormenting her.

Demeter, Mother of all, revenge me.
My son has taken a mortal to wife,
A country girl, impudent and frail.
Revenge my son's wrongs and my own!

But the other Goddesses would not help Aphrodite hurt Psyche. The young woman, far gone in pregnancy, cried on the Great Mother, but Demeter dismissed her prayer. She prayed to Hera, wife of Zeus the Father, and she also rejected her. But her wanderings had brought Psyche near the abode of Aphrodite, and the vengeful Stranger let her in, determined to kill her, and the unborn grandchild that she carried. She poured a pile of what onto the floor, beans and vetch and spelt and millet and poppy-seeds, and required Psyche to sort them into separate heaps by nightfall.

The ants came to Psyche in her despair, and for pity completed her task. But that was not enough for Aphrodite. She dragged the girl to the window and said, 'There are man-eating sheep with golden fleece in that meadow. Bring me a skein of golden wool, and you may live to bear your child.'

Father Pan's reed whispered to despondent Psyche as she walked, weeping, through the meadow. 'They are fierce in the sun, but they sleep in the evening. Go down then, maiden, and gather their wool off the briars.'

But the golden skein did not assuage a goddess' wrath.

Look to the height, maiden,
That is Aroanius, whence springs Styx.
If you climb to the summit and bring to me
In a crystal dish the ice-cold waters,
The heart of Hades river; I may let you live.

It was an impossible task. She plodded, great with child, toward the lower slopes, hoping to die quickly by falling. But an eagle snatched the dish from her hands and returned with it, and she brought the icy waters of death's river to Aphrodite. Eros, meanwhile, had fallen at Zeus' feet, begging for his beautiful wife and his unborn child. Zeus could deny Eros nothing, so called Hermes to catch up the maiden and bring her to Parnassus. There he gave her a cup of nectar, making her immortal.

She drank the honeyed wine.
Still wet on her lips, she was gathered
Into the visible embrace, the familiar arms
And Eros kissed nectar from the mouth of Psyche,
Who had dared great dangers for his love.

The song finished and the bard stretched and yawned. Pylades led him to a bath and a much-deserved rest. I wondered what it would be like to love someone enough to scale a mountain for them, and what it would be like to cherish caresses in the darkness.

◇◇◇

Winter came. We had ploughed the fields in late autumn, when the Pleiades and Hyades had followed Orion below the horizon. The beasts were stalled, the harvest done, the seed grain selected, dried, and stored in pithoi sunk in the farmhouse floor. I looked out of the shutters on a day of sleety winds and a sky presaging snow, and saw Pylades and Orestes trudging out to tend the beasts.

They were warm in my weaving—in my triple woven tunics and leggings, in my well-sewn, pieced skin cloaks, and heavy ox hide boots. I felt proud.

Cassandra

The journey to Troas was much faster than I had imagined. The boat, called *Waverider* by our sailor, wallowed a little and depended much more on sails than on oars, though she could be rowed, and was, by a well-paid crew of sweating oarsmen.

We skipped along from Skiathos to Skiros, then dived across the Aegean in two days, striking Lemnos and catching the rare, beneficent wind that held back the spilling Hellespont and propelled us into the Bay of Troy.

We saw it from the sea and wailed for grief. I had not seen the final ruin of the city, nor had my companions. Troy was gone. Where the solid wall rose from the sea to the Scaean Gate, there was nothing but tumbled stones. Where the Dardanian Gate had looked into the marshes, all was broken, and the swamp had moved to slime the remaining paving. Where the place of Stranger's Gods had been, sanded and swept clean before the Scamander Gate, the river had sprawled, silting and meandering.

Troy was gone.

Chryse, embracing us, asked, 'Do you want to land?'

'No,' I said. I had kept Troy in my mind, the tall towers and the strong gates. Now it only existed in my mind. This ruin had nothing of my city about it.

'On those beaches,' said Chryse, very quietly, 'I watched most of the Argive army die in agony, struck with plagues. I, also, would not be reminded. Come, give your orders, shipmaster. Let us leave this haunted place.'

The kindly wind swept us into the Hellespont, and we lay that night in the last cove before the new city.

We all dreamed the one dream: screaming women, falling gates, the bronze horse forged as an offering to cruel Sun-Bright Apollo to fool the city into thinking the Achaeans had gone. The watch had slept and the gates had opened. All dead: Polyxena, my sister, sacrificed to the shade of Achilles; Hector, my most beloved brother, dead, though I was pleased that he had not seen the city fall; Priam, my father, his white beard wet with red wine and blood, murdered on the floor of his own audience chamber; Pariki, my city-destroying brother, stabbed by a soldier on the beach; Eleni captured; Andromache, Hector's wife, enslaved by the same boy, Neoptelemus, son of Achilles, after he had thrown Andromache's baby, Astyanax, from the headland into the sea. The maidens of the house of maidens, scattered or as dead as Cycne, the Achaean, who would not be a slave again, a suicide in the gutter with her knife in her breast. All that was Troy, its learning and beauty and language and its people, lost in the acrid smoke of burning wood.

I shrieked myself awake and we lay clinging together on the deck. Chryse's dreams were of dying men in filthy sand in the stench of corpses. Eumides dreaming of burning, falling beams and screaming women. We drank wine and threw it up again and drank more and wept.

'We will never be healed,' I sobbed into Eumides' neck.

'Aie! Aie! Troy is lost, lost!' he wailed.

'We will never forget,' said Chryse sadly. 'But we will be healed.'

Waverider turned the corner of the headland and we were flung into the Bay of Troas with enough force to knock us off our feet. When we had picked ourselves up and untangled our limbs, we were rowing into a quiet harbor, perhaps half the size of the Bay of Troy, a little bit taken out of the Hellespont's sheer sides.

'It's small,' commented Eumides, disappointed.

'It will thus not attract envy,' I returned. 'Listen, sailor!'

I could hear children playing, singing in high, innocent voices as they danced down the quay in a long line. One very proud small boy was leading, bearing a bunch of cock's feathers in his golden hair. He carried a kitten on his shoulder. It was evidently scratching him.

> Hector, Lord of Troy,
> Valiant and wise,
> Hector, Golden-haired,
> Protector of Troas,
> Lord of the City,
> Cuirass of Troy,
> Hector sent us here,
> Saying 'Be saved,
> Children of Priam.
> Share not the wreck,
> Share not my death.'
> Hector's pilgrims,
> We came to Troas.
> Built our stone houses.
> Brought with us Pallathi,
> Daughter of Gaia.
> We sleep in peace,
> In Troas our city,
> Children of the Dancer,
> Hector's children.

A bunch of blue-black feathers had always adorned Hector's helmet, soft and shining, with no crest to catch a spear-point. For a moment I saw him again. Hector, my dearest brother, sitting on a bench under a new vine, the cat Stathi on his shoulder, tasting the dark honeyed wine which came from Kriti. Then I blinked, and he was gone.

We came ashore and the rowers leapt onto the pebbles, dragging *Waverider* out of the surf. The dancing children abandoned their song and ran laughing to meet us.

'Welcome!' they cried in my own cradle-tongue. 'Welcome, strangers from afar! What news of the shoreless sea?'

'No news, we come from Corinth,' I said in the same speech, and the boy with the feathers stared.

'Are you of our kind, Lady, sharer of our tongue?' he asked.

'I am,' I said. 'Who rules here?'

'Scamandros and his queen, Peirithe of Phrygia,' said the child formally. 'I am Ormene, son of the palace. I will take you to them, Lady. How shall I call you?'

'They call me Cassandra,' I said. 'Here are Eumides and Diomenes called Chryse, my companions.'

The boy bowed, wincing as the kitten hung on with taloned paws. I wondered whence had come the sacred beast. From Egypt? If they had taken to selling cats, then I would be very surprised. 'If you will follow me,' Ormene said, and we walked up the steep breach and into a small town.

Those of the Troad had wrought well in so short a time. There were fine stone houses and many made of driftwood and mud-brick. Everyone was working. We passed donkeys carrying sand for cement and mud for bricks. We heard the hammering and songs of men perched on the roofs, plastering them for the coming summer to dry and harden. Eumides ducked out of the way of a girl carrying a white-wash bucket and said, 'Do we know this Scamandros, Lady?'

'I can't recall the name—wait. Do you remember, Eumides, in the last days, when the Achaeans had gone on some errand, and the people flooded out of the city?'

'I remember,' he said soberly.

'So do I,' said Chryse, ducking under a hanging net. 'I moved the soldiers off those beaches and inland. We saw them walking across the plain, and were too sick to interfere. Fortunately,' he added.

'Scamandros, the stone-mason, is the son of my brother Cerasimos' wife, Nelea. But I don't know his queen. He led the group which brought the image of the Pallathi out of Troy. Almost the last people to get away before the city fell.'

'The Phrygian marriage was wise,' commented Eumides. 'That alliance should preserve Troas against ordinary depredation. But this child is too old to be a son of that family. He must be six or seven.'

'I am seven years old,' said the boy proudly. 'And apart from the child, who is still with her nurse, I am the last of Priam's sons. The Lord Scamandros has appointed me his heir, above any children he may have with his queen. I don't remember much about it, just the fear as we ran across the plain, the darkness, and then we heard the screams and saw smoke rising. We do not forget the city, Lady Cassandra, or the valour of Hector of the Glittering Helmet.'

'Is that child still here?' I asked quickly.

'Indeed, Lady, and her nurse.' The child stopped abruptly, struck his forehead with the heel of his hand—a gesture so reminiscent of Hector that I caught my breath—fell to his knees and took my hand. 'Forgive me,' he pleaded.

'What transgression have you committed, son of Priam?' I asked formally.

'I did not realize, Princess. You are the fated Cassandra, cursed by the God whom we do not name, daughter of Priam, returned beyond all hope to the city of Troas, daughter of Troy. I did not recognize you, Lady.' The boy bent his head. I laid a hand on his golden curls.

'Rise, Ormene, you are forgiven,' I said ritually. 'I am no princess now, nor do I see lordship in this new, clean place. Take me to the Lord and Lady, and be blessed forever, such blessing as Cassandra has to give.'

He got easily to his feet and led us up a winding street to a stone palace, built into the mountain. It was perhaps an eighth of the size of Priam's palace, but the ground plan was the same.

There were guards at the door, two tall men in Trojan tunics and leather harness. They crossed spears as we approached.

'It's all right,' Ormene assured them. 'This is the Princess Cassandra returned.'

'Lady?' puzzled one of the guards. 'Don't you know me?' he pleaded. I did not until he tore off his helmet and I saw the face of my favorite bronze-smith's husband and dredged my memory for his name.

'I am Polithi,' he rescued me. 'Lady, it is indeed you! We thought you dead—the bards are singing you dead with the Achaean tyrant Agamemnon. I rejoice that it is not so!'

'Agamemnon is dead, miserably and messily, but I was not included in the sacrifice,' I replied.

He grinned all over his broad honest face. 'What do you here, Lady?'

'I came to find a place to dwell,' I said. 'Let me in to the lord and lady, Polithi. Is your wife well?'

'Strong as a giant and pounding the anvil as always,' he replied. 'Let them pass,' he said to his fellow-guard.

We came into a common hall and found the lord and lady of Troas together in front of a charcoal brazier. He was spinning and she was winding the wool onto a shuttle. They were young, well dressed, evidently used to working together, and I liked them immediately.

'Princess!' Scamandros exclaimed, dropping his spindle. 'Lady, this is the Princess Cassandra, strangely returned!'

The Phrygian woman rose and made a profound bow. I saw uncertainty on her face and hastened to dispel it.

'Lady, we seek no rule or lordship here,' I said rapidly. 'I am no princess now, but Cassandra the Trojan healer, and my companions are Eumides, the sailor, and Chryse Diomenes, the Asclepid.'

'You and your guests are welcome to all that is ours,' she said, and a little girl came forward at her signal carrying a platter on which was heaped bread and salt, the hospitality gift of a Trojan household.

We sat down to a feast in the palace that night. Word had spread that Cassandra had returned, and such as loved me had come to find me. Nyssa, my own nurse, leading a three-year-old toddler, clucked when she saw the lines on my face and the wind-burned darkness of my white skin, then dissolved into tears as she embraced me.

'Oh, my nurseling, my own darling. I mourned you as lost!' she sobbed. I held her close. She was old, I realized. Her hair was quite white, but her soft body cushioned me as it had so often in the past. 'Oh, my dearest daughter,' she mourned over my bent head, stroking my hair. 'I had thought that you were both gone, the golden twins, gone with your brothers to the fields of heaven. Now I find you alive, and well, and strong, and beautiful! What of Eleni?'

'I have lost him, Nyssa,' I whispered. 'I've lost him. The thread broke when Apollo released me. I don't even know if he's alive.'

'Now, now, my darling, don't despair,' she chided, as though I were five years old. 'Eleni was the favored one, the God's fortunate child. He'll be alive somewhere, I fancy. Now sit up and drink some wine with me, Cassandra—I am quite faint with joy—and introduce me to your companions. Noble folk, I am sure.'

Nyssa recognized Eumides as soon as she saw him, and pinched his unshaven cheek. 'Ah, I remember you, my sailor,' she chuckled. 'A great provider of sacrifice babies, you were. Many a maiden remembers her homage to the Mother fondly because of you, Eumides.'

But she was stiff with Chryse, though he smiled his rare and beautiful smile and held her hand. 'An Achaean, and one who was at the sack?' she said uneasily. 'Well, you know your own mind, Cassandra. You always have. Greetings, Lord,' she said, and Chryse's smile wavered.

'They say she is returned,' snapped a voice at the gate. 'Let me in, simpletons. It is undoubtedly some imposter, some yellow-headed Carian, and you too foolish to know the difference.'

I sat up with a laugh rising in my throat. I knew that voice. And she was going to get such a surprise when she saw me.

Tithone, my teacher, preeminent healer of Troy, Atropiad, wise woman, stalked into the audience chamber, saw me, and stood stock still.

She was older. Her body had always been spare, and now it was thin as a rod. Her hair, as always, was dragged back under a closely pinned cloth. She had come straight from her workshop. She was still wearing her healer's tunic of sooty grey and an apron of coarse cloth, down the front of which some dark liquid had spilled. The scent of herbs preceded her as she walked toward the high table like a woman in a trance.

I rose and came to her. When I was only an arm's length away, she caught up my hand and turned it over, looking at my wrist. I had been clumsy with a pruning hook when I had been ten, and the scar was still there, barely visible now. Oddly enough Eleni, my twin, had fallen off a wall onto a ploughshare a week later, and given himself an identical wound.

'Oh, my dear acolyte,' she said, slowly, as if the words were forced from her. 'Cassandra, my healer, princess, and priestess, so they lied. I should have known not to trust the word of an Achaean bard, however silver his tongue. How have you survived?'

'I had help,' I said, leading her to the high table and introducing my companions. She knew Eumides—everyone in Troy knew Eumides—and she gave Chryse her hand and a long, considering look.

'Healer, eh?' she asked. 'Well, in a barbarous place like Achaea perhaps even men can be healers. Come and see me tomorrow, healers, sailor. Now I must return. I left my burn ointment on the brazier and…'

I completed the sentence. 'And it must not boil.'

We ate roasted kid that night, and bread made in the Trojan manner, drank wine of Kriti sealed with the goddess' seal and smelled the perfumes of Troy. The five essences—I had distilled them once—myrrh, pine, jasmine, hyacinth, and hawthorn. They hung in the air as the lord and lady of Troas did us honor and the young men sang of the sea and trading to be done north of the Hellespont, in Colchis where all fleeces are golden.

I slept surrounded by my own language, alone with Chryse. Eumides was renewing old friendships along the docks, doubtless sowing more namesakes amongst the waterfront women who remembered him kindly. Trojan women require skill in their lovers, and their services are not for sale.

'It's no good,' said Chryse as we lay down in a Trojan bed together. Our beds are higher than the Argive fashion, and strung with a net to support the mattress. They are very soft, but Chryse was restless.

'What isn't?' I asked, knowing what he was going to say.

'I can't stay here. I am an Achaean and an enemy.'

'Chryse, no, you are a healer, not a soldier.' I protested.

'That will make no difference. You saw how your nurse received me. She is a kind woman, but she flinched at the mention of the name of Argive. Troas might have accepted a male healer—once I had proved myself competent to that alarming old woman—but not an Achaean.'

He was right, but I would not give up yet.

'We will see what Tithone has to say.' I embraced him, and we slept, hair mingled, on the same pillow, as Eleni and I had done so long ago.

Tithone looked up from compounding a cough medicine and offered the spoon to me. I tasted. She then gave it to Chryse and he sipped.

'More colt's hoof,' I said.

'More foal's foot,' he agreed.

'So, you are a healer,' said Tithone tartly, adding a handful of leaves to the mixture. 'I have a word for you, daughter. A bitter word.'

'I know.' I sat down next to a bale of yellow flowers. I have never liked the scent of those yellow daisies and they sickened me.

'You cannot stay,' she said.

'Because Chryse is an Achaean?'

'Partly. If he is a learned and serviceable man—and he seems to be—that might be overcome. But he is an Asclepid, is that not so?'

Chryse nodded.

'Then he is in the service of the God whom we do not name—he who cursed you, my Cassandra, and who destroyed the city. We did not bring him to Troas from the fall of Troy. We carried the Pallathi of the Mother and the cine-staff of Dionysos the Dancer, but we will not have the Sun-Bright in Troas. A cruel God, vengeful and false. Is that not so?'

'It is,' I agreed. Eumides, sipping at the hangover cure which Tithone had thrust into his hand when he arrived, commented, 'But he does not believe in the Gods.'

'The more fool he, then, to serve a non-existent deity who is so cruel to his adherents. It will not matter to the Nameless Once, my son, or to the city, what you believe or do not believe. But it is not just you, Asclepid. It is Cassandra.'

'Me?' I was disconcerted. 'Why? Is this not my home?'

'No,' said Tithone sadly. 'Not any more, daughter of Priam. There is a new ruling house, a new dynasty. You will be a focus for discontent however quietly you live. They are always murmurings in any city. When the fish are scarce, the shorefolk will say, "It was better while we lived in Troy under the sons of Priam." When a house falls or there is an accident in the mines, they will say, "Such things did not happen under the rule of Priam's children." And from there to "There is a daughter of that house living in the city, let us rise up and place her on the throne," is a very short step and one which must not be risked. Do you see what I mean, healer?'

'Yes,' I did see. To Troas, I was still and always would be the Lady the Princess Cassandra, daughter of Priam.

'And also, Cassandra, my dearest, you are cursed of that same nameless God and the city might feel that you are attracting his unwanted attention. He has shown no sign of noticing that Troas exists. Not only might you be a reason for civil war, they may blame any mischance on your presence, as one who had brought the Unnamed's wrath with her. I will not see you stoned from Troas, daughter. You must leave.'

'Now?' I asked desolately, and she smiled and embraced me.

'In time,' she said. 'We have much to speak of, healers together; we may learn much from the combination of Argive and Trojan practice. And I am sure that there are some women in the city that Eumides has not yet met. Stay until next sailing season, daughter. There will be no trouble in Troas if they know that you are not settling here.'

We relieved the mind of the city, announcing that we would leave in the next year. I asked about the kitten. It appeared that an anonymous priest of Bashtet, the Cat-Goddess, had sent three beasts to Troas as a present. I wondered if it had been Dion of the kelp-brown hair. The cats were sandy, barred with black, not ash-colored like Hector's Stathi. They were certainly more equable of temperament, which was perhaps fortunate. They matched Troas. It was also a modest and moderate city.

We settled down to winter in Troas, daughter of Troy, to drink wine, go fishing, keep warm, and talk herbs and treatments with Tithone.

She agreed with me that stonecrop should not be used on broken skin.

Chapter Thirteen

'*It seems that your poor little puppets are without refuge,*' *said Demeter pityingly, looking down into the Pool of Mortal Lives.* '*Where did you purpose they should go, Apollo?*'

'*I have no purpose for them,*' *replied the Sun-Bright.* '*They may go where they wish.*'

'*But they can have no home, a cursed priestess and a stray Asclepid, one of your worship, I might point out,*' *she replied.*

'*My neglect is their blessing,*' *he said, testing the string of a bow.* '*But, yes, there is one small thing. I will break the block,*' *he said, and snapped his fingers.*

Electra

My mother was a wicked woman and I was going to kill her, but she knew how to conduct the business of a palace and she had taught me well. When I swapped my recipe for pomegranate jelly with Abantos for his lentil soup—he added vinegar to it, and oil, and it tasted like nectar—I remembered my mother instructing the cooks in the Mycenean kitchens on the making of the pale pink confection. When I settled quarrels between the slaves or mediated with Pylades on behalf of his workers, I used my mother's example and brought peace to my productive household. I interceded successfully with Pylades when Tauros took a piece out of our neighbor, Stenor, and tried not to laugh when Aulos declared that the poor beast would be poisoned with such unwholesome food. My small establishment needed to be cared for. I ordered honey and wine from the traders, finding a market for my fine-spun wool and my well-made cloth. I folded my fine weaving into the same chest where my doll Pallas lay, my only remembrance of Mycenae. We grew our own grain and ground our own flour to make our bread. Every year the olives were harvested and pressed and the oil stored for the winter. Every year Pylades' flock increased, goats and sheep. We prospered, and Orestes grew in size and in martial skill. The pain settled down into a permanent ache, so that I almost got used to it, and the nightmares faded. Pylades was courteous and never gave me cause to fear him.

Only once had I heard a sound in the night and come down to find out if the house-slaves had left a shutter unsecured. There I found Pylades and my woman, the slave Alceste, lying coupled in front of the fire. He was entirely naked, stocky and tanned from working in the fields. I watched as he kissed down from her mouth to her breast and heard her gasp, saw her body yearn toward his. His hands smoothed her waist and buttocks, her legs wrapped around him. I saw his eyes glow, heard his voice deepen, the contours of his face change from familiar to unfamiliar, blooming with blood. I must have moved, for they stopped and turned. They saw me. Pylades put the woman aside, very gently, and said to me, 'Lady, I am only a man.' I nodded and crept upstairs again.

The next morning, Alceste having been absent all night, I asked, 'Did he hurt you?'

She smiled at me, pulling her tunic up over her soft shoulder, and said, 'No, Lady. He is gentle and kind.'

'He did not force you?'

'No, Mistress, I was willing. He was skilled and loving. He has been a long time alone. Lady, are you angry? He said—my Lord said—that you would not marry him. I would not displease you, Mistress. If you say so, I will not go to him again.'

She knelt at my feet, bending her tumbled head. I could smell the scent of the flesh on her. I put her away from me, trying not to be rough, and replied, 'You shall lie with him as he pleases. It is nothing to me.'

And it was nothing. Slaves have no virtue to lose, and she pleased him. Men have desires and will fulfill them. It was nothing to me. Alceste told Lysane that he was a good lover, passionate and strong, but I was not interested in the love of men, skilled or unskilled.

I enjoyed the evenings. I walked down the stairs, attended by Alceste and Lysane, who carried my basket, my distaff and my spindle. Then we sat down in the main room of the house, near the fire as always, and talked with Pylades and Orestes. My Lord Cousin had been to many places and seen strange things. He talked well and quickly. His face was mobile, reflecting the changing circumstances of the story, and his deft hands moved as he talked, sketching mountains and sails, explaining marvels and monsters, threading the labyrinth below the city of Minos. We listened to him for hours at a time as the fire burned low, and laughed or cried as the story required. Sometimes he spoke of heroes, of Jason and Theseus. But he told no tales of the war against Troy, and I wondered why.

Orestes was well. The God Apollo, he said, spoke to him occasionally, reminding him of his duty of revenge, but the God seemed content to let him grow until he was strong enough. I asked him if there was anything he lacked, and he told me that he had left one person he loved in Mycenae. Her name was Hermione, daughter of Menelaus, fostered with us because she was to marry Orestes when he was old enough. I remembered her. A small, confident child with hair like ebony and very alert black eyes. She was often to be seen speeding down the steps and across the courtyard, playing some intricate game with my brother, her betrothed. One of them had involved setting up a whole house and kitchen in the corner of the gateway. The guards were so amused by her chattering, that they had let her stay there. I had laughed at the sight of full-armed soldiers, helmets and breastplates gleaming, accepting imaginary honeycakes from her leaf-plates and thanking her gravely.

Usually Orestes was with her, giving her orders to mix his wine and bake his bread, which she carried out obediently unless he became too tyrannical, whereupon she would scold him like a fishwife, using words which she must have learned in her burrowings through the market. Her nurse was always issuing forth in a flurry of veils to fetch her from some trader's booth, where she would be found sitting on a table being fed delicacies and talking all the time in her high, clear voice to a fascinated audience.

Ten-year-old Hermione, a pretty child. I had envied her immense confidence. Everyone loved her, no one had betrayed her, and she fitted into her world as though it had been woven especially for her. I wondered if she would miss Orestes, and what had happened to her in mother's city.

Orestes did not speak of her again, but he found no women in Delphi who attracted him. On his weekly visits to the market, Pylades looked for pretty ones to point out to my brother, but he did not even glance at them. Hermione, perhaps, had his heart; or maybe it was revenge. Or maybe it was Pylades. Orestes clung to our cousin, living close to him. When they had been hunting they sometimes slept in the same bed, wet and exhausted. They ate together and rode together and grew in close affection, so that I sometimes wondered. But Pylades had Alceste.

Sometimes there was music, when a wandering singer asked for lodging. One told us that Chrysothemis, my only remaining sister, had been married to a prince of the Paeans and had been sent weeping to her husband, ten weeks' journey away.

Once we had dancers, who had been benighted in a storm on the Delphi road.

I lodged twelve people in that little house, with bedding for all made by my own household, and fed them in the morning. To thank my Lord Pylades for his care, they had danced for us before the fire, young men and maidens, stepping in a circle which grew faster and faster, until veils flew and tunics slipped and their dark hair, bright eyes and white teeth gleamed and blurred in the red light.

Bards came with tales, too. Once Tydeus of the Lyre, a famous Orphean, came and performed the *Fall of the House of Atreus* for us. I saw my brother, now as tall as Pylades, lean forward, listening intently.

> Where is the revenger,
> Orestes the child,
> Far wandering and hidden?
> Let him know this:
> The wicked Queen rules in Mycenae,
> Glorying in murder.

We had lived in peace for four years. The coming of Tydeus of the Lyre was the end of it. There had been so many endings.

'I am going to Mycenae,' said Orestes in the stableyard as we set out for our morning ride.

'No,' I said instantly.

'Sister, I am strong now.' He was, too. He was tall and slim, but now his wrists were corded, his eye steady. Eumides' ring fitted snugly on his finger. I had seen him sword-fighting with Pylades every day, and from being too little to hold up the foil for more than ten minutes, he could now fence with a heavy blade for hours, so that Pylades panted and begged for mercy. His eyes, however, were still the eyes of my little Orestes, who had lain in my arms when he was small and wept for my pain.

'The deed is mine,' I said coldly. He shook his head.

'It is as I said once, long ago, sister Electra. I cannot care for you if you take this dreadful sin upon you. You suffer still, Lady. You still send Lysane to Delphi to the healer for lethos and valerian. But you can care for me, you and my Lord Pylades. And she must die. My mother and Aegisthus must die. For what they did to our father—and to you and me.'

'Wait until we come to the mountain,' I said. 'We must talk.'

We rode up the slope and stopped on the ridge. There was nothing between us and the Gulf of Corinth and the air tasted of salt and last night's rain. I spoke because I had to take the burden on myself. Otherwise no torture would have dragged the tale from my lips—not burning irons, not flogging.

'He came for me when I was eleven,' I said. I could not look at Orestes or Pylades. 'He wept and said that he loved me. He hurt me, though he said he would not. When my mother reproved him and insulted him, he came for me.'

'He came to me also, when I was ten,' Orestes said.

Pylades came forward and helped me down from *Banthos*, for I was faint.

'You also, little brother?' I gasped.

'I, also.'

'Why didn't you tell me?' I cried. His handsome face was as white as linen and his hands were shaking.

'What could you have done, Electra? I knew what he was doing to you. I saw the way you trembled, heard you cry for mercy in your dreams. If you could not prevent him, Sister, how could I?'

'Aie! Aie!' I wailed to the cold wind and the seagulls. 'Ah, my grief! Oh, my Orestes, oh, my son, my son!'

They carried me into the house and tucked me into the chimney corner, wrapped in woollen blankets. They gave me wine and mistletoe. When I had drunk, Orestes sat down on the floor and took my frozen feet in his warm hands.

'Tell me, Electra,' he urged. 'We cannot leave this unsaid.'

'He came when our father Agamemnon was away raiding the coasts of Phrygia at the beginning of the war. Father came home every now and again, when the weather prevented sailing. But the moment he left she let him into her bed. Aegisthus, the destroyer, revenge-child, bred for the destruction of Atreus' House. I saw him come into the city. If I had only snatched a spear from the guard and impaled him, I would have earned immortality.'

Orestes and Pylades were watching me, one horrified, one pale with memory.

'Yes, he came into the city and the Queen accepted him as her lover. What then?'

'She exhausted him with her lust and treated him like a slave. I was sorry for him, though I never said anything. He gave me presents, gifts suitable for a woman, not a girl. Chiton pins, milk-stones. Then one night I heard the latch click, and he was with me. I was eleven. I had never been so close to a man. He said he loved me, needed me, he wept on my breast. Then he hurt me, so there was blood. And he told me that no one would ever believe me if I complained. He said that the Queen would banish me, sell me to a farmer as a dishonored woman.

Then he came—not every night—but often. He wept still, dropping tears onto my face. I never grew used to him, as the slaves say they grow used to violation. My body clenched against him and it hurt—it always hurt. I never spoke. He said that this was how love between men and women was. Pain and compulsion.

Then I began to swell. Learned physicians spoke of dropsy and gave me strong potions, but Neptha knew what it was. I was pregnant and Aegisthus was the father. She gave me other medicines, metallic draughts that made me retch until I swooned, but they did not work.

The Queen came when I was six months in fruit and beat me cruelly, demanding the name of my lover. She flogged me with a vine until I thought I might die, so I told her. My shame could not now be hidden. I was dishonored, a whore, and she could cast me out of the city. She knew. She knew.

And as he had said, she did not believe me. She beat me more for lying. Then she said it was Lapharnes, the slave who sang me love songs, who looked at me from the city and, bleeding and desperate, I said yes.

They executed him that night. To cover my shame, my mother kept me imprisoned in complete seclusion for the rest of the time, giving out that she was herself pregnant. My father visited often enough so that this was credible. She told me that she would save my reputation, that many women took lovers, that I was like her! I bore you, my brother and son, with only Neptha and Clytemnestra to tend me, and I was in agony for almost a day and a night. But I did not care, for I hoped that I would die.'

Orestes bent until his forehead was on my bare feet. No tears fell from his eyes. He quivered with tension and pain, and I could not see his face.

'Then she stole you when you were born. She ordered me stripped, washed and put aside, then donned my bloody tunic and lay down in my bed, smearing her loins with birth blood, taking you in her arms, laying you to her dry breast. She summoned the maidens to attend her, to find a wet nurse for Agamemnon's son, though my breasts were bursting with milk which I could not give you. So short a time I had you, Orestes. Just long enough to hold you in my arms and watch your eyes open on the world.'

'But she cared for me,' he said. 'When I was ill, she was always there.'

'She stole you from me,' I said bitterly. 'She stole from me the nursing of you, Orestes, the care and the loving. I was allowed to play with you, call you brother, never could I call you son, never hear you say "Mother." She stole you. She has stolen everything from me, everything. I died when Aegisthus came into my bed. And she knew. I told her.'

'After I was born…he came again?' asked Orestes.

'Sometimes, when she had humiliated him before the court. But he was careful not to lie with me as man lies with woman, in case I should conceive. When…when did he…?'

'I was ten,' said Orestes. 'He told me the same things, Mother.'

He inhaled deeply and began to cry freely, like a child, and I wept with him. I had never cried openly over my wrongs before, never told a word of my pain, though I knew that the Trojan woman and the healer Diomenes had suspected some of it. Pylades did not speak, but left us in our embrace in the warm corner of his house, and considerately went away.

That night my son Orestes lay in my arms, his head on my shoulder, and we slept without dreams.

The next morning we set out for Mycenae.

◇◇◇

The journey we had made before was easier now. We knew the way and the countryside was at peace. Orestes rode his own favorite, *Hunter*. I rode *Banthos*, my old friend. We were well supplied, well mounted, and it was spring, the season for setting forth.

As we rode out onto the Delphi road, down from the Shining Cliffs toward the port of Kirrha, we saw a caravan climbing the hill and stopped to let it pass.

There were ten soldiers, in familiar battle-dress. They were escorting a curtained litter slung between two horses. In such confinement do Argive women of high station travel. I noticed that the curtains were of fine embroidered wool and the poles of silver. They were conducting a royal woman. Two slave women rode on either side. There were banners which flapped to reveal the ram's head, Perseus' seal. They were from Mycenae.

We stayed, but Pylades went forward in case my mother was escaping to the God. In that case we would have to try to kill her here, on this road, and we would die in the attempt.

'Hail, men of Mycenae,' he said easily, removing his hood so that they could see his face. 'Pylades of Phocis greets you, long away from the Golden Walls. Where are you going, and with whom?'

'Greetings, Lord Pylades,' said the captain, raising one hand to his shoulder in salute. 'We are taking Hermione, daughter of Menelaus, to her wedding with Neoptelemus, son of Achilles.'

The curtains were pulled back and a veiled head was thrust out.

'Where are we?' asked a voice, clear and humorous.

Orestes jumped down and ran in amongst the slaves, calling 'Hermione!'

'By all the Gods!' she swore, and took his hand.

'Do you go by your own will?' he asked, as the cavalcade started again and he was shoved aside.

'Of course not, but I will manage,' she said crossly. 'You know I love you, Orestes. All right, all right, we shall go directly,

Captain,' she said to the guard. 'Try and live, Orestes,' she said, and was carried away, the slave women clucking and pulling the curtain closed.

Orestes watched them until they were out of sight. Then he opened his fist to show a small embroidered handkerchief. Hermione had not forgotten him, and Hermione usually got what she wanted.

Not, however, in this case. I hoped that Neoptelemus had inherited some of Achilles' strength, for he was going to need all of it to subdue Hermione and teach her her duty.

Since I had acknowledged Orestes as my son and he had recognized me as his mother, I had not dreamt of Aegisthus. I could even say his name without wanting to scream. I slept well and ate well and I was strong. Even on a rough passage of the Gulf of Corinth, I was not sick.

But Orestes did not speak or smile. When we stopped at night he sat for hours, honing the edge of an already razor-sharp sword with a mountain stone. The noise ate at my nerves. Our cousin tried to draw him out, but he would not be drawn.

'Lady,' Pylades said to me, as we rode from the city into the road south, for Tiryns.

'Lord?'

'Have you thought—about the future, Electra?'

'The future, cousin?'

'What shall we do if this murder is accomplished? Where shall we go from Mycenae?'

'We shall not leave Mycenae,' said Orestes. 'I am claiming my kingdom.'

'You would stay in that city after the murder of your mother?' Pylades asked, a line dividing his brow, his chestnut hair escaping from its fillet.

'Blood can be washed away,' I said bitterly. 'Stone floors bear no traces of murder. Who knows that better than we?'

He said nothing and we rode on.

Cassandra

Winter passed. When we saw the very first leaves sprouting from the tops of the fig tree, no bigger than a crow's foot, we set sail again. The children waved at us from the shore as we rowed out of the little bay.

Troas could not be our home.

'Well, Princess, where shall we roam?' asked Eumides. He had put on weight and needed less wine and some healthy exercise. He had done nothing at all in Troas, apart from his legendary performances amongst the women of the city, about which some exceptionally indelicate songs had been composed.

'It does not matter,' I replied. 'Leave it to the gods. They might be intending to repair some of the damage they have done to us.'

'In that case, we'll go to Lemnos first,' said my sailor. 'We can trade our cargo for axe-heads there for wood, and is most acceptable to the smaller islands.'

◇ ◇ ◇

We wandered for four years. We traded that cargo of wood for ingots of bronze. The ingots we bartered for sheep, as we carried a bleating cargo to Lesbos where the scour had come upon their flocks. The sheep sold well, but they loaded us with skins for the medicine Chryse and I compounded, which cured the remaining beasts. The fleeces we traded in Kriti for that most valuable of herbs, dittany, herb of immortality.

In Poros we heard that Odysseus had not returned to Ithaca, and we wondered what could have delayed him so long.

In the Chersonese we looked for Hecabe, my mother. The fishermen told us solemnly that she had turned into a black bitch with glowing red eyes and run off howling into the hills, as a certain red-headed Odysseus had told them to say, but a hefty bribe bought from them the location of her tomb.

We made the offerings. I did not grieve. She did not wish to live.

In Malea once, Chryse and I, being utterly exhausted, refused to make love to Eumides, and he had stalked angrily out of the inn, slamming the door. There were lovers, he declared, panting for him on the waterfront, and we bade him go and find some, for we had been tending the survivors of a shipwreck, pounding the water out of sodden mariners all day while they coughed and choked and tried to die out of sheer weariness.

We were woken by a shamed and penitent sailor, who lay down between us to be embraced, saying that there was no love like ours, and no one could replace us, and we made love to him after all.

We treated a plague on Samos. Eumides, now used to the company of healers, had conquered his distaste for retching, filthy humanity and worked two days and a night with us, pouring a Trojan remedy (which we used for cattle scour) down the stinking throats of Aegina's citizenry. We saved eighty percent of the people. No one objected that I was a woman and could not wear an Asclepid's gown while they lay groaning. But after they recovered they gave us a cargo of olives and their best wishes and sent two ships out of the straits to escort us, making sure that the uncanny trios had really gone.

I saw men making the sign against the black sorcery behind my back as we sat down in the marketplace on Thera, and we beat a retreat, showered with stones, after Chryse had dissected the body of a dead man to find out why he had died.

They were all infected with voracious intestinal worms, we knew, but they called us necromancers and we just escaped alive.

It was a pleasant life apart from these little problems. Most places accepted us as traders or as physicians. But there was never an island where we could both have the same status. In some places women were healers, the child-carriers, and no one who could not bear could heal. In some places medicine was the province of men, grave Asclepids in impressive robes, and women's medicine was the province of devotees of Hecate, Drinker of Dog's Blood: sorcery and poisons and charms.

We grew wise with experience, stored with much knowledge and much practice. My skin was tanned with travel and Chryse's also, while our Eumides was as dark as an African and grew an impressive black, curly beard. We were wealthy, well fed, and had friends all over the Aegean.

But we were growing unsettled. We needed a home.

Then one night on the breast of the Ocean I woke in agony, clutching my head. It felt as though someone was driving a needle into my brain.

I knew the fire, knew the voice from the fire. Eleni. Oh, the unutterable relief to know that he was alive; unhappy, tired, frustrated, but alive and mine, mine! I sent what must have been an aetheric shout into his mind, 'Eleni!' and I felt his response, a flood of love and relief.

'Cassandra,' he said. I could not hear any more words, though I strained my senses so that my head throbbed like a drum.

'Where?' I sent, frantically. 'Where are you?'

'Epirus, enslaved,' he said, and then the contact strained and slackened. I searched frantically and found the little glow that was my twin. I could not read him, but he was there. I had not lost him. He was there, a small fire in my heart. My lost one, my love, my dear.

I woke Eumides and Chryse. They sat up, alarmed at my pallor and the pain in my eyes.

'We are going to Epirus,' I told them. 'I have found my brother.'

Chapter Fourteen

Odysseus

They sang, and the ropes bit into my wrists unfelt. I knew that if I broke free they would charm the ship onto the rocks and I would join the dead in the Siren's meadow. They did not sing of love, as poets have reported who never heard them. They did not sing of maiden's yielding flesh or burning desire, nor of war and glory, trumpets or armies, fame or treasure.

They sang of land, of a small farm in the poverty-stricken Ithaca, with the smoke rising from the one chimney and the sound of chickens clucking and pecking in the dirt beside the door. They spoke new-washed linen drying on the bushes, olives laid in press, goats bleating after their dams in spring. They sang of poppies in the grass, children playing on the floor beside the hearth, of the scent of bread baking, of a woman suckling a newborn at her breast in the sun. They sang of cleanliness, of new linen next to washed skin, of sleep, always of sleep in peace.

They broke my heart. I heard it break.

Poseidon, most cruel of gods, sea-monster, if you will not help me home, I will get there in your despite. Men will abandon your worship, Earth-Shaker, and your altars will lie cold in Ithaca, if ever Odysseus gets home.

Then I heard the boom and wash, as of cliffs colliding with immense force. Circe told me of them. Scylla and Carybdis, the Clashing Rocks. The sea was full of wreckage.

If ever Odysseus gets home? I would not wager one obol on his chances.

Electra

There was peace and plenty in the villages as we came through. The Artemision which had been starving was fat and prosperous and they sacrificed a goat for us. The Artemision where someone had tried to rape me and I had killed him seemed strange, and it took a moment before I realized what was wrong. The figures around the well were not female. The men were still wearing the veils there and I asked why.

'The Goddess Artemis ordered it,' they said, making a devout sign. 'She came herself, the golden woman, Bow-Bearer, Divine Hunter. We were lucky to escape her wrath. We will not attract it again. Our village is rich and pilgrims come to see where the Goddess appeared, leaving offerings.'

We slept there that night and no one attacked us. Next morning we rode on. Mycenae lay before us in the dawn light, a closed, grey pile of stones.

'What shall we do? Shall we just go to the gate' I said breathlessly.

'Saying, greetings, men of Mycenae, let us in, we've come to kill your king?' asked Pylades. He was always ironic when he was nervous. I was suddenly angry, possessed of fury, and had to swallow bile or choke.

We saw a procession winding down from the city toward the circle graves outside. The priests of Apollo were leading a bull, and walking in front was a figure I knew.

Dark curly hair, weak face, long legs. It was Aegisthus, wearing my father's robes, and I knew where they were going.

'Come, quickly. We can get to the sacrifice place before them. It's the bull-killing for strangers, there must be visitors expected.

Xenoi, guests, perhaps, to be purified. Come on.' I ran down the path, out of sight of the city, sliding down a grassy slope and hiding behind a bush to remove my veil, put back my hair into a plait, and drape my mantle in man-fashion. No woman could attend the rites of slaughter. They would take me for a boy, even if I looked odd. No Mycenean woman would dare masquerade as a man. The punishment for such presumption was death by stoning.

The priests came chanting hymns into the stony hollow where the altar stone was, carved around with the spirals which denote the Sun.

Aegisthus looked at three strangers and did not know us. I stared into his hated face and saw no recognition in his eyes, no sign that he knew that death was breathing on the back of his neck.

'Greetings. I am Aegisthus, King of Mycenae. Do you require purging of guilt?' he asked, holding up a pitcher of spring water. To allow him to pour it over our hands would make us xenoi, his guests, and increase our crime. Pylades shook his head, smiling.

'No, Lord, we are clean of offense. We are travellers from Phocis and have come to join your sacrifice.'

'King, King!' Aegisthus smiled assentingly and the priests brought the ox forward. It was unwilling, and lowed. This was a bad omen and it was usual under these circumstances to ask someone else to kill the beast. He offered the axe to Orestes.

'You Phocians are supposed to be stout men,' he said. 'Show me.'

'I'll show you, if I can,' said Orestes flatly. He waited until Aegisthus was turned away and then struck with all his force at the usurper's throat.

The blow was so severe that his head was almost detached. Blood gushed over the altar. The bull took fright and reared, breaking his tether and spreading dismay through the crowd as he galloped through them, bellowing with terror. Aegisthus crumpled slowly in the ruin of the king's robes, purple now with blood as well as dye. My heart rejoiced. I only wished that I had been able to wield the axe myself. Despoiler, thief, murderer. He had a faintly surprised look on his face, and I barely restrained myself from spurning his head with my foot. I mired my hands in the wound, trailing my hem in his gore. Dead, dead. The monster was dead, and another monster soon to die.

'Stand off!' warned Pylades, fending back the astonished soldiers with spear and sword. 'This is Orestes, son of Agamemnon, claiming blood vengeance for the murder of his father.'

The soldiers paused, not knowing what to do. 'Who can identify this man?' asked the captain.

'Maybe I can,' quavered an old man. He had been my father's house-steward, and had known us both since we were born. He limped forward to Orestes and peered shortsightedly up into his face.

'Orestes,' he mused. 'Orestes was scalded when he was a child—a bad burn. The scar should still be there.' He tottered around my brother and son to look at his back, lifting the tunic. There was a flat scar just above his waist, where a careless slave had poured boiling water on his in his bath.' And he had brown hair and golden eyes, and he would know my name and the name of his nurse.'

'Your name is Nestor, and my nurse was called Cilissa,' said Orestes. 'I am Orestes, son of Agamemnon.' His voice was perfectly level. 'You taught me to make Panpipes out of elm-bark, Nestor, do you remember? And you gave me a puppy—she grew into a fine dog—her name was Racer. Half wolf—she never learned…'

'Never learned to bark,' concluded the old man. He gave an odd whistle, and a dog came running to the signal.

She skidded to a halt before Orestes, staring. Then she approached almost on her belly, whining and sniffing the air. The crowd grew still. The black dog cocked her ears, identified the scent, then threw herself at Orestes, snuffling and leaping up to lick his face.

'Orestes, son of Agamemnon,' declared Nestor over the bitch's slobbering joy. 'You have avenged your father. The rule of the unholy woman is ended, now that you have come into your kingdom. What will you have us do with the body?'

'What did he do to my father?' asked Orestes.

'Threw him out to rot in the sun. We came in the night and sprinkled earth for him, made the offerings,' said the captain, kicking the corpse. 'Do likewise to this murderer, son of Agamemnon. Expose him.'

'Bury him,' said Orestes, as though he was tired. 'No vengeance can be taken on a corpse. Dig a hole and put him in, suitably disposed. Now we must go up into the city. Where is the Queen?'

'In the palace, Lord. She rises late these days. We will announce you.'

'You will stay here. Complete the prayers to Apollo, pray also to Thanatos who is death and to Hades for favor. Bury the dead. No man will climb after us.'

I looked back as we walked up the hill, and they had not moved. Nestor held the bitch by the collar or she would have followed Orestes.

We came into Mycenae as the walls flushed golden with sunrise. I knew this city; every street that I had traversed as a fearless child, and I knew every step of the marble stairs up to the women's quarters. I had suffered agony here, endless pain, misery beyond measuring—and it looked ordinary. Well-cut stone, well laid. Tapestries on the walls exhibiting the deeds of the House of Atreus as far as they could be told. The smell of floral oils was in the air as we came to the doors of the Queen's apartments.

Old Neptha was there, but Orestes brushed her aside.

'Electra!' she exclaimed. 'Electra with blood on your hands. By all the gods, Princess, don't, don't go in, not with armed men. She is your mother!' She seized me by the sleeve and I pushed her away. She caught sight of my face and stepped back several paces, afraid.

I was not afraid.

The Queen was awake. She had aged. My beautiful mother was gaining flesh, sagging, and her cheeks were marked with the wine drinker's red patches. She was dressed only in her sleeping tunic, and she dragged a gown around her as we came in.

'You!' she said to me. 'Who is this you bring, Electra, your husband?'

'My son,' I said, and she paled, clutching at her bosom.

'We have come to kill you, woman,' I hissed. 'The usurper is dead and his blood is on my hands,' I showed them to her, wet and red. She ignored me and turned to the weaker target.

'Orestes,' she said sweetly. 'Have you come to kill me?'

'I have come to avenge my father,' he said through his teeth. He was as white as clay. Pylades closed the door and leaned on it. No one would interrupt us.

'Your father is avenged, if Aegisthus is dead,' she said. Her hair hung down, black as night, and she came closer to Orestes. He flinched under her smile.

'This is the breast that nourished you,' she said, baring her torso to the waist. 'The arms that cradled you, the womb that bore.'

'I know what womb carried me, who endured the pain for me,' he said quietly.

'When you were sleepless, so was I,' she said, not answering him. 'If you hungered, I fed you. If you had thirst, I gave you milk. You used to lie in my lap and play with my necklace—do you remember, Orestes?'

'You murdered my…you murdered Agamemnon!' he cried. She smiled again, moving closer by each step.

'You cut your first tooth on my beads,' she said, lifting his left hand and placing it on her breast. 'I birthed you with long agony but I was glad of it, for it gave me you. I am your mother. What do you want, Orestes?'

'To kill you, and die,' he said.

I came to his side and laid my hand on the bronze sword. Before she could speak again, seduce him from with holy purpose with words, I pushed it and it entered her side.

She staggered away, and Orestes followed. He seized her by the arm and struck, hard. Her throat was cut and he let her fall.

Blood pooled on the floor, spreading in a red tide. Dead as my father. I would not even look at her face again.

I was avenged. I felt empty, like a house through which the sea-wind is blowing, scoured clean.

Orestes dropped the sword. Pylades picked it up, wiped it, sheathed it, and took our hands.

'Come,' he said. 'We need look on this no more,' and he led us into the courtyard and bade us wash.

They brought us water and we rinsed ourselves clean of blood. The men of the city were gathered in a silent group, watching, waiting for what Orestes would say. They needed to be told that the reign of the usurper was over, that the rule of the monstrous woman was completed by a clean act of revenge, sanctioned by the Gods.

They waited, and Orestes screamed and ran.

We pursued him along the main streets, out through the gate and down the hill. All the way he shrieked and cringed as though under attack, but we could see no assailants.

He stopped where we had left the horses, weeping and shaking.

'The old women, the terrible old women,' he said through trembling lips. 'Three of them. Black rags, snakes—can't you hear their bells? Iron bells, can't you hear them say, "Matricide! We will hound you to death!" Sister? Can't you see them?'

'I see nothing,' I whispered, amazed.

'See how they have beaten me,' he said. He tore off his tunic and I saw long welts as from a whip, curling around his back. The skin was broken and he was bleeding.

'They will not let me enter Mycenae again. I must go to a temple of Apollo. The Sun-God Apollo says I must go to Delphi.'

'But Mycenae and your kingdom!' I said.

'I have no kingdom,' he replied.

Pylades helped him onto his horse and we rode away from the city. I began to believe in the old women when I heard the sound of running animal's feet behind, but it was only the black bitch *Racer*, who had found Orestes again, and did not mean to lose him.

Cassandra

We lived on an island while waiting for the sailing season again. I like islands. This was Skiathos, off the coast of Thessaly.

We dragged *Waverider* ashore there and made new sails for her, greased and mended her timbers, and stored her while the Meltemi blows, the ferocious gales that rake the deep and drive galleys stadia off course. Set sail in that wind, and only Poseidon will know where the wreck lies. I could not come to my twin Eleni yet and I tried to have patience.

Here Diomenes was acceptable, but not I. I was tired of selling magic potions on the sly, visiting cloistered women in stifling houses who did not need medicine but fresh air and exercise and better food. I wearied of procuring abortions for terrified maids in danger of death if their unchastity was known. I was sick even of the Argive tongue, as well as of their philosophy. Toward the end of the winter I found myself grabbing automatically for a veil as I left the small house and thereupon decided that it was time we went to Epirus, sailing season or not. I wanted desperately to see Eleni again. I could feel him all the time now. He was very unhappy. I felt that if I did not come to him soon he might despair.

My companions agreed—I had been snapping at them for weeks. We would leave *Waverider* at Iolkos, Jason's capital. We could not sail around Achaea in such a wind. Eumides' friend Laodamos would bring the galley to Amouda when the weather allowed. To travel in the wrong season, we would leave the sea and buy horses. We would have to ride several weeks through the mountains to get to Dodona, and the tribes there were said to be savage, illiterate, and dangerous.

'Any journey, Lady,' asked Eumides, 'even on horseback instead of on the sea, if you will only like us again.'

'We grieve to see you so unhappy,' agreed Diomenes. 'And there is a temple to the Healer God at Dodona in Epirus. We might be able to stay there.'

'We even have enough treasure left to buy your brother,' suggested the sailor, 'if this son of Achilles will sell him.'

'He will not leave,' I said shortly. 'He is in love with Andro-mache, widow of my brother Hector. It was the gods' doing.' I added.

I embraced them in remorse. I had been unbearable. But I would never live the life of an Argive woman.

Chapter Fifteen

'My Lord and Brother Apollo, your revenge is complete. The terrified children of Atreus flee, pursued by the Furies. I do not think they will survive,' commented Athene.

'Little lost beasts,' grumbled Pan.

'Murderers,' said Hecate.

'I will cleanse them of their deed,' said Apollo. 'They need only get to one of my shrines.'

'You cannot cleanse them of matricide, the primal crime,' said Hecate, breathing venomous breath into the flawless face. Apollo did not recoil, but smiled.

'Your reign has ended, hag,' he said.

'Has it?' she asked.

In the Pool of Mortal Lives the gods heard a whip crack, heard a scream, saw blood creep in a thin line to stain a ragged tunic.

Zeus Father looked at a little ship on Ocean in the Pool of Mortal Lives, driven into landless wreck, and spoke to his brother Poseidon.

'Release that unhappy sailor,' he urged. 'Troy is gone, Brother.'

'I will torment him until the Gods grow old.' The Sea-God struck the marble with his trident. Zeus wiped his brow and tasted salt.

'The Gods do not grow old, but they are tired. Cut the strings, Poseidon, Lord of the Sea. There are others who need your counsel. Leave Odysseus to Fate.'

'Not yet,' growled Earth-Shaker.

Electra

Terror pursued us. It was the worst journey I had ever made, ever known. We stopped by preference at a thicket avoiding the sight of men. The first night we did not sleep, fearing for Orestes.

We could only calm him if I lay on one side of him and Pylades on the other, and even then he thrashed and whimpered.

'Mother!' he cried, then 'Death,' he whispered. My arm lay over him, Pylades embraced him, and our hands met.

I was empty and revenged now. I did not fear the lust of other men. So, when a warm hand touched mine in the pitch dark, where the horses stamped and fretted and *Racer* whined and licked Orestes' feet, I clasped it tightly.

It felt good, in the night and the fear, to touch another human.

I woke in a pine forest. *Racer* had gone off on some purpose of her own, and I made a little fire and heated a mealy pottage. We had supplies for many days. I sat by the fire for a while, waiting for the others to rouse. Pylades was lying on his side. Orestes in his agony had rolled away from him. I examined him idly.

It might have been the first time I had really looked at him.

The new sunlight struck silver lights from his chestnut-husk hair. His face was olive-brown, bony, the jaw firm, the throat rounded. Eyelashes made a delicate fringed line on his high cheekbones. His hands, large hands with well-shaped fingers, were empty and cupped, and sunlight fell into them. Pylades my cousin had both hands full of light, and it pooled in the hollow of his shoulder, the angle of knee and hip.

He woke. Dark brown eyes considered me gravely and I blushed so that I was flooded with heat.

'It's morning,' I said inanely.

'So it is. And you, Lady, have been busy.'

He got up carefully so as not to jolt Orestes and came to sit with me and eat soup. I let him drink most of it before I said, 'Pylades, what shall we do? Orestes cannot travel far, not with this madness on him.'

'We must find a temple of Apollo. We will have to go north, to Corinth.'

'That will take days! Is there nothing nearer?'

'Not that I know of. This country belongs to Artemis and Poseidon. Neither of them are likely to be of any use. The Sun-God set Orestes onto this path, now he must rescue him. To find Pythian Apollo quicker, we would have to go south to Tiryns or Argos, and that is not a good idea.'

'No,' said Orestes. He must have been lying awake, listening to us. 'I am cursed. I cannot go into a city or the Gods may set it on fire. I may not eat with men, or they may choke. I may not drink from a stream, or I will poison the water.'

'If we must find Apollo, then you must go into Corinth and the city will just have to take its chances.' Pylades looked at my son. 'How have you fared the night, little brother?'

'Well enough.' He tried to get up, winced, and Pylades helped him to his feet. Orestes was pressing a hand to his side. When we peeled away the tunic there were great bruises there, as though he had been beaten.

'They have clubs, bronze-studded clubs,' he said. 'Is there something to eat?'

I gave him a clean bowl and began to pack away the gear. *Racer*, returning with a fresh-caught rabbit, sat at Orestes' feet. He ate about half the broth and gave her the rest. Then he took my hand in his and said, 'Electra, you are a woman of virtue. You cannot travel with me and Pylades unattended.'

'Why not? We have made many journeys together. Pylades is my cousin. You're my brother.'

'I am your brother and your son, and I am responsible for you. I love you and Pylades most in the world, and I would have you married. Someone must take care of you when I…when I am gone.' His eyes begged me to take him seriously, so I did. He smoothed my hand. I noticed that my skin was not fine and white anymore, as it had been when I lived in my mother's house. I had spinner's calluses on my forefinger and thumb, and a few small cooking-fire burns. Also my fingernails were filthy and I had not even noticed.

'I know you will not leave me,' Orestes said to me. 'So I am giving you to Pylades.' He put my hand into that of my cousin. 'We will celebrate it at the next shrine we come to, on the way to Delphi. Do you agree, Pylades?'

'That depends on whether Electra agrees,' he said.

Argive women belong to a man—all women, either to father, husband, brother, or son. As my brother, Orestes had the right to dispose of me as he saw fit and I could not have argued. But Pylades was asking me how I felt about it. He was giving me a choice. Like the barbarian women, I could make a bargain for my virtue and some terms on which to live the rest of my life.

'You know my history,' I said to him. 'Do you want to marry me?'

'Yes, Lady,' His voice was deep. 'We know each other well, Electra.'

'I know little of men. I will not please you as the slave Alceste did.'

'You please me.' He said steadily.

'You will not lie with me until I consent?'

'I will not.'

'Then I agree.' I could not think of anything else to ask.

We mounted and rode gently north through the spring flowers, gold and purple, towards Corinth and the temple of the Pythian Apollo. *Banthos* was slow because he had filled his greedy stomach with green barley.

That night we lay, as always, one to each side of Orestes, and he cried in his sleep.

I could not see them, though I strained my eyes. I could not hear the thud of club or lash as it struck my brother-son's cringing body, but bruises bloomed under their assault. I saw no glimpse of black rags and heard no hiss of snake-crowned heads. Pylades could not see them either.

But *Racer* could. A wolf-bitch, fiercely loyal, lay at Orestes' feet every night. She, who had never learned to bark, accomplished this one night. The moon was full. We lay in a pine-wood, under the deep shade. Selene's radiance made inky shadows and ice-light. The stars were damped by her flooding beams.

Racer, who slept little, woke and bayed. Orestes flung up his arms to cover his face. The bitch barked and howled, snapping at the air, for almost an hour while Orestes was assailed. We heard the click as her teeth met on nothing. Then she settled down into an alert crouch, like a dam with puppies watching for anything which might threaten her children.

Orestes, when he woke, joked for the first time since Clytemnestra's blood pooled on the stone. He said that he had two mothers, one human and one animal, and that he hoped he had a divine one as well.

I hoped so, too.

'Is Apollo—has Phoebus spoken to you, Orestes?' I asked cautiously.

'He says I will be cleansed if I come to his temple,' my son replied.

I wondered if he would arrive alive at that temple.

Two nights later we were riding the narrow road between two steep mountains when we saw a shrine and rode up to investigate. It was a small, poor building, with a hearthstone and a wooden image so worn as to be almost unrecognizable. By the hearth, with its carefully tended fire, we assumed it to be a temple of Hera and Hestia, Goddesses of the home and of marriage.

Orestes reeled in a vine of flowers from the hedge and wound it into two garlands. He placed one on my head and one on Pylades'. We came into the shrine and poured a little milk and the last of our wine on the hearth. Orestes took my hand and gave it into Pylades', saying 'I, Orestes, son and brother, give Electra, mother and sister, to Pylades our cousin for his wife. I trust in his honor and courage, to guard her and keep her until he dies.'

'I, Pylades of Phocis, accept the Lady Electra, my cousin, as my wife, and I will guard her and keep her until I die.'

We omitted the customary prayers for fertility. I knelt at the altar and threw a handful of dried gorse on the fire. It flared up and was ash in an instant, and the sacred flame burned hot beneath it. The country people say that this is a good omen.

No one else witnessed this wedding, so simple and strange. But Pylades did not release my hand until we had made the prayers to Hymen and to the Mother.

Then we rode on.

We tended Orestes together, hiding each night in some forest or under the thick woody heath on the mountainsides. One night a bear blundered into our camp. It had been gathering berries and was juice-stained and replete, but bears are very dangerous. One blow of their great taloned paws can unseam a man from throat to navel. Orestes grabbed *Racer* and held her muzzle, lest she should attack it and provoke death in return.

But the bear just looked at us, blinked at our fire, dropped to all fours and padded unhurriedly away, back into the thickets of sloe and whin-fruit.

We were so close to being beasts that the beasts themselves accepted us.

Racer hunted every morning, slipping out before dawn to catch rabbits, and once a hare. First she caught one and ate it herself, then she bought another for her puppy Orestes. She would lay it down at his feet and nudge him with her nose, demanding that he eat it while it was nice and fresh. She could never understand why he insisted on skinning and cooking it. We had a bundle of rabbit skins by the time we came to the cleft in the mountains and rode down toward Corinth.

By then we were ragged and filthy, and Orestes was desperate. He no longer talked about them, but the Erinyes came every night and with increasing violence. The baying of the bitch could not keep them away. I was as guilty as he—I had struck the first blow and drawn my mother's blood—but they did not touch me. Not a hiss sounded or a fang gleamed in my sleep and, for the first time since I was a child, I had no dreams.

'You are stronger, wife, than I would have expected,' said Pylades.

'Stronger, Husband?' He smiled at me.

'You are gently bred, Lady, and I know that you had never walked more than five paces in your life before the strangers brought you from Mycenae with the Princess Cassandra. Now you can walk and ride all day. Your skin is golden, not chalky like the pale maidens of Mycenae. Your hands are deft and tanned by the wind and the sun. Your courage inspires me.'

'I have no house of yours to keep, my Lord,' I said, surprised at this unmerited praise.

'You find wood every day, you carry water, you tend us and the beasts. Orestes is alive because of your care. No woman keeping her man's house could do more.'

I had not noticed. Of course I made the fire and carried the water, cooked the food and groomed the horses. That was my task, the common female work.

'You guard us, comfort us, guide us through the mountains,' I said in return. 'We would be dead and our bones would have bleached in some wilderness, if it had not been for your care, my…my Lord.'

To this he made no reply, but he leaned forward and kissed me, very lightly and fleetingly, on the cheek. I did not draw away, and I almost wished that the caress had lasted longer.

I was becoming used to intimacy. I had slept with women all my life, and never with men. They were rougher, stronger, more animal than men, when they slept. Their breathing was deeper. Orestes screamed and cried for mercy under the invisible blows, and Pylades talked.

I woke once, in deep darkness, to hear him carrying on a sensible conversation with someone I could not see. When I crawled to the fire and blew on the ember, I saw in the little red glow that he was still possessed by Morpheus.

'She is heartless and cold,' he argued. Then he replied, 'She is injured. You must wait. You have been patient for four years. Be patient another year.'

Then he answered himself, 'I burn, I burn!' and woke to find me looking at him across the point of light. I did not tell him what he had said, and he did not remember in the morning.

Corinth was awake when we came in. Pylades was carrying Orestes across his horse, and *Banthos* and I followed, leading *Hunter*. The market drew away from us, perceiving that we were under some curse or blight. We were ragged and filthy yet rode good horses and had good saddles and once-fine clothes. Therefore we were either successful bandits seeking purification for robbery and murder or penitents under a vow. In either case it would have been very unlucky to meddle with us, and we rode into the courtyard of the Temple of Pythian Apollo in good time. The boy who had led us there ran off without stopping for a reward.

I got down and took Orestes from Pylades. No woman can enter Apollo's temple who is not a virgin, but it took two of us to carry him and I assumed that Apollo knew all about me. The attendants led the horses and *Racer* away and we went up the marble steps, between the white pillars, into the antechamber of the shrine.

There we laid our son and brother down and a priest knelt beside him.

I looked at Orestes in the daylight and my heart quailed, so that Pylades hurried to my side in case I should faint. Orestes had never been stout, and now he was bone-thin. The brown eyes had sunk in their sockets. His fingernails were broken from scrabbling against stones, trying to escape. His lips were bitten. Dried blood crusted his teeth. He was clay-pale where he was not black with bruises. Apart from the rise and fall of his chest, he looked like a ten-day corpse.

'Erinyes,' screamed the Pythia from inside the shrine. 'Pursued until almost dead, Furies! Away, hags! Here I will cleanse him!'

The priest brought a bowl of cold water, and anointed Orestes' feet and his hands. As soon as the water touched him, it reddened as if with blood.

'Apollo cleanses you of your crime,' intoned the priest, an old man with white hair under his veil. 'Hence-forward you shall be white of heart, clear of all offense, absolved.' He tipped the dish and water fell on Orestes' face, so that he blinked and opened his bloodshot eyes.

Oh, my beautiful son, my heart cried. *Oh, Orestes, my love.*

'Lift his head,' instructed the priest. Pylades and I knelt on either side and raised Orestes so that he could see into the shrine.

The curtain flicked aside as in a gust of wind. Both Pylades and I shut our eyes, and a white fire flashed on our closed lids. Orestes gave a little sigh, as of a thirsty child who has been given milk, and his body grew heavier with sleep.

Two young priests came and carried him away.

'Three days, Lord,' said the old man, 'for purification. Come back on the third day.'

'Can't I speak to him?' I asked, and he totally ignored me, for Apollo's priests do not speak to women, except for the Pythiae.

'We will come back then,' said Pylades.

We left the temple and retrieved the horses and *Racer*, who was worried. I stroked her ears as Orestes did and told her. 'Three days and we shall have him again,' and she accepted this, although she was not happy.

The waterfront taverns were dirty and lousy. I led Pylades through the market again to the house of Taphis the Corinthian, where I could claim some friendship, perhaps. The Lady Gythia herself came to the door.

'It is market day, all the slaves are busy. Lady Electra!' she said, seeming pleased.

'Lady Gythia, my cousin, Pylades of Phocis.'

'Come in,' she invited, taking *Banthos*' rein.

She settled Pylades on a marble bench while her own maidens prepared a bath for him. I led the horses to the stable and began to groom and feed them, while she watched me with some amusement.

'You are Electra, Lady, are you not? Laodice, daughter of Agamemnon?'

'I am. I have left my brother Orestes in the temple of Apollo for ritual cleansing. We are under a curse—Apollo has cursed us,' I answered truthfully, wondering if she was going to forbid us her household, as she had every right to do.

'Why did Apollo curse you?' she asked, heaving the saddle off *Hunter's* back and laying it over a beam. The horses liked her. She had authority.

'Because we have killed Aegisthus and Clytemnestra. The Furies pursued my brother. We are in blood-debt to them for matricide. Shall we leave?'

She did not even blink, so I assumed that she had known the tale before she spoke. Word spreads fast in the land of Pelops. 'If Taphis has not a good account with Apollo by now, after all the medicines he has sent to Epidavros, then the Gods know no justice,' she said, laughing. 'You will not leave, Lady! You are my guests. Are you married?'

'Indeed, to Pylades, Prince of Phocis.'

'You have changed, Lady, and if you will forgive me saying so, I thought a sworn virgin and destined only to spin for the rest of your life. He looks like a fine man. I hope you will bear many sons,' she said formally. 'Now, having made the horses comfortable, we will see what we can do for the humans. You will wish to attend your husband at his bath. It should be ready by now.'

I had not thought of that. It was the wife's duty to wash and anoint her husband. Somehow I could not explain my equivocal position to the Lady Gythia, so brisk and self-assured. I followed her to the room she had allotted us—the best in her house, which was kind—and she pointed out a pithos full of hot water and a dipper.

'Pour the waste water into the drain,' she said, 'There is meal and lychnis in those little bags to remove the grime. It has been a long journey, Lady?'

'Long and horrible,' I agreed. Coming back into a civilized place, where there were stone-built houses and well-cooked food, wine, clean clothes, and hot water had made me realize how dirty I was, how unkempt. She patted my cheek and smiled at me, a liberty she would not have taken once with Princess Electra. I liked her touch.

Pylades was escorted in and a slave woman removed his outer robes and then his tunic, taking them away to wash.

It was the second time I had seen him naked. He was the only unrelated naked man I had ever seen. Dead Aegisthus had always arrived and left in the dark.

Pylades stood easily, bearing my scrutiny. He was slim, with long thighs, a flat belly, big hands and feet. His hair was torn and matted with mud and leaves. I did not know what to say to him. He seemed beautiful to me, well made, like a *kouros*, the statue of the youth seen in Apollo's temples.

'Will you tend me, wife?' he asked.

'Lord,' I assented.

I helped him into the bath and began to wash him, soaking his hair and combing out the burrs and leaves. Water ran in different patterns over a male body, I noticed, straight down the chest and over the shoulders. I liked the way his body felt, padded and muscular, bony and strong. When I had scoured off the mud and filth of travel, I helped him up and sat him on a bath-sheet while I emptied the bath and refilled it.

I was taking up a towel and an oil-flask, to complete my duty, when he removed them from my hands and put them on a bench. He smiled at me, a sweet smile. Then he unpinned my chiton.

It fell to my feet. I stood still. I did not know if it was fear that made me catch my breath. The tunic came off over my head, snaring in my tangled hair. I was naked. He did not stare at me or try to caress me.

He took my hand and led me to the bath.

Then he washed me, patiently teasing out the tangles in my long hair, sitting behind me on the floor. The scented water lapped my chin—the bath was big enough for a tall man, so I could float in it—and his touch was deft and soothing. I closed my eyes, hearing him chanting a litany, 'Beautiful Electra, golden-eyed lady, my lovely one, my golden one, my dear, my love.'

Finally he could draw the comb right through the wet strands. My hair floated in the bath, clean for the first time in a month.

The slippery lychnis linen pad slid across my shoulders, under my arms, to the ends of my fingers, then across my breasts, very gently and carefully. Something seemed to uncoil inside me, like a leather hinge that had been under tension slackening in the rain. The water was warm, and the soapy cloth was teasing, never staying where it felt good. My feet were lifted, one at a time, and cleansed and laid down, then the cloth slicked up to scrub my knees, moved along my thighs, touched for an instant where something made me gasp, then slipped again to rest on my hip, along the inside of my arms, to my hands again.

There was an itch that grew, demanding attention. The cloth, no, it was fingers now, the palm of a hand, sliding to a nipple and pinching lightly, then slipping down over my belly to linger not quite long enough before it moved away again, to touch the nipple in passing and cup my cheek.

The itch was burning. The fingers returned to find the place unerringly, and a mouth closed on my nipple, sucking, and I grabbed wet hair to bring it closer, closer.

Then a tremor ran through me, an earthquake shock, and I opened my eyes as they filled with tears. Lovely, lovely! I had never felt anything so strong, so sweet.

The mouth moved away, the fingers withdrew. Pylades said, 'Hymen favors you, Lady.'

I reached out my arms, but he was already standing, clothed in a clean tunic. He took my hands and stood me up, then gave me a towel. I dried myself and put on a chiton, as I did not mean to go out. It was not yet noon. I felt oddly disappointed and physically disconcerted, as though I had been climbing stairs and had missed a step.

'What gift did you give me, husband?' I asked, still feeling the earth-shocks along my thighs.

'The blessing of Hymen, Lady. I learned the skill from a Trojan woman. She called it the goddess' gift. Did it please you?'

'I never felt anything like it,' I said with perfect truth.

'I will not lie with you unless you consent,' he reminded me. 'I said that you pleased me, and you do.'

'How can I please you in return?' I asked, sitting down on the bed. I was unsteady on my feet, probably from the hot water.

'I will show you,' he said, sitting down beside me. 'But I would not affront your virtue, Electra. I have waited a long time, a can wait longer.'

'Show me,' I insisted.

He removed the tunic, lying down beside me, and I touched him. The phallus was warm and dry, strong and plant-like. I stroked the stem, as he instructed me, as though I was plaiting hemp. I had never voluntarily touched Aegisthus, though he had ordered me to do various acts which disgusted me, and I had obeyed. Here I could stop, if I wanted. I could turn my face away, let my hands fall, and Pylades would say no word. No other Argive Lord, I am convinced, could have coaxed me from my terror.

I pulled off the chiton and lay beside him, and he ran both hands down my sides, caressing my breasts, my hips, curving inward to the goddess' place, which was wet. The plant shuddered and seeded on my belly and I smelt wormwood.

The smell was different. Sour had Aegisthus' semen been, rank and offensive. My husband sighed deeply and gathered me into his arms, my head on his breast, and I fell asleep to the sound of his heart beating.

Chapter Sixteen

Odysseus

Timing took us through the Clashing Rocks, timing and sacrifice. Some died. Most lived.

When we came to Thrinacie, the Sun-God's Isle, while I slept, the crew massacred several of the Sun-God's beasts, having solemnly promised that they would not touch them.

I don't know why I thought that wouldn't happen. No mariner was as cursed as I, with a crew so bone-headed, greedy and idle, never missing a chance to try to get us killed, or even more cursed than I already am. My life is blighted, or fate cruel. I should never have made that League of Suitors, but I was trying to prevent a war.

Some God must have made me sleep, some God who wanted me to offend Apollo as well. He was, of course, duly offended.

We were at sea, replete with the Sun-God's beef, when lightning struck the steersman and clove him in two. The ship broke her back under a mountain of water and spewed me to the surface.

Nine days I have been drifting in the ruin of the ship. All the others are dead.

What voracious sea-beast is going to dine on Odysseus, son of Laertes? I give him indigestion. May he break a tooth on the mail coat which is dragging me down.

Cassandra

Iolkos was busy, but Eumides had old friends there.

'This is where Jason set out,' he said cheerfully as we came into the harbor among a cloud of shrieking gulls. 'May we have a successful voyage!'

'He sailed, we ride,' said Chryse indulgently.

'He was lucky.' He jumped ashore and I threw him the hawser. *Waverider*'s crew shipped oars and lashed the gear fast, then climbed to the jetty and began stretching and groaning. We had rowed most of the way from Skiathos in an adverse wind and they were pleased to be on dry land, where no one would expect them to row. They were natives of Iolkos, volunteers who needed to get home. They had certainly earned their passage.

'Are you coming with me to Laodamos' house?' asked Eumides. 'I need to arrange with him to bring the boat into the Ionian Sea when the season comes—two months. That should give us time to cross the width of Epirus and do what we have to do there, whatever that is.'

No one is as blithe about the future as Eumides—it is one of his most irritating qualities. I had taxed him with it once, and he had said, 'I was a slave and I was freed. After that, I will never despair again.'

I needed a home, and so did Chryse. We had not found any place where both of us could happily live. Not amongst his people or amongst mine, and not in any of the strange countries which we had seen. Egypt was priest-ridden and stratified, Libya rich in fruit and gold and poor in manners. The islands were narrow-minded and dirty, with many hands reaching for coins. The Lemnian women did not like male settlers, and the women of Lesbos rejected them outright, sacrificing shipwrecked sailors to the Lady of Battles, Hecate. The island of Andros would tolerate no female creature, not even a female goat or a cow, much less a human. Cos and Cnidus, the physician's schools, both refused to allow that women had minds, much less medical skill.

'The world,' I said, exasperated, 'is divided into male and female and there is a mountain wall between!'

'True, Lady,' sighed Chryse. 'Where will we find rest?'

'You can find rest if you leave me and go back to Epidavros. You can take Eumides with you,' I snapped.

A year ago he would have replied, 'I will not leave you, Lady.' Now he said wearily, 'Are you sending us away?'

I thought about it.

'We will make this journey,' I said, taking his hand. 'If we cannot find a place which will take us, then I will send myself away.'

And I thought how desolate I would be without them. I pondered the long nights in which we had talked and played board games and drunk wine and made love. I wondered where else in the world I would find such delicacy, such tenderness, such passion. I wondered who in all of the Earth would be able to make me laugh as they did, the grave physician and the exuberant sailor. Where again, I wondered sadly as we paced the narrow streets of Iolkos, would I watch men making love, so ferocious, mouth locked to mouth, bone clashing against bone. And when my next lover turned to me, oh, then, where would be the extra hands, the extra mouth, the touch that brought me ecstasy? And where would I find the comrade as learned and reliable, as compassionate and skilled as Chryse, my golden Diomenes, or as clever and fearless a sailor as Eumides of the curly hair? I could not lose trios. I would think about it after we had found Eleni.

There must be somewhere for us to live.

When we had concluded our business with cross-eyed Laodamos, we lay down together in his house and made love with passion and desperation, as though we knew that we would part. I looked up into Eumides' eyes, felt Chryse's teeth on my nipple, and dragged someone between my thighs, the papyrus-root piercing me to the heart. As the climax struck me, hard enough to hurt, I bit into Eumides' neck as though it was a fruit.

Then we collapsed in an exhausted heap and wept ourselves to sleep.

◇◇◇

The next day we purchased horses—only a moderate bargain, according to Eumides, which meant that it was good but not indecent. I was pleased, because I had never liked starting a journey pursued by an outraged merchant who has discovered that his trading silver is actually trading tin.

Iolkos' market faded behind us. Ahead was a flattish plain sown with early barley, greening into spring.

'We must follow the road to Kerassia, then north again to Kalamaki,' said Chryse. 'That road goes to Platikambos, where we turn inland for Larissa, thence to Trikka, the birthplace of Asclepius. After that I am not sure and we'll have to get a guide from village to village.'

'That's enough to go on with,' grumbled Eumides. We were being tender of each other, careful. I did not like it. It felt like an inevitable parting.

'We shall not part,' I said firmly. 'Not if we have to gather some disaffected Argives and go and establish a new colony.'

'An interesting thought,' said Eumides, brightening.

It was interesting, though scarcely feasible. But it cheered us, and rose into the flowers which had grown on the path while winter had laid it fallow.

What happened when we lay two nights later in Kalamaki was unusual.

The gods returned to me.

I was alone in our house. Eumides and Chryse had joined a drinking game with the old men and I was preparing for sleep, lying down in the middle of the cloaks as always. When I felt like solitude, I signalled this by taking my mantle to a corner. The others did the same. But I was expecting to lie with one body on either side of me as usual and had just closed my eyes when I heard a footstep.

I said sleepily, 'Chryse?' before I realized that I had not heard a latch, and sat up, pulling the mantle around me.

Tall and bronzed and utterly perfect, the God Apollo was standing in the little hut. His head touched the roof and he burned with a golden light which smelt of honey. I knew that face, that scent. I would not play that game again.

'Lord, you have released me,' I said firmly. 'Your oracle said so.'

'Cassandra, I have released you,' he affirmed.

I felt instantly better. 'Lord, what is your pleasure with me?'

'Cassandra my own, my golden Princess, I know what you want,' he said in that god's voice which shivers mortal cells.

'Lord?'

'A place,' he said softly. 'A home for your heart and those of your two lovers.'

I knew that an immortal bargain was about to be struck, and I also knew that whatever its nature, I wasn't going to like it. Apollo does not stoop to bargain with mortals unless he is asking a steep price. Our lives, perhaps. We could presumably rest comfortably with the dead.

'Will you tell me, Lord?'

'I will tell another,' he said. Typical of male Gods, in fact typical of all gods whatsoever. I don't know if it is their divine point of view or just ordinary malice, but you can never get a straight answer out of a god.

Unless, I remembered, he is trying to tear out your throat with his teeth, as this God had done to me the last time I had offended him. The golden mane shadowed my face again, the rank breath enveloped me, a clawed paw pierced my breast. I shook back my hair, gulped, and prompted, 'Phoebus Apollo?'

'You will find your sweet place, Princess. If you undertake a task for me.'

'Lord, I am at your command,' I said meekly, recalling the teeth.

'When you come to Platikambos, wait there a week.'

'Lord? Why?'

His face grew dark, and he said in a voice which shook the hut and rattled my teeth. 'Do you question me, mortal?'

'No, Lord.' The reverberations were hurting my ears and my eyes filled. I wiped them and he was gone.

When the others came in, more than slightly merry and breathing wine fumes all over me, Chryse said, 'I smell honey.'

'Apollo came,' I said.

The look of patient resignation which he always adopted when I spoke of the gods spread over his face. He pulled off his cloak and rolled it into a pillow, throwing it down. Eumides asked, 'What did the god say? Surely he has released you, Princess.'

He only called me Princess when he was angry or worried.

'He has released me. But he wants us to stop at Platikambos for a week.'

'Why?'

'He didn't say.'

Chryse rolled over and grabbed Eumides' ankle, so that he fell on us with a cry and a flurry of tunic and elbows.

'I am sick of this talk of gods. There are no gods,' he said, half-angrily. 'This is a long enough journey, and now we must interrupt it on a divine whim.'

'He offered to tell me of a home for us,' I said firmly, smothering his protests with my mouth. I kissed him hard, once, twice. 'And if there is a chance that he knows of one, Chryse Diomenes, Asclepius-Priest of Epidavros—which I might point out, is a temple of that same Apollo—then I am staying at Platikambos for the week. It's probably a nice town, anyway.' I kissed him again, and Eumides joined me. Chryse spoke no more blasphemy that night.

I found my despairing Eleni, and told him that I was coming but the God had delayed me. And I heard his voice cursing all Gods wherever they were, and agreed with every word.

Electra

Three days of purification, and they gave Orestes back to us. Each night I had lain beside my husband and stroked and smoothed him, feeling his heat beneath my fingers, and he had evoked the Goddess' gift in me, leaving me sweating and laughing. But the test had not come. I did not know if I could accept him into my body, even Pylades, my dear husband. He seemed unconcerned, saying that there were many ways of making love, none to be preferred above another, and that mating like a beast was not for a son of the royal house of Phocis.

I didn't believe it. The conjunction I had observed with disgust when the Trojan woman and her lovers mated in the goat-herd's hut now seemed explicable, even excusable. I remembered seeing her lie splayed on that dirty floor in a ruin of mantles and tunics, and her cry of delight as the phallus slid inside the willing sheath. Her lover, the golden priest, had mingled his hair with hers as their mouths met, and she had wrapped her legs around his waist.

I was nervous. If I could not accept him I could not conceive.

And the opportunity would not arise, at least for a time. I had to get used to this new feeling, this closeness. All my life I had been alone. Now I was one-half of a person, and the other half was my husband.

Orestes came from the temple, walking, with bowed head. He seemed tranced. The priests hovered behind him.

'It is too grave a matter for us,' they said, making propitiatory gestures. 'He is purified as the Lord Apollo commanded. But the Erinyes still pursue him. You must go to Delphi. There they will be able to talk more directly to the god.'

We left a suitable offering and found a ship. The journey was rough. It was early in the year for sailing. But no pirates attacked us, and we came into Kirrha seasick but in possession of our horses and our valuables.

Orestes had not spoken. He ate when we placed food in his mouth, and drank when a wine-cup was held to his lips. When I looked into his eyes the pupils were almost invisible, the iris wide and colored like honey. Golden-eyed Orestes, my son.

We rode into Delphi, supporting him between us, and the Delphians flocked out to see the Prince of Mycenae, stained with blood-guilt. We had many helpers to lead Orestes up the holy mountain.

There the priests took him from us, and Pylades and I went to his house.

The slaves had done well in the master's absence. Lysane greeted us. Tauros grabbed my hand and shook it to reprove me for leaving him, almost knocking me down with his joy. Graios and Aulos lit a huge fire to announce our return and Abantos, grinning twice in one hour, made lentil soup and honeycakes. The boy Azeus had grown. He was almost as tall as me and greedier than ever. Clonius reported that the house was secure and listed increases in flocks and herds, cloth made, olives gathered and travellers lodged.

One of them had lain with Alceste, and she was pregnant. He had fallen in love with her, and she with him. He wanted to buy her at twice what Pylades had paid, and my Lord agreed, letting the girl take all her clothes and household tools with her, not just the spindle and distaff to which a female slave is entitled. I thought this generous and just, and Alceste was delighted, kissing his feet.

But Pylades went early to his own bed and did not summon me. I slept cold without him. Now that I knew what love meant, I wondered if he had loved Alceste, and whether he would rather have been lying with a willing slave than a frightened wife.

I did not know how to ask him. The next morning we were summoned to the temple and we went, to meet a very old priest who had bad news.

'Apollo cannot prevail against them,' he said. 'Though he has given Orestes a divine gift. The bow of horn may keep them back, and he has a guardian in the black dog. Phoebus has bestowed clear sight on her, so she can warn him. But you must go north, Prince Pylades. North to Olympus, home of the gods. There Orestes will be judged.'

'How can we hope to make that long journey with my brother so weak, so tortured? He will...'

I could not complete the sentence, but Pylades could.

'He will die before we get to the mountains,' he told the old man.

'Phoebus Apollo promises help,' he replied. 'Unlooked for, on the road. You need only begin the journey, and ask at every temple of the Bright One for ways to ward off the hags.'

They brought Orestes. At least he was walking. And as the Furies could not attack him in Apollo's temple, the bruises had faded and he was healthier. But there was no personage behind those blind golden eyes. He seemed empty, like a shining shell when the mussel has been eaten.

Nevertheless, there was nothing else to be done but to attempt the journey. Pylades and I shut up the house again, leaving Clonius and Lysane in charge. Abantos, scowling, made traveller's bread and parched corn for our journey. When I was leaving, he muttered 'This house will be hollow without its Lady.' I was touched, and promised to return with new recipes. Then I told Lysane that I was Pylades' wife, and she scattered pollen over me, praying to Demeter the Mother for blessings on a fertile womb.

'No, I will not bear,' I said, and told her why. She scanned my face, saw something there and kissed me.

'In time,' she said.

We had a litter built; a light one which could be folded if not needed, and took a pack-horse to carry it. While Orestes could ride like a man, we would not affront him by making him travel like a woman. But I suspected that it might come to that, in the end.

We left Delphi in gloom, presaging drizzle, a bad day to begin a long journey. It would take us a month, perhaps, to reach the mountains. As I turned for a last look at the little house where, I now realized, I had been happy, it began to rain.

Through Amphissa to Bralos; Bralos to Lamia, where we lay in the temple to give Orestes some sleep. There the priests shaved his head to buy off the hags with his hair, and we dragged the poor lolling scarecrow another three towns along before they caught up again. Lamia to Domokos, through rich, wet farmland, and round the foot of a mountain to Farsala.

In that city they bathed him in the blood of pigs. Seven pigs yielded enough blood to fill a pool, and they dipped him, witless and slack, seven times under the clotting tide. I could not watch as the birthing, naked head broke through the blood.

I had seen that before.

A week, this time, before the dreams began again. The weather had turned from wet to cold to icy, so that we had woken one morning in our camp and felt our coverings crackle with frost.

All that time he mumbled or whimpered, but he did not talk. I dosed him with the Corinthian potion twice a day, but it did him no good. We had to feed him like a baby and tend him like an untrained child, and my heart was torn. To be killed in battle, yes, that could happen, to die instantly between one breath and the next, ripped out of life; tragic perhaps, but nothing compared to this slow disintegration into death.

I did not believe the God. I did not think we would get him alive to Olympus to be judged.

Cassandra

I had been wrong. Platikambos was not a nice town. In fact, it was neither nice nor a town. It was a collection of badly made dung-and-mud huts in flat clay fields. The inhabitants shared with their landscape the virtues of immobility, inflexibility, and tedium.

Apollo's promise, however, held me there. I was about to quarrel fiercely with Chryse, who was already uneasy, when a fortunate outbreak of a virulent skin disease sent us off in search of suitable herbs and gave rise to a refreshing argument on the relative merits of a marshleaf, milk, and sungold lotion as opposed to a mallow, milk, and Apollo's flower, which was only resolved after we realized, as was often the case, that we were talking about the same herbs.

Then we spent the time compounding and applying it to the sullen villagers and their unpleasant offspring, whom we also treated for lice, fleas, ringworm, blains, cankers, and unhealing sores, largely due to their repugnance for water in any form.

Eumides left us to it and went hunting. He came back at the end of every day with some sort of prey—once a whole string of shining river-fishes—and a bunch of whatever we had asked him to find.

On the last day he came in with four rabbits and a tunic full of mentha and lychnis, saying 'There is someone coming along the road.'

'They'll be sorry,' said Chryse, grinning. He knew that we were leaving tomorrow.

'I think there's something wrong with one of them. He is swaying in the saddle; the others are holding him up. And you'll never guess, friends, who they are.'

We couldn't, having run through a few possibilities—a particularly unlikely one was Menelaus bringing Elene home—so we went out.

The travellers looked muddy and worn. Their horses were plodding, as though they had come a long way, heads down. As they neared us I said, 'Greetings and welcome to Platikambos. The local diseases are not infectious. We are healers. Can we help you? Your comrade looks ill.'

A figure dropped from the saddle into Eumides' arms. He bore him up gently while the others dismounted stiffly, groaning. The woman put back her veil.

It was Electra. A different Electra. Gone was the shrinking maiden. This was a woman. Hard experience and grief had carved lines in her face, but she looked me in the eye and spoke to me like another human, instead of the condescending tone she had adopted with the escaped barbarian slave.

'Lady Cassandra, you remember me, Electra, and this is my husband Pylades. Orestes is tormented by the Erinyes, the revengers. They come every night to him. Apollo says that we have to get him to Olympus to be judged. I don't think he is going to last that long.' There were real tears in those once-stony eyes.

Eumides had already carried the boy into the house and laid him down on his cloak. 'Oh, Orestes, my friend,' he sighed, as I brought a light and we examined him.

The face was skeletal, the eyes hollow, the head covered with a shock of dark hair. I would not have known him from the ten-year-old we had met so long ago. The gaunt hand was still wearing Eumides' ring. The sailor stroked the tormented face, and the eyes opened.

I exclaimed and nearly dropped the lamp. Chryse said sternly, 'What have you been giving him?'

The boy's eyes were blind, the pupils no broader than a pin's point. He was drugged with poppy, that was clear, but it must have been a massive dose. Electra produced a sealed jar. I took off the lid and sniffed, passing it to Diomenes.

'Extract of poppy in wine. Where did you get this?' he demanded.

'The priests at Corinth. They said to give him half a measure twice a day,' faltered Electra. Chryse called upon some Gods in whom he did not believe, including Asclepius.

'They wanted to keep him quiet,' I suggested to my incandescent colleague. 'I would prescribe a cleansing draught. Can we venture black-leaf berry?'

'We must,' he said. 'He'll die if we don't.'

'He might die if we do,' I reminded him. Male healers have a liking for heroic measures. Eumides raised his head and snapped, 'Stop quarrelling and do something!'

'He's poisoned,' said Chryse. 'His breathing is suppressed, there is no flow of urine, is there? When I press on his bladder? Look at the swelling of the abdomen, the yellow tinge to the skin. It's black-leaf berry or he won't last the night.'

'Nothing else for it,' I agreed. 'I saw some growing near the village well and cut down the bush myself, the children might have eaten it. I'll go. Oh, your pardon,' I added to the travellers, who were still standing, amazed. 'Sit down, please, the villagers will bring food and tend your horses, it will relieve them of obligation to pay us for healing them.'

And thank you, Apollo, I thought as I sloshed out into the mud to find a handful of poisonous black-leaf berries. This was the task, this was his bargain. Get Orestes alive to the mountain, and he'll tell someone where we can find a home.

I looked up into the cloudy drizzle and made a private vow that if this didn't work, if it was some trick, I would form a group and sail to where no one had ever heard of Apollo the Bright One, Sun-God, Archer.

We made the infusion together. We always did this when there was some danger that the patient might die, so that we could not blame ourselves or the other physician for failing to save them. Chryse crushed the berries and I heated the water and the honey which was to dilute them.

'Three berries are enough,' I said.

'Four. He has been dosed with a near-fatal draught of black poppy every day for more than three weeks. If we manage to drag him back from Thanatos' clutches I'll…I'll start believing in Gods.'

Electra and Pylades had shed their outer garments in the warmth of the little house. They had washed some of the grime off and were seated either side of Orestes, watching him breathing. Electra was stricken with guilt that she had been administering a toxic potion to someone she loved. I left her to Chryse and smiled at the tall husband, Pylades of Phocis. A handsome man and clearly devoted to the Lady.

'I am Cassandra, healer of Troy and now of Achaea,' I said. 'My companions are Eumides the sailor and Chryse Diomenes, healer of Asclepius, from Epidavros. How came you here, Lord? Were you looking for a healer?'

He smiled, an anxious smile which did not reach his somber brown eyes.

'No, but by the favor of the Gods I have found two healers.'

'If this works, it will take a few hours,' I said, as Chryse dripped the infusion into Orestes' mouth. He swallowed, which argued some chance. When the swallowing muscles are paralyzed, the patient must die. Chryse laid the head gently down on the rolled cloak—I loved to watch the tenderness with which he handled his patients—and said, 'Well, there is nothing to do but watch and wait. Eumides, perhaps you can cook those rabbits. And who have we here?'

Electra

Racer nosed her way into the hut, sniffed suspiciously at Orestes to make sure he was uninjured, then sat down at his feet. The journey had been hard for her. We travelled so long every day that she did not have much time for hunting. Her ribs were showing and her pads were dropping blood on Orestes' cloak.

'A faithful creature,' said Eumides. 'We can have the fish, I'll grill them the way you like them, Cassandra, Chryse.' Then he enticed the bitch away from the garments and gave her a rabbit, which vanished in four bites.

It took her longer to eat the other three, and then she lay down with an almost human sigh to lick her paws. She even allowed Eumides to examine her feet, something which she would not tolerate from either Pylades or me.

Cassandra had changed. She was less careless, more serious, more beautiful than I remembered her.

They were all three beautiful, the golden hair of the woman and her grey eyes and the fullness of her body beneath her tunic, soft and robust. Her movements were quick but a little rough. Those of Diomenes were smoother and gentler, as he dropped a possibly death-dealing potion into Orestes' mouth. Even Eumides, with his curly hair and brown face and glinting earrings, seemed attractive in that house in muddy Platikambos, where we sat and ate grilled fish in the warmth and the light, waiting to see if Orestes, my son, would live.

Chapter Seventeen

'If you let him die,' hissed Hecate to Apollo, 'and rob me of my revenge…'

'Aged Sister, I thought that you wanted him to die,' said Apollo innocently.

'If he dies he will leave my realm. Hades shall have him and Hades is Lord Father Zeus' brother, and could be influenced to release the matricide.'

'What, then, is your will, Queen of Darkness?'

'I want him to live,' she snarled, and all her snakes hissed. Venom dripped on the marble floor.

'Well, I have sent him healers, because so do I,' smiled Apollo.

Electra

The time went past, as time does. The healers told us to sleep, promising to wake us as soon as anything happened. But I could not sleep, and Pylades would not leave me, so we leaned together in a corner of the little house, wrapped in the same cloak.

'Tell me, Lord,' asked Eumides, 'how came the child to this pass? I left him in your care.'

'Not by my will, but the Gods' and his own,' said my Lord soberly. 'This is the retribution for matricide. The children of Agamemnon killed their mother and her lover. As soon as the deed was done, he screamed and ran, crying that the Erinyes were beating him with staves. He has been maddened and running ever since.'

'So he did not claim his kingdom?' asked Eumides, with a pitying glance at the still face. Pylades sighed.

'Shall I tell you what is happening in Mycenae now? The people are leaving. There may have been some attempt to take over power—by a house slave, possibly, which would have been quelled by the guard. But there is no rival household strong enough to take the city for their own, even when there is no child of Agamemnon there. Menelaus is in Sparta, and did not protest when his own daughter, who was betrothed to this unhappy boy, was sent away to Neoptelemus, son of Achilles, in Dodona. He cares nothing and is too far away to hold Mycenae. In the absence of a king there will be a tyrant, some opportunistic farmer, or there will be no one. Unless Argos sends a champion there, the city will be looted by the king's guard and left open to the elements. Even if he lives and comes into his inheritance, Orestes has a lot of work to do before he can live in Mycenae again.'

'That was the prophecy,' I said drearily. 'Only when Mycenae is void and waste will Orestes come home from the north.'

'I never heard that,' said Pylades.

'I did,' said Cassandra. 'That is what Pythia said. On the day that Apollo released me.'

'On the day I met you,' said Pylades softly to me. 'When I took over the care of the last children of Agamemnon.'

'Do you regret it?' asked Cassandra with a smile, as my Lord wrapped the cloak more closely around me.

'No,' he said firmly.

Hours had gone past. I did not know if it was light or dark outside.

'There should have been a response by now,' worried Diomenes. 'Perhaps we should have used five berries.'

'There would have been a response to five berries, but it would not have been the desired one. Have patience,' said Cassandra. Eumides, worn out with worrying, had fallen asleep with his head in her lap, and she stroked his hair automatically, a long practiced movement.

Time passed. Then *Racer* woke and barked. Just once, a commanding, attention-compelling noise. We all jumped.

She was standing over Orestes, licking his face. He was sweating. The healers leapt to their feet.

'Yes,' said Diomenes with satisfaction, moving the body to catch a flow of fluids in a basin. 'Good, Orestes, good. You are coming out of this black trance. Now, don't fail me. Cassandra, call him.'

'Come, boy, come back to the world,' she said in a clear voice, calculated to pierce a fog. 'We are all here, your sister and your friends. Don't you slip away now. Electra, speak to him. Lady Gaia, Mistress of Animals, evoe,' she called, holding up her arms. 'I invoke you, lady of healing and of warmth, spring-woman of the flowery breast. It is Cassandra, daughter of Priam, calls you. Bring him back to us, Lady, out of the dark.'

I did not see anything, but the air of the little house seemed to sparkle, or was it that my eyes were filling with tears. Pylades shouted 'Orestes!' and I called, 'My son, my son, Orestes, return.'

I felt the startled glance I received from Eumides. Everyone else was too busy to notice. But then the sailor spoke tenderly to the boy. 'Hear me, little brother, do you remember playing "one, two, three" with me on the steps of Poseidon's temple in Corinth? It is Eumides who speaks, your old friend.'

'We're losing him,' said Diomenes quickly. 'Stand him up, move his limbs, call him.'

'Orestes!' I wailed as Eumides and Diomenes dragged the limp body to its feet, and Cassandra slapped him across the face.

Once, twice. The smack of palm on flesh was shocking. Orestes murmured, then put up an arm to protect himself, and the next blow fell on his elbow.

'Good, good, fight for your life, boy!' I heard her say, and the bearers shook Orestes, until he moved on his own to maintain his balance. 'Have courage, son of Agamemnon,' Cassandra urged, rubbing both hands over his cheeks, then his neck and chest. 'We are here and we will help you but you must have the courage.'

Naked, his body was slack, hanging between his physicians, but gradually it seemed to be filling with life. I saw tendons flex in thigh and calf as he took a step, resting his weight first on one foot, then the other. His chest rose and fell, his mouth opened, then his eyes.

No longer dilated, they were Orestes' eyes again. He was almost standing on his own and he wailed, 'What is happening? I thought I was safe,' he said, and Cassandra slapped him again, very lightly.

'You're alive, Orestes, and life is a struggle. Don't give up. You have supporters. The Mother Gaia herself came to help you and that is uncommon. Now we will walk. Round and round this nice little hut.'

'Eumides?' he asked, and the sailor kissed him heartily and exclaimed, 'Now, little brother, we will parade. You can lean on me. We've fished you up out of deep waters and you're a little confused, but that will pass.'

'We were sitting on the temple wall, and then we went to Laodamos' house and we must have drunk too much. Electra will be angry with me,' he said fuzzily, then focused on me and said, 'I only drank one cup, sister.'

'Only one cup is one cup too much,' I said crossly, which is what I had said five years ago when this happened. They lurched around the house, taking small steps, and all the time Orestes' hold on life became firmer. 'You bad boy, out drinking with disreputable sailors,' I continued.

'No, that was years ago,' he replied, puzzled. 'I am grown now. Where am I? Pylades?'

'You are on the road to Olympus, cousin. You have been ill. Don't think about it, keep moving.'

Orestes was standing without support, shaking his head, where the hair had grown out into loose curls which fell into his eyes.

'I have been…ill?' he asked, staggering back under *Racer's* joy. He put a hand on her collar and she tugged at his wrist, pulling him, making him take another step and then another.

I don't know how we found ourselves dancing.

Cassandra and Eumides, Orestes and Diomenes, then somehow Pylades and me. We danced the Aegean courting dance, three steps and a dipping kick, round and round the hut to the sound of laughter and *Racer* barking wildly as she tried to join in.

When we collapsed, perspiring, to the floor, Orestes' eyes were clear.

'Tomorrow you will be purged,' said Cassandra, 'and the next day you will be well.'

'No,' he said sadly. 'They will come again, the Erinyes. In my dreams I saw them and there is no escape.'

'We might be able to do something about them,' Cassandra observed. 'I perceive that you have a horn bow.'

'The God gave it to him,' I said, 'but he has been too weak to use it and we could not see them to aim at them.'

'Next time, give the bow to me,' she ordered, casting a sidelong glance at the Asclepid. 'Well, Lord Physician, what is your opinion of the patient? Will he live?'

'He will,' he replied, cocking an eyebrow.

'Then you had better start believing in Gods, Chryse,' she stated, and the three of them laughed.

Orestes endured his purge in relatively good spirits and the next day we rode for Olympus, following the track of the Ennipeas River. For a long way it flows through flat land, but always the mountains occupy the distance. It curls lazily, a slow water heavy with silt, and it was a pleasant journey.

Eight days after his emergence from the trance, they came back.

We were sleeping in a hut in some muddy village when I heard the cry. Pylades woke.

Orestes was lying outside, wrapped in his mantle. He was struggling and calling for mercy.

Cassandra emerged from a tangle of blankets and limbs, naked, and joined the black bitch in defense of Orestes. She was marble and silver in the moonlight and her hair flowed around her in a cloud. She looked like Artemis again, the dog at her side, the fallen boy between her feet.

'Bird bolts for crones,' she taunted. 'Leave him be, Ladies of Guilt and Vengeance. My heart's longing is promised for my defense of this boy. For that I shall risk much. Begone, or I'll spit you, snakes and all.' She looked down on my son with Goddess' eyes. 'You, Orestes, have courage. It is no use asking the Erinyes for mercy. They have never heard of it. Defy them, craven! You are Apollo's child.' She made a sweeping gesture with the bow, as though sighting an enemy.

'Get back,' she said, to me and Pylades. 'Lady Gaia, have I not been faithful? I have healed the hurts and rents, mended the bones and hearts of Earth's children. Turn this aspect from me, Hecate. Lady, call of your dogs or I will wound them if I can. The days of blood vengeance are over. The Argives worship Zeus the father. You cannot recall the old days of Chaos and Night.'

She lifted the bow and shot. I heard the arrow humming, and did I really hear a scream, more of anger than hurt?

Racer dropped to her snarling crouch again. Cassandra reached between her thighs and brought forth fingers red with blood.

'Blood you want, hags, blood you have. I mark him with sacrifice blood, holy blood of the Maiden.' She stooped and drew a sign on Orestes' chest.

Then the night became peaceful. *Racer* rolled over and scratched at an itchy ear. Godhead left Cassandra abruptly. She was gathered into the arms of her lovers, who wrapped her in a cloak and held her close as she shuddered, her hair veiling her face.

Orestes sat up and said in a tone of complete astonishment, 'They're gone!'

'Not forever,' said Cassandra through chattering teeth. 'As long as my sacrifice blood lasts we can hold them off. They are scarcely more reasoning than animals, elemental things of darkness. As long as there is blood they will be assuaged. They didn't like that bow, either. Where did the arrow go?'

But although we searched the next day, we could not find it.

The sacrifice blood lasted five days. On that night, alone in another small hut, I turned to Pylades beside me and said, 'Husband, lie with me.'

He knew what I was thinking and said, 'There will be no blood, Electra.'

'I fear for my brother, my son.'

His voice was kind. 'I will not lie with you until you want me, Electra. Not for any other reason.'

'I want you,' I said. My voice quavered. I was afraid.

Very gently, our hands began the familiar dance, but this time, as the itch grew to a fire, I felt something slide inside me, and it felt good—more than good, suitable. I thought of Aegisthus and dreaded the weight on my body, cutting off my breath, but my husband was lying beside me, pressing close. I had been expecting the clamp of the muscles, resisting the invader, but I felt instead the same muscles close around the phallus and suck, dragging it deeper, embracing, pulling.

He gasped. The climax bloomed and in its heat—more diverse than before, a glow and not a coal of fire—I felt the phallus inside me pulse, and I floated away.

It seemed to be a long time before I came back to my body.

That was what Cassandra the Trojan woman had felt, in the goatherd's hut, her lover in her arms. In that moment of transcendent completion, I believe that I loved her.

Pylades said shakily, 'Electra,' and I said, 'Husband.'

'It was not like that,' he said. 'Not with any woman before.'

'It was not like that,' I replied, 'With…' I could not complete the sentence. I was as weak as though I had climbed a mountain, and I fell asleep in my Lord's arms.

The Furies came back that night, but Orestes defied them and they retreated. Cassandra could see them and laughed as she described their bowed black shoulders as they crowded away from the bow, like old hens in the rain.

Abusing them did not work for long. The next night Orestes fought, and woke bruised and battered. But there was a light in his eyes, and from the sea we were riding back into the mountains. The ground was rising every day, and the villages were scarcer and scarcer, worshipping gods I had never heard of—Dione, wife of Zeus, for instance, when everyone knows that the Divine Consort is Hera.

The highest point is Olympus, which does not rise to a point but a cirque, the Areopagus, the Court of the Gods.

We rode along the gorge of the Ennipeas River, whose waters are cold enough to stop the heart. I was anxious, now that we had come to the end. I was afraid that Orestes would be found guilty and would die, in this far country beyond many rivers. My companions were excited and chattering, and I loathed all of them.

There was a flush of summer green in the grass. Windflowers trembled in the light breeze. The blood of Adonis spotted the slopes. We stopped under the bright fronds of the upland pines and I saw my son's eyes widen as he gazed at the height.

'So high,' he sighed wearily. We had wrapped him in a goat-skin cloak, bought from a peasant. It still smelled strongly of its original inhabitant, but it was warm and it would be freezing on those snowy peaks. Now he drew the ill-tanned skin about his bruised shoulders as if he was chilled, although the morning was bright and warm. The sun, this high, was strong enough to burn unprotected skin.

The dim, resinous shade enjoined silence, but Cassandra spoke cheerfully.

'We do not need to climb,' she said. 'Delphian Apollo wanted Orestes here for judgment, and here he is. Let's find a place to camp out of this cold shadow, and wait. There are gods here. I can feel them.'

'But not see them,' said Diomenes skeptically. It was an old argument but they never got tired of it. Everyone else had.

'Not yet, Chryse dear, but soon,' she returned briskly.

Only gods could scale that mountain. The two monoliths which guarded the approach were high, bleak and bare. Even a mountain goat might fear to trust its nimble hooves to those pathless, vertical hills. For Orestes it was patently impossible. Pylades slung the bundles down and unloaded the horses, and I began to gather wood for a fire. The pine branches catch easily and burn hot but very quickly, falling into ash almost immediately, and I looked for a fallen beech or oak which we could cut into logs with the axe.

Pale grey doves called their sleepy note from the pine trees, '*Coo, coo*,' as we began to dig and wrench up the roots of a dead tree out of the ground and lay them in the sun to dry.

Every noise seemed to echo and wound the silence. Against the sound of running water—you can always hear running water in Thrace—every chop and thud seemed loud enough to birth an avalanche. It was an uneasy place for humans, meant only for Gods and goats. Nevertheless we needed a fire and Orestes was cold, so we persisted, against a growing feeling of sacrilege.

What was a little more sacrilege to Electra, cursed daughter of the doomed House of Atreus; Orestes, the matricide; Cassandra, plaything of Apollo; and Diomenes, Pylades and Eumides, our willing companions?

The sun soared into blue noon. Even at this most fearless time we were subdued. Cassandra and Diomenes Chryse stopped quarrelling comfortably about the factual existence of Gods. Eumides did not tell us he was a simple Trojan fisherman who knew nothing of these Attic mysteries. Pylades did not mention that he was aging by the day and not educated for hard labor. We were quiet, awed by the mountain, which did not loom but occupied the sky, higher than sigh, colder than the ice before the beginning of the world. We felt fragile, unimportant, mortal, and hoped only to be overlooked by the powers that dwelt on high.

We ate goat cheese and stale bread sparingly, for we were not hungry. The resinated wine we had bought in some village smelled sickening, and when Cassandra leaned back to embrace Eumides she sniffed and drew away from him.

'I know I haven't had a chance to wash lately, but you are perfumed with travel yourself, Princess,' he said, mildly offended.

'It isn't that,' she answered, kissing him. 'You smell human. This is not a place for humans.'

'Yet if we must stay here, as you say we must, as Apollo orders,' commented Diomenes, 'then we may as well be comfortable. There is a pool in the river, just down there, where we can wash and thus smell less offensively human.'

'No,' said Cassandra. 'If the gods come I want to be clothed and alert.'

'Very well,' he said, and walked a little way up the gorge toward a small shrine. It was just a pile of Olympus rocks, built into a rough pyramid. A waymarker, perhaps. Someone had fashioned certain stones into rough images of the gods. Father Zeus, Mother Hera, Earth-Mother Demeter. There was Hermes, the messenger with winged heels; Pluton, the wealthy God of the Dead; Ares, the God of War; Artemis, the hunter; Athena the Lady, Pan the Ageless, Lord of Forests; and Aphrodite, the Stranger, with many breasts. They were not finely carved as the masters at Mycenae would have made them, but they were compelling.

'This place is sacred to all the gods,' I remarked. 'No one God can be called upon to aid Orestes.'

'Indeed,' Diomenes said politely. I was nettled by his tone.

'How can you say you don't believe when you've seen them? You've tended the bruises on Orestes; you've seen how the clubs of the Erinyes have wounded him.'

'The mind can make marks,' he said condescendingly. 'Tell a suppliant under Hypnos' influence that a dry stick is a brand and you can blister his flesh. Thus it is with Orestes. He believes that the Furies are attacking him, and so they are. His guilt and fear has created the monsters which beat and injure him, as he feels he deserves to be punished. The same for the place, Lady. This mountain is feared by all men. Even I know that, though I do not believe in gods. That feeling is communicating itself to us, and so we feel afraid. That is men's minds, Lady, not the actions of gods.'

I was so worried that I could not quarrel with him. I took up a stone and laid it on the mound, and he did likewise.

'If you don't believe, why add a stone to the pile?' I demanded.

'Pure superstition,' he said indulgently.

I reminded myself that this supercilious Asclepid had tended Orestes in the most devoted fashion, and bit my tongue. Orestes might need him again. He irritated me more than I can say, so smooth and beautiful, so sure of himself, with two lovers and no history of loss or pain.

Now I knew about love, I knew how much had been stolen from me. I might have ten years with my husband, perhaps less. I could have had twenty if Aegisthus and my mother had not stolen my time. I might have been Pylades' lover when I was clean and maiden, and learned the secrets of the flesh a long time ago. I might have had his children, tall sons and demure daughters, all with the dark hair and eyes of my beloved Pylades. I felt robbed.

And this Diomenes, this Chryse, all golden and beautiful, had two lovers and had been loved and indulged all his life. The sun and rain and mud of our journey had not added a line to his smooth face, or disarrayed his golden hair. It was as fine as floss, held back by a plaited leather band.

I reminded myself firmly that he was wearing that band because he had sold a piece of his silver fillet to buy skin cloaks for us, and blushed.

We walked back to camp in silence.

We sat all day by the banks of the Ennipeas River. We sang no songs and told no stories. We listened to the endless silence, the rush of waters, the calling of the doves, and eventually this formed a pattern which occupied all our thoughts, until it became an end in itself.

We had been mute for a long time. I was leaning against a tree, Cassandra was seated a little apart, her head cocked as if she were listening. Diomenes and Eumides had fallen asleep, Diomenes' head on Eumides' chest, wrapped in their mantle. I could see the dark and golden hair mingling against the dun pine needles of their bed. Orestes was lying on the river bank under his goatskin cloak. Pylades was tending the fire, safely out of the shadow of the combustible trees. The flames were almost invisible in the westering sun.

Then the mountain vanished.

It had been there all day, white and imminent, tall as the sky, the cloven peak like a hoof enclosing the abode of the gods. In a moment it was gone and in its place was a burning cauldron of white flame, too cold to look at. My eyes filled with tears and dazzled, I covered them, blinded.

When I could see again, wiping my eyes with my travelling chiton, Eumides and Diomenes were still asleep, Cassandra was on her feet, staring, Pylades was tending the fire and Orestes was gone.

Without a sound, without a flash. The pressed grass showed where he had been lying. But he was gone.

Then I wept indeed, and not even Pylades could comfort me.

'Hermes carried him, I saw it, cradled in his arms like a baby. He's all right, Electra,' Cassandra chided me. 'This is why we made this journey. Orestes has gone to be judged, and all we can do is pray and wait.'

'We should search for him,' urged Diomenes, waking up and grasping the situation instantly. He was unconvinced by Cassandra's explanation. 'He might have run away while you were blinded.'

'Without a sound?' asked the Princess scornfully. 'Just shifting your weight on these pine needles sounds like rats in a haystack. I didn't hear anything, and I saw the gods, don't you speak Achaean?'

'I speak excellent Achaean,' he returned. 'The difficulty is not in the language but in belief. What if Orestes is lost in the forest, delirious, and we don't look for him because you see gods, and he freezes to death?'

Cassandra scowled at him. He was in earnest, so we searched and called. Voices carry a long way in the mountains, but we did not find him.

Chapter Eighteen

Odysseus

Out of cold into warmth. Out of bitter salt into sweet air. Calypso, the nymph, rescued me from deep water and loved me. Loved me when she saw me, without me saying a word, without a smile, for my lips were too cracked for kissing. My body yearned for sleep, even for death, as long as it was a dry death.

I had lost all that I had, comrades, crew, booty, time. My journey had eaten my years, the children I might have sired, the nights I might have slept and heard nothing but the night birds crying and Penelope breathing in her sleep.

There was nothing to please her in once-elegant Odysseus; I was flotsam, barely alive, yet she treasured me like gold netted out of Ocean.

She was the innocent net for Odysseus' feet, Poseidon's last and cruellest trap.

I knew that the Invaders, the Dorians, were on Ithaca besieging my kingdom, and I had to go home.

◇◇◇

'My Lord Father Zeus,' said Apollo, sweeping away the goatskin cloak. 'Here is the matricide, Orestes, son of Agamemnon, here to be judged. I have purified him of blood guilt. His hands are clean.'

'Who appears on his behalf?' asked Zeus, mounting the steps to his throne and surveying the assembled gods.

'I,' said Apollo, and the Father shook his majestic head.

'Not you, my son. You are a mover in these deeds.'

Orestes blinked and shivered. Gradually he was warming from his flight through the icy air, and he meant to make a fight for his life. But the Gods were too bright to look at, and all the faces he could see were grave and blank, like statues.

'My Lord Poseidon?' asked Zeus. The shell-crowned one made a negative gesture. 'You, Hera?' he asked, and the shining woman said, 'He is a matricide. I will not speak for him.'

'Orestes, will you choose an advocate?'

Orestes, bemused, sighted a warrior maiden, tall Athene Parthenos, and saw that of all the gods she was looking at him. He did not dare to point, but bowed to her.

'Lady,' he whispered.

'Athene, dearest daughter, will you speak for this man?'

'I will,' she said.

The Gods murmured. Putting aside the shield, Athene came to stand by Orestes' side, laying one hand on his shoulder.

'Who speaks against him?' rumbled Zeus.

'I,' said Hecate, striding forward with the Erinyes hissing and snapping at her heels.

'Orestes, are you innocent of the crime of murder?' asked Zeus.

'No,' said Orestes. 'I killed Clytemnestra, Queen of Mycenae, and her lover Aegisthus.'

The gods shifted in their places. The plea of innocence went by ritual in all other cases which they had tried. Athene appeared unmoved. Hecate grinned.

'Then he is mine,' she said. 'If he killed her, there is no case.'

'Wait,' said Zeus. 'There are two sides to this question. We will hear both. Erinyes, what you to say?'

'We are revengers of blood,' said Tisiphone. 'Hatched to follow the matricide, instructed to harry him to suicide and despair.'

'He has shed blood,' said Alecko.

'Clytemnestra lies dead by his hand,' said Megaera.

'He is our meat,' they chorused hungrily.

They scrabbled toward him, and Orestes knelt and touched Athene's garment, burning his fingers. She lowered the golden spear and they retreated, howling. Their dog's voices echoed through Olympus until Hecate herself hushed them with a gesture.

'The case is made out,' said Zeus, looking at his favorite daughter. Born not of woman but sprung full-armed from his own head, she was the divine maiden, sharing no blood with humans.

'There is Law,' she said.

Silence fell. The gods settled down to listen to the exposition.

'When men were savages and knew no laws, Lord,' she addressed Zeus confidently, 'they needed such primitive devices as these to restrain their blood-lust and regulate their desires. When the Titans ruled, Zeus Father, there was no restraint on the evil lusts of men. No man feared the Gods or the censure of his fellow men. In brutish settlements, armed with stone weapons, men slaughtered each other and stole each other's wives. Women slew husbands who had violated them. Men murdered mothers and coupled with their daughters, with no fear of Divine Law.'

'It was an innocent world,' muttered Pan Ageless. 'Before the Son of Cronos came.'

Athene ignored him. 'Then, Lord, revengers were needed. Many a man, lying awake with thoughts of murder in his heart, was constrained from acting for fear of the snake-haired ones.'

'Revenge,' hissed the Furies, and the court echoed to the jangle of iron bells.

'But the world needs them no longer. You, Lord, have imposed law upon men. No man needs now to make his own decision about whether his action is right or wrong. All men know that murder is wrong. All men know that to transgress divine law is to merit punishment, both on Earth and beneath it in the realms of your brother Hades. Is this not so, Zeus, Father of All?'

'It is so.' The gold-wreathed head inclined in agreement.

'Then the Erinyes are not needed anymore, Lord. They are remnants of an earlier time, archaic and senseless.'

'Well, daughter, that is a good case. Now we must consider particulars. What do you urge on behalf of your suppliant, Orestes?'

'*Stand up,*' *she ordered him, and Orestes stood. '*Do not be afraid,*'* *she said, and smiled. The warmth of the divine regard nerved and strengthened him. '*Take off your tunic,*' *she told him, and then turned the naked man by the shoulder to face her.*

'*If he should be punished, Lord, he has borne punishment. Look at him.*'

*She exhibited the blackened torso to the assembled gods. The marks of the studded batons were clear. She turned Orestes to face the gods and said, '*Tell us what you remember of your mother Clytemnestra.*'*

'*She sang songs to me, Lady, Lords,*' *he faltered. '*She tended me and fed me, she nursed me in her arms and her breast was soft as a pillow for my head. She loved me and waked for me and she was beautiful beyond measure. But she murdered my father, and I killed her. Apollo was with me, Lady. He ordered it.*'*

'*And you obey the gods?*' *she asked.*

'*Lady, of course.*'

'*My Lord Apollo wished for an end to the story of the House of Atreus,*' *said Athene, her golden face as cool and set as bronze. '*He set on this little scion of that cursed house, and Orestes did as Apollo wished. All mortals will do as the gods wish. I am defending Orestes because my Lord Apollo interfered in the matter. Agamemnon was my man in the battle of Troy, but I did not order this vengeance. The Sun-Bright wants the tale of the House of Atreus concluded, as though he could order a storyteller to roll up the scroll. These are men, and my concern is with justice. Urged on by Apollo and his much-abused sister, Electra, and by his own sense of horror at her deeds, Orestes murdered his mother.*' *The Furies surged forward, and only the golden spear kept them at bay. '*I say that he has been punished, and should be freed. The Erinyes belong to an earlier time, before my Lord Zeus ruled mortals and imposed the law.*'*

Zeus smiled at his daughter.

'*Well, Athene Parthenos, you have made a case for the removal of the Furies, and the acquittal of Orestes. But the Erinyes are here. What would you have me do with them?*'

'Lord Zeus, this argument strikes at the roots of all propriety,' protested Hecate.

'Lord Zeus, if we have no justice here and are prevented from punishing this evildoer...' hissed Tisiphone.

'...we shall loose our venom on the Earth,' said Megaera.

'Demeter's mourning for her daughter, Persephone, will be nothing to the winter we shall bring,' said Alecko.

'Pestilence and ruin,' hissed Megaera.

'Waste and disease. Nothing shall grow again,' spat Tisiphone.

'Your little mortals will wither, starve, die,' Alecko screamed.

'Not a blade of grass shall penetrate the barren ground.'

'They will eat their goats, then their seed grain, then their children. They will curse all the gods.'

'Law or no law.'

'And the race of men shall vanish from the Earth. Their pitiful little palaces will crumble and fall.'

'And the unjust gods will have no men to play their games,' concluded Alecko.

'They call you Erinyes,' said Athene, thinking deeply. She strode a pace forward, putting Orestes behind her. 'I would have you change your names.'

'Keep back, daughter of Zeus. Your brightness offends our darkness,' they muttered.

'You see that the law has other enforcers. My Lord Zeus makes the laws, and he sees that it is kept. You are hated, women of darkness. Would you not rather be loved?'

The air crackled with dark lightnings as the Furies laughed.

'You are aspects of Demeter, Mother of All. Your nature can be changed. Instead of hunting frail mortals across the Earth, would you not rather be hearth-guardians, women of the home and the harvest? Would you not rather follow the Thesmorphoria home the fruits, preside over the hay-carts lurching home across the rich furrows? Would you rather inhabit the peaks and the barren salt-flats, or the warm meadows where lambs bleat in autumn; snuff not despair and fear-sweat but the scent of baking bread and drying hay? Your altars would be well tended, harvest-mothers, fertile, not *sterile, warm, not cold. Men would sacrifice to you as the guardians of the home, gentle in repose, but as dangerous when attacked as a mother wolf in defense of her cubs. I offer you rest and a new task, Erinyes. They will call you the Eumenides, the Kindly Ones, and they will still fear you, as men fear desperately to lose what men desire. A home, children, peace.'*

The Erinyes wavered, sliding forward to attack, then retreating, confused. Hecate smiled grimly. 'You offer to bribe my hounds with a bowl of broth and a nice comfortable collar and chain?'

'Blood,' the Furies howled.

'You shall have blood,' said Athene Grey-Eyed. 'If you try to poison the Earth, envenomed hags, then I and my sister Artemis will hunt you, I and my brother Apollo will burn you. Down we will drive you, hags, down and deeper down, until Hades' kingdom is above your heads. To the deepest pit, monsters, will you go and there I will seal you until the end of time. Never to fly again, on winged or wingless flight. All the blood which is spilled on Earth, every drop, will drain into that pool, and there you will glut your cavernous appetites until you die, drowned in murder.'

There was silence. Orestes dared to peer out from behind the Goddess, to see the Erinyes who had tormented him so long look at each other and at the Black Mother, uncertain.

'You have punished me,' he said to them. 'I suffered and learned. I will never kill thoughtlessly again; never take a life except in defense. You want my blood. Take it.'

With his bronze knife, he stabbed his left palm, holding out his hand until it filled with blood. Into this the Erinyes, approaching warily, dipped their snakes' tongues, sipping with relish as though they were tasting honeyed wine.

'Release me,' he said gently. 'Be satisfied with my pain.'

There was a pause. The divine sun of Olympus poured down gold on the weary face and the scarred shoulders of the matricide.

'I release you,' said Tisiphone.

'I release you,' said Megaera.

'I do not release you,' said Alecko.

Athene raised the spear to strike, but Hecate fended her off with her staff.

'You, speak,' she said roughly. 'The others have forgiven him, what of you? Will you be destroyed?'

'I do not believe him,' said Alecko. 'Not wholly. My sisters will change their nature, guard the hearths and homes of men. But this Orestes I will follow—only him, perhaps—and I will do no harm to the Earth which is our Mother's breast. When he is dead—and I will not hound him to it, Mistress—then I, too, will leave hatred and revenge and lie down with my sisters. I will not let him forget, but I will not poison his life.'

'Just,' said Zeus the Father, striking the marble floor with his golden staff. 'Harmony is achieved. Orestes, do you accept the verdict?'

'Lord,' said Orestes. 'I accept. Zeus Father, Lord of Lightnings, I ask a favor.'

'Speak,' said Zeus, a little amused.

'I would establish the worship of the grey-eyed one, Athene, Mistress of Justice, in Mycenae when I come there.'

'Granted.'

'And, Lord Father, another word?' he said with great daring.

'Mortal?'

'The Lord Apollo made a promise to Cassandra, daughter of Priam, that he would tell her her heart's desire if she brought me alive to be judged. She has been valiant, Lord, and faithful. I would have died without her. I would not have that promise forgotten.'

'I will tell not her but another,' said Apollo, not pleased at being reminded, but under his father's eye. 'This I promised.'

A bell sounded. As Orestes was carried away in the arms of a silver man with winged heels, he saw two of the Furies melting and changing. The dog's teeth retreated into their jaws, the snakes changed into hair, the black rags were transformed into flowery garments, spotted with gold and purple. But the eyes were the same; ancient, alert, holding the promise of retribution.

The Erinyes were Eumenides, but were still not to be offended.

Cassandra

It was almost dark when I sighted a blur of flesh in the dusk and saw a naked man come walking along the path. He was straight and tall, and I thought he was a god, until he came closer and I saw the bruised body, the curly dark hair.

'Orestes!' cried Electra, and ran toward him. He embraced her and she led him into our camp, where Pylades wrapped him in a cloak and sat him down beside the fire.

'Orestes, how fared you?' he asked anxiously, though we could all see the difference. The bowed head was held aloft, the distracted eyes were clear of doubt, and his only wound appeared to be a deep puncture in the palm of his hand and two blistered fingers.

Chryse anointed and bound the injuries and Orestes did not even seem to feel the bite of the stonecrop ointment (which he will insist on using on broken skin). We heated some soup and he drank it, still glowing with that unearthly radiance, still scented with the honey and woodbine of the gods.

'Orestes, what happened?' Eumides asked, unable to be patient any longer.

All the boy said was, 'I have been acquitted and set free. And Apollo will keep his promise to you, Cassandra.'

Then he fell asleep where he sat, and we heard no more from Orestes that night, though we lay all huddled together because of the cold.

Orestes, the next morning, was dazed, bruised, and freed by the Gods.

After breakfast—we were getting very tired of peasant pottage—we realized that our next destination lay along the same road.

Epirus was ruled by Neoptelemus, son of Achilles, who had married Orestes' betrothed, Hermione, and who held Andromache and my twin, Eleni, as slaves. We journeyed together to free them.

The journey to Dodona was difficult. The misery of Eleni was eating at my courage, and I found it hard to sleep. The clans of wild men in the hills avoided us, and we did not molest them. But we came through their muddy villages sometimes, once interrupting a drive of sacred swine, once staying to celebrate a wedding. The bride, we found, was required to lie with every man in the village—there were ten of them—and she was young and frightened. In order to avoid joining in this mass rape, Chryse explained that he was dedicated to a different god, Pylades feigned illness, and even Eumides, a little green, swore devotion to a virgin deity and said no word about lustful hill-women for three days after.

The customs of the Epirotes are barbarous. We met Selli, priests of Dodona, occasionally, and once one of the Nomads, the original inhabitants. A man in a white loincloth walked unhurriedly to our fire one night, sat down as if he had been expected, and held out a wooden cup for wine.

Eumides filled the cup. We stared at the visitor. He smiled sweetly, showing stubs of teeth. He was shaven, no hair or beard or even eyebrows. His hands, wrists and mouth were stained purple, not, as we found later, with wine, but with cherry-juice. He sat smiling gummily, either unable to speak or bound by some oath to be mute, and we slept uneasily around the fire in his company.

The next day he accepted some bread, which he spread with a strong smelling fruit paste. When he had eaten, he broke an oak-twig, peeled off the bark, and proceeded to deliver what might have been a prophecy, except that even Chryse, who has the best ear for language, could only pick out one word in ten. As he spoke he twisted the bark around his stained fingers.

'He says something about blue and green, the name Molossos, an autumn child, and two golden twins,' Chryse translated.

Without a farewell, the Nomad washed his wooden cup in the stream, smiled at us again, and walked away, straight into the pathless hills.

We had other visitors less pleasant.

One night, near Trikka, we heard *Racer* barking and a neighing plunge from *Nefos*, always a touchy horse. When we made a light, we found a horse thief with a hoof mark on his chest trying to strangle *Racer*, who was making a spirited attempt to tear out his arm by the roots.

We called off the bitch and allowed the thief to leave, which he did in some haste. The next man who tried to steal the horses heard the combined snap of canine and equine teeth and decided against it, leaving a rather good tether behind him, as well as a few rags which Racer had torn out of his tunic.

Trikka, when we came to it, was a pleasant, well-built, well-planned place, with a temple of Asclepius with golden pillars. Chryse, who slept the night there, had some dream which he would not share, saying that it was merely his own mind attempting to frighten him. By the look of his pale face and the fervor with which he burrowed into our bed, his mind had scared him most efficiently.

Epirus was poor and dirty and primitive. Not exotic, like Libya, where men are black-skinned and live in grass palaces. The women were secluded, hungry, and ill-treated, the men sullen, overworked and aged. The soil was occasionally rich but mostly poor and the rain did not improve the roads. We stayed in one village, forsaken by all known Gods, for three nights as we all suffered through a violent flux, brought on, I was convinced, by bad meat. The villagers were not familiar with the use of herbs, and Chryse dragged himself out to pick what we needed. I compounded it as he collapsed, and we recovered as fast as we could. There was no incentive to stay in that mud hut with the lice.

On another comfortless night we woke to the frenzied baying of the hound and found ourselves surrounded by huge men—Cyclopes, wandering masons, and builders. We could not speak to them, for no one knows their language. They considered us with flat, animal eyes. They were heavily armed and they looked hungry.

I knew that my bow was out of reach. In any case, they might just pluck out the feathered dart and laugh. The moment poised on a knife's edge. Orestes gathered *Racer* and held her mouth in case she attacked them and was killed.

Then Chryse stood up very slowly, untying the thong around his neck. Moving cautiously, he held it up to the Cyclop. The massive hand took the pendant gently and it was passed from hand to hand around the circle.

Then they returned it without a word and vanished. For such bulk they moved as quietly as Egyptian cats.

'An old favor,' was all Chryse would say when we begged for an explanation. But we did not sleep well in Epirus.

We were all exhausted before we finally left the mountains and came down into the cleft which houses the Oracle.

Dodona is a polis, a city. Here the King of the Epirotes—as far as that loose collection of squabbling clans can be said to acknowledge a king—has his palace. It is stone-built for the most part, fairly well ordered and old—older than Corinth, the Epirotes say.

The Oracle is of Zeus, though they call him Naios Phregonaios, Zeus of the Oak Tree, and his consort is Naia, whom the Argives call Hera. A priest who, like all the Dodona Selli, made a religion of never washing holy soil from his feet, told us that a sacred dove flew from Olympus to Dodona and perched in an oak, speaking with the voice of men, and demanded that an Oracle be established there. The Thesproti, the sacred clan, became sacred by obeying the dove and building the first shrine, a crumbling clay building now enclosed in the new stone temple. Their Zeus lives in the ground, which made me wonder if they were actually talking about the same God who rules the Argive skies and strikes mortals with thunderbolts.

However, religions are religions and there is no reasoning with them. If they wanted to worship a subterranean Zeus whose sacred animals are pigs, doves and the newborn, all of them attributes of the Great Mother, Gaia, in civilised places like Troy, then it was not for me to argue. We purchased a tripod, made an offering of doves, and asked the Sellos if there were words for us out of the earth.

He shook his head. I had not expected Apollo to keep his promise.

We had business in the palace. Orestes had come to reclaim or to purchase Hermione, daughter of Menelaus, and we rode into the courtyard of Neoptelemus' palace in a light sleet, cold and uncomfortable. Electra, Pylades and Orestes, attended by *Racer*, went into the palace. We went to the adjacent temple of Apollo.

I was dismounting, wringing out my hair in the veranda of the temple, when I felt a glowing shock, and my brother Eleni was in my arms.

'Sister, oh, sister,' he held me close, my beloved Eleni, older, of course, tired, worn out by his hopeless love for Andromache, widow of Hector.

'Eleni, my love.' I held him to my breast. I had missed him almost past bearing, though the twin-thread that bound us together meant that he had known where I was for the last few months. He was never entirely gone from my mind and heart. We had once been so close that our thoughts had flowed, mind to mind. Now I could feel what he was feeling, but not what he was thinking.

'You, here! I have felt you, twin, in pain, lost, enslaved—they told me you were dead, but I knew you were alive. I've been calling, calling for you. You must help me, dearest sister, or I will die. By all the gods,' he added, amazed, catching sight of my companions. 'They are still with you! The healer and the sailor.'

'They are still with me and we have journeyed too long.' I said, as my lovers came wearily to greet my brother.

'I feel—I feel that you will stop soon,' he said, a worried line creasing his brow. 'Come in, come inside, it's cold, I'm sorry,' he called to Eumides and Diomenes. 'I should have tended you before, beloved strangers.' He used the term for previously unmet relatives, and they were certainly all the family I had.

Slaves took the horses and Eleni drew us into a huge, warm kitchen, then into a series of guest-rooms. They were of unfigured stone, but they had a drain for bathwater and we were miserably chilled. It had rained, I swear, all the way from Olympus, and the only one of us not heartily sick of ourselves, each other and the world was Orestes, who had passed most of the previous journey in a drugged trance.

'You are very elegant, brother,' I said. I did not want to let go of him, even for a moment, now that I had found him again. I scanned his face with greedy eyes. He had faded a little, grown thinner and paler. When the goddess had seduced him in Andromache's form, she had ensured that he would love her forever. She was the slave of Neoptelemus, and I could not see that petulant boy selling her to us. I remembered him from the beaches, demanding his father Achilles' armor in a high whine, and stamping his foot when he was told that Odysseus of Ithaca had stolen it, as he stole everything he fancied which was not chained to bedrock. I wondered what had happened to the red-headed Prince of Ithaca, he of the nimble wits. I had extolled as a pattern of beauty, patience, and fidelity. Her fidelity, Chryse said, did not noticeably restrain her Lord's wandering fancy, however.

Eleni clapped his hands, and a train of slaves came in and out, bearing hot water, clean garments, wine, and food.

We looked at each other and decided that we really couldn't allow all that delicious smelling provender to grow cold.

Eleni was watching me as I ate bread and stewed meat, trying not to gobble. The combination of herbs and beans in the pot was interesting though strange, and we did not offer many of the usual conversational pleasantries until fully half the feast was consumed and even Eumides was beginning to look replete.

'How did you come here, Sister?' asked Eleni, filling an Argive kylix with golden mead.

'By a long road, Brother, even from Olympus, where we went to take Orestes, son of Agamemnon, for judgment. The Gods found him guiltless, and he has come here to claim his betrothed, Hermione, daughter of Menelaus.'

'Neoptelemus will not release anything that is his. He is fifteen now, a sour little morsel, ruled by his uncle, Molossos. He has none of the greatness of his father Achilles, the swift runner.'

'That is a mercy,' I said flatly. I remembered Achilles and was glad that his son was not like him. Chryse had the same thought, and agreed. 'Achilles was a monster. The Gods made a stone out of his heart. You rule the temple of Apollo, Eleni?'

'A small temple and a small worship. Zeus Earth-Born is their God, and his consort. Sister,' he leaned forward and I stroked the once-familiar hair, so like my own. 'I have treasure enough to buy Andromache, and she wishes it—she loves me. He keeps her close in the Argive fashion, but he has not hurt her, or lain with her, as she will not have him and he is not strong enough to force her. She has taken no other lover and she is eating out her heart. Every time I see her, at festivals and sometimes, for a moment, over the wall of the palace, she is thinner, sadder. She frets in confinement, has headaches and fainting spells. I fear that she will break her heart and die. Apollo says that I shall be joined with her, he promises that still, but I fear that we will be joined only when she dies, for I will die with her, and before we drink the draught of Lethe and forget the sound of the wind, we will be one. For I will not live without her, Cassandra, I cannot live without her.'

'Then we shall wash, and clothe ourselves, and we shall find a solution,' said Chryse. 'I saved your life, son of Priam, and I will not lose you again.'

Electra

We gained audience with the King of the Epirotes without difficulty. A blond young man sat lolling on a throne, an attendant man behind him. The elder was grey-bearded and hawk-nosed, with an acquisitive eye which reminded me of certain peasants in certain villages.

'I am Orestes, son of Agamemnon,' said my son and brother. We had agreed that he would keep his title. 'I am here to seek the return of Hermione, daughter of Menelaus, once betrothed to me.'

'Yes, we have her,' said the boy unpleasantly. 'She pleases me. Why should I give her up?'

'I can offer a bride-price for her,' said Orestes politely. 'Double whatever you paid.'

'I paid nothing. Double nothing is nothing,' he sneered. 'Clytemnestra, Queen of Mycenae, sent her here, as you were fled.'

'That Queen is dead, and her consort. I am King of Mycenae now,' said Orestes evenly. 'Give me Hermione, most noble King.'

'No,' snapped Neoptelemus.

'Lord, must I plead with you?' asked Orestes, becoming desperate.

'Master, they are offering a great price, and the maiden is obdurate,' whispered the old man, loud enough for me to hear. 'Mycenae is rich in gold, they say.'

'No,' said the boy.

He jumped up, drawing a bronze sword. 'Fight for her,' he said, stabbing quickly.

'I will not fight,' said Orestes, leaping back out of the way. The sword point sought his throat, handled with skill. 'I have shed enough blood.'

'So you don't really want her,' Achilles' son made another pass. 'If you defeat me you shall have her. Pretty Hermione of the black hair and quick temper. How she screamed and wept when her maidenhead broke!'

'Challenge.' Orestes did not waste words. Pylades and I backed away to give them space, and the audience chamber was quickly ringed with Epirotes, yelling in barbarous tongues for blood.

Orestes danced and lunged. He thrust once, and the blade shaved the king's cheek. Neoptelemus swore by Zeus to cut out his heart and stabbed, cutting a furrow along Orestes' chest. I could not turn my face away. They were both panting now, and the boy appeared to be tiring. Orestes had walked a good way across the hills, feeling alive again after such a long penance. He was almost as hardy as a mountain goat and this sneering king had obviously spent his time drinking too much and fighting untrained peasants.

'Kill!' howled the Epirotes.

Pylades drew his own sword and bade me be ready to run for the door. I could not move while the bronze swished through the cold air, seeking Orestes' life.

The son of Achilles lunged hard, the blade missing Orestes' heart as he dodged. Then my brother ducked a sweeping blow, came in under the arm, and stabbed.

The blade penetrated almost to the hilt. He drew it out and Neoptelemus, son of Achilles, fell dead.

Pylades had expected a riot. We did not expect it to be of joy.

Someone brought a lamp down on the head of the counsellor Molossos, killing him. Then the room and the courtyard erupted into a joyful babble, and we stood amazed on the killing floor, listening to voices calling, 'Dead, dead! Dead at last, and by a stranger's hand! Eleni! Eleni! Find Prince Eleni!'

Chapter Nineteen

'The tale of the House of Atreus is concluded, as you wished,' said Athene to her brother. 'Orestes has his Hermione. He will rule Mycenae and, after the death of Menelaus, Sparta.'

'It is the fate of his son Tisander with which I am now concerned,' said the Sun-God.

'What of your promise, brother? Orestes dared much in asking our father for his favor on Cassandra's behalf.'

'I have told someone, as I promised,' he said evasively.

Athene was not satisfied, but Zeus had words for Poseidon.

'Sea-God, it is a time of ending. A new age begins, Lord and Brother. Release Odysseus. He is penitent. Look.'

In the Pool of Mortal Lives they saw Odysseus building a boat out of fresh planks, hewn by hand, laboriously pegging the timbers together, watched by a beautiful young woman who wept, veiled in her weed-brown hair.

'Don't leave me,' she stretched out her pearly arms. 'Don't you love me?'

'I love you,' he returned sadly. 'But I must go home. I am bound by my word, though all of my kin have mourned me and forgotten me. Calypso, I will always remember you, but I must go home or die on the way. I have come so far, suffered so much, and the jealous god sent you to find me and detain me, to lie in your arms and forget my kingdom. No god will deny me my chosen destination, Odysseus, greatest of travellers. If Poseidon's wrath is not abated,' *he said, kissing her, 'and my body washed up on your island, then bury me here, where I can see the coast of Achaea, and look toward Ithaca forever.'*

The Lady of Cyprus was touched by this renunciation.

'Relent,' begged golden Aphrodite, breathing perfumes into the Sea-God's face.

'I will strike him once more, then I will forgive him,' said Poseidon, dazzled.

Cassandra

We were barely clothed when we heard the swell of noise from the interior and hysterical voices crying in what sounded like joy. Eleni went to the door, and was dragged away by many hands, and we ran after, wondering what was happening. I had my dagger and Eumides his sword, and we came into the white stone audience chamber in a riot of noise.

There stood the boy Orestes in a pool of blood, looking bemused. At his feet lay a dead man, struck cleverly under the arm, a recognized Argive killing blow for an armored opponent. Pylades and Electra, stunned, were standing beside their brother. The bitch *Racer* was nosing at Orestes, reassuring herself that he was not badly hurt.

The noise was deafening. The Epirotes had crowded into the room, all shouting and attempting to dance, and we could make nothing of it.

Eleni was carried to the dais on which the throne stood. His followers put him down and he held up his hands for silence. I could not hear his thoughts, but I felt him thinking, as one feels a sandglass quiver as the measure sand falls. I was so overwhelmed by his joy that I started to laugh helplessly, and Chryse looked at me as if I had gone mad. The heat and stench of so many tribes of the sacred unwashed in that space was stifling.

'Orestes, son of Agamemnon,' he announced, and the Epirotes cheered. 'You have slain Neoptelemus, son of Achilles.' The Epirotes screamed acclaim, and it was some time before Eleni could quiet them. 'Do you wish to claim Epirus as your own?'

'No,' said Orestes simply. 'I am King of Mycenae.'

'What do you require of the new King of Epirus?' asked Eleni, grinning from ear to ear and sitting down on the throne.

'Hermione, my betrothed,' said Orestes. He was clearly shocked, but he clung to the reason why he had come to Dodona and somehow ended up in a lake of blood again.

Eleni waved a hand and the women of the royal household were ushered in. There were the three women of Troy, slaves, and Andromache, widow of Hector my brother. Eleni took the hand of a robust young woman who was evidently in a very bad temper and led her to Orestes, who took the hand and stared.

'Hermione, I give you to Orestes of Mycenae as his wife,' announced Eleni. She was dumbfounded. She squeezed the hand, and then touched Orestes' cheek, as though she did not believe it could really be the royal son of Mycenae.

'I, Eleni, son of Priam, King of Epirus, free the sisters Clotho, Lachesis, and Atropos from slave service.' That name was a private joke. They were spinners, and they had called themselves after the Fates. Andromache looked pale and ill. Grief and lack of freedom had eaten her heart. Slavery would not sit easily on such a one as Andromache, Amazon-trained, a fearless rider and fighter. She had seen Hector die, and this same dead Neoptelemus, Son of Achilles, had slaughtered the baby Astyanax, the only memorial she had of his father.

'By the oracle and the divine word, I am King.' I wondered how that had come about. Was Apollo going to start keeping his promises? 'I claim Andromache as my royal spouse. Now, spread the news, men of Epirus. Take the bodies away and bury them suitably. Tonight we shall feast.'

The hall cleared magically. Eleni leapt down from the dais and embraced Andromache. She stood rigid in his arms until she crumpled at the knees and fell.

'Brother, you have no tact,' I said crossly as Chryse and I tended the recumbent woman. She had fainted, probably from lack of fresh air and shock. Joy is just as overwhelming as horror, though it seldom kills. We carried her into the king's apartments, over-decorated with loot from the fall of Troy, and gave her a cordial. She opened her eyes, saw Eleni, smiled lovingly at him, and fell asleep.

Electra

I had no fears for Orestes once I heard Hermione say to him, 'Of course I didn't lie with him. I refused. He was afraid of me. Orestes, my heart, how has it been with you? You're hurt, let me tend you.' A moment later she was scolding him for putting his chest in the way of a sword and Orestes was allowing her ministrations, leaning back with a smile on his face. We left them. We needed a bath and some clean clothes.

There was a large feast that night, at which the Epirotes reviled the rule of the Son of Achilles. He had, it appeared, allied himself with the largest clan, of which the now-dead, elderly Molossos was the head. Together they had looted the tribes, caring not one whit about the hunger in the countryside. The soldiers came to each little village demanding taxes, and threatened or even killed whoever protested.

The Epirotes were so split by blood feuds that they could not combine to form an effective resistance to this oppression. Eleni, the son of Priam, Priest of Apollo, had been chosen as the next king by secret meetings all over Epirus, as the advocate of a new God. All the old gods were claimed by one tribe or another. Eleni was young, intelligent, with golden hair and grey eyes. He was so like his sister, in fact, that I blinked when I first saw them together, thinking that the strain of the journey had affected my eyesight.

They had aged together. Cassandra in her dreadful journeys, slavery, watching the death of Troy, then the death of Agamemnon. Eleni, Priest of Apollo, had left the city before it fell but had also watched the sack, and Neoptelemus, son of Achilles, had tormented him, claimed possession of the woman he loved.

As Epirus had no separation of the sexes during festivals, I could see them all as we sat under a tree—not the sacred oak, but an oak, tall and venerable. Pylades was beside me, leaning back, drinking the mead of Epirus, which tastes like the nectar of the Gods.

The speakers around the little fires grew more vocal. Neoptelemus' deeds became more frightful, and his critics declared that they had always known that a stranger would kill him. Apollo and Aphrodite had both confirmed it.

The women from the temple, sacred prostitutes dedicated to the service of the Lady of Cyprus, had joined in the revel. I saw one lean over Orestes and kiss him deeply, while Hermione laughed and stroked his shoulder. They had been married by declaration at the temple of Zeus, as had the pale widow and the son of Priam. The triad Cassandra, Eumides, and Diomenes were scattered, not close as they usually were. Diomenes was not there, Cassandra was with Eleni and his wife, and Eumides was lying on his back while Aphrodite's priestess dropped mead and kisses onto his mouth.

Someone threw a handful of dried fungus on the main fire and it flared brightly.

'*Evoe*!' the voices called. '*Evoe, evoe*! Come, Dione, come, Aphrodite, come ancient Lord, come Niaos!'

I heard brutish accents and the firelight was cut off by dancing figures. I saw the sacred woman pull Eumides' tunic over his head and kiss his belly. Pylades rose to his feet and took my hand.

'Come, Electra,' he said quietly. 'You will not wish to join the Dionysiac rout.'

He was right. We moved away, into the deep shade, tripping over twined bodies. We got to our room without challenge, but Pylades was excited by the wine and the night, and so was I.

Without a caress, our mouths locked in a kiss. We slid to the floor, tearing at clothes, baring flesh to meet other flesh which hungered for the touch, the voices outside crying to the God, and I was pinned and pierced and screamed aloud in triumph.

Epirus, the next morning, was not happy. Slaves crept heavy-eyed about their tasks. I looked out of a window into the courtyard, where a yawning serf was sweeping up the ruins of the orgy; torn cloth, broken pottery, and the ash from a hundred little fires. The whole court slept late, as did Pylades and I.

I had a headache from too much mead. I walked out into the stoa and sat down in the shade to drink spring water and recover, leaving my husband sleeping.

I saw a rider on a fast horse which looked familiar. It was Cassandra's beast *Nefos*, the touchy stallion, galloping. The woman was riding astride with exultant grace, her hair streaming behind her. I recognized her. The widow, the pale woman, who had fainted the day before. Andromache was riding like an Amazon.

I overheard a conversation as I sat between the columns, too languid to declare my presence. The speakers were Cassandra and Diomenes.

'Sweet golden one,' she said, very gently. 'What troubles you?'

'One last secret and no home,' he said. 'You can lose yourself in the flesh, Cassandra, but I cannot. I went to the temple of Apollo last night.'

'You went to the temple? Why?' His golden head drooped to her shoulder, and he sighed, so sadly that I was sorry for him.

'Apollo said—you said that Apollo said he would tell us where we could live together,' he said drearily. 'And that he would tell another, not you. I went to the temple to see if he would tell me.'

'What happened?'

'I knelt and made an offering of incense. I could hear the orgy raging outside. I knew that you were there, with the priests, and Eumides with the women of Aphrodite. Have you seen him this morning? He's covered with mud and the marks of their teeth.'

'And he's very happy. The mood even caught the Princess Electra, though I'll wager that she lay with her husband. What about Apollo?'

'Nothing. He said nothing. He knows I don't believe in him.'

'Never mind. Don't sound so desolate, my heart. One more journey, my weary one, and then we shall part if there is no hope. Agape mou,' she said. 'One more journey, from here to Amouda, and thence…'

'Thence?' he asked, sounding unutterably tired.

'To the end of the way, in the end,' she said firmly. 'What is this secret?'

I had to admire the way she never lost the thread of a conversation. He touched her breast under the chiton and asked, 'Do you remember your first lover? The first who gave you joy?'

'My brother Eleni, when we were children.'

'No, the first consummation.'

'I never knew his name, and he hurt me. A tall man with a blue bead in his hair. It was the Trojan custom to leave the Maiden with a stranger and join the Mother.'

'They do that on the island of Staphylos,' he said.

'Island customs are always interesting. Why do you ask about my lovers?'

'You have always wondered about this charm.' He undid a little bag from his amber necklace. He unfolded the contents as he spoke. Two maiden's veils. One a plain one, one the red gauze of a bride. 'The first woman who lay with me…the first time I felt that rush of fire…I have never told you her name.'

'Do you want to tell me?' She sounded puzzled.

'It is the only secret left. Arion knew it and never told, and Aphrodite commended his tact. But it is the last thing I have to give you, my love, my golden Cassandra.'

'Tell me,' she commanded.

'Elene of Sparta. We were fourteen. I broke my physician's oath to lie in her arms, to comfort her. I saw her again in Mycenae, where I tended a plague. I never touched her again.'

She said nothing, but folded him close, so that the gold hair lay across his face.

I should have moved, but I was too tired. And this was a secret that I could easily keep. Elene of Sparta had brought ruin on the House of Atreus, she and her mortal sister, Clytemnestra, my mother. They were both beautiful and evil. I could acknowledge their beauty now, and partly understand their evil.

After a week, Cassandra and Eleni parted. The three travellers, two healers, and a sailor, loaded with presents, left by the main gate and rode south towards the coast, where they said their ship was waiting. I kissed Cassandra at our parting, and I wept as I never thought I would for a barbarian and an escaped slave. As she embraced me, she laid a hand on my belly and smiled.

'Good news and a fair child,' she said, mounted her horse, and rode away.

Cassandra

There is nothing to be said for the rule of a hero's son. It's almost worse than that of the hero himself. Achilles might not have shown any talent for politics, but he would not have been so petty and greedy. At least, I assume not. Chryse still shuddered slightly when we mentioned Achilles. I did not fear him—after all, I had killed him. But from what he said, I gathered that although Achilles, the Swift Runner, might have dropped in occasionally and massacred everyone, he would not have watched them die of famine as his son had done.

The villagers were starving. We followed the River Acheron, the river which runs into Hades, and spectres haunted every step. Dead children were piled at the side of the path, because no one was strong enough to hack graves in the stony soil. We carried stores and rode edible horses, and fought off two famished attacks from the villages, killing men so weak that once the initial fury had worn off they could have been knocked over by a child with a stone. We could not travel by night because the paths were mere goat tracks, and our only sure guide was the river. In several of the villages we found bones, human femurs which had been cooked and the marrow extracted. Eleni would have few enough people in his kingdom unless this harvest grew prodigiously.

I had left my twin joyful. Andromache loved him, his oppressor was dead, and his gods, whom he had served faithfully all his life, had proved true. Electra was content with her husband and Orestes with Hermione. The last time I had seen them Hermione had divided her time between agreeing demurely with everything Orestes said, until he pressed her too far, and scolding him so roundly that he had agreed with everything she had said. Presumably this made them happy. The hound-bitch *Racer*, luckily, had taken to Hermione immediately.

My fate was bitter. I could not stay in Epirus, where the only healers are men. It was too late to turn the Epirotes from their strange worship. There was no place for us and now I felt that there never would be. Apollo had deceived me again.

Leaving Eleni had not been so great a wrench as I had thought. The link was renewed. He was in my mind, and he was the only factor which saved me from despair as the villages passed in the wails of famished, abandoned babies protesting with their dying breath the cruelty of fate.

Even Eumides was subdued as we came at last into sight of the sea. In a small encampment by the salt water, we saw Laodamos' men roasting fish, and smelled the clean scent of Ocean.

'We've been waiting three days,' complained Laodamos, looking at us with his crossed eyes. 'Where have you been enjoying yourself, you pirate?'

'Bite your tongue and ship the oars as soon as you've finished whatever meal that is,' said Eumides, angry because he was so relieved that they were there. 'I won't stay a moment longer than I have to in this cursed nation.'

We shared the fish and set the sail. The wind was in the right quarter. I settled down on the stern deck, where I always sat, and let the cold wind blow through me. I saw blue waves, barely rippling, and a strong current carrying us where we wanted to go. The sky was that peculiar Aegean blue, clear as morning and set fair overhead. The horses stood with bowed heads in the center of the galley, resigned. I was becoming resigned, too. I would leave my beautiful lovers and go to Troas, child of Ilium, and I would take no other mate. I would never find such a pairing as this again, so I would not tire my spirit in trying. I would be useful and busy, healing the hurts of the Trojans, and they would manage without me. Eumides could find lovers anywhere, and they would welcome Chryse back to Epidavros.

My eyes filled with tears. I looked over the side to distract myself, and a dolphin, creature of Dionysos, the only God who had not betrayed me, poked its beak out of the water, grinning. It was joined by three others.

All day, as I mourned my lost and ill-fated loves, the creatures sprang and danced tirelessly beside the galley *Waverider*.

We slept on board, as we knew that by morning we should be off Lefkada, where we would have to row into the lee of Cephallenia. Eumides woke early and hauled on the sail, brailing it. We slowed.

'Eumides, have you gone mad?' demanded Laodamos. 'We can't waste this wind.'

'I'm as sane as I ever was,' said the sailor. 'Wreckage in the water—see.'

We hauled it in, sealed barrels and floating boxes, well-built and corded. Eumides examined one. It was full of golden plates, which looked strangely familiar. Chryse inspected the seal and ordered, 'Look for a man.'

We backed oars to slow *Waverider* further, and I saw drifting red weed, which resolved itself into hair. We came about and hauled him in.

I thought he was dead, but his chest rose and fell. Not a tall man but strong and well-muscled, with bright kelp-strands of hair and the remains of a white linen tunic. Toil and travel had deepened the lines in his face, but he had an attractive countenance, even sodden and bruised.

Chryse bared the body's arm, and found an archer's bracelet of fine water gold, figured with dolphins and set with pearls and aquamarines.

'It's him,' affirmed Eumides.

'Whom? I think he's tranced or drugged, Chryse, he doesn't respond even to pain.'

'Odysseus. It's Odysseus. What is he doing in this sea? Can anyone sight any other bodies?' Chryse was amazed, smoothing the battered face. 'He came and talked to me in Mycenae the night I met Eumides, and then at the siege of Troy. He was the strategist of that war, Odysseus, Sacker of Cities. It has been a hard road for all of us, Prince of Ithaca, but hardest perhaps for you.' He moved the streaming hair away from the shipwrecked man's drying skin and covered the body with his warm mantle.

We scanned the sea but found no corpses, only the stern post of a small boat, no longer, Eumides estimated, than a dinghy.

'What was the Prince of Ithaca doing on this sea, adrift in a boat that small? It's suicide,' objected Eumides. 'He must have been blown far from home.'

'If we can get him to swallow,' I said 'we can keep him alive. He's desiccated—he's been sunk deep in salt water.'

'How do you know?' asked the sailor.

'The weed that came up with him. It's black mossweed, the fishermen dredge it up in their nets from the bottom. It doesn't even grow within a fathom of the surface.'

'Trust a healer to know herbs,' muttered Eumides, as we dripped water patiently into the sailor's mouth.

'Lady of Ocean, Thetis, ask Poseidon to speak to me,' he murmured, closing the wide-pupilled brown eyes again as if he was very weary.

◇◇◇

Kelp-crowned, salt drying on the set mouth, Poseidon stared at the impudent mortal, Odysseus, Prince of Ithaca, who had resolutely refused to die and had never begged for mercy.

'Lord,' said the mortal, coughing, 'let us deal.'

'Deal? You bargain with a God?' bellowed Poseidon in a voice like a monstrous conch shell, blown by a giant.

'Of course,' the shade of Odysseus sat up, pushing back wet red hair. 'What else can I do? I am Odysseus of the Nimble Wits. Consider, Lord Sea-God. I have been missing for years. All that time my faithful ones have been praying to you, sacrificing to you. How would it look to all those devout worshippers if your unrelenting hatred was revealed?'

'They would fear me,' said Poseidon complacently, stroking his beard.

'Fear, yes. But respect, no. Does it befit a great God to pursue a petty man with such vindictiveness?'

The mortal seemed to think that he had made a point. He smoothed down his wet tunic.

'You said you would destroy my altars,' Poseidon reminded him, and Odysseus smiled and made a wise gesture with long, beautiful hands.

'A moment of anger, Lord—sailors have hasty tempers. Red-heads even more so. How could I, a mere man, express my agony except to curse the gods, the Fate which could have been kind and was not? Consider me justly punished, Lord. And let me go home. Men ring my palace who know no gods, and will utterly abolish all devotion. I will destroy them if I can but come there. And there is this, Lord, if my other arguments have not convinced you. The miraculous return of Odysseus out of the waters will cause sacrifices to burn on your altars all over Achaea. Men will say, "There is no God greater than Poseidon, Earth-Shaker, Lord of the Sea. Who else could have saved Odysseus?"'

Aphrodite smiled. The Sea-God raised his hand. Taller than a sea-cliff, he loomed over the shipwrecked man, the beard parting over teeth like pearls.

◇ ◇ ◇

'Poseidon has forgiven him,' I said, with absolute certainty. Far away, Eleni echoed my sureness. Odysseus of Ithaca, if we could get him there, was at last going home.

He did not really wake, though our journey took two days. At last we rowed around the point and found the island he had been seeking for so long. *Where had he been*, I wondered, as we carried him carefully ashore and laid him under a tree, piling his boxes and bundles around him. He had retained, through all his travels, one box at least of loot from Trojan Apollo's temple, the gold plates from the walls, and that, perhaps, was like Odysseus of the Nimble Wits and the even faster fingers.

We rowed out again, catching the providential current, and the rowers shipped oars with a sigh of relief.

'Nothing more until we find the channel which will take us past the Peloponnese,' said Eumides. Chryse and I looked at each other.

'For Iolkos?' I asked. Eumides smiled and shook his head, so that the golden earrings flashed.

'For home,' he said.

Chapter Twenty

Odysseus

Walking through the pines over the dry, thorny ground, I, Odysseus of Ithaca, most strangely returned, long since given up as dead, heard a feeble 'wuff!' Three creatures had never despaired at my absence or ceased to wait for me. One of them crawled to my feet, licked my hand, and barked, wagging her tail.

She died as I caressed her, tears spilling from my eyes onto her brown and white fur. She was terribly ancient, toothless, all bones. She had fought off death, waiting for her master to come home.

The other two waited for me in the house, ringed with importunate suitors, patient beyond all hope, Penelope my wife, nurturing in my son, Telemachus, the idea of his father, red-headed Odysseus, traveller and Prince of Ithaca, who would, some day, return. I evaded the watchers easily. I would kill them in the morning.

I opened the door and they saw me. They knew me. I staggered forward into their arms.

Cassandra

As *Waverider* ploughed laboriously up the coast of Euboea, I tried to extract from Eumides some idea of where we were going.

'I woke up knowing it,' he claimed, drawing in his line with a large fish attached.

'What did you wake up knowing?' asked Chryse, taking the fish, killing it and re-baiting the line.

'Suppose I said that there was a land which was originally settled by the people who later became Trojans,' he said, dropping the line over the thwart again.

'Yes?'

'And that later it was settled by your people,' he said to Chryse.

'So? One would conquer the other.'

'But supposing that it was only a little place, and very isolated, and they had a strong king,' he continued, in the most irritating manner possible.

'Eumides…' I threatened, but Chryse put a hand on my arm.

'We're listening,' he said deliberately.

'That king would allow his subjects to intermarry, wouldn't he?' Eumides said slowly.

'Of course, especially if it was a little place, far from anywhere,' I agreed, reining in my temper. Throwing Eumides overboard might be temporarily satisfying, but would delay the climax of his tale.

'And if the Trojan men married Argive women, they would each want to keep to their customs, wouldn't they? And if the same number of Argive men married Trojan women, the same would apply, wouldn't it?'

'I suppose so,' agreed Chryse.

'Well, then,' concluded Eumides, drawing in another fish.

He would not say any more, even when we seriously threatened to throw him overboard.

I thought we were going to Skiathos, and was about to complain that we had already been there and did not want to go again, when we struck east, for a rocky shore which seemed to have no inlets.

The weather turned gusty and the sea became rough. Chryse brewed his infusion for seasickness and even the rowers began to complain. More than usual, I mean. Rowers always complain if they have to row. We were flung from trough to trough, the oars useless, and I began to wonder whether Eumides had really taken leave of his senses, and meant us to live with Hades after all. In which case he could have drowned us comfortably in the Acheron and not brought us all the way into Ocean to die.

We bounced and bucketed along, acutely uncomfortable, the horses whinnying and the rowers calling on Poseidon, and I shouted, 'Eumides? Have you a destination in view or are you just weary of living?'

'Watch,' he said, and in one moment the storm turned to calm. We were in a harbor, wide and flat. The inlet was almost invisible from the sea. I looked back and saw the waves gnashing their teeth against the headlands.

'A king called Staphylos came from Minos' Island when the volcano destroyed it,' said Eumides. 'They told me about him when I was a boy, learning to sail my first little boat. They said that he sailed through smoke clouds black as night and falls of hot stones light enough to float. He was lost and called on Dionysos, and the god sent dolphins, his children. Staphylos was close enough to follow them, fin by fin, as they turned into this harbor. Few people have found it. Some Achaean settlers came, but the Trojan law held. Since he died they have modified it with Argive ideas, but it remains an amalgam of both cultures.'

I saw a hill with a cluster of little white houses roofed in blue stone. I saw lofty olive-clad hills on either side, one crowned with a temple. I saw a deep harborage, a sea-wall ancient as time, and heard voices calling, in Argive and Trojan, asking for news of the outer sea.

'It's called Staphylos' Island, the blue-green isle,' said Eumides. 'They have women healers here, and men. There is no temple of Asclepius, though. I thought we might build it over there.'

He pointed to a bare patch of ground on the opposite side of the bay. My last flash, perhaps, of god-sight showed me a small temple with red-gold pillars and a stone floor, and a house behind it for the Asclepid and the Trojan healer and an itinerant sailor.

We landed and walked through a crowd of welcoming people to the nearest tavern. The tavern-keeper was a woman, unique in Achaea. She sold us sweet wine made of the divine King Staphylos' grapes, dark as blood. I saw a woman in a working tunic with wood-shavings in her hair. I saw a man in the garments of a priest of Apollo sitting by the waterside, talking to a woman sailor, who was cleaning fish, perched on the bow of her little boat. I saw a veiled woman carrying water chatting in a strange dialect—a mixture of Argive and Trojan words—to a man dragging an amphora from the well on a sledge. An unveiled woman walked easily up from the quay, leading a goat and a kid. An herb-gatherer from the temple of Gaia laid her sungold and nettles and Mother's-leaf to dry on the clean pavement near the tavern, sitting cross-legged on the ground under her straw hat.

Donkeys stood patiently as they were loaded with fish and oil and sand for cement to be delivered to the houses being built higher up the hill. Little crooked streets, paved with blue stone, threaded the town to a lookout and fortified place which dominated one headland, though I guessed it would be invisible from the sea.

I sipped the wine, listening to the voices. One man, kicked by a badly loaded donkey, swore by Gaia that it was the four-footed spawn of the Dark Mother. A child, wrestling with another child, tripped, fell, and cried to his father. He was picked up and kissed better by a man in a Trojan tunic who murmured that Athene, Mistress of Battles, would take the pain away.

The crew of the *Waverider* had vanished into the waterfront in the way habitual to sailors. A stout woman, her arms stained to the elbow, whacked one with a dye-stick and yelled that he owed her five obols for the cloth she had colored for him, and that he'd better pay, by various Gods I had never heard of before. Three of the oarsmen had stripped and were lying in a wide shallow pool carved out of the cliff, where cold mountain water leapt down the slope. I noticed that they each made a polite bow and said, 'Honor to the Earth-Shaker,' before they stretched out full length in the cool water and scrubbed off the grime of travel with handfuls of lychnis and barley meal, supplied by a strong-minded young man who demanded a kiss for his attendance—and got it. Old women sat at another table, gossiping ferociously about the loose ways of the younger people and how there was no respect for age—not like it was when they were young.

Chryse raised the cup to me, and Eumides raised his.

'Will this do, Princess?' he asked.

'Possibly,' I said, unable to believe that it was true.

Eumides carried his treasure ashore and stowed it under his bench, collected by Laodamos from safe-keeping. It was enough to buy our plot of land and feed us for many a winter, to build our house and our temple, to secure our future as far as the future can be secured. If we could stay.

We were wary, shocked, unable to rejoice. It was not until we had talked to the priests of Apollo and the priestess of the Mother that we began to believe that we would both be accepted.

'It's a comfortable place,' said the priestess of Gaia, an old woman who reminded me very strongly of Tithone, my own teacher. 'Few people come here and most of them are either lost or running away. We harbor them all. The Staphylos deals with any bandits or pirates. The wine is good and the island-ers as devout as you would expect. Some of our young women have taken to Argive ways—veils, indeed, as though they are too holy to be seen! But most of them are just young women, traders, farmers, and small crafts for the most part, though we have one very good wood-carver. She made the Goddess,' she said, and bowed slightly towards a free-standing wooden statue, the Mother in her most generous aspect, her breasts dripping milk, her rounded arms all wound about with vines and snakes. 'I would welcome another healer,' she said. 'I am getting old.'

Chryse reported from the temple of Apollo, where a bald-ing, nervous man had said 'Welcome, brother! This is a pleas-ant place, except that the young men are taking on Staphylos' barbarian customs. Two of them have become weavers, and you will even see men spinning! Of course it is no use expecting island-born women to wear veils or carry water—not like it is in Achaea. There is no due deference here, no understanding of the divine authority of the husband. And we cannot sell or trade our women without consent, and some of them are so rich that they never marry.'

Chryse was about to suggest that the priest might consider returning to Achaea, where men were men, until he saw the priest's beautiful adopted children and his doting, veiled, male lover. Such an arrangement would not have been acceptable in Argive lands, where men were expected to marry.

'I am glad you are here,' said the balding priest. 'Fifteen of us were crippled last year in a blight which affected the genitals of men, and we could not allow the Mother's priestess to tend us. Apollo owns the land you want. He would want me to sell it to you, Asclepid.'

We reported to the Staphylos, an affable young man who appeared to divide his time between training his twenty shore guards and sleeping in the sun.

'Delighted and honored,' he murmured as we presented our plan for a temple. 'It will put both the priestess of Gaia and the priest of Apollo's noses out of joint, and that will be amusing. You are welcome here, healers. And we can always harbor another sailor.'

We set a broken arm and promised some of Chryse's seasickness mixture to the shore guards, who were sitting in a row on the white stone wall between the Horns of Minos, eating grapes and spitting the pips at the Staphylos' chickens. It was the most relaxed place we had ever seen, but the shore guards were healthy, well-armed, and alert, and pirates might get a surprise if they raided the blue-green isle.

We hired free workers to cut stone for us. When our house was finished, we hauled Eumides out of the waterfront tavern and half-carried him up the hill. The house-building had been a bad influence on our friend. Now that he had a place to stay that did not sell wine, he might sober up. If remonstrated with, he would protest that the fishing was done for the day, King

Staphylos had invented wine and he was merely honoring his royal and semi-divine memory.

Our house had three whitewashed rooms. Later we might be able to afford a fresco, but now the walls were clean and bare. There was a central room with a raised hearth and chimney and two sleeping rooms, one for us and one for guests. Our floor was of well-laid island stone, cool to the bare feet. There was a bath, and we had not even had to introduce the workmen of Staphylos to the concept of drainage. Our roof was sound, our lamp lit, our loft stored with firewood, and baskets of dried herbs, roots, and flowers. The most beautiful well-made bedding that I could find was laid out on the wooden furniture. On the square table was our one reminder of Troy, a piece of blue cloth, patterned with dancing dolphins.

I brought the consecrated flame from the Mother's temple toward the hearth. Once lit, it would never be allowed to die again as long as we lived. Eumides and Chryse knelt down, one on either side of me. They cupped their hands as I lowered the ember, and the fire caught and burned high, washing all our faces with golden light.

'Oh, my loves,' I said. Chryse smiled at me.

'Was it a good bargain, Eumides?' he asked.

The sailor said in an awed whisper, 'A very good bargain.'

Electra

She was born when the leaves fell, my autumn child. I laid my doll Pallas in her cradle. Pylades was delighted, and held her up to the stars, proclaiming 'This is my child!'

She was a good baby. She hardly cried, except when she was wet or hungry. She was ten months old and sitting up when Orestes sent to us to come as see his coronation as King of Mycenae.

We made the journey. The city had been laid waste by the departing soldiers, as my Lord had predicted. There were pavers working in the streets, and slaves white-washing the insides of houses and sweeping out leaves and rats' nests. Two priests stood at the door of the new temple of Athene.

The Palace was devoid of terror for me now, leaning on Lysane's arm. No Erinyes danced on the roof, proclaiming torture and death for the matricide. No blood stained the marble floor of the king's hall.

Orestes looked pale and determined as he walked into the city, as my father had walked so long ago, armored, clanking up the path under the Lion Gate. Orestes moved with grace and strength through the ritual challenge of the sentries.

Still not entirely joyful, my solemn son and brother. He did not speak of it, but Hermione said that he sometimes had bad dreams. But today he was sure, kingly, and beautiful, and the elders of the city and the priests crowned him, not with Agamemnon's crown, which had been lost, but with a new golden fillet figured with laurel leaves.

We joined in the feasting but retired early. Pylades, lying beside me, slid an arm under my shoulders and said, 'My Lady?'

'My Lord?' I asked, kissing him.

'Would you like to stay here, Electra? Your brother is king.'

'No,' I said surprised. 'I have to get home, the baby will be forgetting me, the spinning isn't half done. Neptha has given me a new recipe for solid honey sweets—thank you for allowing me to bring her home with us, Pylades, she will be wonderful with Tisimene—and Abantos will enjoy making them. The pruning isn't half done and there's all the olives to pickle in brine—and I don't like the quality of the salt that Clonius always buys if I'm not there. There are all the preparations to make for winter, cloth to sew and boots to mend. And Tauros is sure to have bitten someone again. I must go home.'

'So you do not regret it, Electra? Leaving your home and your royalty and marrying me?'

'You are a prince of the royal house of Phocis,' I said, thinking about it, 'though that would not matter. Regret it, my Lord?' I kissed him again. 'Even if we die tonight, I never thought that the sins of the House of Atreus could ever merit a fortunate ending.'

'Lady,' said Pylades, smiling, my beloved husband.

'My Lord?'

'Are you happy?'

I thought about it. Then I said something that I never thought I would say.

'Yes, I am happy.'

Afterword

The House of Atreus

The progenitor of this singularly doomed family was Tantalus, son of Zeus, who liked offending the Gods. He stole nectar and ambrosia and sold it to men. He also gossiped about Olympus. He cooked and served up his son, Pelops, to Zeus, who took offense, and sent him to stand in crystal water but never be able to drink, to be in biting range of apples and never eat. Zeus resurrected Pelops, replacing his cooked shoulder with an ivory one.

Pelops, King of Phrygia, inherited these mischievous tendencies. He courted Hippodameia, Princess of Pisa. Her father challenged each suitor to a chariot race which he always won. She got tired of this and sawed the royal axle half through. The wheel fell off, Pelops won and killed Oenomaus. Hippodameia married Pelops and bore Thyestes and Atreus.

Atreus married Aerope but she fell in love with Thyestes and bore him two children who Atreus cooked and served up to his brother at a reconciliation supper. At this point the Gods cursed the House of Atreus, and one wonders at their patience in waiting until this dreadful deed amongst such a profusion of dreadful deeds.

Subsequently, Atreus' sons were Menelaus of Mycenae, who married Elene, and Agamemnon, who married Elene's mortal sister, Clytemnestra, and sacrificed his own daughter, Iphigenia, at Aulis for a wind to Troy. Subsequently she took up with Aegisthus, Agamemnon's nephew, incestuous child of Thyestes and his own daughter, born as a revenger for his father, and they killed Agamemnon when he came home from Troy.

The children of Agamemnon and Clytemnestra were Chrysothemis, Laodice called Electra, and (technically) Orestes. Orestes and Electra murdered Clytemnestra and her lover, Aegisthus. Orestes was pursued by the Furies and finally acquitted by the Gods. Then Orestes killed Neoptelemus, son of Achilles, and reclaimed his betrothed, Hermione, daughter of Elene and Menelaus, whom he married. They produced one son, Tisander. Electra married her cousin, Pylades of Phocis, and bore several children. With the peaceful transition of power to Orestes, King of both Mycenae and later Sparta, since Menelaus died without an heir, the tale of the House of Atreus had a happy ending, against all the conceivable odds.

Mount Olympus burns with a cold white light, so bright that one cannot look at it even through sunglasses at about five p.m. in the spring. I have seen it myself.

Athene's Argument

In the Aeschylus play *The Libation Bearers*, Athene explains that mother-murder can be forgiven because men are the important sex, women being 'just the field for the seed,' an unacceptable argument which I suggest reflected the opinions of the playwright rather than the goddess. She talks the Erinyes out of revenge by explaining that there was someone else to enforce moral law, and that, I believe, is the ratio decedendi, the pith, of Orestes' defense. I have left out the anti-female bias and the pro-Athenian one, which places the trial on the Acropolis and establishes Athene as Athene Polias, the city's patron. It would have been very popular with the Athenian audience, but the home of the Gods was definitely Olympus.

Atreidae and Their Motives

I have taken the bold step of assuming that the children of Atreus had a motive, apart from pure revenge, for killing their mother and stepfather. I have studied modern cases of matricide and found that it is usually carried out either by psychopaths or by children attempting to stop or revenge abuse.

Epirus

In the north of present-day Greece, Epirus had a bad reputation. Strabo says it was savage, dirty, and barbarous, and Herodotus, most tolerant of all historians, says it was strange and its customs 'unusual.' This from a man who took cannibalism, sacred prostitution, and animal sacrifice in his stride. A sample quote, 'In that village recently a goat tupped a woman—a most unusual sight.' If Herodotus thought that Epirus was unusual, it must have been very strange indeed.

Herbal Medicine

I have derived most of my herbs through Dioscorides who, although he was fourth century and with the Roman army, has been extensively quoted by Culpeper, and therefore I am sure of which plant he is describing. Hippocrates' herbs are also identified by Dioscorides (there must be an easier way to do this) and the maxims are from Hippocrates. The Complete Herbal and English Physician by Culpeper is reprinted by Harvey Sales, London 1981.

Ancient herbal practice was somewhat different from today's. Go and see a practicing qualified herbalist.

Orestes' Flight

I traced Orestes' path through Greece in April and May 1995. Sometimes I have had to guess at roads and distances between ancient settlements. Purists are implored to forgive me.

Religious Ceremonies

Luckily, although there is still little known of the Elusinian Mysteries, a lot of the others were written down.

When I was at Delphi I saw the places where the original temples had been built, of clay and beeswax and feathers and laurel boughs. The ancient authors described the formalities in consulting the oracle, and I have followed them.

Much digging at Dodona has revealed what looks like an Earth Mother cult later taken over by a father, which explains the Zeus/Oak Tree and the association with the Sky-Father of the attributes of the Earth Mother.

Herodotus is my main source for ceremonies. He mentions them often because he was constitutionally interested in everything.

Minoan religion had no animal sacrifice. Its ruling deity was Gaia, the Earth Mother, Mistress of Animals. The male God was the irresponsible but powerful Dionysos, the dancer. I posited in a precious book *Cassandra* that Troy was settled by the Minoans, who fled Crete when the volcano Thera erupted. Some Minoans would have been washed up on Staphylos' Island at about the same time.

Stadia

A stadion was about one hundred and eight metres. Plural, stadia.

Staphylos' Island

The present-day Skopelos, this is the most beautiful of Greek islands. It is also called the Blue-Green Island, has few tourists, and is otherwise as described, having been settled by first Minoan and then Argive people. They are digging up the ruins of Staphylos' palace at the moment, and there are a few stones left of the temple of Asclepius to the right of the bay.

A Note on Pronunciation

English pronounces all Greek names with a long 'e', as in *IrEEnEE*. Actually it's a short 'e,' more like the 'I' in 'bit'. Very approximately, and Greek speakers must try and forgive me, this is how Greek sounds. A 'c' is pronounced 'k' and 'ch' is a soft sound, like the 'ch' at the end of 'loch'. The 'g' is always hard. 'Au' is 'ow.' No one is sure how Phrygian was pronounced, so Cassandra was probably pronounced as it is spelled. The 'd' in Diomenes and Eumides is a voiced 'th', as in 'thing.' Transliterating a language always produces problems, and some places are spelled diversely. For example, Chania in Crete is also spelt Chanea and Hania and is pronounced *HanEEa*. I've picked whatever spelling seemed to reflect the way the word is pronounced.

Bibliography

Re: Abused Children and Homicide

Easteal, Patricia, *Voices of the Survivors*, Spinifex Press, Melbourne, 1994.

Leyton, Elliott, *Hunting Humans*, Penguin, London, 1990.

Leyton, Elliott, *Sole Survivor*, Penguin, London, 1990.

Mones, Paul, *When A Child Kills*, Star Books, New York, 1994.

Wilson, Colin and Pitman, Patrica, *An Encyclopaedia of Murder*, Pan Books, London, 1964.

Wilson, Colin and Shearman, Donald, *An Encyclopedia of Modern Murder*, Pan Books, London, 1983.

Re: Ships and Galleys

Models and maps from the Naval Museum, Sitia, Crete and the War Museum, Athens.

Severin, Tim, *The Jason Voyage*, Hutchison, London, 1985.

Severin, Tim, *The Ulysses Voyage*, Hutchison, London, 1987.

Primary Sources

Hippocrates, *Hippocratic Writings*, Penguin, London, 1983.

Homer, *The Iliad*, Penguin, London, 1965.

Homer, *The Odyssey*, Penguin, London, 1967.

Secondary Sources (Ancient)

Aeschylus, *The Oresteia*, Penguin, London, 1981.
Aeschylus, *The Suppliant Maidens*, Penguin, London, 1967.
Euripedes, *Electra*, Penguin Plays, London, 1981.
Euripides, *The Trojan Women*, Penguin Plays, London, 1985.
Herodotus, *The Histories*, Penguin, London, 1935.
Hesiod, *Works and Days*, Penguin, London, 1968.
Sophocles, *Electra in The Theban Plays*, Penguin, London, 1985.
Strabo, *Collected Works*, Penguin, London, 1992.

Secondary Sources (Modern)

Kerenyi C., *Heroes of the Greeks*, Thames and Hudson, London, 1974.

Maps and guidebooks produced by the Greek Government, and the *Lonely Planet Guide to Greece*, Lonely Planet, Melbourne, 1994, which I unreservedly recommend, not least for its excellent commentary on ancient sites and ancient history.

Numerous works on archaeology beginning with Arthur Evans and Schliemann to digs presently happening in Albania.

Pomeroy, Sarah B., *Goddesses, Whores, Wives and Slaves*, Pimlico, London, 1994.

To receive a free catalog of Poisoned Pen Press titles, please contact us in one of the following ways:

Phone: 1-800-421-3976
Facsimile: 1-480-949-1707
Email: info@poisonedpenpress.com
Website: www.poisonedpenpress.com

Poisoned Pen Press
6962 E. First Ave. Ste 103
Scottsdale, AZ 85251